Collision

Book 1 of The Confession Series

T S Reed

Contents

To those with scars that run deeper than the surface: you are worth so much more than you have been taught to believe.

x

NVJ
I said a lot... I hope I said it well.

x

A Note

This story contains elements of domestic violence and its lasting effects. If you choose to read on, please *always* put your mind first.
Sending love and comfort,
T.S.Reed
x

Playlist

Scan the QR code below with your device's camera to
access the Collision Playlist, curated by T.S. Reed.

x

Two roads diverged in a yellow wood,

And sorry I could not travel both

And be one traveller, long I stood...

Robert Lee Frost

Prologue

One Year Ago

Mikaela

There is a silence that hugs against my skin and a weightlessness that sinks into my bones. I know I should feel something as I wait here, but my mind is heavy and I can't remember what I'm waiting for. I can't remember what I am hoping for. I can't remember what I am supposed to feel anymore. I can do nothing but stare out of the shattered glass, past the billowing smoke, and watch as he cries on the sidewalk.

He isn't moving. He isn't coming to me. He isn't getting up. He is just crying.

Slowly, with a finality I should be more afraid of, darkness creeps into my vision and latches onto my mind. I welcome it with open arms. As the keening and crying of sirens and metal shatters the silence, I let the darkness in. And as it takes me, it brings me one last gift.

Jamie's voice.

Chapter One

Present

Mikaela

A small groan slips from my lips as I double over, heaving for breath and clutching at my side. It's been months since I've attempted to even walk for an hour without short breaks, so now, while I desperately try to gasp through the sudden urge to vomit, I'm beginning to regret my life choices.

Ahead of me, Jamie pounds the pavement - his breathing even despite the sweat coating his t-shirt and sticking it to his back - and the sun glistens on the golden hue of his skin. His legs are long, and lean muscles stretch and contract with each easy stride away from me. Years of recreational running have kept my brother trim and toned, with wide shoulders and a subtle strength, and when he glances back to me, for the slimmest second, his face is beaming with pure enjoyment. But his bliss disappears instantly.

"You not up for it, Mik?" Concern laces into his voice as he doubles back and immediately I feel it; that flame of pride that scorches me from the inside.

I am not weak.

"Perfectly up for it," I spit through clenched teeth as I straighten and remove my hand from my side. The ache lingers, but there is no way I want to show him that. Looking like a broken doll in front of Jamie only leads to doting and sympathy, and I don't need any more of either. "Besides, it's doctor's orders, remember? Exercise and fresh air. It's good for the mind."

"Mik -"

"Don't, Jamie." I yank at my hair, the tug burning my scalp as the band catches on my curls and snaps tiny strands in half, before tying it back again. We both know I am just trying to gain some precious breathing time, but he says nothing. Instead he just chuckles.

When Jamie laughs it's always easy and light, even when he feels the complete opposite. It's one of my favourite things about my big brother, watching the laugh lines crease around his eyes and his whole face crumple into a mix of happiness and ease. That and his bone crushing hugs and inability to cook a decent meal without burning the ass off of a pan (or his hand). He throws his hands in the air - palms to me in surrender - and backs away slowly, a wicked glint hiding behind the blue of his eyes, and I can't help but smile.

"If this kills you, I'm telling Mom I told you to stop," he chuckles, pulling a hand through the thick waves of his blond hair.

I huff out a laugh as I push forwards into a painful jog again.

"If it kills me, I'm haunting your ass for telling Mom."

This is not where I should be. I glance around at the few men who rush in with leather briefcases and the handful of women in high-quality suits and perfectly pointed Louboutin heels who waltz through the space, flashing ID cards at me without so much as glancing in my direction and I feel the distinct sensation of not belonging. It's a gnawing, creeping, crawling sensation - like fire ants making a home of my skin.

My eyes drift over my skirt - too cheap and poorly fitted - and I brush myself down, crossing my ankles as I try to hide the threadbare flats I threw on in my rush. The lilac blouse I'm wearing does a little in lifting my outfit from disaster to simply drab, but it hangs in weird places where it used to sit perfectly; a constant reminder of who I once was.

I twist my fingers in the sleeve as I wait for something to happen - an email, or a phone call; anything that isn't just sitting here while people pretend I do not exist - and begin my plan for the long, drawn out murder of my beloved *Golden Boy* brother whose assurances that I'd "fit right in" now feel like the words that enticed Eve to eat that God damned apple.

Around me, the day isn't even beginning. The bustle and business of the morning doesn't exist yet, and early risers mingle in small clusters in the open space of the office. Coffee cups from local cafés perch on the edges of glass topped desks, while people laugh and catch up, and check their emails for the morning ahead. The space is modern and sleek, all open except for two large offices - doubling as meeting rooms when needed - tucked into the back of the building, and a small divide has been set up between myself and the rest of the office in the form of simple, white bookshelves - spilling with new prints and signed editions made out to Jamie and his small team of editors.

It feels like hours pass as I sit and watch them all, tapping a pen against my notebook and waiting for the day to begin, but it can't have been more than thirty minutes. Eventually, I move my attention to the computer - no sharp and snappy ideas and concepts bubbling to the surface of my subconscious and pushing into the world of creation - and begin to open and close different tabs and files.

Familiarising myself with this system won't take me long at all.

As time continues to crawl past me, dragging out each painfully long minute into chasms of lost meaning, my mind wanders again and names and faces begin to mist and dance beneath the thin veil of the block in my mind. If I could cut them out and bind them to my pen, then at least I would have something to do.

When the sharp trill of the phone pulls me from my daydream the images dissipate and I reach to answer. The office isn't open for another ten minutes, but surely it's good practice to get ahead with calls for the day?

"Wilcox Writings. This is Mikaela speaking, how may I direct your call?"

"Oh! Now isn't that just the sweetest little phone voice you have." The familiar laughter of Benjamin Haston rings through the line and a tight coil twists in my stomach, knotting into a mess of pain and anger and nausea, and for a moment I contemplate hanging up. *Jamie wouldn't fire me for hanging up on Haston, would he?* "How's it going, Little Mik?"

I pinch the bridge of my nose, an attempt to stem the automatic onset of a Haston induced headache, as I take a deep breath and will the nerves to roll off of me.

"Don't call me that, Haston." I roll my eyes as I swivel in my chair and listen to him chuckle. *Infuriating. He is infuriating, even after all this time.* "I'm not fourteen anymore."

Ben

Even on the phone Mikaela Wilcox has a way of getting her meaning across without having to say the words. *I'm not fourteen anymore and I like to imagine a world where you died in some horrific accident or were never born and didn't ruin my life.* It's cute really, in an *I really will kill you one day* kind of way.

I cradle the phone between my cheek and my shoulder as I adjust my tie in the distorted reflection of the opening elevator doors and smile to myself.

There, behind a ridiculously large glass desk, her chair twisted to the side and her face away from me, is a vision. The lilac of her blouse is gentle and warming against the soft white of her skin and the spattering of freckles that runs up the side of her neck are peeking out from behind the long, golden curls that are pulled over one shoulder. She pinches the bridge of her nose and I can almost hear her whine that it's my fault she has a headache again. She looks good. Skinnier than I remember, definitely a little uncomfortable, but still, she looks *really* good.

"No, you certainly are not," I say.

She spins herself around to face me with wide eyes and her mouth puckers open into a small o as she holds the phone to her ear, and suddenly the room feels a little too small.

I've seen her once in the last five years. Just once since she told me to stay the fuck away and it was two years ago. We didn't speak then. In fact, I'm sure she didn't even know I was in the same city as her that night, let alone the same bar. She'd seemed happy then. But now? Now I feel like the pressure of what I have agreed to might be too much, because she is looking at me with the surge and babble of volcanic rage clawing its way into her emerald eyes.

13

Those same eyes run over me slowly, head to toe, as we both pull our phones away from our faces and I feel the need to move. To say something. To do something. Instead, I just smile. It's an awkward kind of smile, one that's almost a grimace and only pulls up half of my lips, and I want to take it back. Mikaela doesn't smile at me. She appraises me cooly, with a detached disinterest, and I feel my cheeks flaming under her scrutiny.

How on earth did Jamie convince me this was a good idea again?

"It's good to see you, Mik." My voice catches in my throat and I think I might just turn and walk away. I think I might just run.

I swallow my pride and walk towards her.

Mikaela

He's aged a little since I last saw him; soft laugh lines framing the ice of his steel blue eyes and a dark stubble lining his jaw where he had once been clean-shaven and baby faced. But so many things remain the same.

His nose has a small bump where, years ago, it had been perfectly straight - the tell tale sign of that one high school fight that landed him in the ER. His hair, such a dark brown you might mistake it for black, is pushed back, small curls forming in the short cut and he smiles lazily as he looks at me. It's a crooked sort of smile that would have set my heart racing when I was eighteen, but now it makes me want to cry. Even now, in his neatly pressed, deep navy suit - a suit that screams designer - and his baby blue shirt, he looks like trouble. The same trouble that had an eighteen year old me talking myself down from a very precarious ledge just days after Jamie came home from college. The same trouble that had me swearing at nothing and everything at once as I drove downtown to pick Jamie up from some back alley fight he definitely hadn't started before Mom got home from pulling another double shift. The same trouble that has always caused heat to rise in my cheeks.

"The feeling is not mutual, Haston."

Ben watches me as I busy myself by clicking through tabs on the computer, and I try to ignore the way he perches down on the desk and moves closer than I want him to be.

I can feel the heat of his body and I curl my fist momentarily.

I see the way his eyes skim over me, noting the ill-fit of the purple blouse that hangs limply from my shoulders with no shape and the way my skirt scrunches above my knees, and I flush a burning red. I set my gaze ahead, avoiding his eyes as they burn into me and trying desperately not to recall the last time we spoke.

"No?" He grins effortlessly now as I ignore him, chuckling to himself when I still refuse to look back to him and my heart squeezes painfully. *He's really just going to pretend? Act like the last five years didn't happen? Absolutely, irrevocably, determinedly, fucking infuriating.* "It's probably not good news that I'm here to stay then, huh?"

My head snaps up instantly, eyes wide and jaw slack, and Ben smirks. The fire of betrayal blazes beneath my skin where embarrassment had settled and my mind does exactly what I have been praying it would not do since the second I heard his voice: it pulls up her face.

"What?" My voice is stronger than I anticipate and, by the looks of it, it surprises him too. I don't feel strong though. I feel like reality is slipping away from me again.

He frowns deeply and stands up from the spot on my desk, holding his hands out in a *look at me and see that I'm impressive* kind of arrogant display, but his jaw tightens and I can't be sure, but I think I see him swallow a lump before he speaks.

"Who do you think gave this place a much needed cash infusion, Mikaela?" He shrugs, shaking his head slightly. "You're looking at the new CFO of Wilcox Writings."

I'm looking at...

My heart is in my stomach and my body launches into movement without another word.

I can feel Ben watching as I stalk away from him and towards the two glass paned offices at the very back of what I now understand is to be our shared work place. Heat seems to ripple off of me with every step and as I hear him call out to me, I let the sensation embrace me.

"Come on, Mik," he almost shouts and I know if I turn around he'll be rocking back on his feet and smirking at me like he knows exactly what I'm thinking. "You know you've missed me."

My hands shake as I push forwards, ignoring the questioning glances of everyone now appraising me as if they've only just realised I exist, and I fold my arms across my chest. Ducking my head, I weave past whispering women who all look me up and down and turn back to each other to discuss my outfit and my face and my very presence in this hell-hole of an office in hushed judgements until I get to my destination.

My brother's office.

I don't knock.

16

"Are you kidding me?"

"Josh, I have to call you back. I'm so sorry." Jamie holds a finger up to me, as if to put me on pause, and I feel my blood boil. Taking a deep breath, I turn to close the door; grimacing when Haston nods at me, his signature smirk resting against his lips, before entering the office next door. "Great. Thanks, Josh. Right. Yeah, I'll call again this afternoon."

Less than half a second passes when the phone hits the receiver before I find my words spilling from me and a familiar sense of painful disappointment washes over me.

"Haston? Really?" I keep my voice measured, even as my temper flares, and watch as Jamie's shoulders slump slightly. "After everything, you hired him? No. Worse. You brought him in as what? A partner? Damn it, Jamie. I thought you were smarter than that."

"Mik."

"No. Don't 'Mik' me right now. Every single time that man has shown up in our lives you've ended up in situations I've had to try to fix. Every damn time, Jamie. And you let him back in without question." I throw my hands up in exasperation. "You can't do this."

"Mikaela." Jamie raises his voice only slightly but I flinch. He freezes, immediate shame washing over him, diminishing him and making him look like a chastised school child, before his eyes soften and frown lines crease his forehead. "I'm sorry." He pushes to stand and I shake my head. He doesn't continue to move. "Listen, I know you don't like Ben but he's been my best friend for over a decade, Mik, and he's good at what he does."

"What he does is reign chaos over our lives, Jamie." I swallow the pain rising in my throat. "Or do I need to remind you of what happened five years ago?"

Beneath the shock and anger of his gaze something dark flashes and I steady myself for what is to come.

"No one needs to remind me of what happened five years ago." He glares at me, all sympathy slipping from the sea blue eyes and anger spinning between us. He's pissed I'd go there even after everything he's done for me in the last year. I'm pissed he'd hire Ben after everything I've been through. We're both pissed and we're both stubborn. But, like a knife being twisted, Jamie doesn't stop with the first injury. "And it's not like you've been around the last couple of years, Mik, or as if your life isn't full of mistakes either. Now, if you don't mind, I didn't give you your job for you to criticise mine. The phones won't answer themselves."

I clench my jaw as I feel the prickle of tears threatening to show. It angers me to no end that my tears usually come when I'm angry as opposed to just when I'm upset, and that only makes the whole crying thing worse.

I clear my throat as I brush away the moisture from the corner of my eye and watch as Jamie diverts his gaze.

Bastard.

"Right," I say, the t hanging in the air between us as he flicks through a stack of new manuscripts on his desk, and I turn away from him. "I guess I'll get back to my desk then, Boss."

Holding my head high as I hear him sigh behind me, I begin the agonising walk back to my desk, feeling the watchful eyes of those around me burning into my skin and boring into my skull. I try not to think about what he implied. I try not to feel that constriction around my throat. I try. I don't want to think about that. I don't want my mind to return to that place; not now, not ever.

Rolling my neck, I close my eyes and sigh. I'm not entirely sure when, but work got busy. Most of the morning passed answering the phone and desperately searching for the right connecting line to patch each author, agent and enquiry through to the appropriate person, and now, as I finally hit that midday lull, I find myself staring down a mountain of notes to pass on to members of staff I do not know and trying to ignore a growing bundle of nerves knotting in my stomach over and over.

I hear his approach before I see him and push my notepad aside. Turning to face him I paint a sickeningly sweet smile across my face and sit a little taller, my best perky receptionist impression perfectly in place by the time he stops awkwardly in front of my desk.

"I've got to head out for a lunch meeting. Ben too." Jamie holds his head low and tucks his hands into his pockets, shuffling on the spot. "We'll be gone for two hours."

"I'll make sure to take any messages that come through. Will that be all, Mr. Wilcox?"

The snort from behind Jamie only makes the burning hatred simmering in my chest increase.

"Damn, J." Ben approaches with the cool air of a man who is too confident, smacking his hands onto Jamie's shoulders as he laughs loudly. "Whatever the hell you said to her this morning has done a better job of getting under her skin than I ever have."

"And yet the problem is still you." I mutter.

"Sorry, what was that, Little Mik?" He smirks at me, determined to keep up this infuriating antagonism, and Jamie shrugs out of his grip.

"Right, let's not do this you two," he groans. "You don't like each other. Fine. But as of this morning you're both members in my company so the least you could do is keep it civil, for my sake. Alright?"

I sigh when I look at my brother. His eyes are a warm Grecian sea - crystal clear and calm, just like Mom's - and as he looks over to me they are scrawled with one hundred begged apologies. My fake-ass smile drops for a moment and I take a deep breath.

"Fine," I huff, "but only because I need this job."

"I know you do, Mik." Jamie smiles softly at me and that last little sliver of anger I have been desperately trying to keep hold of disappears. "I know."

"Okay. So." I pull my eyes back to the computer screen as the sting of the past builds in the corners of my mind, and begin typing in the new meetings and appointments I've been jotting down all morning. "I guess I'll see you both in a couple of hours."

"Don't forget to take your break, Mikaela." Ben's voice is deep and gritty and my fingers still at his command.

"Civil does not mean you get to tell me what to do, Haston," I retort before I begin typing again.

"No, but I do." Jamie shrugs with a smile, leaning over the desk and grabbing my dark green tote bag from beside me. "There's a nice little café about two blocks from here. It's quiet and packed with authors all the time. It's a real *you* place. Go."

"I'm not particularly hungry, all things considered."

"Mik." Jamie shakes my bag at me, his eyes fixed on mine as he raises his brows in challenge. "Go."

Jamie's right, of course. The café is exactly the sort of place I would have lost my days to years ago. It's busy and there's volume to it, with groups of men and women and teenagers all nestled into small tables and corners of the room, with their mugs steaming and their fingers dancing over keyboards as they fashion worlds and creatures and lives that are not their own out of letters strung together with the beauty of pearls.

My mind slips away from me as I take it all in and I revel in the magic of it.

I turn slowly, breathing in the scent of freshly ground coffee beans, warm chocolate and vanilla, and gaze around. The back wall is exposed brick with hundreds of small planter pots hanging from silver loops. Fresh herbs and flowers stem within them and spatter the wall with color as exposed lightbulbs hang overhead from thick black wire. Heavy beams stretch out across the ceiling and my eyes trace the patterns of the wood. It's a truly beautiful sight and the tug of a smile ghosts the corners of my lips as I make my way to the queue.

Digging for my purse in the bottom of my bag feels like a criminal offence. I can practically hear the eye rolls around me as I pull notebook after notebook out, followed by some pens, a bag of hair-grips and my keys, before finding any sight of the card I need. With each new item dragged from the depths of what might as well be Mary Poppins' bag itself, my cheeks turn a deeper shade of red.

"Hey." The soft voice behind me is as unexpected as it is uplifting and a small squeak bursts from me as I spin to face the man standing a few inches too close.

"Oh, I'm sorry. Please go around me." I try my best to smile apologetically, painfully aware of how easy it would be for him to reach out and touch me; grab me. "I'm just trying to find my purse."

The man lets out a soft laugh and shakes his head, and my heart hammers in my throat.

"It's Mikaela right? The new receptionist?"

What?

My chest caves as the breath is ripped from my lungs and the world begins to creep in towards me, every hair on the back of my neck stands to attention and the silent grip of terror wraps its bony fingers around my throat as my eyes automatically scan the room. I can't move. I can't make a sound. I can only stand frozen. And then suddenly the stranger is backing away, his eyes wide and his words streaming from him at an obscene speed.

"Oh God, that sounded so creepy. No. I'm so sorry. I'm Max. One of the Editorial Assistants at Wilcox. I promise you, I neither followed you here, nor did I intend to make it seem like I was a crazed stalker or something. This is my favourite lunch spot. Total coincidence, I promise." He huffs out an awkward laugh as the choke hold loosens and I laugh stiffly, shoving my things back into my bag before extending a hand to him.

"Nice to meet you, Max."

There's a crawling sensation on the back of my neck, lingering even now.

"Yes, that's how normal people start a conversation. You're right." He beams at me as he shakes my hand and somehow this simple thing - this stranger's smile - puts me at ease, as if I have known him for a lot longer than the last two awkward minutes. "Can I buy you lunch to apologise for my awful manners?"

"Sure." This time when I laugh it sounds freer - it feels easier - but I can't stop myself from glancing around at the faces surrounding us. "Thank you, Max."

"You are most welcome, Mikaela."

Max Kingford is unapologetically beautiful. His deep, dark skin is smooth - the perfect canvas for the abyss of dark brown that pulls its victims into the depths of his eyes - and his smile is wide and carefree. When he laughs, it's as if an entire chorus sounds from him - booming and bright and unencumbered - and the first time I heard it, I think I got lost in it. Now, I find myself wanting to hear it again.

The walk back to the office is somewhat shorter than the walk to the café, probably due to the conversation and the laughter that keeps me from checking my watch every five seconds, and for a moment genuine shock ricochets off of me when I look up to see that sophisticated, all glass high-rise that homes my brother's company.

"Thank you again for lunch, Max. I really appreciate it."

Max smiles another of his award winning smiles as he flashes the half-sleeping security guard his staff badge and leads me to the elevator.

"It was my pleasure." He pushes the button for the tenth floor and turns to face me. "I remember my first day on the job and honestly, if any of them up there had even bothered to ask my name it would have made my day." He shrugs. "Buying the newbie lunch seems like a pretty good way to make sure the first day isn't completely awful."

Although his smile never falters and his eyes still shine with open kindness, his words seem to draw out a melancholy that neither of us expect and my smile is wistful, if not a little sad. I could like Max if I stay here. I could really like Max because he's right. If anyone else - other than Jamie and his aggravating, obnoxious friend - had stopped by my desk just once to say hello I would have felt ten times better than I had as I slipped out unnoticed for lunch. But no one had. No one except for Max.

"Well." I sigh as the elevator doors slide open to reveal the busy bustle of the office once more. "My first day is officially not completely awful."

He laughs loudly, his dark eyes shining bright as he throws his hands into the air in a dorky display of celebration, ignoring the disgruntled looks and murmurs of disapproval from all around. "Well then, mission success!"

I can feel his eyes on me still, watching as I slip back behind the giant desk and I smile to myself, pushing my hair back. It's a long minute before he speaks again.

"Same time tomorrow?" His voice is light, possibly even hopeful, and I turn to him with my first genuine smile in this ridiculously uncomfortable office.

"Sounds perfect." I turn to face him. "But this time I'm buying."

"Oh, you have a deal," he calls back over his shoulder. "EA's are hardly living the life of the rich and famous, sweetheart. You can feed me."

Ben

Jamie's office is unseasonably warm in comparison to the rest of the floor. He says he likes to keep it 'toasty' which is why I'm standing with my hands in my pockets, my jacket thrown over the back of a chair and my sleeves rolled up. I loosened my tie and undid the top button of my shirt within thirty minutes of being in this greenhouse, but even now I can feel the gnawing sensation of discomfort crawling up my skin.

It's just too warm.

Across the space, by the front desk, Mikaela tucks her hair behind her ears and her head is ducked down as she laughs. Her eyes crease slightly around the edges when she smiles like that, wide and toothy, and her nose scrunches when she shakes her head. She glances back towards the guy she just walked in with, whispering conspiratorially while others around them shake their heads, and that uncomfortable warmth seems to kick up a degree.

I run my hand over the back of my neck, the damp sweat sticking my collar to my skin, and bite down the urge to tell them both to get back to work.

"Damn." Jamie sighs beside me, ignoring the way my body flinches at his proximity. *When did he sneak up behind me?* "It's good to see her laugh. Sometimes I forget what it sounds like."

"What?" I turn to him, my brow furrowing, only for him to turn away quickly - something akin to shame clouding his features. "Why would you forget that?"

"Never mind." Jamie shakes his head quickly and practically sprints towards the door. "I should go let her know the meeting ended early."

"Right. Yeah, that's a good shout." I follow suit, grabbing my jacket and swiftly moving into my own, much cooler, office and finding immediate pleasure in the gust of air conditioning that brushes over my skin. "I've got to get through a few contracts and files today. Familiarise myself with your books. Mind asking her to hold my calls?"

Jamie smiles and immediately I know what he's thinking. And I know how wrong he is.

"This is going to be great," he had enthused weeks ago. *"The three of us together will be like old times, before the chaos. Honestly things have changed. I know it will work."* Even now Jamie can't help but cling to youthful optimism of earlier decades and I sigh as I feel myself give in to a smile.

"Yeah, no worries."

"Thanks, Boss." I grin.

Jamie groans. "You know I hate it when people call me Boss."

"Yes." Honestly, I don't mean to take so much pleasure in his pain, but he makes it so easy sometimes. "I do."

Chapter Two

Mikaela

The thick aroma of fried bacon drifts through the apartment, tempting me out of a much needed sleep, and I roll to my side. Reaching for my phone a swell of darkness comes, bringing in relief as I stretch down to my bones, and I let out a small sigh. It's only six fifteen, but Jamie is a creature of habit and I've grown used to his early rises in the last six months.

Listening carefully, I can hear him padding around the apartment, opening drawers and talking to someone - probably another one of his frat buddies on the phone - and I grumble to myself. Unlike my brother, I do not function well in the mornings. In fact, I don't function at all.

One glance in the mirror confirms my suspicions that the fact I had another shit night's sleep is written in the pallor of my skin and the groggy look in my eyes and I kick my feet a little in frustration. I need sleep. Lots of it.

I clamber out of bed, grabbing a pair of ridiculous socks from a drawer, and shove my feet into them as I stumble out towards the promise of breakfast, burnt or otherwise.

At least I get food this time. Usually I'm the one who cooks.

My stomach growls and I grumble through a yawn.

Ben

"You know, Jamie." She yawns as she falls out of the spare room, yanking on a sock. "I think I'll enjoy my mornings much more when I find my own place."

When I glance back at her my skin prickles. Her hair is a mess of curls bursting from a knot on top of her head and it seems to bounce as she trips a little. There's a simple beauty about her when she's half asleep.

Don't fucking stare, Ben.

"Why is that, do you think?" I try to level my voice into something light and can't help but laugh when she stops moving.

Her eyes snap up, her hands now knotted in her hair as she tries and fails to tame it, and a small squeak slips from her lips. I can feel my smile slipping. It falls out of place entirely as I trace over the tight fit of a tank top that has seen better days and shorts that leave very little to the imagination. Still, my mind does a pretty good job of imagining certain things anyway and my heart is a jackhammer in my chest. For one terrifying moment I find myself wondering what it might feel like to run my fingers over the slip of skin that peeks over the waistband of her shorts - what it could feel like to trail kisses along the exposed white of her shoulder and up her neck.

Fuck.

As she crosses her arms over her chest and a mask of stone cold indifference slips across her face, I shake my head, willing away the thoughts that have absolutely no place in this fragile little thing between us, and turn back to the stove.

"What are you doing here?"

If she wants to sound intimidating she needs to give herself time to wake up.

I smile as I focus on the eggs that are now over-cooked. "I was invited."

Mikaela

He's just standing there with a spatula in his hand, staring. Neither of us speak and my skin tingles underneath his steady gaze.

Why is he breathing like that?

I shift and fold my arms around myself, wishing I'd thrown on a sweatshirt before I left my room, and he shakes his head as he turns away from me.

"What are you doing here?" My throat croaks with sleep and I grimace.

"I was invited." He sounds like he's smiling. "Breakfast?"

"It's six am, Haston. Why are you in my kitchen?"

"First of all, this is your brother's kitchen, and you're the one who pointed that out. Although, I will admit you didn't realise it was me you were pointing it out to so, I'll allow it." Waving the spatula in front of him, Ben chuckles.

I roll my eyes as I move around him, opening the refrigerator and grabbing a water.

"Secondly," he continues, "I'm going for a run with your brother in ten. Care to join?"

My hand stills and my body heats. Memories of watching Ben and Jamie compete on the track in high-school, Ben's muscles slick with sweat and his smile mischievous, slink into my mind and my breathing thickens.

Oh, hell no, Mikaela Wilcox. Do not even go there. You hate him. Hate.

"Erm. Sure." I close the refrigerator and look back to my bedroom. "But no to the breakfast. Thanks."

"As you wish."

I practically sprint to my bedroom just as Jamie steps out of the bathroom.

In the safety of my room I close my eyes and lean against the door, my mind spinning and my stomach knotting. I am almost entirely sure I imagined the way his eyes trailed over me, drinking in every single inch of my body, undressing me without so much as taking a single step towards me. I'm convinced, wholeheartedly convinced, that in my half-sleeping state my mind has conjured up something that does not exist, that is not there. Something that has *never* existed. That, despite the fact I now feel flustered and confused, I did not feel the delicious tightening of desire when he looked at me like that. I can't feel desire when he looks at me like that. Not now, not ever.

Pushing forwards I make my way to the closet and dig for a gym set in the mountains of clothes I haven't bothered to put away since laundry day.

He is trouble, Mikaela.

I shake my head clear of the image of him standing there with that stupid spatula and that look that burned right through me.

You've had enough trouble with men to last a life time.

I pull a pair of cobalt blue shorts and a matching sports bra from the pile and throw them on before grabbing one of Jamie's black hoodies I stole weeks ago from the chair in the corner of the room.

You want someone calm. Someone good.

Bending over to slip on my shoes, I feel the phantom tightness in my gut - a constant reminder that I have to take it easier than I used to - and I huff out a disappointed sigh before moving to the mirror.

When I look at myself I want to put on a t-shirt; I want to hide. Instead, I run my fingers along the line across my stomach and take a breath. I grab the comb from my dresser and pull it through the knotted mess of my hair, forcing it into some semblance of control and trying to tie it back. Flyaway's stick in twenty different directions despite my attempts to flatten them and I grunt in frustration. It will do. It's not like I want to impress Haston of all people.

Ben

Jamie frowns as Mikaela slips out of her room, her headphones tangled in her fingers while her phone hangs from her lips.

"You have pockets, Mik." He grunts over to her as he spots the hoodie she has slung over one arm and she rolls her eyes. "And by the looks of it they're mine."

Bringing my glass to my lips I try to suppress a smile. It seems Mikaela still steals her brother's clothes and that small detail makes me happy. At least that hasn't changed. Her phone is precariously balanced between her teeth when she smiles and she drops the black sweatshirt over the back of the couch, before twisting towards her brother.

Beneath the dark blue outfit that might as well be a second skin is a pink line, starting somewhere beneath her bra and running down her stomach. It puckers out, a visible ridge against her skin that screams for attention, and I can't tear my eyes from it. It's fresh - not brand new, but new enough that it hasn't transformed into that silver string of something old - and neat. Surgical.

I watch as she grins and moves to Jamie's side, nudging him with her hip, before drawing my eyes back to my plate. My mind swims in questions I have no right to ask.

Growing up I had very little to do with Mikaela. She made sure of it. I'm pretty sure she thought I was an irritant that her brother refused to put down and, on the odd occasion she hadn't wanted distance, Jamie made sure she got it anyway. He made sure that our paths only crossed in wider circles for a long time. Mikaela had been quiet and focused and determined to make better for herself than the life she had been living in the tiny apartment her mom could barely afford and I had been the opposite. I was chaos and trouble all rolled into a charmingly good looking face with a wide smile and gleaming eyes. I knew it too, which only made trouble more fun. My parents had money, so there was little I couldn't get away with – not to mention my grandfather's connections – and truthfully, I revelled in the facade of freedom it brought me.

Jamie followed in my ways; drinking too much as teenagers and spending nights at parties, cozied up to new girls every time. Mikaela had loathed me for that – the trouble Jamie got into. In her eyes it was reckless and destructive. It wasn't how their mother was raising them. In mine, it was living life while you could. Before responsibilities took over and made you stop playing. In hindsight, I wonder if it was an escape for Jamie.

I glance up to Mik again as she takes her phone from her mouth and wipes it on Jamie's arm, grinning when he recoils from her and pushes her away from him. When she smiles there's a mischief in her that I haven't seen before and she throws her head back slightly as she laughs.

I can't look away.

I trace the freckles that run down her neck and across her chest as she slips into the giant hoodie, pulling up the zip, and pull my lip between my teeth. This is definitely a dangerous game, but I know I'm not imagining what I see when her eyes meet mine. The peach blush that rises beneath her skin and the way her breath hitches slightly. Mikaela may hate me, but she isn't immune to me and, for some stupid reason, I am greeted with a sense of pride in making her blush.

I want to do it again.

"Shall we?" I stand from my seat at the breakfast bar and move to put my plate in the sink.

"You've just eaten. Don't you need to wait?" Mikaela cocks her head to the side and - *fuck me sideways* - it's absolutely adorable.

"Don't worry about me, Little Mik."

She grimaces and Jamie rolls his eyes.

"Besides," I continue, "you wait to swim after eating and I don't intend on finding a pool."

"This is going to be great fun," Jamie complains, watching his sister scowl as she shoves her headphones into her ears and glares at me.

"Whatever." It's kind of sweet when she grumbles. "Let's just go."

33

Mikaela

"Mik?" Ben's hand is on my shoulder as he crouches beside me, gently brushing the stray tendrils of my hair from my neck as I gasp for breath. There are black spots floating through the space around me and my head is thumping as my heart sputters and stumbles. "Are you okay?"

I don't have the energy to shrug off his touch as I sit with my head between my knees and try to focus on breathing. My lungs are burning and my insides started screaming at me to stop twenty minutes ago because I was stupid and tried to match the pace of the two of them. It was a bad idea, I know that, but I didn't want Ben to see that I'm weaker now. Benjamin Haston knowing I have been so reckless with my life is not something I ever want. I take another burning breath as I tell myself it's because he'd never let me forget it - he'd hold it over me and judge me harshly and I have had enough judgement to last a lifetime - but the idea of him seeing me so damaged makes my heart squeeze painfully.

"I'm fine." I close my eyes for a moment before pushing myself up to my feet.

Darkness encroaches quickly, blanketing where I stand, and I stumble, my head suddenly light and my limbs detached.

"Shit." His breath releases on a hiss as a horn sounds and warm hands grip my waist, pulling me back into a wide chest, away from the edge of the road and into his arms.

His palm is flat against my stomach as my hoodie hangs off of my shoulders and I freeze. My whole body seizes up beneath his touch.

"You should sit down again, Mik."

I try to breathe, my mind reeling as ice floods my veins, and his touch remains firm against me.

"Let go of me." I am weak. I am fearful and pathetic and I don't care. I don't care about anything except for the fact I can feel his hands on my skin and I can't breathe.

"Mik?" His hand slips from my stomach, but he remains close against me, spinning me to face him. His fingers rest against my waist with ease, as if he has always held me like this, and he furrows his brow and ducks down to look at me. I can feel my lips trembling, my heart rate spiking again, and I drop my eyes to the floor. "What's wrong?"

"I said let go." I don't know what to do. I don't know where to turn or look. Jamie ran ahead of us earlier and Ben held back when I started to lag. Now, as he holds me close and people continue their morning routines around us, I feel like I'm suffocating.

Because, despite the fact I *know* it's Ben's hands on my hips, I don't see him.

I push him off of me and back away. He steps forwards just the tiniest amount as my hand cups my throat and I feel my last shred of control slipping. When I start to run again, I run alone, straight back to the apartment. This time the desire to puke isn't coming from the pain in my side, or the complete lack of exercise I've had for months. This time the nausea comes with a face and a name and hands that I can still feel all over my body, and I need to shower. I need to scrub him off.

Max pulls his chair through the office, nodding politely at every single person who stares at him with interest or disapproval, and whistles to himself. When he gets to my desk, he throws himself down and spins dramatically as he eyes me with an intense sort of intrigue. "Why so frowny today, Mikaela?"

I chuff out a laugh as I continue to scratch ideas down in my notebook, hoping something might stick while I have a brief lull from enquiring phone calls and authors with too much authority barking demands at me. "Just busy today, Max."

"Lies."

A small scream leaves me as Max snatches my notebook from my hands and for a moment I forget that we aren't alone, only to be brought back to reality by the judgemental tutting of the ice blonde Queen Bee office manager as she struts behind my desk towards Jamie's office. Glancing back to me, Max laughs that joyous laugh again, cracking my own smile in half as he spins away and I give in to his playful demeanour, desperately trying to crawl over him to retrieve my notes. I laugh while I claw at him and he pushes me back into my chair.

"Max, give it back!"

"There are some really cool concepts in here." He muses aloud as he pushes away from me, holding the arm of my chair so that I'm trapped behind the desk. "Like, really cool. I've read a lot of manuscripts that are well written but have no original thought. These are original."

"You know for a stranger you're really quite happy to just insert yourself into my life, aren't you?" I throw my hands up in exasperation as I kick back in my chair, giving up the fight while he grins and flicks to a new page.

"You ever tried to publish?"

"No." I turn back to my computer, suddenly feeling the weight of vulnerability as he scrutinises the characters and concepts I've spent countless hours scribbling tiny little lives for.

"Why?" He focuses in on an idea I half conceived this morning and grabs a highlighter and pen from my desk, marking phrases for me and adding notes.

"Nothing ever stuck enough to finish it, I guess." The phone, now glowing with a small red light, flashes up at us and I hold a finger up to Max, taking a deep breath.

"Yes?" I hook the phone between my ear and my shoulder and grimace at the voice on the line, despite knowing it is his extension.

"I was thinking of grabbing an early lunch. Jamie's busy." Ben spins on his desk chair in his office when I turn to face him and watches me through the window. "Join me?"

I can feel Max watching me as my eyes bug and I spin back to face the front of the office.

Lunch. Me. And Haston. Alone?

"No thanks. I have plans."

"You're going to eat? Because after this morning -"

I roll my eyes as I cut him off. "Yes, I'm going to eat with Max."

Ben

I focus in on the assistant now pointing something out in her notebook and the way she grins over to him; comfortable, easy, like they're familiar.

"Right. Well, enjoy that then."

Good. I'm glad she's going with him. I don't need to babysit her - make sure she's looking after herself. It's not my place to do that. Never has been.

I put the phone down instantly, watching as she stares at the handset for a moment before turning back to the man at her desk and I realise, I'm pissed. Pissed that I asked her to go with me. Pissed that she said no. And pissed that she's sitting there laughing with that guy when he has a fucking job to do.

Mikaela

"So, what's with you and Baby Blue?" Max unscrews his water bottle as he grins over at me.

"Who?" I push the last bits of salad across my plate, my stomach full and uncomfortable from the burger Max insisted was *to die for*. I feel like I will die if I eat anything else.

"You know, Baby Blue? The other new kid? The swoon-worthy one." He leans back in his chair with a dreamy sigh and raises an eyebrow at me when I glance up at him.

"You mean Haston?"

He nods, his face impassive now, but those dark eyes glimmer with suggestion.

"Nothing is *with* us. He's Jamie's best friend. Has been for years." I feel my face contort into an automatic scowl as I put the fork down and take a sip from my bottle. "And he's a giant pain in my ass."

Around us, the breeze picks up and people chat as they pass on the sidewalk. Birds flit between potted trees that line the sidewalk bistro and the sun beats down on my back, pulling a light sheen of sweat that seems to cling to my skin and my blouse, leaving me uncomfortable and jittery.

"And the three of you grew up together?"

I laugh as Max waits. Often, I forget that people don't automatically connect me with Jamie. We share the same hair color, a sandy blonde with dark streaks hidden within, and our noses are similar too, but the connections seem to stop there. My eyes are a mossy, dirty kind of green while Jamie's are brilliant blue, and he towers over my five-foot-three frame by almost a whole foot. His skin is sun-kissed gold, while mine could give Snow White a run for her money, with a spattering of freckles that seem to spread out over every inch of my body.

"Yeah." I sit back, letting my hair fall behind me as I bring my face up to the warmth of the sun. "Jamie's my brother."

Max nods thoughtfully as he picks at his own food and I glance to him when he clears his throat.

"Well I guess this is the end of a beautiful friendship." He sighs dramatically. "And to think, it had only just begun."

I can't help it. I bark out a loud laugh, the woman on the table next to me jumping at the sound, and he grins. "And why does it have to end now?"

"Because I can't have the boss finding out the things I say at lunch."

"Oh, well that's an easy enough fix, Max." I shrug with nonchalance. "I just won't tell him."

Max smirks as he holds his bottle out to me, waiting for me to tap my own to his. "That sounds like a much more enjoyable arrangement. You're right."

"I usually am," I laugh.

As I fish through my bag for the key card I know I threw in here before we left for lunch, Max stands and stretches. A small frown pulls his eyebrows down, and he glances behind me.

"Everything okay?" I look back to him before my fingers catch on the cold plastic and I finally find it.

"Yeah." His voice is distant and he shakes his head slightly.

My skin prickles. The hair on my arms seem to lift as a chill that has nothing to do with the weather settles over me and I twist in my seat, catching a flash of messy auburn hair in the crowd. My stomach twists and nausea bubbles in my throat.

"Just thought some guy was staring at us but, I don't know." Max's smile is back as he looks at me, but I'm staring at the retreating figure.

He's not here, Mikaela. It's just your mind playing tricks on you.

"Shall we?" Max is holding his hand out for me.

I swallow the lump in my throat.

"Yeah. Sure." I take his arm and we move away from the spine chilling sense of dread as I do my best to push aside another flare of pain.

Ben

"Stop that." Jamie peers up at me over the manuscript he's spent the last three hours pouring over and I sit throwing a small ball up into the air repeatedly. "What's gotten into you today?"

"Nothing," I grumble.

Fucking observant dick. Convinced me to take this stupid job.

I glance back to the empty desk in the front of the office and grunt.

"Mhm." Jamie nods to himself as he scratches out something he doesn't like. "And I'm the next American

Idol. Seriously, I thought you ran in the mornings to get the temper out of you, not to draw it out for you?"

"I'm not in a temper."

"Again I say, American freaking Idol, Ben. Go get some lunch or something. I'm busy here and you're making it hard to focus."

I scoff as I get to my feet and sulk out of the room. I need to get out of this funk and quickly. Sweeping my eyes over the faces in the space around me I find that my appetite is gone, but I make my way over to the nearest desk anyway.

"Hey." I plaster on a smile, bright and wide - the type that I spent my teenage years perfecting - and lick my lower lip as the wide brown eyes of the girl in front of me meet mine. "How's it going today?"

I run my eyes over her, appreciating the thin white blouse that's buttoned one button too low, and the charcoal grey skirt that sits just above her knee. She's pretty in that overdone, always perfect kind of way - her hair is an almost white blonde and her lips are just a little too pouted - and a tiny voice in my mind makes note of the fact she's wearing way more make up than Mik does.

"It's going well." The girl smiles as she flutters her eyelashes at me. "How about you?"

I nod as my eyes slowly travel back to hers, deliberately dragging out the moment and pausing for a second too long on those lips.

"It's going a lot better now." Lowering my voice, I revel in the way her eyes drop when I speak. "I don't suppose you need a coffee right about now?"

She gets to her feet with a sultry smile and leans forwards to reach for her purse, no doubt a deliberate ploy to press her ass against me, and I hold in my urge to roll my eyes. *Perfectly predictable.*

Quickly, I lead the girl out of the office with my hand on the small of her back and my eyes straight ahead, laughing with her at some stupid little joke she makes as we approach the elevator.

When the doors slide open Mikaela is laughing, leaning into that assistant's side as he draws in a laboured breath. I can feel my jaw tighten as I watch the guys hand withdraw from her waist and they step around me. She hardly acknowledges my existence, save for a quick glance in my direction, and they walk back into the office. It's like I'm just some stranger in her way and it enrages me.

Fuck.

My hand slips away from the girl's back and I shove both hands in my pockets as we step into the elevator and she comes to a stop far too close to me. She smiles coyly up at me, shuffling closer, and I stare directly ahead. My eyes don't leave Mikaela. Not until the doors close and my shoulders slump.

Chapter Three

Mikaela

The only way to describe the sound that leaves my chest is a cackle. A witchy, heartfelt cackle. Max leans in to me as he wheezes, his hand holding my waist while I dry my eyes and try to calm down.

"He didn't?" Another burst of laughter comes when I look into his wide eyes and he silently begs for me to believe him.

"I swear." He sucks in a short breath. "He looked like he'd been caught shitting on someone's doorstep as soon as he saw her and she was ice cold. No reaction."

My head rolls back as I lean against the wall, still crying, still desperately trying to steady my breath before I have to see Jamie again, and Max leans against me. Our bodies shake in silence before he starts choking on another round of hysterical laughter.

"No one ever said anything about it again?" I push off of the wall as we both straighten up and he shakes his head, his eyes going wide with alarm.

"God, no." The thought alone sobers him up enough to stop his laughing. Unfortunately, it only adds to mine. "I don't think anyone wanted to get fired. I mean, he was so embarrassed. And then, when she published the story, she painted him as a bashful bachelor and girls were calling here all week because she published his photo with it. I think it was revenge. The whole office decided he was going through enough. It was our first big bit of press."

"I can't believe he never told me."

"Why would he tell you, Mikaela? He slept with the girl, span some lie about having to leave town for a year and ends up interviewed by her the next week. That shit's just embarrassing."

I fall into another fit of breathless giggles as I lean forwards, my hand resting on Max's forearm, and the doors slide open.

Almost immediately I feel the cool gaze of discontent washing over me and I twist my body to step out of the elevator, avoiding Ben's eyes. Instead my gaze falls on his arm, tucked behind the office administrator, his hand clearly resting possessively on the small of her back. She's staring up at him all doe-eyed and smiley and I step carefully out of their way as Max's hand slips from my waist.

I don't look back, even when I get to my desk. Instead, I take my phone and notepad out of my bag and try to ignore the burn of his eyes on me. I can see him from the corner of my eye, standing with his hands now shoved in his pockets and his focus completely trained on me. Max grunts something beside me, throwing himself in my desk chair, and watching the doors close in an excruciating display of time slowing down to extend my misery.

"Erm. Up please." I smile softly at Max once Ben is gone.

"You know the pain in the ass has a thing for you, right?"

My stomach twists and I bark out a grim laugh.

"I'm glad you said that now and not before lunch, because that's a sure fire way to put any girl off of her food."

"Mikaela." He raises his eyebrows at me as I push him out of my chair and roll my eyes.

"Max."

"I saw the way you froze up when he looked at you." There's a playful shrug of his shoulders when he plonks onto the desk and picks up the stress ball I brought in this morning. "You sure there's nothing there on your part?"

Putting my head in my hands I can't help but feel drained already. This is one of the things I always hated when Haston would appear in my life; constant questioning. Constant doubt and justifications and not being believed. Just like that fucking night two years ago when he showed up in Boston and landed himself in our favourite bar of all places. Taking a deep breath, I remind myself that Max doesn't know this.

"Completely sure, Max. There was just a thing this morning that has me on edge with him." I smile softly as I look up, determined not to ruin a great afternoon with the heaviness of my life. "That's all."

Max nods, pushing himself off of my desk and smiling widely.

"Okay. You've got one smooth playboy incoming, FYI." Max backs away towards his desk and pretends to cover his eyes in embarrassment as I stifle a giggle. Gratitude floods my senses and I thank the heavens for the way Max can ease back into simple fun so quickly.

Jamie stops at my desk with a pile of papers in his hands and an apologetic smile. The same smile he used one hundred times when we were kids. The same smile that usually means I'm going to have to do something he should be doing, or I'm going to have to cover for him.

"What do you want?" I frown and he sucks in a breath.

"I've got a potential new signing coming in in twenty. He's big news, Mik. Publishing him could really put us on the map here."

"But?" I prompt, knowing he's not done.

"But I also needed to read and make decisions on these manuscripts that were sent in… by yesterday."

Of course he did. And of course he's now flashing his signature puppy dog eyes at me as he waits for my response.

Bastard.

"Don't you hire editors to do that for you, Jamie?"

"They're swamped. I wouldn't ask if it wasn't necessary. Besides, you're the fastest reader in this place by a long shot. And your ma-" he pauses as he realises what he was about to say. Now I just want him to leave me alone.

"My major was supposed to be in Creative Writing. Yep."

"I'm sorry."

I sigh and hold my hands out for the two manuscripts he's gripping tightly. "Decisions by yesterday, huh?"

Jamie grins as he ducks down quickly, planting a swift kiss against my scalp, and I swat at his chest. Heat floods my cheeks and I twist to check no one is watching.

"Jamie," I groan.

"What would I do without you, sis?"

"Fail." My voice is a grumble and nothing more, and Jamie grins down at me before ruffling my hair a little.

When the intercom buzzes I shove my highlighter into the mess of curls I've scrunched on top of my head, holding it in place, and pick up the phone.

"Yes, Boss?"

"Stop calling me that."

I can hear Jamie's smile. "Will do, Boss."

"Right, whatever." His smile is probably now a pout which feels like a mission completed. "Josh should be here any minute now, but I've got to make a call. Can you just keep him with you until I'm ready?"

I glance up just as the doors of the elevator open and my voice catches in my throat. "Sure thing."

I take a second to collect myself as I put down the phone and rise to my feet. My eyes run over him and suddenly I feel gawky and awkward.

His hair is a mop of ruffled curls, a soft brown and unruly, and his eyes are so dark they're almost a piercing black. They feel like cold water running over my skin. His skin is sun kissed and a gentle red splays over his prominent cheekbones. Deep grey jeans and a black shirt, the top few buttons undone, cling to his body and this guy oozes confidence.

I smooth my hands over the pale pink dress I had chosen to wear today and thank every deity there is for the foresight to wear heels. He's tall. *Very* tall.

As he steps forwards and into the office, he smiles. And it's a beautiful, wide, breathtaking smile. His eyes run over the length of me and I try not to shift under his gaze.

"Welcome to Wilcox Writings."

Why is my voice so breathy?

"You must be Jamie's sister." He speaks softly, with a gentle English accent and a warm smile.

"Yes. Josh, I presume?"

"You already know my name?" That smile shifts into something playful, boyish even, and a shiver runs the length of my spine. "Now I feel like I'm on the back foot here, because your brother never told me yours."

He holds his hand out for me to take and I feel my blush spreading up my chest and into my cheeks.

"Mikaela. It's a pleasure to meet you."

Josh rakes his eyes over me again, making no effort to be subtle in his appraisal, and holds my hand for a moment too long. I can see it in his eyes; he knows exactly what effect he has on me and he's unashamed of the fact he's enjoying it. "The pleasure is most definitely mine."

I need to say something - anything - but he's looking at me as if we aren't standing at the front of a very busy office and my veins are on fire.

"So, is your brother about?" His eyes flick to my lips and I force myself to look away - break the contact.

Sitting back in my chair, I gesture to the seats against the wall. "He's just on a call. If you'd like to take a seat I can let you know when he's ready for you."

Josh nods slowly as he steps back and relaxes into a leather seat, his hand coming up to brush over the five-o'clock-shadow forming on his jaw as he watches me work, and I struggle to focus on the words in the manuscript in front of me.

As time creeps forwards I sneak glances at him, expecting to find him on his phone or doing something other than watching me, and each time he smiles as if he's caught me doing something I shouldn't.

Something beneath my skin tells me he *has* caught me doing something I shouldn't.

After being caught looking at him for a fourth time, I remove the highlighter that is jammed in my hair and let my curls cascade down to form a barrier between us. I highlight a passage of the text in front of me and write down my suggestions as I pray for Jamie to finish on the phone quickly.

The intercom buzzes and I jump. Josh smiles.
Great. Now I look nervous.
I reach for the phone and smile over to him.
"Hey, Boss."

"I hate when you call me that." A noisy rustling seems to crackle down the phone, making it nearly impossible to hear Jamie, and I roll my eyes. I'm on speaker and he's searching his desk drawers. "Is Josh here?"

"Yes. He got here about ten minutes ago."

Josh shifts in his seat.

"Great. Send him in?"

"Will do, Boss."

Leaning forwards when I speak, Josh smiles as something flickers behind his eyes - amusement maybe? - and my stomach flips.

"You can go on back now. Do you know which one's his office?"

He rises to his feet swiftly, brushing down his jeans and pausing to look at me again. "Yeah, I've been here before. Thanks, beautiful."

I can't help the smile that escapes me. It's small and embarrassed, and still it's intoxicating, and for the briefest moment it hits me that maybe I enjoyed feeling his eyes on me? For the first time in a long time, I think I could have enjoyed the attention.

As Joshua Lucas waltzes through the office with the command of someone who knows how important he is, Max slowly slinks towards my desk, breaking into a mini run when Jamie gestures to the small meeting table in his office and closes the blinds.

"Okay." He grins, his eyes shining as they dart between the closed door and me. "You might claim Baby Blue isn't interested, but that beautiful London boy, who just so happens to be sitting across from your brother in what I am assured is a meeting *way* above my pay grade, just spent ten minutes trying to figure out how to get you out of this office and into his bed." He's shaking with excitement.

I bury my face in my hands and laugh as I groan.

"Okay. Okay. You might be right." When I glance up Max is positively beaming with pride. "I'll give you that one."

Max grins as he perches against the edge of my desk with his back to the elevator.

"I mean, Mikaela Wilcox, I am not condoning workplace rendezvous." He raises an eyebrow as I twist in my chair, my fingers pressed against my lips as I steal a glance in the direction of the office. "Actually, forget that. I really am. Rendezvous my gorgeous girl. *Ren-dez-vous.*"

"I'm sure you're not paid to sit around at reception and flirt all day, Mr Kingford." The icy acidity of Ben's tone cuts Max through and stops his laughter in its tracks. My eyes widen slightly at the sight when I turn to see Ben standing with two takeaway cups in his hands and a scowl on his face. "You were up early this morning. I figured you might need some caffeine." He places a steaming cup of coffee onto the desk and turns to Max, who's still standing awkwardly beside me. "Your job, Mr Kingford?"

"Yes. Of course." He shoots a worried glance my way and I nod. "Sorry."

As Max scurries back to his desk across the open space, Ben rounds back to me and I feel my chest tighten.

"How's your day going?" He smiles slightly and I furrow my brow. Right after he's just been so rude, now he wants to be nice? His eyes shift slightly, following Max back to his desk, and I snort. He glances back to me at the noise, an amused smile pulling at his mouth, and his teeth graze the fullness of his lower lip.

What the fuck?

"It was going swimmingly until you swanned in with that attitude, thanks."

That sounded cutting. Good.

"Oh come on, Mik. I saved him from a breach of contract issue or something." He flashes a dazzling smile and I huff in return. "Right." He grunts as he throws a hand in Max's direction and his scowl returns. "Do you want me to go and apologise? Bring him back? I'll do it. I'm just trying to make *this* friendly."

Rolling my eyes as he waves a hand between us, I return to the manuscript I've been working through and shake my head. "Thank you for the coffee Haston, now if you don't mind, I'm sure I'm not being paid to sit around talking to you either."

Ben grunts an incoherent response and storms past me as I scribble notes on the page.

Despite every nerve in my body telling me to let him leave, I glance back at him as the blonde he'd left with earlier stalks in and glares at his retreating frame. His shoulders are hunched as he runs a hand over his face and mutters to himself.

"What a fucking waste of effort." He glances back to me and I turn away quickly. "Kingford can do what he fucking likes. What am I even doing?"

I look down at the coffee in front of me. Oat milk caramel latte. Just like I used to order.

When I glance back he's stopped in the middle of the office, glancing between my desk and his office, and I choke on the possibility of an unexpected realisation.

"Ben?"

He turns to me with confusion in his eyes.

"Max is gay, by the way."

I watch his shoulders shake as he chuffs out a laugh and closes his eyes, shaking his head slowly. I can feel the amusement dancing off of me as I watch him turn back to his office and take another step away from me.

"Good." The word slips from his lips in a whisper and the whole atmosphere shifts. There's a tension in the air. Something unspoken hangs with the word, something unwanted and off-limits, and he moves away faster, slamming the door behind him.

I watch him throw his coffee straight into the bin.

As I pack away my things and neaten the desk after the last few people have left, I hear the door to Jamie's office open. He walks out laughing, his hand on Josh's shoulder as they speak between themselves and I smile at the sight.

Sometimes it's so easy to forget just how much time and effort went into Jamie building this business. How many sacrifices he had to make. How much this place meant to him when he really needed it. Especially seeing as I missed most of it. Now he seems to glow when he speaks with authors and agents, and I feel a swell of pride as I watch him.

In the corner of my eye I can see Ben, sitting with one hand running through the dark crop of his hair while the other holds his phone to his ear. He sighs in frustration at whatever's being said, and I watch him close his eyes and lean back, as if trying desperately to remain calm.

Good, he had said. *Good.*

The approaching laughter pulls me back to the two men before me and I smile warmly up at them both. "Looks like the meeting went well?"

"Very well." Josh smiles at me as if he's known me for decades and my stomach flips a little.

When Josh turns back to Jamie, Jamie's head is cocked to the side as he watches me intently. I glare at him, silently screaming for him to stop, and a slow smile slips over his lips when he turns back to Josh.

"It's going to be good to be part of such a great group, James."

I watch my brother as he takes Josh's hand in a firm grip and smiles with the warmth of the sun, and happiness settles in my bones while I return to shutting down the computer and locking the drawers of my desk.

"I'll get our team to draw up the contracts and have them sent over for you to have your lawyer to look over ASAP. Okay?"

"Perfect." The gentle lift of that British accent settles into something soft, enticing me to look back to him and I hold my breath when our eyes meet. "You heading home?"

"I am, yes."

"I don't suppose I could tempt you with a drink?" His grin is wicked and my blush is furious as Jamie wags his eyebrows and backs away as my eyes shoot to him.

It's one thing to imagine Josh might be looking at me with any form of desire, but it's something else entirely to find out my imagination was right. My heart hammers in my chest and my breathing becomes light.

A drink is innocent enough. I could go for a drink.

"Go," Jamie encourages, "I'm gonna drag Ben out for a few anyway. Have fun."

Trying not to hyperventilate, I turn away from my brother and shake my head as I suck in a deep breath and smile.

"Sure." Nervous, I push my hair back behind my ear. "A drink would be nice."

The room is heaving and I find myself pressed up against Josh as we squeeze towards the last open seats against the bar. Music throbs through the floorboards, pulsating with a lazy kind of drawl that drags the crowd around the room as friends call out to each other, and Josh's hand rests against my waist.

"Sorry." He leans in and shouts into my ear above the noise of constant conversation and the drone of the singer's voice. "I'm not from around here. I genuinely thought this would be a quiet little bar."

"Wait." I can't stop myself from laughing as I push up onto my tiptoes, my hand resting against his chest, while I try to speak into his ear. "You mean that accent's not local?"

"You're funny." He smirks as his hand shifts to the small of my back and he holds me closer. "I like that."

Flames dance beneath my cheeks as his eyes trace my lips and my breathing hitches. Behind him a couple starts to move, gathering their stuff and pushing away from the stools perched beside the bar, and I push him away gently.

"Seats." I nod to the open spot, trying not to melt under the heat of his gaze, and he smiles as he guides me to step ahead of him.

Once seated, Josh immediately moves to call the bar tender over and I tuck my hair behind my ears again, taking a deep breath and trying to remain calm.

I haven't been on a date in years. And this, sitting in a bar with a handsome stranger, feels like a date. In fact, when he looks at me the way he looked at me just two minutes ago, it feels like the kind of date I have always had rules about. Rules that I need to remind myself of if he keeps touching me.

"What would you like?" He turns a dazzling smile to me as the bar tender leans over the counter and listens for my order. Josh's hand is placed lightly on my knee, a simple touch, but possessive somehow - like he's claiming me in front of this man - and I swallow.

Don't read what isn't there, Mikaela. People touch.

"Oh - erm - just a beer please."

"Any preference?" The bartender looks stressed as he glances around the busy room and the emotional fool in me feels a squeeze of pity as I follow his eyes across the crowd. He's alone back there.

"No, whatever's easiest for you. Thanks."

When he moves from us, Josh cocks his head to the side with a slight smirk. "I wouldn't have pegged you for a beer kind of girl?"

"Well, there's a lot you don't know about me." I laugh as two drinks are placed in front of us and he nods slowly.

"I think we should fix that." He leans casually on the bar, one hand still placed on my knee, his thumb brushing the edge of my dress with casual ease, as the other swirls the glass of water he's holding. "Three things I should know about you? Go."

My laugh is stiff as he waits. This man is confident and forward. My heart seems torn by the way he smiles at me like he wants me; like I should be happy that I don't have to wonder what was going on in his head when he looks at me like that, but something unknown stops me from revelling in it fully.

I tell myself it's nice. It's refreshing.

"Okay." I take a sip of my beer, glancing around at friends laughing in corner booths, colleagues celebrating successes over drinks and awkward first dates making polite chit-chat as they avoid checking their phones. "I'm feeling the pressure now. Hmm."

There is a softness to his smile as he sips from his glass and waits, and I feel my mind scrambling for information to share with him.

"Okay, so Jamie and I grew up just two blocks from where his office is, before it became all corporate buildings and business central. I moved out of town for a while and haven't been back long, and number three?" I click my tongue as I try to think of anything other than the one thing screaming in my mind. "When I was a kid, my neighbour had a dog called Snuffy and I told everyone she was mine."

Josh nods slowly, rubbing his chin as he pretends that these three things are the most important pieces of information he will ever be given, and I stifle a laugh.

"Your turn," I prompt.

"Right." He sits a little taller now, shuffling slightly on his stool so that he is just the tiniest bit closer to me and I glance down to his hand still cupping my thigh. "I'm from London, obviously." He smiles as I feign surprise and I can't help but smile back. He really does have a charming smile. I take a sip of my drink as he continues. "I have two brothers." He leans closer. "And I think you're beautiful."

Suddenly beer is coming out of my nose and my eyes are streaming as I choke on my drink.

Reaching past me to grab napkins from a pile perched on the bar, Josh grins - biting back his laugh - and I groan as I try to wipe at my face. The skin of my leg is warm still where his hand had been and I twist myself to face the bar, accepting the offer of paper towels and burying my face in my hands.

To Josh's credit, he regains his composure swiftly and his voice softens when I don't look back to him. "You alright there?"

"Sorry. Wow that's embarrassing." I laugh half-heartedly and roll my eyes.

Ground just swallow me whole.

"You can change your third thing now, if you want."

His smile is endearingly soft when I finally look at him and the world seems to pull out from under me as he says, "no, I'm good."

56

Chapter Four

Mikaela

In the stoop of Jamie's apartment building, a little drunk and full of laughter, I reach again to take my bag from Josh's shoulder. He pulls back quickly and I stumble forwards, placing my hand on his chest to steady myself.

"Come on, I need that." I'm giggling like a school girl and I can't seem to stop.

Gone is that charming smile. Now he grins wickedly, his grip tightening on the handle as his free arm wraps around my waist and he pulls me in.

"If I give you your bag back, Mikaela," he whispers, "then you'll fish those keys out and go inside, and I'll have to accept that tonight is over."

His eyes focus on me and my laughter dies. I take a steadying breath and try to ignore the mingling scent of musky leather and sandalwood.

"But tomorrow has so much potential." I can hear the shake in my voice as I look up to him and feel myself sinking. I focus on his eyes, eyes that contain whispers that bubble beneath the dark surface, and my chest tightens.

"You know." He drops his voice to a whisper as he moves to brush my hair back from my face, before caressing the back of my neck. "You might be right."

Kissing Josh is like a drug - intoxicating and irresponsible - and I want to accept the thrum of it in my veins. It's hurried and rough and, as his arm tightens around me and he pulls me closer still, I try to give myself to it. I try to stop thinking. His tongue swipes against my lips, pushing them apart as my hands press against his chest. Breath becomes shorter and harder to find and his hand slips from my waist to my ass, grabbing me firmly, as I gasp against him.

Relax.

Pain, like a simmering volcano, lies beneath my skin; pulling to the surface with every frantic grab and he pushes me back into the guard rail, his fingers gripping the hem of my skirt and scraping up my thigh while his lips move along my jaw, down my neck.

Breathe.

I close my eyes to the world - focusing solely on the feeling of his body pressing against mine, on the man that is holding me, focusing only on this moment in front of me - when the door swings open and the world comes crashing back into full view.

My hands, still pressed against Josh's broad chest, push, and he steps back smirking. He doesn't so much as glance in the direction of the person interrupting us. He doesn't seem to care. Instead, his eyes slowly work their way up the length of me again as I press my fingers into my lips, my eyes stinging, and spin to face reality.

Blue ice freezes me to my core and I feel sick. Instantly.

Ben

It hits me with the force of a thousand trucks. Rage. Unadulterated, disgusting rage. And I hate it.

Mikaela's head is rolled back as he hitches her knee up and her lips part. Her eyes are screwed shut as she takes in a shaky breath.

Without thinking, I push the door open with as much strength as its hinges can take. The hard crash of it pulls them apart.

My eyes never leave her. Not as he steps back, looking way too sure of himself for a guy whose face could easily be ruined if he makes one wrong move. Not as she straightens her dress and awkwardly pushes at her lips, as if she can somehow wipe away hidden stains of the kiss I just witnessed and it could be like it never happened. Not even as her glassy jade eyes meet my own and widen slightly.

Glassy. Because she's been drinking.

And the rage shifts. It disappears so suddenly that she must see it, she must be watching it run from her, concern stepping forwards to take its place, because hidden in the depth of her shock is something absolutely painful. I would recognise it anywhere. Mikaela is ashamed.

"I didn't mean to interrupt." I make the effort to keep my voice level and disinterested when I cast a smile towards her, but she's no longer looking at me. She stares at her feet, avoiding my gaze, before glancing towards Josh who's just standing there, grinning at her like she's some prize to be won, bathing in self-satisfaction. The rage crawls back. Just thinking of his lips against her makes my skin itch. "I was just leaving, so you two can resume whatever *that* was in a moment." I bristle as I run my eyes over the asshole once before turning back to her. "Mik, can I have a word?"

She gawks at me, her eyes bugging and her jaw hanging a little slack, and incoherent noises spill from her lips as she shuffles away slightly.

When she doesn't respond in anything akin to a sentence, I place my hand against her arm and guide her down the stairs and onto the sidewalk, just far enough away to avoid prying eyes and listening ears.

"Mik, what the hell are you doing?"

I can see the confusion searing behind her eyes as mine burn into her and I wait.

Those eyes are like pages of a book when she's had too much to drink - something anyone who paid any attention to her would know - and I watch as all of her emotions – every thought that crosses her mind – write themselves into them before she finally settles on one. My shoulders square a fraction and I stiffen just a little before she can utter a word.

"What the hell am I doing?" She repeats my words as if they're incomprehensible, her arms crossing over her chest as she mirrors my stance, squaring her shoulders and wobbling slightly in the process.

The asshole on the stairs doesn't look like he's had a single drink.

"More like what are you doing, Haston? You're acting like my brother and I have news for you." She jabs at my chest with venom. "We're not related."

I scoff and the fire burns brighter in my chest.

"Trust me, I know." The retort is automatic and I feel that shift again; the one that thickens the air and has my skin burning and my heart racing. Except this time she doesn't look embarrassed. She looks furious.

She glares up at me, shaking her head. "What does that even mean?"

What do I mean?

We both know there's nothing but bad history between us and maybe, yes, there had been a time I had possibly thought there could be more, but now? My comment was pointed and sharp. Even now it slices through my own defences as the picture of that sleaze pawing at her skin creeps unbidden into my mind. Followed by a fantasy of kicking him swiftly in the gut. It's entwined in my thoughts with the same ease that dragged dreams of skimming my teeth and tongue over her neck into existence this morning. And watching her wait for me to answer her I realise something. I am screwed. I am completely and utterly screwed, because all I want to do right now is pull her back into the apartment, carry her to her room, and lock us away in there for the rest of the night. I want to erase every touch and trace of Joshua *fucking* Lucas, and I want her to want that too.

"What I do in my free time is absolutely nothing to do with you, Haston. Do you understand?" She seethes as I stare at her.

Blinking, I find some sense of sanity and soften my voice. "Mik. You barely know the guy. This isn't -"

"No." Her voice is measured but venom drips from it, cutting me off before I can utter another word. I've only seen her like this once before and picturing that now is ice in my veins. "Let's get something straight here. You do not know me. You think you do, but you don't, Haston, and I don't *want* you to. I do not like you. I do not trust you. I do not want your opinion on this. You are my brother's friend and a colleague. I am being civil because it is important to Jamie, but make no mistakes with this." She doesn't shake or sway. The glassy intoxication fades from her eyes. She ignites with her anger. "I remember what happened five years ago like it was yesterday and I will *never* forget it. So back off."

Something inside of me breaks with her words and, as she turns her back to me and moves away, I reach out. I know I shouldn't. I know I should just let her walk away. But I'm desperate. I'm desperate not to end this with her angry at me again. I'm desperate not to be the bad guy in her story.

"Mik!" My fingers wrap around her wrist and her body tenses on contact - as if some deeply ingrained instinct tells her to stop moving, not to pull away - and her breath stops. Her eyes are wide and frenzied when she swings to face me. My stomach becomes lead.

I relax my grip, stepping back, as she gasps for breath and tears spill. It's as if she's looking right through me, staring up at something or someone else, and her chest moves in ragged, disjointed gasps.

I can't move. I can't speak. I just watch her as the color that had drained from her cheeks begins to rise again and she blinks away whatever ghosts surfaced behind her eyes.

"Go home, Ben." Just a whisper and yet it claws at me with violence.

"Mik, what's wrong?"

"I said go home."

Mikaela

"Is everything okay?" Josh watches as I dart up the stairs and ring the buzzer for my brother's apartment, too frantic to look for my keys.

I'm biting back tears and my hands are shaking. My stomach rolls as I shake my head and try to erase the thought of that face from the depths of my mind.

"I'm fine. I'm so sorry, Josh. I -"

He steps forwards and grabs my hand and I feel the tug of my stomach as sickness threatens me again.

"Hey." He waits for me to look over to him, keeping his hands on me when I tremble under his touch. "It's fine. Whatever that was, it's fine." He reaches up, his fingers brushing against my cheek and I still, closing my eyes and struggling to breathe. "I'll call you tomorrow?"

My smile is small and all wrong. It feels foreign and broken. As fake as I have been all night, pretending to be anything other than what I am. I told myself the kiss had felt right in the moment; it was exciting and thrilling and not something I would usually do. But maybe I was lying. Maybe his fingertips on my skin feel cold and unwelcome. Right now, everything feels wrong.

I take a breath.

The problem, I tell myself, *is not Josh*.

"Okay," I nod before taking my bag from him and stepping inside as the door clicks open.

Walking into the lobby and away from his kindness, I let myself sink into the pain and anger and exhaustion of it all.

And I let myself blame Ben.

Ten Years Ago

Ben

Avoiding my father was a skill; one I mastered at a young age - mostly thanks to Mom's insistence that I spent time with Jamie out of the house. So college, in many ways, became an extension of this. I rarely return to the city, finding perfect excuses in study groups, part time work and summer internships to keep me away, and when I do come home it's only for a weekend every couple of months.

It works for me, this arrangement.

My father wasn't often a cruel man, but when he was it was as if another person took over his home. I know that now, but I had seen the way a person could change and I ran from it. I'm still running from it.

In public, Richard Haston carved a reputation for my family to be proud of, a legacy to leave behind for future generations, and he spent many nights reminding me I was not enough. I would never be enough. No amount of education or effort or time would change that. And now, at twenty-one, I finally learned that 'too little, too late' has a bitter taste.

I'm proud of you is a lie that I will never un-hear.

It feels like hours have passed where I stand, shaking the hands of people I've never met and never heard of.

My mother is a stone wall beside me - calm and strong - never letting a stray sob escape her lips despite the fact I can see she's breaking. Even after everything, she's still breaking for him.

I know my eyes are glassy and distant, no doubt a side effect of draining good, old Richard's best bottle of Scotch last night, and my head is swimming with the words burned into my mind from a conversation with a dying man.

"I'm not proud of you," I had responded. *"I'm not proud to be your son."*

With the nastiness of our final conversation wrapped around my throat and threatening to empty the contents of my stomach right here, in front of everyone, I feel like I'm blind to the people in front of me. I am blind until she steps forwards. Because when she steps forwards, it's like she brings in light.

In the three years since I last saw her she's gotten taller and less awkward. She's slim still, but her figure has changed too. Where she had been a beanpole at fifteen, eighteen year old Mikaela is all curves. She has beautiful curves. Her hair, a shock of blonde curls, frame her slightly rounded cheeks and wide eyes and her smile is kind. Even in the darkness of a funeral there is a softness to her. A softness in her smile. A softness in the way she holds on to her mother and glances at the devastation around us.

I look to Elizabeth and my chest tightens. She seems frail from another round of treatment, finished last week if I remember Jamie's last message correctly. And then Mikaela speaks and I am pulled straight back to how good she looks.

"Jamie couldn't get back for the funeral," Mik tells me what I already know. "He'll be home tomorrow night though." She smiles at me, a real smile - not one of those sympathetic smiles everyone else perfected in the car ride to the church - and somehow, behind the haze of it all, I find some focus. "Let me know if there's anything I can do."

She squeezes my hand gently before going to let go, pausing when I tighten my grip on her and hold her in place.

Her simple offer is the most sincere thing anyone has said to me since he died and I throw my words at her without thinking; without caring. "Will you sit up front?"

As I stare at her, seeking comfort in her, she nods and my heart does a jittery thump.

Slowly, she wraps an arm around her mother's frame and guides her to the pews, taking a seat in the second row, directly behind where I will eventually sit.

She places her hand on my shoulder at the start of the service and I reach up to hold it.

I hold on to her until it's over.

I hold on to her until every last remnant of my father is gone.

I'm wallowing.

Jamie and I are sitting in a dark corner of some local bar neither of us really like and he's letting me drown my sorrows in a stormy silence.

Jamie's good like that.

I'm not really sure how long we've been here when she walks in, but suddenly my whole body is on high alert.

Mikaela's hair is scraped back straight and her eyes are darkened with make-up. It's like her laugh fills the space before she really enters and I lean forwards just a fraction as she grins. She glances around the room, her friends looking back at the complacent security guard in astonishment, and even though I know she's seen me - even though our eyes met for the smallest moment - she skims right past me.

A tight black dress clings to her body, cut a little too low to be innocent, and the way she slips into the room with an air of cool countenance and control intrigues me.

This is not the first time Mikaela Wilcox has been here.

My eyes follow her as she makes her way to the bar, leaning forwards to shout over the noise into the barman's ear, and I shift in my seat; itching to walk over to her. To talk to her.

Part of me wants to drape my jacket over her shoulders and march her out of here: remind her she is underage and over-exposed. Another part of me - a part that fucking terrifies me - wants to pull her over to the booth. It wants to sit with her all night; talk to her all night. I'd leave Jamie behind to flirt with the bar staff just to see her smiling at me.

"Earth to Ben." Jamie laughs. "Who's got your attention this time?"

He turns quickly, following my gaze to where Mikaela stands before I can drop it, and his smile slips from his face. "No."

My attention snaps back to him and I try to fake a smile, my eyes narrowing in a flash of deceitful confusion.

"What?" I steal a glance again, quickly, before frowning.

It doesn't go unnoticed.

"No, Ben. Not Mik." Jamie glares at me, his jaw tightening and his lips setting in a grim line. "She's my sister. She's - just - no."

"Honestly, Jamie, I have no idea what you're talking about."

Lies.

The truth of his words smother me with their weight and something uncomfortable squeezes in my chest. Of course he's right. It's Mikaela, for God's sake.

Across the bar a guy has his hands on Mikaela's waist as he leans in to speak to her and she takes a sip from the straw in her ridiculously fruity drink.

My grip tightens around my glass.

"She's off limits to you, Haston." Jamie practically snarls at me as he snatches the glass from my hand and snaps my focus back to him, the amber liquid spilling and splashing off of the sticky surface of the table. "Off limits. Always. You got it?"

"Not that this was an issue to start with." I brush down the splattering of bourbon on my shirt as I level him with a stare before I signal over to the waitress clearing glasses between booths. "But yeah, I've got it."

"Great. Now we're leaving, before you do something I'm going to have to punch you for."

I roll my eyes and fish a card out of my pocket, holding it out to the waitress. "I'd like to settle my tab."

I don't risk looking at her. Not when Mikaela is right behind her, oblivious to how difficult she has just made it for me to leave.

Mikaela

I've had too much to drink. The girls squeal with bubbles of giggled gossip and the room spins around me. The tiles shift beneath my feet as I stumble, laughing when the floor comes up to greet me and a firm hand wraps around my waist, pulling me backwards, saving me from smashing to the ground.

"Jesus, Mik." A gravelly voice sighs against my ear as fingers dig into my skin, bringing a blissful kind of pain that sends a shiver running down my spine, holding me upright.

I twist slightly, looking up to my saviour with blurry eyes and groan, loudly.

Ben rolls his eyes with a smirk in response.

"I thought you left." I can hear how my words slur as I move out of his arm and trip again.

Why does this floor keep shifting like that?

Ben shrugs with feigned nonchalance and winds his arm around my waist once more, leaning towards the bar to grab my bag. "I did."

"But you're back."

"I am."

I can't help it. He sounds so silly and light hearted and I laugh as I twist to face him, smiling dopily at him as he raises an eyebrow.

His face is really close now and he smells nice.

"What's so funny, Little Mik?"

I try to shrug but the movement feels too big and I place a hand on his chest, taking a deep breath in while my head spins and my eyes search his face. He smells like lemons and pine mixed with a little whiskey.

"You smell nice," I tell him. His smile dances with amusement. "Why are you back?"

Ben pauses.

I'd seen him leaving with Jamie over an hour ago, just after I'd spotted him tucked away in the corner. His eyes had scanned the room before he ducked into the street to call his driver and I had glanced around me as he left, wondering which woman was the one he was clearly searching for. *Maybe he's back for that girl.*

"Well." He looks around at the faces of my friends, either happily pressed up in some corner with men who are probably a little too old, or too lost in raucous conversation to notice that I am currently wrapped in my brother's best friend's arms, and he sighs. *Maybe his girl left.* "Who else was going to make sure you get home safe, Mik?"

As he leads me to the car waiting outside, I glance up at him repeatedly. His lips are set in a straight line and his eyes are pinned to the sleek black Mercedes that sits waiting for us. His fingers brush gently over my hip as he holds me against him, wrapped around me to stop me from falling and when he pulls away, his fingers skimming across the small of my back, my skin hums beneath his touch.

I stop looking at him.

"Ladies first." He motions to the back seat when he opens the door and I slip into the car before he follows.

In the darkness, I can feel every nerve in my body as if each one is on fire, and when Ben follows in behind me, sidling into the open seat and keeping a large space between us, it feels like the whole car is going to combust and burn me to cinders with it.

I watch as he signals to his driver, someone I recognise from snapshots from the past, and I smile widely.

Norman.

He's old, maybe in his seventies, and the way he smiles, all toothy and twinkly, gives the impression of mischief. His eyes are kind and for a second I feel like I'm thirteen again, following Jamie out of the apartment and watching as he dives into the back of the car with Ben. Back then, Norman would shoot me an apologetic wink before driving off to places I wasn't allowed to go to. Right now, seeing him shoot one of those secretive winks in the rearview mirror, years after I'd last thought of him, brings a strange sense of comfort to the car and I sink into the leather a little more easily.

"Miss Wilcox." His thick Dublin accent lifts through the vehicle and I feel my cheeks pulling up into a wide smile. I had forgotten that about him. "There's water stowed in the compartment between your seats, should you need it, and young Ben can adjust the heat if you're cold."

The ghost of a smile flickers on Ben's lips as he speaks. "Thanks Norman. You know where to go."

"Thank you." I repeat, smiling at the man in the front seat as he pulls out into the traffic. By the time he glances back in the rearview mirror, the two of us are sitting stiffly apart, unsure of where to look or what to say.

I swear, he shakes his head and chuckles.

The drive home is half an hour from the bar - on the subway it's just fifteen minutes - but twenty minutes into the silent crawl forwards, I can still see the faint glow of the neon sign behind us and hear the throbbing music of surrounding clubs and bars.

I twist a bottle of water in my hands as I push my knees together and try not to glance over at Ben again. He hasn't said a word and I'm beginning to feel like a burden.

He huffs, making me jump slightly, as he runs his hands over his face and slumps lower in his seat. His legs are tucked together in a way that can't be comfortable, not dissimilar to my own, and he glances over at me with a storm in his eyes.

I know I should at least try to look like I wasn't staring at him just now, but I don't look away.

"Sorry about the traffic," he mumbles, looking back out of the window.

I twist in my seat, facing him as I lean my shoulder against the leather of the chair and rest my head, and I am looking directly at him. No hiding it. For the first time since he came to my rescue tonight I let myself *really*-look at him, and maybe it's the alcohol, or maybe it's the way his eyes keep shifting back to me like he wants to say something, but I feel a tightness in my chest.

He hasn't shaved since before the funeral and the dark stubble that coats his jaw is thicker than usual. Messier. His eyes are heavy too, not just from drink, but from carrying the weight of his father's death. Dark rings puff beneath the surface of his skin and I know I haven't imagined that the usual shimmer of his eyes is duller somehow.

He is suffering. My heart aches for him.

"Ben?" I whisper his name and he turns his body towards me, his knee brushing against mine as I shift closer. My heart sputters at the contact. Slowly, with his eyes following my every move, I reach towards him and take one of his hands in mine, my fingers brushing over his knuckles. "Are you okay?"

For a moment he doesn't say anything. He just stares at my hands, wrapped around his, and I wait with bated breath. Eventually he sighs and closes his eyes, his head rolling to the side and resting on the upholstery like mine.

"I'm fine, Mik." With that lie he tries to smile and I shuffle closer. When he looks at me again his eyes are burning with silent pleas and I sigh when he shakes his head.

"Ben."

This time his smile is a little less forced as he says, "I will be."

A shiver crawls up my spine, chilling me to my core, as Ben's eyes drop slightly, tracing my lips and I take a breath. I tell myself to ignore that feeling; that my legs pressed up against his and our fingers intertwined means nothing. I tell myself I'm just cold. The window is open. There's nothing more to it.

When Ben frowns I smile a little. He always ends up looking so serious.

"Are you cold?"

"I'm okay." I shift closer again and Ben's breathing hitches in a painful way. The thought that he is trying not to break hurts and I don't fully understand my reaction to that pain.

Slowly, I place my head against his shoulder and close my eyes, shifting so that I can lean against him. In the drunken haze of the night, it feels comfortably normal nestled up next to him and, as he wraps his arm around me and brushes his hand against my skin, I drift into a soft sleep and dream of crystal blues.

Chapter Five

Present

Ben

"This is getting fucking ridiculous." I slam my coffee cup down on the desk, grunting as its contents splash out over my hand, and grimace as the idiot in front of me clears his throat. "What won't she come and say this time?"

"Well." To his credit, Max tries to stop himself from smiling but I can see the amusement in his eyes. "Your three o'clock has pushed back by twenty minutes and she won't be available this afternoon to minute your meeting with Jamie and the other investors, so I'll be stepping in."

I shake my head as I frown. It's been two weeks of avoiding each other and Jamie is already riding my back about it. Two weeks of picturing that asshole touching her every time I so much as glance in her direction. I'm going to need to fix it somehow.

"Tell her, if I get any messages she needs to bring them to me herself. It's her fucking job, not yours."

"Would you like me to use that exact expression, or do you maybe think that might not work?" Max quips back with a smirk.

"No." I admit with a sigh. "I don't want you to say that. But you have to admit, this isn't exactly working."

"I don't know." Max shrugs. "My watch is clocking almost three times my normal step count these days."

I stare up at him with mild disinterest and he grins like an idiot.

"Get out, Mr Kingford."

"Okay. Yep." He pushes out of my office, papers piled high in his arms for his boss, and I swivel in my seat.

In the front of the office she's packing up her stuff, her hips swaying slightly as she moves around her desk, and Jamie sits in her seat. His feet are on the glass surface and he's twisted back to look at me. He frowns and I grimace.

Yeah. I need to fix this.

Mikaela

Jamie sighs dramatically as he twists back to see Max scuttling out of Ben's office. I chance my own glance, meeting Max's eyes and mirroring the small smile that still plays on his lips. One unintentional perk of avoiding Benjamin Haston like the plague is the amusement it brings to the man who is quickly becoming my closest friend. I'm sure the second I leave the building Max will text me a play by play of Ben's complaints, but, for now at least, I need to focus on getting out. And not looking back at the blue eyes that feel like they're boring a hole in my skull.

"I'm worried about him," Jamie muses aloud and a far too familiar feeling settles in my stomach; like thousands of little needles pricking me with the constant reminder of the approaching anniversary. "You know it's ten years since his dad passed tomorrow."

"I know." *It's hard to forget.*

Jamie continues on as if I haven't spoken. "He's always moody around this time, you know?" I watch as my brother picks up a pad of post-its from my desk and flicks through them as if they're uncovering a story for him. "But this year it's worse. I don't know. I think he's drowning in it."

Somewhere, buried deep within my subconscious, is an image of Benjamin Haston I wish I could forget. He is tired and sad and vulnerable and there is nothing but open air and half-truths between us as we hold onto each other. Jamie's words tug that image to the surface and I chew my lip as I bury myself into tidying up papers that are already organised on my desk.

Ten years could change a lot, but it doesn't mean the idea of his pain doesn't still leave my own chest hollow.

"I have three places to look at this afternoon." My attempt to change the subject doesn't go unnoticed, and neither has the fact I've actively avoided being in the same room as Ben for the last two weeks, but this time Jamie makes no comment.

"You know, I really don't mind you having the spare room for a while longer, MikMak." He shrugs as I grab my phone from the top drawer and roll my eyes.

"Call me that in public again and you'll regret it, JimJam."

He grins when I shove his feet from my desk.

"And I don't want to stay at yours," I continue. "I want some space - something that is mine - for once I want to have somewhere that no one else gets to control." I swallow the lump forming in my throat as the weight of my words settle over me like an inescapable fog. "I think I *need* that."

Jamie reaches forwards to take my hand and squeezes tight. Three times. Just like Mom.

"I can come with you?" he offers, his words soft and his eyes littered with unasked questions.

I smile at my big brother, always trying to protect me, even when I haven't let him, and close my eyes for a moment.

When I open them again Ben is approaching, a sorry look on his face and his hands in his pockets. I shake my head.

"I don't think I need you as much as someone else does right now, Jamie." I nod over to where Ben comes to a stop a few feet away, glancing nervously between us. Even in my anger I find myself aching to soften the blow; to fix up the broken pieces and hold him together if he needs me to. I hate his pain. I hate thinking of him as someone alone, someone who struggles, because if I picture him like that then maybe he isn't the villain in our story.

Maybe I am.

With the memory of him broken and lost in the cold expanse of that church burned into my mind, as it had been in the weeks following his father's funeral, as it is at this time of year every year, I sigh and shake my head. "Take him to dinner or something, yeah?"

"What happened with you two, Mik?" Jamie whispers as he leans forwards, his elbows on his knees.

"I don't know what you're talking about."

"Yes you do. The whole office knows what I'm talking about." We both look back to Ben who shifts uncomfortably. "You two didn't ever..." His voice trails off suggestively and I scoff at him.

Now he's being ridiculous.

"Hell no." My cheeks are burning and I force out a laugh. "Now stop digging for something that isn't there and I'll see you at home. Okay?"

Leaning in, I press a quick kiss to his cheek before making my way to the elevator.

In a moment of weakness, as the doors slide shut between us, I find myself looking over to Ben and, for the first time in a long time, I let my mind draw the painful image of his face at the funeral up to the surface.

Blue eyes meet mine and I offer him a small smile as the doors finally form a shield between us, and for a short, painful moment I'm not sure he even saw it. And then my phone chimes.

Ben: Truce?

I close my eyes and rest my head back against the cool metal of the wall before replying.

Me: Truce.

The third apartment I see is a small and shabby studio in a rundown block in Inwood. It's just one room with a small fire escape landing, a bathroom that seems too big for the space it belongs to, and a view of another apartment block wall.

I run my fingers over the wooden counter that sits against one wall and smile to myself as the overly-enthusiastic realtor babbles about the potential of the property.

"You know, it's hard to find somewhere like this for such a low price." He holds his arms out as he spins on his heels and smiles. "Now of course, we'd need references and a credit check, and there is another interested party-"

"I can put the deposit down today." I grin as I take the two small steps to the raised platform I want to use as my bedroom, picturing the way I could press my bed against the exposed brick, box off the open ledge with bookshelves and push my dresser up against the back wall. I could wind an exposed bulb over the beams above me and hang it over the space, let its glow be the warm light of my room while the rest of the studio has brighter, cooler light. "It's exactly what I'm looking for."

"Fantastic." The man claps his hands together and smiles. "We can get the paperwork over to you this evening and everything should be ready for you to move in within a week if everything runs smoothly."

We talk through the paperwork quietly in the small, unkept area that would make my kitchen and breakfast space, before running over finance requirements.

Everything is within my budget. Everything is what I need and want. For a second I just sit with that and breathe. It's as if the universe heard my pitiful admission earlier today and decided I deserved a break.

I deserve a break.

Thanking the man politely as we exit the apartment block and enter the bustling street, I pull my phone out of my bag and feel that giddy lightness in my chest finding weight again. Funny how a name can make you nervous like that. I click to call him back and lift the phone to my ear; laughing when his breathy hello fills the line almost immediately.

"Well hello, stranger." I can hear the way his lips turn up as he speaks.

"Hi," I speak softly, desperate not to show my nerves as I move down the busy street.

"Where are you right now?"

"I'm just heading home." I hesitate. Although Josh and I had text after that night on the stoop, he'd returned to London for a visit home two days later and I'm suddenly unsure what this *thing* with him is and wary of oversharing. But he called me while I was viewing, right? That means something. It has to. "I actually just found an apartment."

I hear him let out a low whistle and a laugh bubbles from my lips.

"Congratulations are in order then." His voice is smooth as silk and intimidatingly sure. "Text me when you get home and put on something pretty. I'm taking you out."

My heart hammers in my chest and my stomach flips. "Okay."

"I'll see you soon, beautiful."

I stumble as I struggle to hook my foot into the black stiletto heel I kept from the days when I had been able to go out regularly; the final artefact of a life long left behind.

Catching sight of myself in the mirror I pause. The poppy red dress hugs my figure tight, wrapping around my waist and cutting in a smooth square across my chest. The colour is striking. I adjust myself, smoothing the fabric as I turn to the side to appraise myself a little more and frown. Objectively, I look good. I have never been under any misguided impression that I'm not what my mother would call *chocolate box pretty*, but staring at this image of me - all dolled up and trying to impress - something just feels wrong.

Fixing my hair so that it falls in smooth waves down my back and adjusting the shoulder of my dress to cover the small scar there, I take one last look at myself before opening my bedroom door. I need to let go of the nagging voice telling me to change my dress. That voice does not belong to me.

Moving through the space slowly, I begin to hum as I search for my keys. After assessing the kitchen counters I figure they have to be on the couch, so I pour a glass of wine and head over to the seat I'd thrown my jacket on in my rush this afternoon.

As I lean over the back of the couch, rummaging between cushions, the front door opens and closes and I half shout a quick hey over my shoulder, without looking behind me.

My hand is buried beneath the cushions, trapped between pillows that refuse to give to my touch but drag me in still. My hair falls forwards, like a curtain between me and the room, and I grunt as I try to blow it out of my eyes.

I should have taken the five extra seconds and gone around.

With my ass in the air and my face dangerously close to the pristine cream fabric, I hear Jamie's keys clunk on the counter and the fridge door open.

"Gotcha!" I mutter as I hook my pinky finger through my keyring and pull hard. The key snags, but another tug and they're free. "I found a place!" I push myself up from my precarious position, legs flailing slightly before I teeter in my heels, and shove the keys into the tiny bag beside me. "It's small and it's quirky and I love it."

"Quirky in what way?"

"Oh." I still at his voice.

Yes, I pity Ben right now.

Yes, I offered him a smile and agreed to a truce.

Yes, I did these things as a willing participant.

Truthfully, I know I need to say something. I need to answer him because our truce is new and fragile. I want to say something. I really do. But when I look up at him and he smiles tentatively at me, his lips curving into a lazy sort of half smile and his eyes still a little sad, my mind goes blank. No. That's a lie. My mind flashes right back to that torn and broken expression from ten years ago and I *ache*. I have nothing I can say. I offer him a tense smile instead and he nods before dropping his gaze to the floor.

"Jamie, I'm going out. I'll be back late." I look to the floor too, just as Jamie rolls his eyes.

"Don't do anything I wouldn't do." My brother jumps over the back of the couch as if he's some eighteen year old gamer and not a thirty-one year old business man, and I chuckle a little. "Or do. Up to you."

As if on cue, the buzzer sounds and I scuttle to the door, leaving without another word and shutting down the bubbling feeling of anxiety building under the heat of sea blue eyes that follow me out to the corridor.

"I'm telling you." Josh smiles and his eyes sparkle with something akin to mischief as he leans forwards in his chair and pours more wine into my glass. I can't help but notice his is still barely touched. "I remember it clear as day and I've never seen so many mice. The poor man was just screaming and the four of us were hiding in the bushes, crying with laughter. How we weren't expelled for that I'll never know."

"So they caught you?" I place my napkin down as I watch him intently. He's so relaxed and calm here, whereas I feel out of place and on display, and it's jarring how different we are.

Josh nods as he laughs. "Oh God, yeah. Apparently, having one hundred live mice delivered to your room in a boarding school is really easy to track."

He furrows his brow as a wicked grin spreads over his lips, and suddenly I feel a little silly; like I've given the wrong answer in class only for the teacher's pet to pipe up with corrections. Trying to smile through a wave of self-doubt, I take a steadying breath and glance behind me.

"I'm sorry." I look back at him with an apologetic smile as I rise to my feet and Josh stands too. "I'll be right back."

"Of course." His eyes roam over my body and I feel awkward under his scrutiny.

Slowly, I make my way through the restaurant and towards the toilets, looking back to Josh as he takes his seat, his eyes glued to me with an intensity I can't escape.

Watching my fingertips turn white, the tremors pulling through my body as I cling to the marble of the counter, I try to breathe. My eyes move, fixing on the spark of darkness hidden deep beneath the green that stare back at me, and I can see it still. Never too far from the surface. Always too close to escape.

"He is not Matthew." It comes as a whisper and yet it cuts at my throat like razor blades dragging up with his name. "He is not Matthew."

Wiping away my tears and closing my eyes, I try to bring down the mask. For years I had it perfected; cool and detached and pain free. It had been such a perfect disguise, so well worn, that people recognised it as my face and yet I can't find it now. Now, when I need to, I can't make myself hide the panic.

I take a deep breath, preparing to face my date, as pain circles like a vulture; waiting to pick the skin from my bones.

Three Years Ago

"Mik, please open the door." Desperation clings to Jamie's voice as I sit with my back against the wood, my chest heaving and shattered glass all around. "Please."

I shouldn't have called him. There are two years of apologies to make. Two years of silence to account for. And now, sitting here in the mess I've made, I can't say a word.

I won't let him see me like this.

My hand covers my mouth, pushing back my sobs, as I close my eyes and wait for him to leave. I need him to leave. I can't face him, not now, not with the faded yellow that lines my upper lip because I burned the dinner last week. Not with the soft purples blossoming around my eye from a text message I received about a job two hours ago. Not with blood staining the white of my blouse from the cut on my shoulder.

I can feel my chest caving in as I listen to my brother plead with me and I know there's no way out.

"I can hear you, Mik." I hear him place his hand against the wood and picture the way he is pressing his forehead against the door. His voice trembles and I feel it. I feel all of it. "Please just let me in. I can help."

I shake my head as I pull my knees to my chest and close my eyes. If I could close my mind as easily, then I wouldn't have to feel this.

"I love you, Mik. I love you so much, okay? And I'm here." Jamie whispers and I shatter. "I love you."

Fresh pain consumes me.

"I am here," he repeats, resignation hiding behind his words and I whimper. "And I will be here when you are ready to come home."

Home.

I want to go home.

"I'm so sorry." His apology clings to my skin, like mist over the sea, as Matthew's voice swims beneath the surface.

"I'm so sorry, baby."

Bile rises in my throat and I crawl over splinters of glass and shards of broken promises. All the pain and anger and fear threatens to spill from my lips with each tremor that pulls through me.

"I didn't mean to. Please, baby. I didn't mean to."

He never means to.

Present

"You alright?" Josh cocks his head to the side as the waiter pulls my chair back for me and I fidget with Mom's silver ring on my middle finger, the smooth surface soothing me as I breathe in.

"Of course."

Something about my smile seems to feed his curiosity. He raises a brow and waits. Expectant.

"Honestly, I'm fine."

Those observant eyes run over my face slowly as I try to keep the half smile from fading and reach for the bottle of water on the table, moving to fill the empty glass in front of me.

I can feel the pool beneath my eyes, no doubt leaving a slight shimmer in the glow of the soft lights, tears waiting to be shed, and my lips feel tight over my teeth.

I feel vulnerable.

I feel *alone*.

Without another word, Josh holds his fingers up and signals for the closest waiter. I glance up at the man who appears almost instantly and guilt fogs my mind.

"Can I get the cheque please?" Josh smiles warmly and the waiter disappears with a silent nod.

"No, Josh." Shaking my head, I look around and try to get the man to come back. "We don't have to-"

"Listen, Mikaela." He shrugs as the waiter returns, passing him his card without so much as looking at the bill. "I like you. You seem great. I would quite like to get to know you, but tonight you're acting strange. So, let's call it a night. I'll take you home, we'll say goodnight, and in the morning – if you want to see me again – you can give me a call."

He rises to his feet, buttoning his blazer while I stare up at him, before holding a hand out for me. His jaw is clenched slightly, but he smiles as he reaches out to me.

I take his hand in my own, chewing the inside of my lip as I let him lead me through the crowd and out to the open air of the bustling city streets.

"I'm sorry." It's almost a whisper and I can't bring myself to look at him.

The drive back to Jamie's is quiet as I search for the right words. Kicking myself for ruining a perfectly nice evening, I open my mouth to speak countless times, only to close it when nothing seems to come. Over and over, I try to find a way to explain that I get paranoid sometimes. I try to find a way to say that I don't know how to feel okay anymore. I try to find a way to say anything, but instead I sit in silence.

When we pull up outside the apartment block I currently call home, my mind is still spilling with things I know I should say, but don't know how to voice.

"It wasn't you." The words tumble from my lips as I open the door and Josh pauses. "Just so you know."

He nods before slipping out of the car and making his way to my side. He holds out a hand once more and a slow sort of calm seems to wash over him, sinking into me as I stand. His fingers wrap gently around my hand and his thumb brushes over my knuckles. I focus on *that* - the soothing way he touches me.

"I didn't think it was." His voice is calm and he smiles playfully when I glance up at him. "But it's good to be sure."

Slowly, he pulls my hand to his lips, his eyes remaining on mine, and presses a gentle kiss against my skin.

Gentle. Josh is gentle.

"Sleep well, Mikaela."

As I watch him walk away and climb back into the car, I can't help but feel like maybe I'm a fool. Sighing, I turn my back to his car and take a step towards the building when the whir of a window opening causes me to spin back.

"Hey?" He's leaning across the passenger seat and I duck down to see him smiling one of those wide, easy smiles that steals all of my breath and all of my sanity. "I really hope you call."

A shy smile dances over my lips when I watch him drive away and I let out a slow breath.

This is all so much harder than I anticipated it would be.

Ben

Jamie's head snaps up at the sound of Mikaela's keys in the door and my eyes flick to the clock on the wall. Only nine thirty. My stomach knots. She said late.

I watch silently as she slips her heels off and kicks them aside before walking straight to Jamie's side. Her eyes scream with worry and I watch as Jamie opens his arms for her without hesitation.

"What happened?" He squeezes her tight as she closes her eyes and breathes in the comfort of her brother, and my heart thumps heavily. This all feels too private, too vulnerable, and I can't help but feel uncomfortable as it unfolds in front of me.

She doesn't want me here for this.

"I panicked," she admits feebly, curling into his side and tucking her knees up against him.

Jamie nods when she pulls back a little to meet his eyes and a sad sigh fills the air.

"It was all so lovely, JimJam." She shrugs as he picks up the remote and mutes the TV before he turns his attention back to her. "It was all going well and it scared me."

I feel a twist in my stomach and get to my feet, clearing my throat as she looks up to me.

"I should go." I try to smile, but her eyes are shimmering and I feel my heart jump to my throat. Here and now, the fine balance of our entire relationship seems threatened yet again. Some dark part of my mind seems to run its nails down my spine, drawing out a shiver of anger as her last three words echo inside me. She was scared.

She said it was lovely too, I remind myself as I take a deep breath. *She said it was going well.*

"You don't have to leave on my account." She sniffles as she pulls away from Jamie, wiping her cheeks, and I shake my head.

"It's not you, Mikaela." I can't tear my eyes from her. "I just think I should go."

Jamie pushes to stand up, shifting out from beside his sister, but I step aside quickly.

"I can see myself out."

Mikaela nestles back into Jamie's side and I slip away quietly, giving her the privacy she needs.

Mikaela

When the door closes and Ben is gone, a strange emptiness settles over me and Jamie runs his hand over my arm.

"You've gotta open yourself up to the idea that there are good men out there, Mik. Even after everything. Even when you're scared."

My eyes fix on the closed door. I know he's right. There are good men out there.

I close my eyes for a moment and allow myself to think it all over. I had enjoyed the company when we first went for drinks and I think I was excited when he called me. I'd even found myself looking towards our date with eager anticipation earlier tonight. And Josh seems nice. Josh could be a good man.

He could be someone who would hold the door open for me, and carry my bag just because he wanted to. He could be kind and caring. He could be wonderful.

But, clawing away at any glimmer of excitement and hope, six little words gnaw at the edges of anything good. Six little words that haunt me: *Matthew was wonderful, until he wasn't.*

"How was your night anyway?" I push away from Jamie and try to shake off the pain as I make my way to my room. Maybe I'll try writing something. Or maybe I'll start packing.

"You know." Jamie sighs as he gets up to follow me, grabbing a roll of tape from the drawer in his coffee table and holding it out to me as if he's asking a question. "Ben didn't say much, but he never does when it comes to his dad."

Chapter Six

Ten Years Ago

Ben

"I feel like I should apologise." Mikaela walks to the small kitchenette with her head low as she pulls her sweater sleeves down over her hands, twisting them between her fingers. "Do you want a drink or anything?"

I follow behind her, closing the door to her mom's apartment, and watching her closely. Her hair is thrown into a messy knot on the top of her head and her face is make-up free. Under the grey men's sweatshirt, three or four sizes too big for her, are tiny black shorts that cling to the shape of her and, as she moves, I watch her closely.

Part of me wants to reach out and pull her towards me. Demand to know where she got the damn top. Who it belongs to. Another part of me is already screaming at that urge as if to say: *This is Mikaela Wilcox, big guy. Calm the fuck down.*

Unaware of the constant stream of internal confusion going on in my mind, she pads through the cramped living space, avoiding looking anywhere in particular, and I find myself wishing she would turn to me - even for just one minute - so I can see what's going on in her head.

"No, I'm good. Thanks." I watch as she picks up dirty mugs and bowls from the counter and dumps them in the sink, busying herself as I stand leaning against the doorframe. I smile to myself as my eyes roll down the shape of her, admiring the way her hips naturally sway as she walks away from me. "Why?"

"Why what?"

"Why should you apologise?" I smirk when she finally meets my eyes and a small laugh slips from her lips.

I'd noticed that last night. She has a beautiful laugh. I'm not sure why it's taken me this long to hear it.

She shakes her head, her hand moving to the back of her neck as she leans back against the counter and drops her eyes to the floor, and I watch the soft pink of her blush pool beneath her skin.

"I was a complete mess last night and you - well, you had to do the whole big brother's best friend thing and rescue me from myself." She glances up at me and I smile. For a moment, it's just the two of us looking at each other in silence.

Her eyes are warm and inviting and her chest rises and falls with every shaking breath.

I trace the shape of her lips, the fullness and the cupids bow, and allow myself to wonder what it might be like to run my thumb across them, to brush my lips against them... To taste her.

Her eyes darken as I take a short step forwards and my mouth goes dry.

Once. I just want to touch her once. Then I'll stop.

"So - erm - Jamie is feeling worse than I am." She breaks eye contact and glances to the hallway, ultimately severing that pull between us, and I stop in my tracks. "Although I'm really not sure how because I was - well you already know what I was like."

I clear my throat and force myself to blink away the thick fog of thoughts that taunt me as I watch her turn from me, her hands trembling as she busies herself with more cleaning. "You were fine, Mik."

"I don't know about that." She mutters, more to herself than for me to hear. "I think I fell asleep on you."

"I didn't mind." I shrug a little. She stills again and a rose blush spreads underneath her pale skin once more, creeping over her neck and flooding her cheeks.

She turns back to face me, her lips slightly parted and her eyes wide as they run over me, and that blush deepens. And, just like that, the pull is back. I do not tear my eyes from her once; not as she stumbles over words that just don't come or as she brings a hand up to her neck. Not when she stops trying to talk and simply stares at me with the smallest smile.

Instead, I watch her and, *my God*, I want her.

"She's off limits to you, Haston."

Jamie's warning from the bar rings like a knell in my mind as the sound of his footsteps coming down the narrow hallway pulls my focus to the door behind me. And Jamie's right; this is Little Mik, for Christ's sake. I couldn't touch her even if I wanted to. But right now? In this moment? I realise I really, *really* want to.

Mikaela

"I thought you were leaving last night?" Jamie's voice is groggy and thick with sleep as he pats Ben's shoulder and makes his way over to my side. He pokes me three times, sharp in the ribs as I groan, before he reaches up for the cereal boxes balanced on top of the refrigerator. "What made you stick around?"

I move aside, putting down some toast and busying myself gathering pills for Mom.

My heart thumps in my chest while I wait for Ben to speak, holding in the smallest breath. My palms are clammy and my fingers won't catch the lip of the pill bottle and I can feel my mind growing thicker with each passing second - thick with the ideas of Ben's arm wrapped around me as he held me close to him in the car. Thick with the citrus and pine scent that clung to my skin even after he'd walked me to the door and pushed me up the stairs, laughing when I'd stumbled slightly and holding my waist until I could get my key in the door. Thick with the terrifying hope that maybe what I have been feeling since I'd seen him standing in that lonely church isn't some one-sided, silly infatuation.

"Oh." Ben pauses and I can feel the weight of his eyes on me, but I can't move to face him. Instead, I line the bottles up as if they have an order and aren't just going to be shoved in a cupboard until I repeat this process in three hours. "Nothing important."

Two words. That's all it takes to remind me of my place. Two very little, brutally honest words.

I shake my head, clearing away any lingering hope for a different answer, and bite down on my lip. Silently, I make my way out of the kitchen, smiling over at my brother and avoiding Ben's gaze completely, and make my way down the hall to my mother's room.

It's time to wake her up anyway.

Present

"That's the last one," Jamie puffs as he puts the box down before throwing himself onto the small couch I found in a charity shop down the street. "So this is it, huh?"

I slump down beside my brother, my overalls hanging from me at an awkward angle and the grey bralette beneath damp with sweat. Glancing around the space, I let peace settle over me and I breathe it in.

Hanging baskets now descend from the exposed beam that seems to separate the living space from the kitchen area and Devil's Ivy winds it's way down above our heads in twisted rivers of green. The bedroom is almost set up; my bed pushed against the wall on the raised platform and a small dresser against the opposite. Instead of a single bulb as planned, I've wound small lights around the beam that runs around the sleeping space, and now they hum with a gentle glow as the sky grows darker outside. There is a soft breeze from the open window and I smile as Jamie throws his arm around my shoulder and pulls me in.

"This is it," I sigh.

"It's very you." He chuckles as he takes in the tiny apartment. Where his is sleek and minimalistic, a manifestation of his need to control, mine is small and cozy and mismatched; chaos and creativity combined. There's a real feeling of finally gaining my independence here, and when I glance up at Jamie I feel the swell of pride in my chest. I am proud of who he is and what he has achieved. I am proud of who I am becoming because of him.

"Take out?" He grins. "My treat."

I laugh as my stomach grumbles and pull myself to my feet. Moving to the small kitchen, I search for the box with plates and cutlery and begin to pull things out, putting them in cupboards as I move through the space.

"There's a Chinese two blocks away. If you phone it in we can take a walk and collect?" I stretch, trying to put the few bowls I have on to a top shelf, as the buzzer sounds.

No one else knows this address, not even Max, and my head cocks to the side as Jamie moves to where I am, taking over for me so that I can reach for the small phone hanging on the wall.

"Hello?"

Jamie watches me as I place the phone down slowly, press the button to open the external door, and turn to him with an ice cold glare.

Sometimes, when we were younger, he would do this; tell people things he knew he shouldn't and then expect me to forgive him for it later. That was how Ben ended up crashing my fifteenth birthday on the pier. And apparently it is how Ben is now crashing my first night in my own place.

Jamie frowns and steps forwards, his mouth opening to ask why I'm looking at him like this, feigning his innocence, when the front door pushes open and he furrows his brow. For a second I genuinely believe the shock on his face, but then I turn to face Ben - Ben, who is smiling impishly at me, carrying two bags of takeout – and I find my common sense.

I don't want to admit it, but I'm kind of grateful for the food. It's been a long day and as we sit around the small coffee table I liberated from a pile of thrown out furniture on the sidewalk - Jamie and I on the couch with Ben sprawled out on the floor in front of us - it kind of feels like when we were kids. Except now Jamie can't send me away and Ben keeps glancing over at me rather than ignoring my existence.

Looking around the room, I contemplate how much there is left to do. My desk is only half built and my TV sits on the floor with wires spewing from its frame as some show no one is really watching plays in the background. My walls are bare and I know I want to find a way to incorporate art into my new home, a way to make it bright and up-lifting, and the exposed wooden floors need some love and life put into them. It needs work, that's for sure, but I grin as I consider the fact that it is mine to fix.

"So." Ben clears his throat as he lies back and stretches out, his thin black T-shirt lifting slightly to reveal the band of his Calvins and the hint of rock hard abs, and I look away quickly, focusing on the beam of wood that runs the length of my apartment above us. "What made you pick the first place you saw?"

I push to my feet, grabbing the empties and bringing them to the trash can, as I clamp down on the snarky retort that threatens to spill from my lips.

He brought food.

We have a truce.

I still want to throw something at him.

"It wasn't the first place I saw." My tone is clipped but I didn't tell him to leave so that's a win, right?

"Really?" He pushes up on his elbows and Jamie sighs, pinching the bridge of his nose, as Ben continues with his thought. "So you *chose* this neighbourhood?"

"Sorry." I stare at him as he raises his eyebrows at me. That truce lasted long. "Not everyone wants to be surrounded by people who compete with flashy cars and homes that feel like museums."

Ben grins as he lays back down and crosses his hands behind his head, clearly pleased with himself, and my blood boils.

"You've never been in my home, Mik." His voice is all bubbly and amused and I hate it.

"And I don't recall asking you to come to mine, Haston," I retort, flipping him off when he laughs.

Ben

She turns away from me, her finger still in the air, and returns to boxes that sit on the floor around her. She moves through the space leisurely, finding homes for pots and pans and glasses and coffee cups, and I watch her.

I watch as she crouches beneath the counter and pushes pans into corners and as she climbs up on the workspace to reach the top shelf for her coffee cups. I can't help myself when she hops down, all pleased with herself and proud, and a huge grin splits over my face. At some point she's going to change her mind about that placement, but right now she looks so goddamn happy.

My eyes skim over her body as she reaches up to another shelf, pushing spices and sauces into the back corner. She's standing with one leg stretched out behind her and her weight balanced on the tips of her toes, as if leaning like this gives her some extra height, and I shake my head. My eyes linger on her hips and I grunt a little as I shift where I lay. As much as I have spent years trying to deny it, I have always loved to look at Mikaela.

The sting of the smack yanks me from my thoughts as a small parcel hits the side of my face and ricochets under the couch.

Jamie hisses at me. *Hisses*. "Stop."

I grunt and twist to see the fortune cookie that had been perfectly aimed.

"Why are you throwing shit at me?" I fish it out from under the couch and tear off the wrapper.

"Because you're ogling my sister like I just fell into ten years ago." Jamie whispers as he glances to where Mik stands tying her hair up into a high ponytail, oblivious to the whispered conversation just a few feet away from her.

"First of all, I'm not." I scoff, breaking the cookie in two as I avoid meeting his eyes. "And secondly, I wasn't ogling her back then either."

"Like shit you weren't." Jamie pushes forwards on the couch and drops his voice further. "She's *off limits*, Ben. She is not the girl you fuck and fuck up. Just remember that."

Sometimes I fucking hate Jamie and the person he still thinks I am.

I huff as I adjust my position on the floor and glance up at Mik as she walks back to us, three beers in hand. This conversation with Jamie will have to wait.

When she extends a bottle towards me I take it with a smile and she scrunches her face up as she looks at me.

"What?" She raises an eyebrow.

"What do you mean 'what'?"

Mikaela drops back to her spot beside Jamie and passes him his drink, clinking her bottle against his before taking a sip. "I mean, why are you smiling at me?"

"*Jesus Christ*, the two of you are such suspicious people." I groan before drinking. "Must be a family trait."

Mikaela laughs as she looks to Jamie for an explanation. "The two of us?"

Jamie shrugs, his eyes burning a hole in the side of my face. "Yep. The two of us."

Mikaela
Somewhere in the mess of half unpacked boxes and piles of books, cushions that have been strewn over the

floor, and empty beer bottles is my phone. And it won't stop ringing.

Jamie groans as I lift his legs from my lap and stumble away from the couch, careful not to step on Ben as he snores on the floor. The soft glow from the TV helps me find my way to the kitchen without making too much noise, following the buzz of the phone against the worktop, and I answer quickly, not stopping to check the caller ID.

"Hello?" I whisper, blinking as my eyes adjust to the dark.

What time is it?

"I know I said I'd leave you alone if you didn't call, but I couldn't help myself." Josh laughs and suddenly my stomach is knotting and turning. "I hope you don't mind me calling."

"Oh. Erm." I turn on the spot. Once. Twice. "I don't mind." I push myself onto the counter and run my thumb over my ring as I try to wake my mind up a little. I had meant to call him. "Sorry I haven't called you. I was going to, I swear. I've just been moving."

I hear people talking in the background as Josh hums and glasses clink.

"How is it? The move?"

"It's going well. I have a lot of unpacking to do this week but I'm in. Jamie helped." I glance to my sleeping brother, wary of disturbing him, and feel my chest tighten at the sight of Ben sprawled out on the floor. Ben helped too. Even if he did it all with that infuriating little grin.

"Good. That's good."

"Josh?" I chew on my lower lip as I listen to him speak to someone off the line.

He answers after a beat.

"Yes, Mikaela?"

"Why are you calling me at two in the morning?"

I can hear the noise of traffic; of sirens and taxi cabs.

"I want to take you out again. Try it once more."

I take a deep breath and remind myself to smile. As I answer, I pick at the rip of my overalls.

"Friday?" My voice is light and gentle, but my stomach is doing somersaults. "But maybe a different restaurant?"

"I'll pick you up at seven."

"Okay."

I can hear the way he's grinning as the street noise dies down into a dull hum behind him. "I'll speak to you before then."

"Mhmm."

I push off of the counter as I hang up, spinning my phone in my hands, and slowly, make my way past the sleeping men, towards my new dresser.

With my mind racing to catch up with the idea of another date, I grab an oversized jersey from the bottom drawer and glance back quickly before unclipping the straps of my overalls, the denim stiff and uncomfortable from a day of heavy lifting and a night on the couch. I pull off the tiny grey bra and throw it towards the hamper, covering myself with my arm despite the fact neither of the boys have woken up, before pulling the top over my head. Wrapping myself in the long sleeves and shimmying out of the denim brings a comfort I didn't realise I need and I take a deep breath.

I'm here; in my new home, with my brother, and I have a date. Granted, when I think for too long about that last point my heart rate spikes and a cold sweat starts to cling to the back of my neck, but it's a start.

Maybe things are finally looking up.

Ben

I roll to my side and grunt as my leg knocks into the coffee table, my back aching from laying across the floor for too long, and I glance around the tiny apartment. In the darkness, my head is cloudy, a steady throb over my right eye reminding me why I cut down on drinking two years ago. The headaches aren't worth it.

Drawing in a deep breath, I try to focus on anything other than the dull throb brewing behind my eye.

A soft giggle draws my eyes to the kitchen and my heart picks up its pace. She's whispering as she perches on the counter, picking at the hole on her knee and smiling to herself, and I tuck my hand under my cheek as I watch her in the soft glow of the TV.

She's nothing more than a silhouette in this light, but I can see the way her head tilts to the right and she twists a thread between her fingers. I can see the way she curls into herself, making herself smaller as she tries not to wake us. I can see that she's nervous.

When she laughs, I feel a bitter pang in my chest and I close my eyes again. But it's no use. Even behind my eyes, I can trace the tiny dimple above the left corner of her lip when she laughs, and the way she tucks the flyaways of her hair behind her ear as she leans with her phone between her ear and shoulder. I can picture the way she presses her fingers into her lips as she listens and tries to hold back her smile. I know the exact shade of forest green that mingles with the jade of her eyes. It dawns on me that in the short time she's been back in my life, I've been memorising her again.

Jamie's right: this is exactly like ten years ago and I need to get a grip.

"Friday?" She sounds nervous, unsure of herself, and I could laugh. *Does she really think that whoever is on the end of the line will say no to a date with her?* "But maybe a different restaurant?"

102

And there's the feeling that I'm becoming far too accustomed to when it comes to Mik; a clenched jaw and a stiff neck, the roll of nauseating disappointment.

Of course it's Josh.

When she hangs up she tiptoes past me and I still. My heart hammers as I try to keep my breathing deep and even. If she knows I'm awake she might ask me to leave and all I know right now is that I don't want that. I'd shown up because I wanted to help. I wanted to see her and not be weird and tense, and I didn't want to spend another night alone when all I can think about is her. And now I want to stay. I want to stay because even when she's irritated by me she smiles, and I have always liked watching her smile.

I open my eyes when she's passed me and my breathing hitches.

Mikaela stands with her back to me as she slips out of her overalls and peels off the tiny scrap of fabric from underneath. I know I should say something, or close my eyes, or just do anything other than watch as she slips into a giant top, the smooth silk of her back to me, but I don't do anything.

The top skims against her backside, brushing darkness against her pale skin and ripples over her as she turns back to the rest of the room. She glances to the sofa and then to me. And I hold my breath.

When the mist of her eyes meets mine I don't look away. I think I might want to, but I can't.

I watch as her mouth opens in a small o and her hands fly to the hem of the T-shirt, tugging it lower.

She doesn't look away from me though.

She just stands there and, despite every cell in my body screaming for me not to, I move carefully. Despite every whispered warning and every insult thrown, despite every second of history I know we can't erase, there's something I want to do. Something I've wanted to do for what feels like a lifetime.

Mikaela

I swallow as Ben gets to his feet, heat flaming in my cheeks as his eyes rake over my body, and he takes a step forwards.

His eyes remain glued to me, intrigue swimming in the brilliance of the blue, and, with every painfully slow step that brings him closer to me, another surge of adrenaline and fear mixes and melts in my veins. Blood rushes behind my ears - a flooding, screaming noise - as he stops at the foot of the stairs.

I don't know why I'm not moving.

I don't know why neither of us are speaking.

I don't know why it suddenly feels like I'm eighteen again.

He swallows hard before taking those steps towards me, and I don't think I'm breathing.

With the gentlest of touches he trails his fingers across the side of my neck, pushing stray tendrils of hair back, his eyes following his fingertips, and my body ignites.

"What are you doing?" I whisper, my eyes trained on his lips as he smiles with an innocence that doesn't seem to match the moment.

"Testing a theory," he breathes.

I don't pull away. I don't flinch. My breathing becomes heavier and his other hand moves to my hips, his fingers digging into my skin with delicious pain as he pulls me closer, pinning me against him. He leans in, his breath fanning my skin, and my eyes flutter closed as his lips brush against my jaw with a feather touch.

I'm dreaming. I have to be dreaming.

"Ben." My hands are pressed against his chest. His pulse is racing beneath my palm. I can't think beyond the heat of his lips.

I wrap my fingers around his T-shirt and tilt my head automatically, allowing him access as he presses soft touches into every point of contact. He kisses my skin as if I am fragile, as if I might disappear in a cloud of smoke if he applies any pressure, and my heart sputters. He kisses me as if he sees me - *all of me*. His lips dance over my skin and his fingertips press into the nape of my neck as he moves to my lips.

And it is *volcanic*.

I can't think straight as heat pools in my core when his tongue swipes at my lips, coaxing them open, and we're a clash of teeth and lips and tongues. His fingers press into my skin and I can't be sure I'm not hallucinating the rush of pleasure as I moan with his touch.

Ben

Electricity sparks in my chest as I feel the silk of her lips against mine. I've only had one hit and I never want to stop.

My tongue swipes, tasting her, and the soft whimper that sounds from her lips leaves me aching for more.

I want her.

I have wanted her for so long.

Her hand moves to my hair, twisting, as my own slips down her body with tantalisingly slow precision. Every inch of her responds with delicious shivers as I touch her and I want more.

When she moans, I smile against her lips. My grip tightens and my hands move to cup her ass. When she gasps, I deepen the kiss; pulling on her lip with my teeth when she hesitates. I can feel her pulse racing as she groans and wraps around me, her tongue tasting me, her inhibitions melting away.

I lift her swiftly, my fingers gripping her thighs and her legs wrapping around my waist, as I move. My mind is lost in her, in the illusion of it all.

With her in my arms, the ache in me screaming for attention, I try to navigate the unfamiliar space and my hip crashes into something hard. The damn rail on her bed. I grunt in pain, my lips never leaving hers as a bubble of laughter escapes her and *fuck*, I don't think I could have ever imagined how my body would respond to that. I need her.

And yet there, in the corner of my mind, is an all too real kind of pain. Pain that carries a warning.

She's off limits, Ben.

The sound of Jamie shuffling on the sofa breaks through the bubble that envelops us both, and something inside me cracks as she pushes against me, trying to jump away.

Slowly, desperately hoping to keep this moment alive, I place her down. She pulls away from my lips; her eyes widening with realisation as she lets go and tries to take a step back.

She's off limits.

I step with her by instinct and her hands push against my chest while she glances to the sleeping figure on the couch.

"No," she whispers and her eyes snap back to me. Gone is the forbidden desire that had just been burning when she looked at me. Gone is that intoxicating smirk I felt against my lips just moments ago. Now she's staring at me with anger and confusion. "What the fuck was that?"

"I-"

She pushes me away from her and I shake my head.

"You need to leave." Her voice trembles.

"Mik." I reach for her one last time and she flinches. She *flinches*. I drop my hands and let them hang limply beside me. They feel empty. "Come on Mik. Don't act like that was all me. Please."

Mikaela

My fingers press against my lips as he stares at me, his eyes pleading and my lips parted. He's right. It wasn't all him. And I don't understand that. My mind is reeling and I can't get the heady scent of citrus and pine and beer out of me.

It's all around me. It's all over me. It's Ben, and Ben is my brother's best friend. Ben Haston is an arrogant ass. Ben Haston has been a nightmare for years. But he also just kissed me with a softness I didn't think he was capable of and left the flames of longing lapping beneath my skin where his fingers had been. Ben Haston kissed me and I wanted him to. Oh God, I wanted him to. And now I feel sick.

"I said leave." I look to the floor, afraid of the blue of his eyes.

Ben

I feel my face drop as I stand staring at her, disappointment and rejection washing over me where excitement and confusion had just mixed in a potent bliss.

I don't know why I did it. I don't know why I want to do it again. I don't know why her pushing me away now is scratching out a pit in my stomach, but I do know I don't regret it. I wanted to kiss her then. I want to kiss her now. And I don't want to stop.

Fuck.

I bite my lip as I stand there like an idiot, listening to her shut me out when she was just wrapped around me; wanting me. She wanted me. And now it's so much worse than ten years ago.

When she looks back to me, with doe eyes and a heaving chest, the whisper of reality slowly creeps over my mind. My hair is mussed and I can still feel the sting of her pulling it as my whole body aches for her. But standing in front of me is Mikaela Wilcox. The same Mikaela who, just two weeks ago, had seethed at me for mistakes she didn't fully understand. The same Mikaela Wilcox who had told me she didn't want anything to do with me. She didn't like me. Still doesn't like me. But friends don't kiss friends like that, and enemies definitely don't feel that fucking good pressed up against each other.

I nod tightly, turning from her and moving quietly through the space. Glancing back to her as I grab my keys from the little table beside the door, I sigh and she stares.

I don't regret it, but I wish I understood it.

Without another word I push through the door and make my way down the stairs and onto the street.

Fuck.

Mikaela

He leaves and I stand staring at the space he had just occupied. I stare for what feels like a small eternity, before sinking to the floor and leaning back against the bed.

What on Earth just happened?

Chapter Seven

Mikaela

"Where did Ben go?" Jamie rolls over onto his stomach, stretching out, before propping himself up with his elbows as he runs his hands over his tired eyes and looks over to where I'm sitting.

I haven't slept for a second. My heart still pounds like a jackhammer in my chest every time I close my eyes and my mind plays tricks on me; convincing me his fingers are still holding my hips or brushing over my thighs, and his lips are pressed against my throat, or gliding over my own. I can't close my eyes without drowning in Ben.

So instead, I did the safest thing and stayed awake. Now I sit with my knees up, my pyjama top stretched over my legs, and a coffee trapped in my hands. My eyes feel dry and itchy as exhaustion scratches at their surface, and I chew on my lower lip, trying desperately not to think about the way my body ached when he pulled it between his teeth.

Jamie walks over, pulling a chair out from beneath the breakfast table and sitting beside me. Slowly, he places a hand over mine and lowers my mug to the table as his voice brushes over me and cocoons me in its warmth.

"Mik. What's wrong?"

When I look at him, panic floods my senses. With his eyes wide and worried and his hand resting on mine, I feel a surge of heat behind my cheeks and my head whirs with thoughts of Ben's lips on my neck, his fingers pulling pain and pleasure from my hips.

My brother's best friend *kissed* me.

I kissed my brother's best friend.

Jamie waits as I blink back the memories and shove them deep inside the recesses of my mind, calling on anything else I can find to replace them.

"Josh called." I blurt out the first thought that comes to mind that isn't consumed by how gentle Ben's kiss had started and a furious blush spreads over my cheeks as the truth sits silently between us, waiting to explode.

Josh called and then I made out with your best friend while you were passed out on the couch.

"I thought he would." Jamie shrugs as he gets to his feet and begins rummaging in one of the boxes marked *food.*

"You did?" I push out an awkward laugh and cringe at how forced it sounds. If Jamie notices, he doesn't say anything.

"Yep."

I roll my eyes at my brother's indifference. "And what made you so sure?"

Jamie grins. "Because he called me and asked about you."

Slowly, I bring my mug back to my lips feeling a wave of nausea and flutters of nerves. "Oh."

Jamie cheers loudly as he yanks a box of Cheerios from beneath a pile of jars and I jump in my chair.

"So when's the date?"

God, he's chipper.

"Friday."

Jamie nods and smiles over his shoulder as he retrieves a bowl and the milk from my fridge. "I'm out of town for the night."

My brow furrows and I frown at him. "Out of town?"

"Yeah." He watches me as he raises a spoonful of cereal to his lips, a mischievous smirk appearing for just a second, and I can't help but grin. "For work."

"Does *work* have a name?"

A flash of boyish excitement spreads across Jamie's face as he pretends to zip his lips.

"Right." I shake my head and push myself to my feet, moving to my bedroom to get ready for work. "You'll be back Saturday though?"

"I'll be back Saturday."

"So we're still going to see Mom?"

Jamie nods with a tight smile. "I wouldn't miss it, Mik."

Ben

One. Two. Three. Four.

I push the air from my lungs as the burn in my chest builds.

Around me, the city still sleeps as I remain completely wired – my body wound with enough tension to keep me racing forwards - even as the air I inhale burns my throat. Every single step brings new flickers of her to me; the heat of her lips, the taste of her skin, the shake of her fingers as they pressed into my chest. Every second is flooded with Mikaela. And for every wave that comes, a thought I don't want to face follows: I broke my promise.

As the elevator doors pull open, I breathe out a sigh of disappointment.

Her desk is empty.

Jamie is going to kill me.

Jamie is going to kill me and I don't particularly care.

All I want to do right now is see her and speak to her. I want to find out what she's thinking. If I'm honest with myself, I just want to breathe in the air around her and feel her close to me. And the reality of that is dangerous.

I move through the space quickly, pushing down any thought of her as I focus on the day ahead. I have meetings, contracts to read over and a tonne of papers I neglected last night. Maybe if I just focus on that then I'll be able to block out the feeling of having her legs wrapped around my waist and the sound of her breath hitching as my fingers gripped her thighs.

I shake my head and push forwards, aiming for my office and groaning as the elevator doors shift behind me and an all too familiar laugh lilts through the air.

"Ben!" Jamie calls out as he pushes through the half open doors and glares at me. Mikaela's laugh skids to a halt. "What the hell?"

My blood turns to ice and I hold my breath as I turn slowly. Mikaela isn't looking at me. She's staring at the floor as she pushes her hair behind her ear and slips towards her desk. She's hiding. My eyes are glued to her as she twists away though, placing her phone into her desk drawer and firing up the computer for the day ahead, moving as if nothing has changed. Moving as if her brother isn't barrelling towards me, ready to rip my head off.

"Jamie." I blink and turn to face my best friend as nausea rolls over me. "I can -"

"I mean, I know you two hate each other's guts, but I had to get an Uber home this morning just to get changed." Jamie shakes his head as he laughs and my words stick in my throat. The tremor of my hands slow as I push them deep into my pockets and tilt my head. Jamie looks expectantly at me and I fumble for some sense in his words. "You couldn't have woken me up and dropped me home?"

"I - what?"

Jamie doesn't know?

"I told you, JimJam," Mikaela says, her voice quiet and soft. "He had a family thing. I told him not to wake you."

Her eyes meet mine for a fraction of a second, wide and pleading, before she turns back to the glowing screen and begins to input passwords to the programmes she needs. My chest thumps.

Jamie doesn't know.

"Right. Yeah. Sorry, I just -" I stare at Mikaela. "Erm - yeah."

Jamie's laughter bounces off of the walls as he claps his hand across my shoulder, knocking me forwards slightly, and starts to make his way through the office.

"I'm messing with you, man. Everything's okay though, right? With your mom?"

"Mhmm. Yeah." I shake my head and fake a smile as Jamie walks away from us both. "False alarm."

With the click of the door telling me we're alone, I move to Mikaela's desk, closing the distance between us with just a few strides, before stopping beside her in silence. She flinches slightly as she pretends to busy herself with yesterday's email list and double checking the day's schedule and I wait, watching as her fingers swipe over the keys quickly.

She refuses to acknowledge me.

"Can we talk about it?" I glance over my shoulder before leaning past her and moving the mouse so that she can't deflect by doing anything else.

"Your office is in the back, Haston." Her voice is cold and unfeeling, and I feel it like a knife twisting in my gut.

"Mik, come on. We can't just pretend –"

"Yes," she spits, "we can. We can pretend it didn't happen because it *shouldn't* have happened and it won't happen again. Now go away, before Jamie comes out here and wonders why the hell you are still at my desk looking at me like that."

"Looking at you like what?" I challenge.

"Like a sick and wounded animal, Ben. Like last night meant more than it did." Anger flashes behind her eyes as she glares up at me and I feel my hackles raise.

Last night *did* mean something, and I'm not going to pretend it didn't.

She continues on as her eyes dart to Jamie's closed door and pulled blinds, and her nostrils flare. "Like it was more than a drunk mistake in the middle of the night."

"Maybe it was more than that, Mik," I bark back. "Maybe it did mean something. You can't tell me you really think it didn't."

I step back when she pushes to her feet and barges past me, making her way to the kitchen without so much as a glance in my direction. "It didn't."

"Bullshit." I push into the room behind her, standing close enough I can feel the heat radiating from her, and place my hands on the counter on either side of her body. "It meant something and you know it."

Her shoulders tense as I stand pressed up behind her, my voice unashamedly low and desperate. I can feel her heart racing and her breath becoming short and rushed as I lean in to her, my lips brushing against her skin, and I whisper. She closes her eyes.

"It meant something to me, Mik." I press a soft kiss into her shoulder. "And I think it did to you too."

"No." Her voice is shaking and she stands as still as stone, waiting for me to take a step away from her. My chest caves when she shakes her head. "It was a mistake, Ben, and we're lucky Jamie didn't see anything. So no. It didn't mean anything and you need to drop it. It won't happen again."

Moving away, I say nothing as a lump forms in my throat, thick and heavy and carving pain into the depths of me as it makes its way to my gut.

She still hasn't turned - she still won't look at me - but her words cut at me with every syllable.

"Please." It's just a whisper, but it smashes into me forcefully. That word, that final utterance, the plea for me to understand. It's all it takes. I turn on my heel without another word and move from the room with a painful silence.

The drone of this man's voice is sending me to sleep. There is something lifeless and dreary about the way his pitch always drops down at the end of a sentence and the sound of a hacking cough punctuates every other phrase.

I rub my eyes, sighing as Jamie mutes the line and presses the intercom button.

"MikMak?"

He watches her as I stare blankly at the file in front of me. I hear as she snaps her laptop closed and Jamie shudders with the impact before she responds.

I want to look at her.

"I told you not to call me that here," she grunts.

I glance her way, a small spark of me desperately hoping to see her staring back at me, only to be shattered within an instant.

Her shoulders are tense and her jaw is tight. "What do you want?"

"I need coffee." Jamie grins as he watches her place her head on the desk and I hold back the urge to walk out. "And cake. I need cake."

"Then take a break and get coffee and cake, Jamie," she snaps. "I'm not your PA."

"I know." He laughs when she swivels to look at him, before he shoots her wide eyes and an apologetic pout.

My body tenses when her eyes brush over me and my entire being bristles under the weight of her indifference, even from the other side of the office.

"But," he continues, "I'm stuck in the worlds most boring negotiation meeting. I'd ask Ben to get it but -"

"Fine. Just stop talking." She slams her finger down to cut off the line, before ripping her bag from the back of her chair.

Jamie laughs as she storms towards the stairwell and disappears from sight before turning his attention back to the conference call we're stuck on.

I watch the door to the stairs swing shut slowly.

"We'd consider another sixty considering the success of his last publication," the man drones on when Jamie unmutes us and I pull my focus back to the matter at hand with a grunt.

"You can tell your client that we do not care what his successes were with his last book," I bark down the line. "He wasn't signed to Wilcox Writing and we are not in the business of handing out deals of that measure before we have evidence that that figure will be matched, and then some, in profits. The deal offered is the final offer. Joshua Lucas can like it, or leave it."

"I think," Jamie jumps to action, glaring at me as he speaks, "what my colleague is trying to say, Gentlemen, is that when Mr Lucas decided that we were the publishing house for him, he was aware that we are an independent company still functioning within our first five years of business and we simply cannot justify paying our authors above the offer we have provided on their first book with us. Once this book is out and a profit is made, we can reconvene and discuss higher advances and rates for future work."

I push to my feet and make for the doorway, ignoring the incredulous look plastered on Jamie's face, before storming out of the office entirely.

Mikaela

"What the hell is with you and Ben today?" Jamie grunts at me from behind his computer screen as I pick at the salad he ordered in for me.

My cheeks flush and I put the pot down. "What are you talking about?"

Jamie glances over the frames of the glasses he hates to wear and raises his eyebrows. "I'm talking about the fact the two of you are definitely not cut out for late nights. You're grumpy as shit, Mikaela."

I swallow the lump in my throat and try to roll my eyes. "Yeah well, I don't know about Haston, but I'm fine."

"Yeah." Jamie scoffs. "You're absolutely fine. You haven't been a raging bitch all morning. And I'm really Superman."

"You know." I stand and grab my bag from the other chair. "I think I want to go out for lunch. I need more than a salad."

"Go then," he sighs, "and come back with a smile, yeah? You're kinda the first face of the company, Mik."

"You're kinda an ass, Jamie."

"Only kinda?" He smirks as he types.

"Shut up."

"He kissed me." I stop walking in the middle of the street, passers by swearing at me as they narrowly avoid smashing into me, and Max freezes. I've kept this from him all day, and now it feels like it's choking me.

"I'm going to need you to repeat that." His head does this weird little roll as his eyes widen with glee and my stomach churns.

"Ben. Ben kissed me."

"Holy shit."

"Yeah."

Max grabs my hand and drags me into the road and across the street, straight to a little bar with a simple neon light stating the most unimaginative name possible: The Bar.

"Wait!" I grunt as he yanks me through the simple red door and straight to the empty counter. "Max. I want to go home. Stop!"

"Mikaela Wilcox, I love you and I say this with complete and somewhat overbearing adoration, but you just told me that Baby fucking Blue himself kissed you and your shoulders are up to your ears. You need a shot. And honestly, so do I."

I slump over the bar as I fall onto an open stool and watch Max flag down the bartender standing around on his phone. He's right, I need a shot. Or six.

"Two tequilas, please." He smiles at the guy serving us and I grunt.

"Each." I look up and the guy grins. "Two each."

"One of those days, huh?" Mr Barman raises an eyebrow and Max cackles.

"Oh," I pout. "You have no idea."

My bag is dumped on the bar and Max fidgets with the straps, tying them in knots as he nods silently, and I play with the peanuts I've been given.

In the two hours since we left work, Max has managed to get every little detail of my encounter with Ben, and the more I speak about it, the more I think about it and the more I think about it, the more I feel the ghost of his lips and that phantom ache between my thighs that I have been desperately trying to ignore. Especially since Max seems to be comparing Ben to Josh, quite vocally.

The bartender, who we have since learned is Alex - twenty-three years old and stupidly easy to talk to - leans forwards with his tattooed hand supporting his chin as he listens to us ramble, offering his own advice that essentially adds up to *bone them both* every so often.

"So, what are you going to do about it?" Max holds up his beer in a signal for two more and Alex pushes himself up off of the bar, fetching us more drinks.

I think I could like Alex. He's useful.

"Nothing." I untie my hair and run my fingers through it as Max raises an eyebrow at me. "There's nothing to be done. It shouldn't have happened and I'm not planning on repeating it."

"But Mik." His voice takes on a whiny tone as he places his hand on my knee and leans in. "That kiss sounded epic. It sounded steamy and heated and when you described it you..."

His eyes slip to the door as a gust of wind blows in and his voice trails to a stop.

"Max?" I twist in my seat and my heart drops into my stomach. The effort it takes to breathe suddenly makes it feel like I've stepped into a vacuum.

"Incoming," Max murmurs and Alex glances over to the man who just entered this little hole in the wall as he places the drinks down in front of us.

"This the blue guy?" Alex whispers.

"Not quite." Max clamps his smile shut and widens his eyes.

"Well, shit." I can hear the laughter in Alex's words.

I swallow. "Yep. Shit."

Chapter Eight

Mikaela

His eyes hone in on Max's fingers, still resting on my thigh from his pleas moments ago, and my heart hammers. It hammers in the sort of uncomfortable way that tells me I either need to run or stay, stop or go... make a decision.

I feel the color drain from my cheeks.

A spark of ice cuts through his gaze and freezes me to my core as he makes his way over to me, his jaw set and his smile fixed in place with a saccharine kind of superficiality. He walks with steady control and there's something familiar in the way his eyes seem to skate over the scene; something uncanny in his detachment.

"Hey, beautiful." Josh places one hand on the back of my stool while the other remains in his pocket. My breathing hitches. "We're leaving."

"We are?" Can he hear the tremor in my voice? See the fire in my bones? The way his eyes fix on mine tells me he can't. Or he doesn't care.

I shake my head slightly, clearing the fog from beer and tequila and memories that I wish would stay locked up, before glancing back to Max. Josh still hasn't spoken and waves are crashing in my gut in the silence.

Something in me must be screaming for help because Max shakes his head slightly and moves to stand.

"Mr Lucas." He offers the hand that was just resting on my leg to Josh as he gives one of his effortlessly beautiful smiles and Josh turns to him stiffly. "It's so nice to officially meet you. I'm Max."

"Yes." Josh's tone is clipped and a current of flames simmers beneath it. "And we're leaving."

His fingers wrap around my arm and I stumble from my chair, the alcohol making it harder to stand, as his fingers dig into my skin. Floods of pain and anger threaten to overwhelm me, threaten to spill from my eyes, as he grabs my bag from the counter and yanks me out of the bar with him.

I haven't said a word.

I can't find my voice.

Am I about to do this again?

As the crisp evening air slams into my skin and my mind starts to shift into action, I register the pain. His fingers are leaving angry marks of white around his tips where he holds fast to my arm, and the lack of circulation causes my muscles to ache.

"Josh," I whimper. "Josh, you're hurting me. Stop."

I pull my arm back, trying to free myself, but he pulls harder and my body crashes against his. He holds my arm still and my tears fall.

"Who the fuck is he?" His voice is low. Dangerous.

"What?" I can't stop shaking.

"I asked who the fuck the guy is that had his hands all over you, Mikaela."

"Max." I wince when his grip tightens. "It's Max. From work. The EA I told you about."

His eyes widen slightly as my tears spill, a sense of self beginning to settle back into the cold blue, and he lets go of me.

I step back instantly, my own hand flying to where his had been, holding in the pain as if it will somehow wipe it away.

"Shit. Mik, I'm so sorry, I don't know what came over me." He steps forwards and I step back. "I just - shit - I saw his hands on you and I just - I like you, Mikaela, and I thought for a second that it was a date I'd stumbled in on and I hated it. I hated thinking you were there with another guy and that he was making you laugh and touching you. Shit. I'm so sorry."

"You hurt me." It's all I can muster.

"I know. I'm sorry. Fucking hell, Mik, I really like you and this isn't me. I'm not like this. What the hell are you doing to me?"

It took seconds, just seconds, for his anger to fade and shame to take its place and when he looks at me with pleading eyes I stare up at him.

He is not Matthew.

"Mik."

I shake my head as I swallow my pride and close my eyes.

He is not Matthew.
He is not Matthew.

"It's fine." The words claw at my skin and catch in my throat. "But if you hurt me again Josh, if you ever touch me like that again, we're done. Whatever we are, it will be over."

He nods, a sober expression over his face, and he steps forwards. This time as he reaches out to me I let him touch me; I let his fingers brush over my cheeks as he leans in and kisses me softly. I let him kiss away my shame as the door swings open behind us and Alex and Max barrel out of the bar.

Max: I don't like it Mik.

I stare at the words burned into my screen for what feels like a lifetime as Josh chops onions and peppers and hums to himself in the kitchen. I had seen the look Max had given me when I told him it was fine, I had felt the weight of his worry on my shoulders as if it were a real burden to bear, and I hated it. I hated seeing his pity.

I shut off my phone completely and curl up on the couch.

Josh's place is the antithesis to my own. Decluttered and minimalist, it feels like he hardly lives here at all - like the shell of a home that desperately needs some warmth. The walls, all a stark white, have no personal photos, but a splash and pool of red hangs above a large fireplace and I stare at it as classical music swims through the space around me. It's not the kind of home I'd picture for a writer. There are no books and no cozy corners. Everything in here has a place and a purpose. Everything in here has been chosen for style.

My head hurts as I look around, and I can feel the throb of alcohol leaving its fingerprints behind as I long for sleep.

I crawl off of the small couch and walk around the empty space. His coffee table is empty and I run my fingers over the slick, white surface.

I pad to the kitchen, my arms wrapped around myself, and lean against the door. Josh moves with precision, the knife slicing even strips of peppers as he focuses solely on the task at hand, and I feel my mind slipping away from me.

Four Years Ago

Every slice of my knife is clean and precise and I wait for his comment. The bottle sits empty beside me and I wince as I catch the scent of it on the breath that caresses my shoulder.

His fingers brush the back of my neck, skimming the scabbed stitches from three days ago, and I freeze.

"Don't do that." His voice is a broken whisper. "Please, don't do that."

I take a deep breath and will my hands to move as his lips press into my neck and his hands grip my waist.

"I'm making lasagne." I keep my voice even and resume slicing onions to mix in with the meat. "Is that okay?"

Matthew buries his face in the crook of my neck.

"I'm sorry, Mik." He moves his hand down my arm and takes the knife from me, placing it on the counter. His fingers entwine with my own as he kisses my neck once more, moving to my jaw as he waits for me to respond. "I love you, so much."

I turn my face, the ghost of his fingers still searing beneath the skin of my throat, and let him kiss me.

I let his fingers dance over my wounds as he pulls me away from the counter and over to the table.

I let his hands grip my waist as he lifts me and lays me before him.

I let him push my skirt up as he kisses apologies into my flesh and sinks his sorrow into me.

I let him erase his pain in connection as I numb myself.

I give him grace and forgiveness and acceptance where he has given me bruises.

Present

"Mikaela?" Josh tilts his head as he stares at me and I crawl back to reality. "Is that alright?"

"I'm sorry. What?"

"I said I'm making lasagne. Is that okay?"

I nod tightly and he places the knife on the counter before walking over to me. His hands run down my arms, rubbing in soothing motions as he ducks his head to look at me, and his eyes are an abyss.

"Do you have any painkillers?" I can't will myself to smile and Josh's hands move down to my wrists. His eyes drop with them and his lips press into a thin line.

On my right arm there are five are small marks, barely turning from red to purple, but potent enough a mix that I know what shade of foundation I'm going to need to conceal them.

He lifts my arm gently and places soft kisses to the skin as he speaks.

"I really am sorry, Mikaela." He kisses another bruise. "I don't know what came over me. I've never been like that before. I won't be like that again."

"It's fine." I lie, to him or to myself I'm not sure, but it's a lie all the same. "I just have a headache from the drink."

"Of course," he soothes. "Aspirin is in the cupboard in the bathroom."

"Okay." I nod, turning to leave, but his hands wrap around me before I take a step away.

"Mik?"

"Yes, Josh?" I face him and my heart splinters. His eyes are wide with pain and his lip trembles.

"I really am -"

"Please don't say sorry again," I interrupt. "It's okay."

This time the lie feels more dangerous. It feels more risky. This time, as he kisses me, I tell myself it's true; it's okay, he didn't hit me. His grip had just been too tight.

Chapter Nine

Ben

Flowers were delivered to the office bright and early this morning - a garish bouquet of pinks and whites and muted purples - and they are currently sitting on Mikaela's desk as a near constant reminder of the truth.

She has a guy.

She has a smart, talented, British guy who she doesn't push away and who she doesn't want to hate.

She has a guy and I, at two o'clock in the afternoon, have a raging headache.

"I need some air." I huff to no one as I get to my feet and rummage in my desk drawer. I'm halfway through searching for my phone when the door opens and closes quickly and I glance up to see Max staring at me with a wounded look on his face.

"What now, Kingford?" I bite at him as I shove the drawer closed.

"It's Mik."

My heart shudders and my anger skitters away. *What about Mik?*

"What?" I try to keep a tone of indifference and end up with a shaky voice. "She needs you to pass on more messages?"

"I think she's in a bad situation."

My stomach twists. My throat dries up. I say nothing.

"And I know," he continues, "that it's none of my business but she told me about the other night and I just think that - as much as I hate to admit it and as much as she denies it - she'd listen to you on this and not me. So I'm breaking her trust and I'm asking you to help."

"Max," I sit back down, gesturing to the seat opposite me, and try to keep a calm head, "I don't understand."

"I know you two kissed. She told me two days ago and then Josh showed up and he was acting really weird - like possessive and cold - and he yanked her out of the bar so quickly. Physically. He was pulling at her arm and I know she was in pain, it was all over her face, but then when we got outside he was kissing her and she said it was fine and she left with him, but I don't think it was fine and I don't know what to do." His hands shake as he speaks and I feel something inside me snap.

Josh hurt her?

"And you're only telling me this now?" Rage fuels my mind.

"I didn't know what to do." His voice is so fragile it almost hurts and I nod tightly. "She won't talk to me."

My eyes drift to where she's sitting, the pale pink blouse covering her arms as she pushes out of her chair and moves across the space to the small shared kitchen with her head down. I don't think past what Max has said, not even to glance in his direction and utter a response. I just get to my feet and start walking.

I push into the small space behind her and watch as her shoulders tense in response to me and her face twists away.

"Mikaela." Under the husk of my voice is thinly veiled contempt, even to my own ears, and my hands are balled into fists.

"Not today, Ben. Please."

"He hurt you?" I choke on the words and she flinches. I hate that she keeps fucking flinching. It's all the confirmation I need. "I'm going to fucking kill him. Is that what those flowers are? Some form of shit apology? I'm going to rip his fucking head off of his shoulders."

Every cell in my body is vibrating with the need to move, to do something, and my breath comes thick and fast. When she turns to me her eyes are wide and her lips tremble.

The room feels too small, like the whole place is closing in on us and she could get hurt. I back away, my voice still tumbling from me with words I know she doesn't need to hear but I can't stop them.

"Tell me what to do, Mik. Tell me what you want me to do, because I want to kill him and if I leave this room I am going to hunt him down and I am going to make sure he fucking hurts for hurting you. So please, just tell me what you want me to do, because I'll do it."

"Ben." Her voice is stern even though she still looks fragile. "Just stop."

My words dry up and I stare at her as she places a hand on my arm.

"He didn't hurt me." *Lie.* "I'm okay." *Another lie.* "I don't need you. Thank you, but I don't need you." *Truth.*

Mikaela

"He didn't hurt me." *Not intentionally.* "I'm okay." *Am I?* "I don't need you. Thank you, but I don't need you." *I don't want your help because you scare me in a way that no one else does.*

Ben is shaking under my touch, like every nerve is frayed and exposed, pain radiating through him, and I pause for a moment.

Together we stand in silence, just breathing. Just looking at each other.

The air grows thick as tension rolls off of him. Slowly, with excruciating tenderness, he raises a hand and brushes his thumb against my cheek. I close my eyes as he cups my face and takes a deep breath.

"Mikaela, if he hurt you -"

I swallow hard before pulling away and turning back to the coffee pot.

"I told you he didn't, Ben. But thank you for your concern."

The door closes behind me and I give in to the tremors.

I won't do this again.

Nine Years Ago

"Mikaela Wilcox, what on earth have you done this time?" Mom sits on my bed in my dorm as I get ready for dinner and her eyes bug at the sight of my skin.

My pulse quickens.

"Oh, that's nothing." I brush it off as I yank the thick, cream sweater over my head and cover the purple of my ribcage.

"Nothing?" Her voice is incredulous. "That's one hell of a bruise for nothing, sweetie. What happened?"

She moves across the room towards me as she speaks and starts pawing at my top, pulling it up to inspect me closer. My hands push at hers as I force a laugh through my lips and shake my head.

"I went to a frat party, Mom." I lie through my teeth. "I drank too much and fell off of a table. It was stupid and completely avoidable and I am fine."

Mom sighs with relief, her body sagging slightly, and my chest aches. She's been looking frail again, the skin of her chest barely covering the bones of her; stretching taut and translucent. She doesn't need to be worrying about me when she's getting worse again.

It was a one off - a moment of weakness and fear.

It was my fault.

The truth of the matter is that I had gone to a frat party, and I *had* had too much to drink, and I had danced on a table. But I didn't fall. I pulled a guy up to dance with me. I knew Matthew was watching and I wanted him to dance with me, but he wouldn't, so I danced with a stranger and I laughed when he placed his hands on my hips.

Matthew's eyes had burned as he watched me, his drink to his lips and his chest rising and falling slowly. His friends surrounded him, talking in animated voices about shit he didn't hear, and he pushed away from them all. He pushed his way straight to me and he pulled me from the table and out of the room. He dragged me up the stairs and shoved me into an empty bedroom and when he pinned me against the wall the air was knocked from my lungs. My eyes streamed and my head span when he shook me.

"You think that shit's cute, Mik?" He had pulled me back and twisted, pushing me across the room. "You think it makes you look like anything other than a slut? You think it makes me look like anything other than a fucking idiot?"

I couldn't keep up with him. He was talking so fast and moving so quickly. He had grabbed my arm and swung me to face him, his fingers stinging my skin, and I remember that I cried out when he shoved me sideways, crashing straight into the dresser. My ribs ached. My voice was stolen. And then he was holding me. He was kissing apologies into my hair. He was soothing me.

"Shit. Mik, are you okay? I didn't see the dresser. I didn't. Are you okay?"

I had cried as he held me and as he drove me home. I had cried until I fell asleep and when I woke he was beside me, holding me and sleeping so soundly. His lips were parted and his breath was thick with the stale stench of alcohol as his arm was draped over me, and the ache in my side mirrored the ache in my chest.

How can you love someone so much and hate them too?

When I had brushed my fingers over his cheekbones I told myself it was okay. It was only once. I'd leave if it happened again.

"You've got to be more careful, my little MikMak," Mom croons, pulling me from the memory. "I need you fit and fighting."

"I know, Mom. It won't happen again."

Present

"Josh, I really wish you had let me pick the place." I twist my fingers beneath the table as another waiter passes by our table, spinning Mom's ring over and over on my finger.

The ceiling is covered with soft, twinkling lights and smooth jazz oozes from speakers hidden in corners and behind billowing white gauze. Couples sit around us, whispering across tables, as men and women in white shirts and black ties weave between us all, topping up glasses and recommending dishes.

It's intimate and expensive and I *hate* it.

"I wanted to make it up to you, you know, for the other day." He lifts his glass and holds it out to me.

Whiskey. Tonight he's drinking whiskey.

I glance down, nervous but sure of what I need to do, and take in a deep breath.

"Josh." My voice trembles and my hands shake. "We should talk."

Chapter Ten

Mikaela

"What the fuck happened?"

My eyes snap away from the sidewalk at the sound of his voice and I stop moving. Ben's eyes burn into me while the sound of sirens in the distance wail, like a warning that came too little, too late. My chest aches.

Why are you here, Ben?

Slowly, I find my footing and push forwards, stepping around him without another word as he watches me intently. My heart hammers in my chest and tears threaten me with the all too familiar sting of fear, but I keep my head high.

I will not let him see me crumble, even now; even with the angry red marks of fingers burning against my arm like a brand that I will *never* be able to forget and the stickiness of dried blood clinging to the skin of my back.

"Mik?" He pushes himself to his feet, and follows me into the building. The silence is deafening and shame floods through me as he fails to pull his eyes away from the tear in my dress that exposes too much of my skin.

"Go home, Ben." There's a break in my voice; a drain that I can't quite plug before I speak, and he clenches his fist, no doubt registering the defeat beneath my words. "Please."

"I'm not going anywhere." He takes my keys from me as I fumble, my hands shaking despite my resolve, and crouches down to my eye level. "Did he do this?"

"Why the fuck do you care?" I look away, the venom I had intended missing, as the tears finally come.

He hesitates for just a second before placing his fingertips beneath my chin and lifting my eyes to his.

"Mikaela."

I know he heard it. I know he heard how I whimpered when he touched me.

Ben

The tiny cry that slips through her lips is agonising.

She won't look at me.

"I need you to tell me what happened, because right now I -" I clear my throat as I close my eyes. In the darkness it's worse. I can picture hands on her skin. I can see her as she's pulling away, fear in her eyes. I can imagine it all and my imagination is slowly killing me. "Did he - did he make you do anything?"

"No." She shakes her head quickly and a sigh of relief washes over me like stormy ocean waves as I gently brush away her tears. Her eyes meet mine. "But he - Ben - he was so angry."

She shakes violently as a sob rips from her chest and she heaves for breath that just won't come.

My arms encase her, holding her against me, as we sink to the floor. Over and over, I stroke her hair and rock her gently. I hold her as her nails dig into my skin and as she trembles with every cry. I hold on to her as she drowns in pain.

As she clings to me, it takes every ounce of focus I have to keep my rage from bursting out of me; to keep the fury and anger and agony from spilling out and twisting me into someone unrecognisable. Focusing on her fingers, on the pressure of her nails digging into my skin, I close my eyes. Focusing on the way her shaking calms and her sobs become whimpers, I take a deep breath. Focusing on what she needs now - someone to tell her she's okay and to mean it, someone to keep her safe - I find a way to keep calm.

"I've got you." I whisper as my lips brush against her hair. "You're okay now. You're okay."

She presses closer against me, her grip tightening and her heart pounding against my skin, and I breathe her in.

I can do this.

I can hold her until she doesn't need to be held.

Mikaela

When there are no more cries left in my throat and the river of tears has ebbed to an end, he is still holding me.

I don't move. I don't try to push him away. Instead, I keep my eyes closed and listen to the steady rhythm of his heartbeat as his fingertips gently brush against my arm.

His voice has been constant and now, as silence settles over us, a fresh wave of fear twists in my gut.

"Ben?" My voice is hoarse and thick.

"Yeah, Mik?"

"I don't - I don't want to be alone." The words disappear from me and his fingers still on my skin as my breathing hitches.

"I'll stay on the couch." He resumes the steady back and forth of his fingertips and my body, still aching with ghosts of pain, releases its tension.

"Thank you."

Eventually, I pull away from him and Ben watches as I wipe my eyes.

He moves slowly, brushing the curls away from my tearstained cheeks, his fingers lingering for just a moment too long as my eyes close, before pulling his hand away and pushing up from our spot against my door. He guides me with him when he moves, helping me to my feet as he smiles softly and I lean into him. He wraps his arm around my shoulders, pulling me tight against his side, as he unlocks the door and leads me to my couch.

Every step threatens to shake more tears from me.

Every creak of the floorboards beneath us threatens to expose my cracks.

I curl into myself almost immediately once I'm seated, and the questions I know Ben quashed earlier seem to push themselves to the surface once more.

His eyes burn with an intensity I have never seen and his hands clench into fists and then uncurl over and over again. As he watches me wrap my arms around myself, trying and failing to cover the tear of my dress and making myself as small as I can, he runs his hands over his face and takes a seat beside me.

I can feel the way his blood is boiling and his mind is racing with each passing second and I stare at the nothingness ahead of me.

"Mik." His voice is barely a whisper. "Are you okay?"

I want to tell him I'm fine; that everything is going to be okay and that this is nothing, because really, considering everything I've seen before, this *is* nothing. But when I open my mouth to speak there's nothing that comes out. There's nothing I can say.

This isn't okay.

I am not okay.

"I don't know," I admit. I'm tired and I'm cold. "I'm cold."

Ben

Her voice is so small and her eyes are empty.

Without speaking I get to my feet and move to the bathroom adjacent to the living room and twist the taps over the tub that sits beneath the window. I grab a bottle, something luxurious by the looks of it, and empty half of it into the steaming water. Immediately, the scent of jasmine and honeysuckle mists in the air and I move to the small basket in the corner. I grab a towel and hang it on the rack beside the sink before making sure that everything is just right.

Every step I take is automatic, just as they were years ago when I did this very thing for Mom - helping her wash away whatever horrors had just existed.

After a few minutes I make my way back to the living room and move back to her side, crouching down before her.

She's laying on her side, her arms tight around herself and tracks of tears staining her cheeks.

"Hey," I whisper as her eyes open and my fingertips stroke her cheek. "Come on. Let's get you cleaned up."

She gives a tired nod and pushes to her feet.

I take her hand carefully in my own and lead her to the bathroom.

The tub is half filled with suds and bubbles, and steam clouds the mirror and window.

A pocket of laughter bursts in her chest as she watches the suds rise and the steam dance and I hold onto her with my thumb brushing lightly over her knuckles. Cautiously, I cock my head to the side and look at her, still standing with one arm wrapped around herself, the tear in her dress exposing more of her chest as she giggles.

"It's not that I don't want to hear you laughing." I watch her carefully. "But what's so funny?"

Mikaela takes a shaky breath, her laughter slowing as she registers the concern barely hidden in my eyes.

"This." She gestures around the room and ends looking at me. "It's just strange." She sighs when I let go of her hand. I want to take it back; to hold it tight for my own sanity. Instead, I watch as she shrugs and looks to her feet. "You know, you don't have to do any of this."

I nod as I take a step back from her, my eyes darting between the living room and where she's standing. The idea of leaving her alone for just a second is tearing at a gaping hole forming in my stomach.

"I know." I give her a smile I know doesn't reach my eyes when she looks to me. "Have a bath and I'll be right out there if you need anything."

Mikaela

When I'm alone, I peel the dress from my body, the black satin now a skin I need to shed, and drop it where I stand.

I want to burn it. I want to tear it to shreds, douse it in gasoline and light it where it lies. My chest pounds as I strip from my underwear and step into the heat of the water, flinching at first, but slowly submerging myself into the sting, welcoming the sensation as it burns the layer of skin *he* touched.

I feel my blood rise to the surface, the burning red of me beneath the water, and I lower myself until my shoulders are under and I am nothing but a face in a cloud of bubbles.

I close my eyes and listen to the pour of the water as waking nightmares plague my mind.

One Hour Ago

"I don't see this working." I shake my head as a chasm of anxious energy tears at my stomach, my voice lowering to just a whisper while Josh stares at me with expectant eyes.

There's something familiar in that look, something unsettling, and my mouth goes dry.

I will not do this again.

"Why?" He lifts an eyebrow, a smirk settling on his lips, and I know he believes he can talk me out of walking away. I know he has the words ready, the apologies and the promises and the sweet whispers. But he doesn't know I've heard them all before.

"I think -" I force myself to look at him as I speak "- that we are just too different, Josh, and I - I'm sorry but I just don't want to keep pretending." I watch with bated breath as the hair on the back of my neck stands on end. He purses his lips and nods silently - a reaction I wasn't expecting. "I should probably head home."

I lift my fingers as the waiter glances to us both and pulls the small tablet he uses for orders from his apron as he approaches.

Josh frowns.
My head is foggy and my balance unsettled.
In trying to build up my courage I drank too much.

Present

I lean forwards and shut off the tap.

My cheeks are damp.

I'm not sure if it's from the steam or tears but I don't care.

I'm exhausted.

Pulling my knees to my chest and closing my eyes again I press my knuckles against my lips, clamping down as my cries threaten to resurface and memories, both old and new, twist and contort into one torturous stream.

Three Years Ago

I shake my head as I bite back my tears, my hands shaking as he stalks towards me and I stumble backwards, crying out when I step on shattered glass.

All around me are remnants of the meal I had prepared; across the walls, spilled over the floor; ruined.

I feel the blood pooling beneath my foot as I stand in the sea of shattered crystals. Mom's wine glasses.

"Matty." His name is a plea, a desperate shred of hope before the inevitable. "I wasn't going to take the job. He was just being a nice neighbor. I promise."

His breath is hot on my face, the whiskey burning my eyes as he brushes against me, his fingers wrapping roughly around my neck and holding me tight. I gasp when he squeezes, my tears falling quickly as he pushes me backwards, tearing my feet from the floor and slamming me against the wall.

"Matty, please." I claw at his fingers as his face swims out of view. "I can't - I can't breathe."

"You're killing me, Mikaela." He cries as he pulls me back and slams me into the wall again. My eyes roll back in their sockets and my chest burns. "You're killing me!"

Present

I flinch as the door opens.

He doesn't step in.

"Mik?"

My cries rip through me as I hold myself together. I have no doubt he heard me wailing from the room next door.

I know I'm breaking.

I'm falling apart and I can't breathe.

Why can't I breathe?

My chest is heavy and light all at once. I feel sick. Really sick. Like the contents of my stomach are about to come up and I'm going to pass out all at once kind of sick.

"I can't - I can't." I gasp for breath as I try to get to my feet. My knees shake before they give out and I fall back into the scalding water.

And then I'm not alone.

Ben

Within an instant I'm by her side, ripping the towel from the rail and wrapping it around her, still in the tub.

Once she's covered I lift her, ignoring the splashing of water against the tiles and the way my clothes now stick to my skin as she wraps her arms around my neck. I carry her to her bed, placing her down gently and pulling away.

My imagination is killing me. She is lost in a panic and as she sits shaking, wrapped in a sopping wet towel, my mind is weaving intricate stories of how she ended up sitting before me, bruised and breaking, and the whole room is tainted red.

"Please," she whispers, her eyes meeting mine. Beneath the surface of the green is a flicker of something so fragile and so fearful that, for a moment, I feel a tear opening in my chest.

My breathing stills.

She stares up at me with so much pain and sadness, and I feel a pang of guilt in my gut. She doesn't need anger. She doesn't need to see my pain.

"What do you need, Mikaela?" I crouch in front of her, my eyes never leaving hers, even as her towel slips and she moves to lay down. My fingers move quickly, pulling the sheet up over her, covering her, as I throw the wet towel to the side.

"Hold me?"

I stop moving and swallow hard.

Her eyes are locked on mine; forest green burning with something dark and twisted and desperate. "Please?"

"Mik. I-" I'm leaning with my elbows on the edge of her bed as I place my head in my hands. I want to comfort her, to let her seek safety in my arms and make her feel better, but I shouldn't. I know I shouldn't. I can't hold her like this, with the pain of another man's hands bruising her and the echo of Jamie's one rule rattling in my brain. *Her own words* rattling in my brain. "I don't think you really want that."

Mikaela

I shift so that I'm sitting up slightly and watch his conflict write itself over his face. I can see he's torn as he looks away from me, our kiss is probably a twisting regret in some dark corner of his mind now that he's seen how broken I am, and I know it's wrong. I know it's selfish to want this from him right now, but I need someone to be soft with me.

I need *him* to be soft with me.

"Please." I place my fingers against his, pulling his hand away from his face. "I want you to hold me."

His eyes are tear soaked and I glance away from him, ready for the swell of pain that is going to come with his refusal.

Ben sighs. He moves quickly, opening drawers to retrieve a t-shirt and underwear for me, before perching on the side of the bed with his back to me.

"Okay." He holds them out and I take them gingerly, my breath caught in my throat as I wait for his next words. "Put these on."

I can feel his breath fanning against my neck as his arms wrap around me and he pulls me against his chest. I sigh, expelling pain and finding a strange release, when I feel his hand flat against my stomach and his legs tucking up behind mine.

"Is this okay?" he asks.

I nod.

In the warmth of him, I feel safe. His arms are strong and his chest is firm. I feel his skin against me, and as his lips press against my head, I close my eyes, ready for what I fear is still to come.

"No. Josh, stop." My voice is broken and hoarse.

I should have gotten a taxi.

I should have gotten a taxi.

"Come on, Mik," he whispers in my ear as his fingers paw at my dress.

I feel the rip of the fabric and my knee jolts up, connecting with his groin as he grunts. I push him away from me, my back raw from the way I've been shoved against the car door.

Something sharp scratches between my shoulders and the sting of torn skin screams for attention.

His weight is heavy on me.

"You fucking bitch!" His words are venom in my ear, his voice an acid that drips over my skin, as he grabs my

arm and pushes me down further. I cry out from the pain of his grip and he pushes me back again. "You're a tease, Mikaela. A fucking tease."

Bile rises in my throat as his fingers squeeze my body and his words rip through me.

"Get off of me." I sob as he bites down on my shoulder and his hand trails up my thigh. "Get off of me now!"

"Come on, Mik." He repeats himself. "You can't tell me you don't want this."

I scream.

"Shh. It's okay." Ben holds me tight as I thrash in his arms, a scream tearing through the darkness of my tiny apartment. "You're okay. I'm here. I'm right here, Mik."

"Ben?" I turn to him, burying my face in his chest as he pulls me closer and holds the back of my head.

I tremble as the tension of my nightmare seeps out of my skin.

"I'm right here, Mik." His voice is the softest caress.

"Okay." I pant as I blink against his skin and his hands rub my lower back in small circles. He holds and hushes me as my breathing starts to settle to a steady pace and he presses another soft kiss against my forehead. "Okay."

He holds me silently, not moving and not pushing for me to speak. He waits for my breathing to be completely even and my hiccups to disappear before he says a word.

"Mikaela." His fingers comb through my hair and a shiver travels the length of my spine. "What happened tonight? I need to know."

I peel myself out of his arms, moving slowly so that I can look at him, still longing to be touched by him.

His eyes are dark as the strength of his anger simmers beneath the blue, but he chews his lip, softening his expression as he looks at me. My heart aches just looking at him and, as if he needs the contact too, he brushes his fingers over my cheek and holds onto me as I lay facing him.

I know my face is blotchy and red and my eyes are swollen from tears and I don't care. His fingers trace the creases between my brows, and I smile sadly at him as some stray tears spill.

"I - erm - I told him I didn't think we would work," I begin with a strained voice. "I don't even know why." *Liar*. I close my eyes and take a deep breath. "That's a lie. I do know. He - Josh - he reminds me of Matthew and I just can't do that again and I felt like the whole restaurant was closing in around me and I needed to get out of there. But he offered to drive me home and I thought - *God* - I thought it was sweet."

"But you were walking?"

"He pulled up a couple of blocks away," I whisper. "He said he wanted to talk about it."

His whole body tenses and I open my eyes to him, knowing where his mind has gone. I bring my hand up to his cheek and brush my fingers over the dark stubble along his jaw, watching as he tries to breathe deeply, slowing his racing heart.

"I can stop," I whisper.

He shakes his head and his voice rasps. "I need to know, Mik."

I take another deep breath.

Why?

"I told him what I'd already told him. That we're just too different. And that I would walk from there. I just - I didn't want to stay in that car. But the door was locked and he -" My voice cracks as Ben's jaw tenses and he closes his eyes. "His hands were... he was *everywhere*.

And my dress." I shake my head, bile rising in my throat. "I kicked him and tried to get out, but he pulled me back and I think I screamed. Some kids were nearby, well, not kids but a group of boys, and they came running and he let me go. I think I lost a shoe."

His blue eyes open to mine and for a moment it's just this; it's just us, laying together in the darkness and I don't want it to disappear.

"I should take you to the hospital, Mik."

I shake my head. "I'm not hurt, Ben. Not really. I don't need to go to the hospital."

"Then I'll call Jamie? See if he can come back to town now?"

The air is too thick and my head throbs.

I won't do this again. Not after everything I've put Jamie through already. And what about the deal? Surely by now a contract has been signed? And now I'll have to see Josh at work. I'll have to face him when all I want to do is forget he exists. And Jamie will kill him. He would have killed Matthew if I hadn't needed him.

"Please, don't."

"He's gonna find out, Mik."

My eyes are screaming as I look to him. "I'll tell him Ben, but..."

He raises his eyebrows at me - a challenge for me to continue my lie - and I close my eyes.

"I just don't want to talk about it anymore. I just - I just want to be held and I don't want to have to think about any of it."

Ben

Mikaela's eyes are closed, but I can still see the dimming of the green as if she is staring right at me.

I pull her to my chest again. That last part was true at least, even if I know she'll avoid telling Jamie, and I need to feel her safe in my arms. A small voice in the back of my head tells me I shouldn't hold her like this - it's only going to make everything else harder - but I push it down and focus on the woman curling in to me and nestling in against my chest.

"Okay." I stroke her hair repeatedly.

"And Ben?"

"Yeah, Mik?"

"I'm sorry if you saw anything earlier."

I can feel the embarrassment flood through her, warming her skin and staining her cheeks, and I feel the first hint of a smile since I saw her stumbling towards me this evening.

When I don't say anything, she clarifies. "You know - in the bathroom."

I chuckle, a rumbling kind of chuckle that vibrates in my chest. "Trust me Mik, I didn't look."

"You didn't?" She smiles against my skin and I roll my eyes.

And then I say something stupid.

Mikaela

"When I see you naked for the first time it's not going to be because some lowlife has done this shit to you." His voice is almost too quiet to hear and yet the timbre sends shivers down my spine.

My heart jitters and my core tightens.

When.

We say nothing else as we lay there, waiting for sleep to come, but my mind plays his words over and over again.

Chapter Eleven

Ben

A tiptoeing warmth creeps over us both as she sleeps peacefully. The sun sneaks into the sky and over the space with comfort and the promise of a new day, breaching the wide window beside the bed as a soft breeze brushes over where she rests and I move from her side.

She spent the entire night curled into me, her hand over my heart and her leg tucked over mine and I had lay still - terrified to wake her.

I shift slowly, untangling our limbs and slipping out of the bed without jostling her, and move to the window by the fire escape. I climb out and I let go of all the pain I've been afraid to release in front of her.

All of it.

I sit with my head in my hands in the early morning briskness, my mind reeling as I sneak glances over to where she is, peaceful for now. I think over every tiny detail of her night with painstaking intensity. In her fear, her arms wrapped around me like a vice, her face had been buried into my chest and I had obsessed over the details she had shared; memorised it all as if I had been there. But if I had been there she wouldn't have had a single mark left on her skin. If I had been there, she would have come home laughing, probably calling me names, but laughing still. If I had been there, she would have climbed into bed safe and alone and calm. She wouldn't have needed someone here all night to hold her and to comfort her. She wouldn't have needed me.

I sigh as I lift my eyes to the street below me. People go about their Saturday morning with a lazy ease - some wandering without care to their next destination, others taking quick steps to another morning of work. I watch as a woman, a little older than Mik, walks hand in hand with a little boy; swinging their arms and laughing as he grins up at her, and I feel myself soften.

The breeze ruffles the dark curls that bounce over the boys eyes and he pulls from his mother's hold, running to another woman, older and grey, with wide arms and a warm smile. In an instant she's on her knees holding the child, grinning from ear to ear, and I pause to imagine that I can hear her voice over the steady hum of city traffic. I imagine it's soft and comforting. I watch her pull a parcel out of her bag and hand it to the child just as the first woman reaches them. The older woman pulls her into a warm embrace before glancing down to the boy and laughing as she says something; eyes wide and welcoming.

The three of them walk together, the child holding them both and I imagine them taking my worries away with them, banishing them with their laughter and smiles.

This whole exchange takes place so perfectly before me and my mind wraps around it. I want to cling to it. I want to hold it as a reminder that the world isn't as dark as it had seemed last night; that there is good out there to counter the shit in the world. There is good out there to counter the shit Mik has been through.

Mikaela

When I wake up, Ben isn't beside me. He doesn't hear the way I whisper his name, or see the way my arms reach out for him only to come up empty as my eyes open. He doesn't see the bitter disappointment that I woke without his arms around me.

I push myself up when I realise I'm alone.

For a moment – a single, blissfully kind moment – I consider the idea that it may have all been a brutal nightmare. A nightmare that felt real but wasn't. I stretch out, yawning as my t-shirt rises and glance down.

The familiar phantom ache is different today; much more raw, more intense, and when I see the splattering of obsidian against the white of my hips I know why. The nightmare is very real. Images flood my mind and I stumble out of the bed and towards the bathroom as nausea rushes through me.

Ben

"Shit," I jump as Mik flies past the window and darts into the bathroom.

I follow quickly, clambering back through the open window and racing to the door left ajar, as she throws herself over the toilet bowl and heaves.

Pushing to her side, I crouch behind her and gather her hair as she pukes, stroking her spine with my free hand.

"That's it," I soothe. "Get it out."

Mikaela

I choke as I cling to the toilet, tears streaming when I gasp for breath between each heavy convulsion of my stomach, and I screw my eyes closed. Focusing only on the slow, steady movement of his palm against my back, I try to drown the world out as I expel everything I have inside me.

When there is nothing left in my stomach, I drop against the tub and grab some tissue to wipe my mouth before flushing it all away.

Ben gets to his feet, glancing down at me as I sit trembling, and sighs. I know that look too well; I'm a mess.

"I'm going to get you some water and you need to eat something. You have anything in?"

His voice is gentle and I think that makes everything worse.

I sniffle as I shake my head, staring up at the ceiling.

"Right." He shuffles where he's standing. "Then I'm going to the store. I'll be back soon, just -"

At his hesitation I turn my face to him.

"Just let me in, okay?"

I watch him and he watches me.

His eyes are dark and stormy, like an ocean that can't rest, and his lips are turned down in an uncharacteristically uncertain frown. Ben has always been so sure footed, so confident and ready for action.

He's always known how to act; how to shine and how to darken a room. He always knows what to do.

But in this moment?

I study his features as he studies me and I realise that for the first time since the day I met him, Ben Haston is truly at a loss. And I don't know what he is really asking of me anymore.

"Sure." I push to my feet and move around him, walking through the space on autopilot, putting on a fresh pot of coffee and placing away the plates and mugs that had been left to sit on the drying rack last night.

For a moment it's silent. He makes no move to leave and I don't know what else can be said.

And then he's gone.

I don't turn when I hear the door close softly behind me - I don't dare to - because, if I turn to watch him leave, I think I might follow and I think I might ask him to stay. I might ask him to never leave me alone.

But I can't ask that of Ben.

I place my glass on the dresser before stripping down to my underwear in front of the mirror shoved into the darkest corner of my room. I've done everything I can to avoid this. I've brushed my teeth three times. I've thrown out the dress and shoved the bag into the garbage chute. I've made coffee and polished all of the surfaces. I have nothing else to distract me.

It takes me a while to look up; to face what I know I don't really want to see. Tears sting in the corners of my eyes as I suck in air that is too thin and my stomach churns. I ache with emptiness.

I meet hollow eyes first. Deep set and darkened by sadness. They stare back emptily as I sink into the darkest corners of their pain. After an eternity, I glance down at my body only to be hit with the weight of memory.

My hips are blackened with the marks of fingers; shades of mulberry and onyx mingling where he had held me against him. My wrist is stained too. Bangles of bluish black blossoming against the snow of my skin where he had pulled me out of the bar just days ago. My chest aches as I turn slightly and lift the curtain of hair that covers what I know is the worst of it all: my back.

My shoulders are angry with scratches torn into them; crimson splotches scream at me as I hold down quiet sobs. Where my skin has torn there is a thin layer of burgundy that protrudes, scabbing over the breaks of flesh and meshing my back together. Steppingstones of peeking purple guide my eyes down my spine where bone had hit against the door, the e-brake, everything that fought against me, and I feel my tears washing over my cheeks.

"This is okay," I whisper to myself with gut wrenching resignation. "This isn't even close to bad, Mikaela."

The sound of keys in the door startles me and I dart to my drawers, pulling shorts and the first top I can find out quickly and throwing them on. As I pull the thick cream knit over my frame I hear him suck in a breath.

My heart sinks.

"I thought I needed to let you in." I mumble as I move to the side of my bed and begin pulling the covers up. My eyes remain glued to my hands as I feel him move into the space and across to the other side. Immediately, he's helping me – pulling up the sheet and handing me cushions that were thrown from the bed last night – and I chew my lip as he moves quietly around me.

Once the bed is made, he pauses and waits until I look up at him. In an instant, I feel a little less damaged.

His eyes are soft and he is smiling. It isn't the sort of smile I expect, where it doesn't meet the eyes and is partnered with a sad tilt of the head and softly raised eyebrows, instead it's calm and warm. His eyes crinkle slightly at the edges and he stands straight and tall. This is a smile to remind me I'm still *Little Mik* and gratitude washes through me with unexpected strength.

"I thought I'd make omelettes?" He motions to the kitchen.

The swelling in my chest pushes me to smile back at him as he eyes me with a lazy grin and when my heart starts a light pattering, I find myself blushing.

"Omelette is good." I drop my gaze, peeking through my lashes as he moves away from me and over to the brown paper bag on the table, where he unpacks enough groceries to get me through the next few days.

"Come on." Ben gestures to the seat beside where he's standing as he unhooks a pan from its place above the cooker and starts to rummage in drawers for chopping boards and knives. "Sit."

Ben

As I chop and dice, I can feel Mikaela watching me intently. She's pulled the heels of her feet up onto the chair and tucked her knees under her chin, focussing on the silence of it all as she watches my fingers move.

"Where did you learn how to cook?" She asks.

"My mom taught me the basics." I try to sound casual as I weigh the fact she's talking against the fact she sounds like she's not asking the questions she really wants to ask. "And then at college I picked up a few skills."

She doesn't speak again.

When I'm done chopping tomatoes and mushrooms, ham and cheese, I crack eggs into a bowl and begin to whisk. Eventually, I glance over to her and sigh.

Her face is contorted into a mask of confusion as her brow furrows and she chews on the corner of her lip. Darkness swirls in the green of her eyes and every now and then she rubs her temples as if trying to stave off a headache.

"Ask," I command and Mikaela bites back a frown before she speaks.

"Why were you outside my door last night?" Her voice is stronger than I think even she thought it would be and I see a flicker of pride in her eyes.

"Because I came to apologise," I state simply. "And I was worried about you."

"Oh." Mikaela shakes her head and her lips purse into a thin line. "Why?"

Placing the bowl and whisk down on the counter before turning to face her, I breathe deeply. Now this feels even harder than before.

"I came to say I was sorry for how I behaved. I was here to tell you I was an idiot, because you're Jamie's baby sister and I should never have kissed you or pushed any of my feelings, whatever they may be, on to you." I watch as she swallows hard before I close my eyes for the briefest moment, telling myself the dejection I saw in her is my own and not truly hers. "I came to tell you I'm going to stop pushing you to talk about it, or give me answers you can't give me. I just - I want us to be okay again, but it's harder to say all that than I thought it would be. And I came because, even though you said you didn't need me, I was worried you were getting yourself into something that could - something that could take you from me again, and the thought of not speaking to you again... I hate it."

"Were we ever okay, Haston?" Her head tilts to the right as she smiles and I sigh with the relief of seeing laughter dancing behind her eyes.

"Touché." I grin as I return to the cooking; pouring half of the eggs into the skillet.

"Ben?"

"Yes, Mik."

She moves to my side quickly, taking the pan from my hand as I watch her, placing it away from the heat, and quickly wrapping her arms around me.

She buries her face in my chest and I wrap around her, holding her close as I breathe in the smell of honeysuckle from her hair.

Wrapped up in her, I close my eyes and try to steady the aching thud of my heart. The softness of her, of having her holding on to me with such ease, is a comfort I know I'm beginning to crave.

Or maybe, just maybe, I aways have.

Mikaela

"Thank you for staying."

His hand brushes against my neck as he holds me and I shiver beneath his touch.

I pull back slightly, my face upturned as he looks down at me and, for a second, it's as if nothing dark has happened. Nothing dark, nothing painful. The sting of it all just melts away as he looks at me, his fingers soft against my skin, and I take a deep breath.

Slowly, I push up on my tiptoes and my eyes close. For the briefest of moments I can feel his lips hovering over my own, I feel his breath fanning over my skin and taste the coffee on his breath, and then he sighs and he's gone and his arms are no longer around me and my chest hurts again.

"You don't want that, Mik," he murmurs as he adds ingredients to the pan and shakes his head. "Not really."

Heat floods my cheeks as I step back and turn away from him, desperately biting back any tears that might spill. I move back to my seat and curl in on myself.

When he places the food in front of me I mumble a thank you and push bites around the plate, aware of his eyes burning into the side of my face.

"Eat, Mikaela."

I spear a piece omelette and bring it to my mouth. As I chew, I groan. I don't want to admit it - not when he's just pushed me away so easily, not when I'm angry at myself for thinking that after his little speech, after I pushed him away without even thinking of what it could be to hold him, he'd even want to kiss me again - but the food is good and my stomach needs it.

Ben

I watch her as she eats. Her eyes don't meet mine again and she remains in silence the whole time we sit together, but I watch her. I watch her and I hate myself. I hate that I pushed her away, even though every single cell in my body pulls me to her, even when all I can think about is how much I want to erase her pain; to hold her and make her see that she is safe. I hate myself for wanting that when what she needs is a friend, not someone who would take advantage of her vulnerability.

I hate that she is vulnerable and I hate that I want her. I want every single piece of her.

Occasionally, she shifts uncomfortably in her chair and my mind roams to the raw red scrapes on her back, scrapes that seem so much harsher in the bright light of day. Pain radiates from her, and she curls in against herself the longer we sit together.

"Mik, I thi-"

"I'm not talking to the police." She cuts me off quickly and brings her empty plate to the sink.

Of course she knows what I'm thinking.

I slump forwards and she turns on the tap. "Just think about it, Mik. He hurt you. Your back is scratched and torn and the bruises..." My throat grows thick and my heart hammers with my words.

It isn't until Mikaela turns to me with fire in her eyes that I snap out of the pain of it all.

"Why does it matter to you, Ben?" She quietly seethes at my concern as she storms past me and back up to her bed.

Hearing the scrape of my chair as I push myself up to follow only seems to spur her anger.

She's tired, and in pain, and afraid. And now I'm forcing her to feel what she doesn't want to feel.

Guilt eats away at me as I speak, but she needs to hear it. Someone needs to say it.

"It matters to me, Mik, because, believe it or not, *you* matter to me." I speak softly despite her rage. "You have marks all over your body from what he did to you and I hate it. I hate knowing he is out there right now and nothing is going to happen to him if you don't speak to them. I hate knowing he could hurt someone else, Mik, but mostly, I hate that he could hurt you again."

"You're right, Ben. I have marks on *my* body." Her words come out like acid, burning me as she chokes them up and spits them out. She faces me with tears streaming and as I step towards her she pushes me back.

"Mik." I step forwards again, my hands outstretched as I reach for her, only for her palms to slap at my chest again. This time I don't step back and she closes her eyes.

Her voice wavers with pain but her volume remains low. "I have physical reminders of the fact I was too *weak* to push him away from me. I have the reminder that I had his hands on me without my consent. The last thing I want to do now, the last thing I *need* to do, is relive it when I already see him every time I close my eyes. When I know how little will be done about it when it's his word against mine." When she glances up at me there are pleas in the set of her mouth, the darkness of her eyes. She needs me to say I understand, even if I don't. "I didn't get to choose what happened to me last night, Ben, but I get to choose what I do about it and I want to choose to move on with my life."

She stands there for a moment, waiting for a response, before she realises her hands are still pressed against my chest. She pulls back quickly, moving her hand to her wrist and instinctively rubbing the bruises there.

"Okay," I sigh, my entire world crumbling as she moves away from me, and I watch her open drawers and ready herself for the day.

She rummages through her belongings, pushing aside shirts that don't have long sleeves or that are too sheer to cover her wounds and my chest aches with every discarded option. "What are you doing?"

Mikaela moves to the bedside unit and picks up the small, silver ring she wears constantly, slipping it onto her middle finger with a frown before turning to face where I stand uncomfortably at the foot of her bed.

"Jamie will be here in an hour. We're visiting Mom." Her eyes soften as she tries to smile and I nod.

Today is not the day to push this then.

"I'll get out of your way then." I move back to the living area and pick up my jacket from where I threw it over the couch. "Need me to do anything before I go?"

She simply shakes her head and watches as I make my move to leave.

Mikaela

"Okay." His eyes are shimmering and the steady rise and fall of his chest seems to falter when the word comes out.

Pain.

Since I stumbled home to Ben last night he has been in pain too. His fingers wrap around the door handle and as he pulls it open, I feel my chest tightening and my own pain resurfacing. I rush forwards three steps, until I'm standing at the edge of my makeshift bedroom, longing to take the next few steps and reach out to him.

"You could come with us." Now that the words are out of my mouth I feel the flush of embarrassment. I heard the desperation there. I feel the way my chest aches for him not to leave. But I can't admit that I want him to stay here and hold me until Jamie comes. I shouldn't want that. "I mean, only if you want to?"

Ben pauses in the doorway.

"Mom would probably like that." I tack on the justification with a huff and Ben turns to me with a sad smile.

"I need to get changed." He glances back to the door.

My heart thuds and I nod.

"I'll be back in an hour. Okay?"

Chapter Twelve

Mikaela

The drive never takes long, but I twist in my seat as anxiety builds in my chest before we even set off. I say nothing to Jamie about last night as I slip into the back seat of his car, and I pray I won't have to.

"Why are you getting in the back?" Jamie laughs as he pushes his sunglasses up his nose.

"Because I-" My reply is cut short by the image of Ben hurtling down my street, three coffees balanced precariously in a cardboard holder, weaving past a group of speed walking moms.

"I'm here. I'm here!" By the time he skids to a halt beside Jamie and glances apologetically down at me, he's out of breath. "Sorry I'm late. The cafe around the corner had a bigger queue than I thought it would."

I swallow hard.

He looks good. The deep burgundy of the long sleeve jersey emphasises the hard lines of his body. His sleeves are rolled slightly in the brisk air of the day and the front is tucked haphazardly into his dark jeans, giving an impression of looking good without trying.

I smile warmly for the first time all morning as my eyes run over him and my hands reach for a cup. His smile in return is heart breaking, and suddenly I don't care that he pushed me away this morning. He also agreed to visit Mom just because I asked and even though the idea of

166

bringing him to her lodges tears in the back of my throat, it also makes my heart feel a little lighter, as if I've been carrying too much weight for a little too long until right now.

"That's okay," I muse. "Jamie was fifteen minutes late anyway. Thank you for the coffee."

Jamie stares at me. He doesn't move to get into the car, or look at his best friend, or take a coffee. He just stares as I gaze up at Ben and smile. In the years he and Ben have been friends I am sure he could count the times I have been genuinely nice to Ben on one hand. And none of those times happened in the last five years. Not to mention the fact Ben has clearly been invited without his knowledge and the topic of our mother has been off limits between Ben and I. It has been that way for years. Jamie isn't even allowed to utter our mother's name in the same sentence as Benjamin Haston.

Or at least he wasn't.

Until now.

"Well." Ben extends a cup towards Jamie. "Let's go then, shall we?"

"Right." Jamie blinks a few times and I look over to him for the first time since Ben's arrival. "I'm sorry, what?"

I close the car door with a roll of my eyes and Ben grins. "I said 'let's go.'"

"Yeah, I got that, but what are you doing here?" Jamie climbs into the drivers seat as he asks and Ben glances at me, unsure of what to say.

"He's here because I thought it would be nice, Jamie. I'm making an effort, just like you asked me to." Impatience mars my voice and guilt knots in my gut. I remind myself it's not his fault he's in the dark. I remind myself to breathe. "Now can we go? Please?"

A cloud of discomfort hovers over the three of us as we sit in the sounds of radio chatter and chart hits. I stare out of the window, watching as buildings that climb the sides of each other slowly break apart; opening up to wide, green yards and landscapes that seem worlds away from the sprawling city behind us.

Occasionally, I feel the pull of eyes on me and I look ahead, meeting Ben's gaze in the rearview mirror, or the confused glare of Jamie as he tries and fails to make sense of it all.

Jamie glances between the road, me and Ben all too often. It isn't subtle.

Time moves very slowly.

"So, Mik." Jamie checks his mirrors before signalling left and turning onto the winding road that will lead us the rest of the way. "How was your date?" He glances at Ben only to be greeted by a stoic expression as he avoids looking at me.

Jamie's eyes switch between us again and I feel panic rise. Sometimes he can be very perceptive.

My heart sputters and my eyes dart to Ben before dropping to my lap. I pray silently that what I say now won't trigger that hero complex of his, one that I'm beginning to both hate and kind of adore, and relief rushes over me when Ben remains silent.

"Not great," I murmur. "I won't be seeing him again."

"Shit, Mik." Jamie glances back with an apologetic frown and I shift in my seat. "I'm sorry. If it makes you feel any better, his agent called me this morning - pulled out of the deal - so you won't have to see him at work either."

Tension I didn't realise I have been carrying seeps from my pores as I slump back in my chair and close my eyes.

"Thank God," I breathe and Ben twists in his chair.

"You okay?" His voice is laced with concern and Jamie furrows his brow as he watches me open my eyes and shake my head.

"I'm fine." I fight the urge to throw my coffee cup at him for being so blatantly obvious.

That's more like it. This snappy, short response is a return to normality between us. But as Ben watches me carefully, as if I might fall apart any minute now, and my frustration gives way to a short burst of something different - something heated and delicious and altogether terrifying - Jamie grunts.

"What's go-"

"We're here." I interrupt, pointing ahead so that Ben will turn away from me and Jamie will stop talking.

There is a stillness in the air as the three of us make our way down the winding path across the green. Although birds take flight overhead and the sky is clear and blue, there is pressure in the atmosphere. Our footfall feels heavy and the silence that hangs over us all is suffocating.

I feel Jamie's hand wrap around mine, squeezing gently, and I take a deep breath as I stop at the edge of the pathway.

"This way," I nod my head to the left as I step onto the grass and begin making my way through the stones.

I listen to Ben as he takes in a deep breath and steps after me.

In five years I've never allowed him this close. I've never let him come to her. I've never let him mourn her.

Five Years Ago

"Jamie, pick up. Just pick up."

I sink down the wall and curl in to myself as doctors pass in the otherwise empty corridor. I stare at the floor, watching the flickering of the florescent lighting overhead in the polished surface. I wonder how often floors have to be cleaned in a place like this; where blood and urine and other fluids probably make cleaning a tiring, thankless job.

As I hear the familiar sound of my call being patched through to voicemail again I splinter and fray at the seams. My chest burns as I choke on strangled sobs and palm at my face in a desperate attempt to push my tears back in, my mother's words echoing in my mind.

She wants Jamie.

She has been *begging* for Jamie.

"You're through to Jamie Wilcox. I can't get to the phone right now, but leave your name and number and I'll get back to you as soon as I can."

"Jamie, where are you?" I whisper as my throat tightens. "It's Mom. Jamie, you need to get here. Please. I - I can't do this without you and..." I suck in a shaking breath as I pull the phone away from my face and close my eyes. I bring my head to the wall; hitting once, then twice, then three times. I bring the phone back to my ear. "I don't know how long she's got left in her, Jamie, and I'm all alone here. Matthew - Matthew couldn't come with me and I need you. I know we haven't spoken

in a while but I need you, JimJam. I need my brother.
Please."

As I sob, I let the phone drop from my hand and I pull
my knees to my chest, making myself as small as I can.

Waves pull me under, my body shaking violently, and
I break over and over again.

Ben

"Okay, so that's the last stitch." The doctor pulls off the
latex gloves and rubs her eyes before turning to the bin.
"The police are outside. They want to talk to you, but I
can give you a minute to check on your friend."

"Thanks." I press my fingers against my forehead, the
sting fresh across my brow. I should have let her give me
something to numb the area first. "Is he okay?"

"He's back from radiology. I can't tell you anything
else." She frowns as she watches me roll my sleeves, my
own blood staining my white shirt.

"Okay, Doc." I huff. "Out with it."

"What do you mean?" Her eyes don't quite meet mine
when she glances up from where she's scribbling down
notes on a chart, but I can see what she's thinking
anyway.

"I mean you're giving me a look that suggests you have
an opinion you'd like to share."

"Not my place," she mutters.

I want to laugh as I watch her, but I know it's not the
time. She's young. A resident maybe? And she's tired.
Her hair is tied back in a shock of red and her scrubs
are crumpled. She's definitely at the end of a long shift.

"Listen, I'm guessing you've had one hell of a shift
and you've probably spent most of it biting your tongue

171

because you never know how a patient will react if you give them a piece of your mind. Right?"

She rolls her eyes and continues to ignore me.

"So," I continue, "I'm giving you a free pass. Say whatever you want to say and I'll sit here and take it." I shrug and she sighs, placing the pen against the chart in her hands and glaring at me.

"Fine," she snaps. "Do you know how much I hate people like you?" Her eyes are burning with intensity and I nod calmly. "How stupid do you have to be to get behind a wheel and drive when you've had that many? How stupid to do it after one! I see kids in here that get hit by assholes like you. I have to tell their parents their kids won't walk again or - *God* - I have to tell them their kids are gone." Her voice is shaking as it raises to a shout. "People like you kill people, because you are reckless and arrogant and fucking stupid. You're lucky it was a tree and not someone's Mom or Dad or kid. Just - fuck. *Fuck.*"

I watch as the doctor slumps against the wall before a small smile creeps over her lips and a bubble of laughter bursts from her.

She has a pretty smile.

"Feel better?" My eyes dance over her face as she closes her own and places her head against the wall. It's like watching the tension roll off of her.

"Much." Her laugh is warm and I get to my feet, pleased to have made someone smile today. "Thanks."

"No problem, Doc. Now about my friend?"

"Second door to the right, bed three."

I nod and glance towards where my doctor stands before leaving the room. "Thanks. For the stitches and the telling off." I chuckle to myself when she nods. "Not many people are willing to call me out like that. You've got balls."

I leave the sound of her laughter behind me as I fish my phone out of my jacket and punch in a number I know I'll live to regret.

Walter Haston, retired police commissioner and imperious grandfather, answers on the third ring.

Mikaela

When I was six years old my father left. He just woke up one day and decided he was done. I cried for three weeks. Every night I would crawl in beside Mom and curl up to her. Together we talked it out. Together we cried through the worst of it. Together we kept moving forwards.

"Just keep your head above the water, baby girl," she would soothe. "Head above the water."

Now I'm fully submerged. I'm fully submerged and I can't see which way is up and which is down. There's a numbness that encases me as the ice of it all settles in my chest.

Someone puts a hand on my shoulder as I stare at the emptiness of her eyes.

Someone should close her eyes.

They speak softly, words that they've probably said a thousand times over. Words I've known would come, but never prepared for.

"Is there anyone we can call?" The nurse crouches before me and I look down at my mother's hands.

"No." My breath comes in short gasps and my world falls out from under me. "No, there's no one."

Ben

"He's dealing with it, Jamie."

A headache is brewing behind my left eye as Jamie shoves his legs into his jeans, trying to pull them up with one hand.

"What does that even mean, Ben?" He grunts. The sling holding his left arm in place shifts slightly and he winces from the pain.

"It means there's nothing to be done. Nothing to worry about. It's sorted." I move to his side and grab his jacket from the bed while Jamie works on catching his breath.

"Nothing?"

I nod.

"Okay." The sigh that leaves Jamie's lips seems to expel all of the panic of the last four hours. "Pass me my phone, will you? I should probably check on Mom."

Mikaela

A soft mist of rain swirls around my skin and soaks through me as I clutch the small bag to my chest. I don't step forwards. I don't move out of the way of passers by.

I simply stand and wait.

I wait for the world to start spinning again.

I wait for my head to be above water.

The sound of wheels against tarmac pulls me from my daze and my chest caves at the sight of him.

He's been drinking again and his dishevelled, autumn red hair and wild eyes tell me he's hurt without having to see any injury. Another bar fight.

"Mik." His voice is too loud. Too heavy. "I'm sorry."

"Just take me home, Matthew." It takes everything I have not to fall apart on the sidewalk. "I just want to go home."

I'm stepping towards the car when I hear it and pain flares in my chest. Spinning back to the doors I walked out of almost an hour ago, some internal fire burns and my heart shatters with the pressure.

"Mik! Mikaela! I'm so sorry. I - Mik." Jamie's face is contorted with agonising guilt as he races to me from inside. *Inside*. His arm is held across his chest in a sling and his left eye is swollen shut.

And I can't bring myself to care.

The smell of whiskey smashes into me before he does. I push him.

"Don't touch me." My voice is weak and broken.

"Mik -"

"I called you." I think my eyes might be just as hollow as my voice. "I called you so many times, Jamie. Where were you?"

"We were in the emergency room." Jamie answers quickly. He keeps reaching out for me and I keep shrugging out of his hold and backing away. "My phone was off and I was getting my shoulder fixed and I - Mik, I'm so sorry. I should have been there."

"We?" I don't really need to ask. I know as soon as he says it. I know before his best friend steps out of the shadows and I push out a disappointed laugh. "Of course. I should have known Ben was involved."

Jamie steps closer again and I hit him. My fist smacks his chest as fresh waves of excruciating agony tear through me.

"Don't fucking touch me." I sob, hitting him repeatedly. "Don't touch me. You were supposed to be there. You promised her. You promised her you'd be there, Jamie. But you weren't. You fucking weren't. I hate you. I hate you so much."

My fists slam against him, again and again, and he takes every blow. I know every connection hurts him but I don't stop. I can't see past the silent pain that had hung in her eyes as I held her hand and whispered to her. I can't see past the way her lips trembled with every rasping breath. I can't see past the way her lips formed his name with her last one.

I can't see past the emptiness.

When I stop hitting him, when I crumble against him, he holds me tight, brushing his free hand over my hair and whispering apologies.

"You said you'd be there," I weep. "Why weren't you there, Jamie?"

He opens his mouth to explain just as Ben speaks.

Jamie's hand stills when he does.

Ben

"I crashed my car, Mik. It's my fault he wasn't there." I hang my head low, shaking it slightly as Jamie glances back to me.

The sound she makes is not human. It is visceral. And broken. Agonised.

I can't look at her. I'm afraid that if I do, I'll see how broken she is and it will kill me. "Don't blame him."

Just one glance at her is agonising.

Her tears keep falling, but a mask of emptiness takes the place of her pain as she pushes out of Jamie's arms and stares past me. Without another word she turns away from us both and walks towards the car half pulled up on the sidewalk.

"I'll let you know the funeral arrangements when they're finalised." She pauses with her hand on the door and her eyes on the floor. "And then we're done, Jamie."

My stomach drops.

Jamie chokes on a sob as he steps towards her and my gut churns with the pain between them.

"And Ben?"

My eyes meet hers and I feel it all - the pain and anger, the desperation, the deep seated need for blame - I see it and I take it. I take all of it so that she won't have to shoulder this burden.

Let her blame me. Let her hate me.

"Yes, Mikaela?"

She appraises me with cold indifference before she says: "stay the fuck away. You are not welcome anywhere near her. Ever. Do you understand me?"

I nod as the knife of her words twist in my gut and the man on the other side of the car laughs.

He laughs loudly.

My eyes snap to him as hatred blurs my vision and Matthew smirks, as if in on some little secret no one else is privy to, before climbing into the car. As if he *wants* this.

"Get in, babe." His voice is like nails on a chalkboard.

"Mik, please." Jamie's pleas fall on deaf ears as she climbs into the car, hugging Elizabeth's belongings to her chest. "Please don't leave."

"I want to go home." Her voice is void of life.

The engine sputters to life and wheels screech against tarmac as Matthew speeds away. Neither Jamie nor I make a move to leave. Instead, we stand with the weight of our actions resting on our shoulders, the ghost of grief creeping over us both as her taillights fade into nothing more than a blip in the distance.

Chapter Thirteen

Present

Mikaela

There isn't much to do other than sit and chat, but I feel lighter somehow just being here. A cool breeze dances over us as we sit on the grass, leaving goose bumps where it brushes past me, and the rustle of branches overhead is a constant reminder of the life that surrounds us.

As I lay on my stomach, my arms folded and my cheek resting against them, I watch Jamie excitedly and animatedly share memories with Ben; from the first time Ben visited our home, arrogant and self-assured even as a child, to the times our mother had stormed into bars and pulled both underage boys out by the back of their shirts. Those ones are my favourite. Especially when they make Ben throw his head back like he has now.

His laughter rings out loud and I close my eyes. Listening, I loose myself in the musicality of it that I haven't heard before - a rise and fall in the cadence and pitch that sounds like a spring celebration - and the lure of rest pulls me into a gentle darkness as I slip in and out of peace.

Ben

I glance towards Mikaela. Her arms are tucked up beneath her cheek and her hair is brushed out behind her. She dozed off an hour ago and in her sleep she's peaceful. I take a second to appreciate that.

"So," I mumble, turning my attention back to my best friend who is watching me with cautious eyes. "Josh pulled out of the deal?"

Jamie sighs and runs a hand over his face. Disappointment is a stale smell in the air. "Yeah. His agent said it was about the money, but I think -"

"Yeah." I cut him off with a tight nod. Neither of us has to say it - no one has to announce that Josh pulled from the deal because of Mik - but Jamie is looking at her with so much sadness that I can almost taste the saltiness of tears. "Why aren't you saying this to her?" I glance back to her and frown. Her breathing is too even and her lips are too tight. She isn't asleep anymore. "Maybe she could tell you what happened."

Mikaela's shoulders tense ever so slightly.

At least she knows that was meant for her.

"Look Ben, Mik has her own stories to tell and her own demons to fight. She wasn't keen on dating anyone for a while and I pushed her towards Josh. If shit went bad that's on me, not her."

I suck in a harsh breath as the weight of Jamie's words hangs over me. This. This is why Mikaela asked me to come today. She doesn't want to be alone with Jamie and this is why she doesn't want to tell him. Although Jamie's words are just an assessment of a failed signing, I can't help but hear them the way Mikaela definitely heard them: Jamie set her up with a man who hurt her. He pushed her towards a man who pinned her down and touched her when she cried. The guilt of that would destroy him.

"I understand." I say it for her, not for Jamie. And I do. I understand and I won't make her talk about it to anyone, not if she doesn't want to. "But you know, whatever happened with them, I can guarantee it's all on him. It's not on you. It's *definitely* not on her. Shit, if someone doesn't know how good they've got it with Mik then that's on them."

I see the corner of her lip tug up in a smile just as Jamie whacks my head.

"Stop fucking simping for my sister, you dick."

I laugh loudly as Mik stifles a giggle and Jamie's eyes dart to her.

"Is she awake?" He shifts where he's sitting, leaning over to her slightly.

"Doubtful," I shove him back, covering for her eavesdropping and saving her from what I'm sure would be an awkward conversation. "Now stop hitting me when I compliment your sister, okay? I didn't mean anything by it." Jamie scowls at me and I grin. "What the hell is simping anyway?"

Jamie's answering smile is amused. "Fuck if I know. Some kid we signed last year used it in a book and honestly, I still don't think I used it right. Ever realise we're pretty old?"

I grin at my best friend. "Nope. I'm young at heart."

"Whatever, douche." Jamie laughs as he pushes himself up to his feet. "This old man is cold. I'm gonna grab a blanket from the car. Need anything?"

"I'm alright." I shake my head with a smile and watch as Jamie makes his way back through the thick of headstones, towards where he parked.

Once he's out of earshot I turn to her and lay myself down, facing her in the grass.

"I get it, Mik."

Her eyes flutter open and the shimmer of unshed tears greets me. "Yeah?"

I nod, moving a hand to brush her hair out of her eyes, and pause as my fingers rest against her cheek. "I wish you'd tell someone, but I get why you won't. I won't try to make you."

Her eyes close again as we lay face to face in the silence, and she sighs. "Thank you, Ben."

"Anytime, Little Mik."

She grins with her eyes still closed and for one split second I consider leaning in and closing the small distance between us.

"Dick." Her voice is just a murmur as I toy with her hair and her smile is playful for the first time since she stumbled home last night.

Mikaela

Jamie lays across my bed, his hands tucked behind his head, as I yank at his shoes and scowl.

"Get your filthy boots off of my sheets, you child."

As if to prove my point, he sticks his tongue out at me before rolling to the side and slipping from my grip.

"Mik." Despite the boyish grin, his voice is deep and serious. "Why was Ben there today?"

I stop moving and Jamie turns his face to me.

"I'm not complaining," he explains. "I'm grateful actually. You know how much he loved Mom and it's been hard not sharing that with him. But you - Mik you made your position on all of this pretty clear five years ago. And I stuck with it - even when you were gone - I didn't let him see her, so I'm just confused."

I huff as I turn away from him, unsure of what to say now that Ben is gone. A small perk of him being there was that Jamie couldn't ask *why* he was there. Now I miss the buffer.

"I asked him to come." I try to shrug but the sting of my shoulders leaves me stiff and uncomfortable. "I just felt like it was time."

"What aren't you telling me, Mik?"

I groan inwardly, cursing the fact Jamie chose today of all days to pay so much attention.

"I'm just - I'm ready to put it behind me, Jamie. All of it. I want to put Matthew, and what happened with Mom, and just all of it behind me. Forgiving Ben? Well, it seemed like the easiest place to start, okay?"

"You sure that's all it is? Because I hate to be *that* brother, but please don't start sleeping with my best friend."

This time I groan out loud. "You know you're a pig, right?"

Jamie laughs, pushing himself up and off of my bed. "Just laying the law, MikMak. Making sure you don't get hurt. Ben's a good guy, you know that, but he's never been serious with anyone and you deserve something real."

"Well." I watch as he moves through my tiny apartment and digs through cupboards as I speak. "I'm not sleeping with anyone, thanks."

"Good." He huffs as his search comes up empty. "Keep it that way."

"Sure." I roll my eyes. "What are you looking for?"

His head is halfway into the darkness of the corner he's searching in. "Mom's crystal glasses. I thought we could toast to her, you know. Say happy birthday."

The breath fades from my lungs and I feel the splinter of shattered shards all over again.

"Jamie." My throat closes around his name; around my confession.

"Yeah?" He opens another cupboard.

"Jamie, look at me."

His back straightens and he turns with the mist of questions swirling in his eyes. "Mik?"

"The glasses - I - God, I should have told you. They - he -" My chest is caving in on itself and Jamie is holding my hands and shaking his head and I can't see past his eyes.

"Hey. Hey, Mik. Eyes on me. Come on."

I can't breathe.

"Remember the steps. Come on. Five things you can see?" His voice is distant.

"The scar on your lip," I choke.

Jamie nods, smiling encouragingly.

"The paint peel on the cupboard under the sink," I continue, my voice shaking as I try to take a deeper breath.

"Next?"

"Plates on the rack."

"Good. Two more. Take a breath and two more."

The pressure in my chest is lighter now.

"Your first grey hair." I try to smile as Jamie feigns offence. "You have Mom's nose."

Jamie cocks his head to the side as he prods my nose with his finger. "So do you."

I laugh as my tears fall.

Jamie sighs. "Better?"

"He smashed them, Jamie." The confession cuts me. "Matthew smashed them."

A darkness clouds his features, a mist of regret and shame mingling with something undiscovered; something shoved deep into the hidden depths of himself and left to fester.

"I'm so sorry, Jamie."

He shakes his head slightly as a sad smile twists his lips. "It's not your fault, Mik. None of it."

Jamie left three hours ago and the apartment is too quiet. Even with the glow and whisper of the television screen permeating the space, I feel alone and exposed. My skin itches and every sound has me skittering to the door - checking the chain and sinking to the floor - or the window - double checking locks and pulling the flimsy curtains tighter. My heart is permanently in my throat and the thought of closing my eyes to sleep leaves me shaking and nauseated.

I'm right back where I started.

Slamming my laptop shut, I pull the blanket around myself and let my mind take a break from the blank page staring back at me. I shuffle from the couch to the kitchen and push onto my tiptoes, reaching for a coffee cup as I try and fail to think up a way past the opening scene of the story I'm stuck on and glance at the time. The clock on the oven flashes an irritating red, reminding me I never set it, and I push the knot in my throat down. I'll fix things in the morning. Right now I need coffee. I need it if I want to stay awake.

As my fingers brush against the lip of a cup and I hook one through a handle, a gentle rapping on the door startles me.

Suddenly the cup is no longer precariously balanced on the edge of the shelf. Instead, it's falling almost painfully slowly, clipping the counter on its way down, and exploding into large chunks of sharp edges and tiny chips that scatter everywhere.

"Shit!" I jump back as a broken piece ricochets off of the floor and snags on my calf before skittering to a stop beneath the table.

The knocking resumes, a little more frantic now, and my head snaps up at the sound.

What if it's Josh? What then?

My blood starts to scream behind my ears as I take a shaky step over the mess and towards the door. Slowly, terrified of whose face I might see, I hold my breath and place my eye against the peephole. A strangled kind of cry catches in my throat and I slump against the door - my breathing now heavy and disjointed - and my fingers move to the chain, unhooking it before I open up.

Ben

Her cheeks are tearstained again and her bottom lip is red and swollen from biting hard as she chews on her own skin.

"Hey." Mikaela breathes in a way that screams with relief.

"You shouted in there. Everything okay?" I peer over her, glancing into the relative darkness of her apartment and spotting the mess of a broken cup on her kitchen floor.

"Yeah. I'm fine. I just -"

"Didn't realise it was me at the door."

I sigh when she nods, her lip quivering and tears pooling again.

She steps aside, letting me in, her eyes lingering on the ratty gym bag in my hand, and I give her a small smile.

"I couldn't sleep," I confess, "because every time I tried, I thought about you all alone here and probably not sleeping. I was worried. So I packed a bag, got in the car and came here. I stopped at that little shop down the street too. The one that never seems to close. Got snacks and hot chocolate. I figured if neither of us could sleep, maybe we could not sleep together."

Her laugh is as unexpected as it is soft and I knit my brows together in confusion.

"Sorry," Mik chuckles. "It's just your phrasing. You reminded me of something Jamie said. I'm sorry. That's really sweet, Ben. Honestly."

As she speaks her features smooth into something more akin to the Mikaela I know – she's warmer now and definitely more forthcoming with me, but she's still Mik Wilcox – the girl who would mock me endlessly when we were young.

"Make yourself at home. I just need to clean this up." Her eyes flick back to the coffee cup shattered on the floor as mine run over her, catching a streak of red running down her leg.

"Wait." I reach out to her as she steps away, wrapping my fingers around her wrist before she can move, and I step closer. She sucks in a sharp breath, but doesn't pull away. "You're hurt."

"It's nothing." She smiles too sweetly. "Just a cut."

I shake my head at her, the ghost of annoyance flaring in my gut as I realise Mikaela Wilcox has given up when it comes to looking after herself.

"Sit down." I drag her to the table, pulling out a chair for her as I sweep remnants of stoneware away with my foot. "Where do you keep your first aid kit?"

Mikaela

Everything about Ben has authority and a calm control that leaves me with no choice but to do as I'm told, and truthfully, I'm grateful for it. My head is pounding and the sting in my leg is beginning to burn with every step I take. And I am tired. I am *so* tired.

"Bathroom. Under the sink."

He nods as he pushes me to sit down, before turning quickly, his jaw tight.

I watch him as he rummages in the bathroom, his shoulders tense, and as he makes his way back to me, his eyes burning with an intensity that seems to simmer in the blue. I watch as he slowly gets to his knees.

"Put your foot here." His command is partnered with a small gesture to the seat next to him.

"Ben, I appreciate this, but I can -"

"Mik." His eyes are trained on me, all of the intensity and compassion and worry searing into my skin. "Just do as you're told for once and put your foot on the chair so that I can look after you. Please."

I try not to smile as I do as I'm told.

His fingers move with a feather touch, skimming over my skin and wiping away the slow stream of blood with an antiseptic wipe, and his mouth remains set in a tight line. I watch as he swipes over it gently, coating the wound with a gel, before pressing a dressing to it and taping it to my skin.

The whole time he takes care of me, I wonder what might happen if I run my fingers through the dark mess of hair, or what he would do if I place them under his chin and tilt his face so that he is looking at me. What he might do if I lean in as I hold him like that.

"Stop looking at me like that, Mikaela." His voice is a low growl, but his smile is pure mischief as he watches his own hands.

"Like what?"

I gulp when he turns his gaze on to me. Like *that*. Stop looking at him like that. Exactly the same way he is looking at me now; like he's starving and I am the only thing that could ever satisfy his hunger. My lips part slightly and I watch as he shakes his head while his fingers caress the angry skin beside my wound.

"You don't want me, Mik." His voice is twinged with something so painful it twists in my stomach, even though his smile never falters. "Not really."

"What if I did?" It's a whisper, a secret that grows in the safety of the darkness - something that should never have seen the light - but here it is; hanging in the air between us. "What would happen if I did?"

Hope. I see it just as he feels it. Just as he tries to claw it aside and bury it beneath concern.

"You're hurting, Mik, and you're afraid. You don't want me. But if you did?" His fingers brush tentatively down my calf as I move, lowering my leg and leaning forwards. "If, when some of this has passed, when you aren't scared to go to bed alone in this shitty little apartment... if you wanted me?" There is nothing but simple honesty in his eyes. "You'd have me, Mik."

My breath hitches and he shakes his head, dropping his gaze to the small pile of bloodied wipes and tissues.

"But that's not important, because you're just vulnerable right now. So, go pick a movie and get comfortable. I'll clean up over here and make us some drinks. And I'm going to stay on your couch for a while."

Chapter Fourteen

Mikaela

"This is weird." I stare at the ceiling, my hands over the sheets and my eyes wide open.

Ben sighs on the other side of the room. He's sprawled across the couch, his feet hanging over the arm of the chair as he tries to shift into a more comfortable position. We turned off the film half an hour ago and since then we've remained awake, stewing in the silence in separate corners of my apartment.

"No it's not." He grunts, twisting again.

"Yes," I groan as I roll onto my side and look over to him. "It is."

Even from this distance, I can see his shoulders rise and fall in a silent huff.

"Why?" He asks.

"Why what?"

"Why do you think this is weird?"

I sit up, the cover falling from me as I push myself to the edge of the bed and grunt with the ache in my back.

"Because," I sigh, "I can't sleep and I know what will help me sleep, but I can't ask for that so I feel weird and uncomfortable."

Ben brings a hand to his face, closing his eyes and breathing deeply. He knows why I can't ask for what I want.

"Okay." His voice is low and strained as he gets to his feet and walks over to me. In the dim light of the streetlamp streaming through the window every line of his abdomen is strengthened and hardened and it really is a spectacular sight. My heart thumps a little louder with every step he takes and as I stare at him, approaching in nothing but old grey sweats, he rolls his eyes.

"Okay?" I glance up to his face and he's biting back a smile.

"Stop drooling and move over." He pushes me back a little, a smirk forming on his lips as he pulls the covers back. And then he groans. "And put on some shorts or something."

I glance down at myself as he stares at me. I have a t-shirt on, and that covers everything that needs covering, but Ben's eyes are lingering on the hint of red cotton that peeks out from under the hem.

"What's wrong with what I'm wearing?" I smile sweetly when I look back to him.

He rolls his eyes and climbs into the bed.

"I'm a man, Mikaela. And if I am going to hold you so that you can sleep, I need you to wear something that covers you up a little more so that *I* can sleep. Put on some shorts, please."

I grin.

"Mhmm. Okay. One pair of shorts coming up."

As I move over to my dresser, I swing my hips a little, smiling to myself when I hear a muffled groan from behind me. When I glance back to the bed Ben has a pillow over his face and I can't stop the laugh from bubbling in my chest. "You okay there, Haston?"

"Yep." He pulls the pillow away. "Just reminding myself you don't want me."

Another groan sounds as I bend over and I'm giggling.

"I never said that." I shake my head and shrug my shoulders.

"Shut up and get into bed, Mik."

Shimmying into a pair of shorts, I can't stop the fizzing in my chest as Ben rolls to his side and pulls the covers back for me.

His eyes close as I crawl in beside him and his arm snakes around me, pulling my back against his chest and wrapping me up in him. I close my eyes as he buries his face in my hair and sighs.

"Are you sure you're okay with this?" I whisper, my heart pounding as he shuffles closer, his body warm through my t-shirt.

"You need sleep, Mik." His breath is soft on my skin. "If this helps then, yeah, I'm okay with it."

"Okay."

"Okay."

I close my eyes, smiling to myself as his breathing becomes deeper, and wait for sleep to come.

Moments pass, silence enveloping us, as I lay in his arms and I hold my breath when his fingers weave between mine.

"This only works if you actually try to sleep, Mik." His voice is low, already thicker with the heaviness of rest, and my stomach knots.

"I can't," I admit.

Ben sighs as I twist. His arm remains around me, even as I move to face him, and I tuck my hands up beneath my cheek.

"Why?" I ask.

"Why what, Mik?"

His eyes are still closed, so I wait. When he opens them, I'm greeted by the calmest blue. In the depth of the crystal are flecks of navy and hints of green. Up close they resemble an artists palette, a mixing and melting of hundreds of shades just searching for the right one.

How have I never paid attention to the subtleties of those eyes before now?

"Why do you think I'm lying?"

He shakes his head gently and his fingers move up my spine, tenderly brushing over the sensitivity of the marks left on my back.

"I don't think you're lying, Mik. At least, not intentionally." His fingers skim over the surface of my t-shirt, snagging slightly on a wound, and I close my eyes as I try not to flinch. He moves his hand lower instantly, resting it at the base of my spine, and resumes drawing patterns with his fingertips. "I think you *think* you want me, but you don't. Not really. There's too much history behind us. Too many bad choices. And I think right now - as much as I want to think you do want me - what you really want is to feel safe and comforted. And I'll give you that, Mikaela. I'll stay until you feel safe and I'll comfort you until you don't want me to, but I can't give you more than that. Not when I know you'll just regret it one day."

I open my eyes to him again, focusing on his words - his fears - and I smile softly. Slowly, with a shaking hand, I reach up to his face and brush my fingers over the little lines creasing around his eyes. I move tentatively as his eyes close, skimming down to his neck and holding him there. He sighs with my touch and my heart thumps. He's right, of course, that there is history that needs to be unpacked and there is pain that needs to be talked about too, but he's also wrong. He's wrong to think I would regret it. He's wrong to think I would regret *him*, or that this is only comfort.

Ben is so much more than that. Ben has always been so much more than that. At times the thought of him makes me so angry I could set the world on fire, but then he says or does something disarming and sweet and, even when I hate myself for it, I catch myself smiling at the thought of him.

So yeah, he is unexpected and infuriating and frustrating, but I want all of it.

"You know," I muse aloud as he lays still, "I'm going to prove you wrong, Haston."

He smiles and my lips curve to match.

"Of course you are, Wilcox. Now go to sleep."

I laugh when I move closer, placing my head on his chest as he tightens his arm around me, and I close my eyes. Somehow, I am going to show Ben that he's scared of nothing.

I am going to show him I want him.

Ben

Waking up next to Mikaela for the second morning in a row is messing with my head. She looks peaceful wrapped around me, one leg hitched over my waist and the sheets kicked off of us, and my heart kind of stumbles in my chest.

What on earth am I doing to myself, letting myself get so caught up in her?

I move carefully, not wanting to wake her, as I brush some hair off of her face and she smiles as her eyes open.

"Morning," I whisper, and I try not to laugh when she grimaces and nuzzles in closer.

"Morning," she croaks, pulling herself tighter against me and placing a small kiss against my chest.

My heart does that stupid stutter again and she grins.

"You're like a freaking furnace." Her comment is made with a small grunt, but no effort to move.

"You're hardly an ice-box, Mikaela."

She laughs as my fingers run up and down her arm in soft strokes.

"So we're agreed. We're two hot people in bed together. Remind me why our clothes are on?"

I bark out a laugh and she grins again as she pulls her head back to look at me.

"Because -" I start, only for her to cut me off.

"You don't think I want that." She finishes, rolling her eyes as she untangles herself from around me. "Right."

"Is that a pout?" I wink when she scowls at me. "Are you pouting?"

"No." She pouts again as she sits up and I tug on her t-shirt a little.

"You know, I can't get a read on your mood right now." I breathe in and watch as she shakes me off and gets to her feet.

"I'm fine, Ben." She shoots me a quick smile as she shuffles down towards the kitchen. "I just need coffee."

"Mik." I push myself upright and watch her. Her shoulders are tense and her movements are suddenly stiff and awkward. "What is it?"

She fills the coffee pot with water and digs in a drawer for a filter. "Nothing."

So it's something.

I stretch as I stand up, watching her still, before moving down to her. She's scooping coffee into the machine, a small v puckering between her eyebrows as she concentrates. I take the spoon from her, placing it on the counter, and slip between her and the coffee machine.

Wrong move.

Like this, she's so close I can breathe her in and the lazy haze of early morning has left my guard down. I want to lean in, to trap her lips with mine and to hold her hips as I pull her close. I want to believe her when she says she wants it too.

"Mikaela." I breathe her name as her eyes darken and she gazes up at me. "Talk to me."

"I don't want to talk, Ben." Her voice is barely a whisper. "I want - I just - dammit."

She takes a step back and I just stand watching her.

"I want you to believe that I know what I want. I want you to stop looking at me and seeing what he did. I want you to see *me*, Ben. But you don't. And everything you are doing - everything you keep saying - it all reminds me you don't."

"I'm sorry." I drop my eyes, hanging my head low as she paces before me. What else can I say? She's right. I see what he did to her all over her. "I do see you, Mik. I promise. But how can I not see what he did?"

She turns to face me and I step forwards.

"Your wrists are bruised, Mik. Your back is torn up." She flinches and it kills me, but I continue. My voice stays steady even though just saying it hurts. "You have fingerprints on your hips. And every time I see a single mark on you, I want to put his head through a wall, Mikaela. I see you, but I see what he did too. And I just want you to be okay."

She nods, her lips set in a grim line, as I take another step towards her. Gently, I place my fingers beneath her chin and lift her face so that she will look at me.

"I want you, Mik. Please don't think I don't. But I want you to be sure. Take some time to heal, okay? Then, if you really want me, I'm yours."

She nods again, this time with a sigh, and I take one of her hands, pulling her towards me and wrapping my arms around her.

"How much time?" She grumbles against my chest and I laugh as I run my hand through her hair.

"I don't know, Mik. Let's just take this one day at a time."

"Where are you going?" Mikaela steps out of the bathroom in a light green dress, her hair wet as she scrunches it with a towel.

"I told Jamie I'd go for a run with him today." I crouch to tie my shoe and Mikaela furrows her brow.

"You brought running clothes?"

"Mik, I brought running clothes, work clothes, shoes, pyjamas." I shrug while she stares at me. "I said I'd be on your couch for a while."

"About work." She's twisting the ring she's always wearing again.

"What about it?"

"If we show up together people will talk."

"And you don't want that?" I straighten up and place my hands on my hips as she bites her lip and shakes her head, her eyes dropping for a second as her cheeks flame.

"Not because it's you." The words flood from her quickly as she steps forwards. "Just, if it was anyone... I hate being gossiped about."

I brush her hair off of her shoulder, toying a little with the strap of her dress as I smile. "It's okay, Mik."

She smiles up at me as she speaks. "You're not going to take this as a sign that you're right, are you?"

"No," I chuckle. "I get it. So what do you want to do?"

She glances around the space, chewing her lip again as she takes a deep breath and squares her shoulders. "Maybe you shouldn't stay here tonight."

She looks absolutely terrified but her voice doesn't waver.

"Mik."

"No, hear me out." She looks back to me with wide eyes. "I'm going to need to stay here alone at some point, right? And not just to prove that I'm not lying to myself, but because this is my home and I need to feel safe here. So, why not bite the bullet and just do it?"

"Mik," I murmur as she smiles sadly. "Are you sure you're ready?"

"I don't know," she admits, "but I think I need to try. And if I'm wrong and I can't do it -"

"One phone call. I'll be here in ten minutes."

"Ben, you live at least twenty minutes away."

"And I will get here in ten, Mikaela."

The smile that breaks over her lips is breathtaking. It pushes her cheeks up and creates little lines beneath her eyes as she squints slightly.

"Okay." Its the softest breath, and the happiness behind it steals the last part of me that wasn't already completely and hopelessly lost to her.

"Okay," I repeat. "I'll be back for my stuff in a few hours. Need anything?"

She shakes her head, her eyes on mine as I absentmindedly twist the strap my fingers are still holding onto.

"Okay."

She grins again. "You going to go, or just stand there looking at me?"

The playful teasing has me wishing I could stay.

"I'm going." I let go of her and step back. "Right now. I'm going right now."

She follows me to the door, watching as I move into the hallway, and I look back to her again.

She needs time.

Time is officially my nemesis. Because looking at her right now I want to go straight back in, lock the door and lose the day in kissing her. Instead, I take a deep breath and smile.

I say, "text me if you need anything."
And then I walk away.

Chapter Fifteen

Ben

If someone asked me why I loved to run, this is what I would tell them: there is a clarity that comes from it. A sense of ease and comfort that cleanses the mind and makes it easier to breathe and be. It makes it easier to exist. This morning is no exception to that rule.

As my feet hit the sidewalk with rhythmic precision, I feel the pressures and pains of the last two days begin to unknot and unwind from my muscles. I feel them seep from my skin, dripping out of my pores and escaping into the day. Here? Now? I feel closer to myself than I have in what feels like a lifetime. Certainly closer than I was in the six months I spent traipsing across Europe, avoiding responsibilities, when I heard Mik was back in town. And yet, with every clarifying step, a sense of loss and discomfort that I'm not familiar with seems to creep into me. I want to get back to her.

"So. You and Mik." It's not a question, but it's weighted.

"What?" I grunt as I shake my head at him. Mikaela doesn't need Jamie snooping around her feelings when she doesn't even know what they are herself.

"I'm just wondering when the two of you got close enough that she's talking about forgiveness." Jamie is scowling as I come to a slow stop. My chest is tightening and my calves are burning while I bend forwards and grimace, and Jamie is staring.

"What's your problem, J? We spoke briefly over the phone because *you* were being difficult about us not talking. She asked if I wanted to come with you guys and I said yes. Why is that an issue?" I feed him a lie I'll need to inform her of soon.

His shoulders raise as he rolls his jaw. "I don't have a problem. I just don't understand when you and my sister got close."

"You know." I roll my shoulders back and pull my phone from the strap across my arm. "You don't get to have it both ways, Jamie. You can't lecture me about making an effort and then get suspicious when I do. It's fucking draining."

"I'm not suspicious." His denial is bitter and weak with dishonesty.

"Yeah." I pull open my messages, my heart lifting a little at the appearance of her name. "You are. And it's getting boring. You don't think I'm good enough for Mik, I get it. We agree on it. Now stop acting like I'm doing anything and everything in my power to get her into bed, because I'm not." *In fact, I seem to be doing the complete opposite and I don't completely understand why.* "Especially when you're the one who was so desperate for us to put the past behind us. Just be happy we're trying."

Jamie's face is a picture; a strange mix of incredulity and shame gliding into place and battling for dominance as he stares at me.

I glance back to my phone as I continue. "I'm going home. If you feel like reminding me of all my short comings again today, don't. Okay?"

"Ben, I didn't mean -"

"Yeah, you did." I sigh. "But I get it, she's your sister. Just give it a rest. Alright?"

I turn away from him, heading down a narrow street that will lead me the short walk home, my fingers already flying across the screen to reply to her.

Mikaela

I lay across the couch, my phone on the coffee table, and I wait. This is going to backfire massively. It is going to blow up in my face and I am going to end up having to apologise. My cheeks are still burning and my heart is pattering against my rib cage as I fidget with the buttons of the shirt I dug out of Ben's bag and minutes drag past me. And then my phone buzzes.

I try to avoid looking at the photo I sent him; his shirt wrapped around me, skimming my thighs with a few too many buttons undone.

Ben: You're really going to make this difficult for me, aren't you?

My heart beats a little easier.

Me: I just think you should know what you're pushing away. Keeping the shirt by the way.

Ben: You know exactly what you're doing, and you're playing dirty. Need a shower and then I'll be back to get ALL of my things.

I get to my feet and wander to the kitchen as I type.

Me: All? Shirt included? Only one way you're getting me to take it off, Haston.

Ben

I groan loudly as I step into the elevator, my eyes dancing over the photo she'd sent. It's innocent enough, just her smiling at the camera - her phone held out just above her to get the full picture - but it's what she's wearing. Mikaela very clearly has nothing but my shirt on. And even that is hanging off of her.

The spattering of freckles that runs down her throat and between her breasts creates a very real, very tempting road I want to travel and the sparkle in her eyes tells me she knows it too. And then her next message comes in and my heart rate spikes.

Mikaela: All? Shirt included? Only one way you're getting me to take it off, Haston.

That idea will be burned into my mind for the rest of forever; me peeling the fabric from her skin delicately. Or even better, ripping it off of her as I kiss her.

I'm in trouble.

I shove my phone into the pocket of my shorts as I turn down the corridor and make my way to my apartment and then I stop moving. I definitely locked the door when I left last night, and yet it's swinging open slightly and her signature calling card drifts through the air with a soft sort of homeliness that twists my gut for some unknown reason.

Only one other person has a key to this place and she never drops by unannounced. Not unless I fuck up. I steady my breath, ready to lie through my teeth for the next God knows how long, and take a step into my own home; nervous for what is about to greet me.

Her perfectly manicured nails tap expectantly against the rim of her coffee cup as she crosses and uncrosses her ankles, slowly. Julia Haston is observant and far too persistent to drop an enquiry half way through an interrogation and as I sit here, my own palms sweaty and my face flushed, I can't help but feel like the naughty kid caught selling old porn magazines at school all over again.

She's unimpressed that I missed her messages last night and this morning.

"I'm getting bored of the lies, Benjamin." The long name. Only used when I'm in deep trouble. How fun.

"I'm not lying, Ma."

She nods as she pushes to her feet and glances down the hall to my unmade bed, visible through the very open door I know I closed on my way out.

My mother: the professional snoop.

"You know, I've never known you not to make your bed. Even as a boy you did it every single morning." She hums quietly as she moves across to the bookshelves and skims her finger over the surface. "You don't have to tell me who she is, darling, but at least pretend you respect me enough not to hide that you're dating someone." That deliberate twinge of sadness in her voice is designed to break the strongest of men.

I sigh loudly.

"I'm not dating anyone, Ma. I crashed at a friends because she needed help with something. That's all."

Her eyes flick up to mine and there is absolutely no denying the simmer of something light and excited dancing behind the shade of blue that matches my own.

I shouldn't have said *she*.

"But you want to?" Mom smiles. "Date her?"

My head drops into my hands as I release a low groan. How, when I am so desperate to keep my mess untangled and my mind less misty, is my mother of all people making it harder for me?

"Yeah," I admit with a slump of my shoulders. I lean further forwards, my elbows on my knees, and avoid looking at the celebratory smile that blossoms over my mom's face as she comes to sit beside me. "But it's complicated and I don't know if it's a good idea."

"Okay." She places one hand over my own and pulls it gently, imploring me to look at her. "Talk it through, explain it to me."

When I was a child, I always thought my mother was the hardest person I knew, in a different way to my father. It was never a negative with her. She was solid and dependable and a fantastic mom; the perfect counter for the shit show my father turned out to be. She protected me from far more than I realised. She pushed me to hold tight to my friendship with Jamie. She forced me to see the world outside of our little bubble of privilege. But I found it hard to talk to her. Now, as she smiles a sympathetic little smile and tilts her head slightly to the right, I look closely at her.

Age and experience has withered her slightly; creasing her sharpness into something a little softer, a little smoother. The cold behind her eyes has long since melted away, and perhaps it's the familiar smell of freshly made coffee and walnut loaf that wafts through from my kitchen, or the way she perches herself beside me and pulls me back against the couch cushions, cradling me as if I'm a ten year old child and not a thirty-one year old man, but I realise something. My mother was never really hard. She was *strong*. She was strong because she had to be and that made her colder. Something about the way she looks at me now, partnered with the memory of the mother she had been, pulls memories of Mikaela to mind. And I *want* to tell her. I want to tell her everything.

"She - erm - she's this strong, beautiful woman, Ma. Honestly, she's incredible and she doesn't even realise it." I admit this with a shaky breath as I let my mother wrap me in her embrace. "She doesn't let me get away with anything. She never lets me forget that I can be an ass and she makes me want to be better." My mother sighs this happy, little sound that brings a smile to my face before reality sets in again. "But she's been through a lot. And there are other factors, other people, this would affect."

I feel my mother nod before she presses a kiss to my temple. I want to say, *it's Mikaela Wilcox, Mom. You remember her. Jamie's baby sister. You adore her.*

"So you worry she'll reject you because of these things?" Her voice cuts through my conflict and I close my eyes, thinking of the woman I left behind this morning: her features soft and her voice steady as she looked up to me... Her smile uncertain.

"No," I whisper. "She'll give herself to me, Ma. She'll say she wants me too."

"Then what's the problem, Benjamin?" Her palm brushes against my arm as she chuckles and I let my fear surface.

"What if I'm not actually what she wants? What if I do this - I go for it - and she wakes up one day and realises I'm not who she wants?"

Mom's shoulders seem to shake with quiet laughter as she squeezes me a little tighter. "Whoever she is, she means a lot to you, doesn't she?"

I let her hold on to me for a little longer, the only answer I can give right now, and she sighs in contemplation. Silence wraps around us for a while and it blankets us, smothering us in its comfort.

When my text chime breaks through that sacred barrier, both of us jump and I shift out of her hold. Mikaela's name lights up my screen and I twist nervously, shielding her from the lovable snoop beside me.

She watches my face intently as I read the message twice over and shoot back a very rushed reply.

Mikaela: Are you coming back today or in a year? Kinda miss looking at you right about now.

Her words are like tiny drops of honey, trapping me in the fantasy of the two of us being more than everything I know we really are.

Me: I'm on my way. Unexpected visitor. Can I use your shower?

I get to my feet and roll my eyes as my mother grins a wolfish smile and pushes herself up from the couch. She picks up the purse from my coffee table, before moving through to the kitchen to cover the walnut loaf she clearly baked while waiting for me.

Mikaela: Yours broken or do you miss me too?

Playful Mikaela is going to break me.

"You know." Mom pauses to look at me as she stands in the doorway, her grin softening into a small smile that screams of pride and hope. "You won't know if you don't try, Ben."

I nod thoughtfully, guiding her to the door before bending down to kiss her cheek in a goodbye.

When Mikaela's next text comes through, I follow my mother out and down to the basement car park, smiling to myself the whole time.

Fear is a funny thing.

Mikaela

Maybe this is a step too far.

I'm in the bathroom, the door to my apartment unlocked and the entrance to the building propped open with an old shoe, staring at the tub as it fills with suds and hot water. Steam dances up towards me as I bend forwards, twisting the tap to stop the flow, and bubbles catch against my chest, soaking through the shirt.

Okay, this is definitely a step too far.

I run from the bathroom and begin to hastily unbutton the shirt that now clings to my skin. I need a t-shirt and some goddamn shorts or something. Ben will be here any minute now, and there's one button that just won't open, and the sensation of fizzing seems to swirl in my stomach, anticipation and nerves battling for first place as my fingers fumble and snag. And suddenly my heart is in my throat and my breath is gone.

Ben pushes through the door with purpose and determination. His eyes lock on me as his chest rises and falls in staggered breaths. His skin glistens from the thin sheet of rain that started to fall a little while ago and his throat bobs with a gulp as he steps up to me. When he stops, he's so close I can taste that heady mix of citrus and pine and something that is distinctly *him.*

My fingers still on the button an inch below my breasts and his eyes move slowly, searing into every exposed piece of me as I try to remind myself how breathing works.

We're on the edge - the precipice - balancing between what was and what could be. Where we will land is a mystery. Which way we will fall is still undetermined. But I can feel it. Sense it. Everything will be decided by what happens next.

His fingers move like the ghost of touches, trailing down from my collarbone, skimming between my breasts and tracing the pattern of my freckles, before meeting mine; still clinging to that fateful button. If he choses to undo it there will be no return for us, no stepping back and away from the truth that I have pushed aside for years; I want Benjamin Haston.

I have wanted him for longer than I can admit.

He peels my hands from the button and pulls them away. His fingers still hold mine, but he shakes his head and closes his eyes.

My heart sinks.

I want to lean in. I want to taste his lips again and pull him in to me. I want him to take his shirt off of me and claim me as something that is entirely his. But I don't.

"Slow." His voice catches, so beautifully strained, and his eyes remain shut.

"What?" There's no disguising the wanton breathiness of my own tone.

"If we do this -" His breath comes in ragged jolts as he he steps closer, pressing himself softly against me and his hand moves to my spine. I have to tilt my chin up to see him clearly. "- then we have to go slow."

I nod quickly, despite the fact his eyes are still closed, and when he opens them I'm hit with the electric blue of his desire. Slow. I can do slow. In fact, I want slow. I want to savour every soft second I can steal away with this man.

"But can I keep the shirt?" I whisper, a triumphant smile tugging at my lips as his breath whooshes from him in a laugh.

"Absolutely not."

Chapter Sixteen

Mikaela

This is what free-falling must feel like. It's like the earth simultaneously stopped moving and sped up. Like gravity has been suspended, and yet something is still pulling me hurtling towards a bone-crushing landing. This is exhilaration and freedom and stupidity all bundled into one all-consuming thought: *Ben Haston is kissing me.*

His lips brush against mine slowly, tentatively, and I sigh as my fingers press into his shoulders. I wrap around him - sink into him - as tension seeps from his skin. Every second that passes brings comfort and closeness and a familiarity I didn't realise I knew until this exact moment. His hands slip from my waist, his fingers brushing against my ass as he pulls me against him, pinning me to his skin, and I'm smiling.

He pulls his lips from mine, breathless and flushed, and his eyes shimmer with something exciting and new... Something unleashed.

Everything inside of me tightens in response.

"Slow," he repeats, reminding us both, his voice husky now.

"Slow," I agree, still flush against him and aching for more contact.

Standing like this, my hands splayed against his shoulders and his caressing my skin beneath his shirt, it feels like possibility is all around us.

I stare up at him, moving slowly as I pull one hand towards his face. My fingers press into the stubble, scratchy against my skin, and Ben smiles warmly. I pull my fingertips up to his lips - lips that are swollen and parted, still sucking in heavy breaths after our kiss - and he grins further. He presses a kiss against my fingertips and my heart stutters.

"I - erm - I ran you a bath." My voice shakes and Ben twists his head just the tiniest amount, nuzzling into my hand as he does so. "I know that's probably weird."

His laugh rumbles in his chest as he leans in and presses his lips against mine again. "You ran a bath for me?"

I nod, my breath catching in my throat with the simplicity of a quick kiss. "You did it for me and I just thought - I don't know what I thought - it was strange and I can let it out. It's just that a bath is always better than a shower, you know? And I thought you might - never mind - I'll go let it out."

I pull back, my rambling embarrassing me, as he shakes his head and pulls me back to him by my hips. His fingers spread over the shirt, pressing lightly, and my chest aches with tenderness when I realise he has placed his hands over the bruises. He has placed his touch over the marks of violence and changed the way my skin feels.

"Thank you." His fingers move to my face as he holds me gently and brushes hair out of my eyes. "I'm going to go take my bath now, and then when I'm done, we should talk."

He must feel the way my pulse quickens and see the gulp of fear I push down, because his voice softens even more and his fingers massage gently against the back of my neck as his thumb caresses my jaw.

"We need to define slow. Lay out some ground rules." His eyes darken into stormy seas again as he glances down at the semi-transparent shirt still clinging to my skin. "Or I'll end up ripping that off of you way too soon.

Ben steps out of the bathroom with a towel wrapped low on his hips and my mouth goes dry. His hair is pushed back in messy waves where he hasn't had it cut in a little too long, and drops of water glisten against his flawless skin as he looks over to where I sit on the couch, his shirt now dried and partnered with a pair of ratty old shorts.

I curse myself internally for the choice as his eyes roam over me.

"I just need to grab jeans from my bag and then we can talk, yeah?" His eyes meet mine as he smiles.

I nod, lifting my glass to my lips.

"I ordered some food." I mumble as I try to look anywhere other than at the man on the other side of the room. His perfection is distracting and definitely doesn't invite restraint.

"Good idea." He moves over to the couch, grinning when I glance up at him. The towel really does hang low on his hips and my fingers itch to trace those incredible lines of muscles that line his hips and dip down below the white cotton. I swallow against the dryness of my throat as he leans in, his voice low and gritty. "Just need to do something before I go in there and get dressed."

He leans over the arm of the couch and over me with such casual confidence, his fingers wrapping behind my neck and tangling in my hair as he pulls me closer to him, and pauses. His breath fans over my lips as he runs his tongue over his lower lip and my entire being seems to hum with unbridled lust.

"Yeah." He whispers to himself as I wait, practically panting. "This was a good idea."

Before I can respond he traps my lips beneath his.

His kiss is slow and sensual and I shift to my knees, desperate to keep the contact before he can pull away from me again. My fingertips scrape over warm skin and, despite the fact I feel every single cell in my body humming and dancing with desperate need, his kiss is unhurried. He tastes like peppermint and some tiny, distracted part of my mind - the only part that hasn't already been infiltrated by Benjamin Haston - notes that he must have used my toothpaste since he last kissed me.

When he breaks from me my eyes are still closed and my lips fall into a sad little pout, pulling a chuckle from deep within him, and I feel him back away from me slowly.

"I'll be two minutes." His voice is back in the bathroom before I open my eyes and throw myself back onto the cushions.

Kissing Ben is going to be the death of me if I can't remember how to breathe each time his lips meet mine.

Ben

When I emerge from the bathroom, throwing the towel I used into the empty hamper by the door, Mikaela is at the front door. Her voice is gentle as she passes the boy some cash and tells him to keep the change and

I lean against the door frame, watching her. The tiny caveman inside of me is fucking pounding on the ground as he dances around the fire that spreads in my chest at the sight of her, and I wonder if that should scare me; the fact I want to claim her so completely when I know I shouldn't.

The boy glances at the crumpled bills in his hands and a huge smile erupts over his face before he glances back to her. "Are you sure?"

"Of course." She laughs in a way that just emanates pure joy. "You got here quickly and you were polite. Plus, I'm really freaking happy right now so I thought I'd spread some of that happiness."

Mine, the caveman grunts. *All mine.*

The boy is practically bouncing with excitement and Mikaela rests the pizza box on her hip.

"Thanks, Ma'am," he whisper laughs.

She grunts and I grin.

"Wow. Call me Ma'am again and there's no tip next time." Her laugh is positively buoyant.

As the door closes, I move across the space to the kitchen and grab two glasses. I note the coffee cups have moved to the lower shelf and the wine glasses are now on the top shelf, and every ounce of self restraint I have goes into refraining from laughing and shaking my head.

Mikaela bumps her hip against mine as she moves into the kitchen space and I turn to face her, placing the glasses down and grabbing her before she can move past me. She pushes onto her tip-toes as I lean in and kisses me quickly before glancing to the couch. Part of me hates the pizza. It's keeping her body from being pressed up against mine.

"Kitchen or couch?" The longing in her eyes is definitely for the comfort of cushions at this point.

"Couch." I push her towards the living room and move to the sink, filling our glasses with cold water before following behind her.

Fuck, this is easy.

"You could sit closer, you know." She sulks between bites of pizza and I grin, throwing a napkin at her before pointing to the corner of her mouth. She wipes at the sauce as she rolls her eyes.

"I know." I run my eyes over her slowly and she shudders. I like that; that she reacts so easily. "But this is... safer. While we discuss rules."

Mikaela huffs as she glances at the small pile of cushions placed between us and I bite back my laughter. As silly as it seems, I need the barrier. Especially with her sitting there in my shirt, the shadow of her nipples drawing my eye to her chest every five fucking seconds.

"Okay." She shuffles closer and raises an eyebrow at me. "Hit me with the rules, Haston."

"We need to agree them, Mik." She nods as I continue. "I want us to take things one step at a time, make sure we're good before we dive into anything we can't take back. So." I'm not even pretending that I'm not imagining her naked in front of me as my eyes skim slowly over her body and I set the first rule. "No sex."

Her eyes widen ever so slightly and her jaw slackens momentarily before she regains her composure and reaches for her water.

"Right. Of course, slow would definitely mean no sex." The twinge of disappointment in her voice is matched with the slight downturn of her lip and I breach the barrier for a moment, my fingers brushing the hair

216

behind her ear, and I hold her until she looks back at me.

"Do not mistake this rule as me not wanting you, Mik." I am practically growling and I take a sharp breath when her eyes flick to my lips. "Because I want you. I just want it to be right."

Mik licks her lips and I feel it in my groin. *Yeah, rule one sucks already.*

"Okay," she whispers. "No sex. Rule two?"

I pull my hand back and grab another slice of the veggie pizza balanced precariously between us. It is seriously good pizza, but I'm only eating more to stop myself from touching her again.

"Considering we're not having sex, I think it's safer if we minimise sleepovers." I bite back the lump in my throat that forms with the thought of her alone in this tiny apartment and wait for her to respond. She stays silent. "I don't mean that they won't happen if you need me here, Mik." My voice is hushed and I hope she doesn't register the tremor of fear beneath it. "If you can't stay here alone, I will be here. But I -"

"I can stay here." I expected fear, maybe even anger, but there's strength in her voice; determination. "Sleepovers are reserved for absolute necessity until further notice." She nods to herself as she leans forwards and pulls open a small drawer on her coffee table.

I watch as she rummages for a moment before pulling a pen out and grabbing a napkin.

"What are you doing?" My lips tug into a smile when she bites the lid of the pen and pulls.

"I," she mumbles around the pen lid, "am writing these rules down."

There's a strange tightness in my chest, watching her furrow her brow and concentrate on her handwriting while the napkin crumples with each stroke of the pen.

What the fuck?

"No sex. No sleepovers." She repeats as she writes. "What next?"

I swallow hard. This one will be make or break. I have three rules and only one of them makes me think she might back out of this. Only one of them really, truly tests how much she wants this. And I couldn't blame her if this one pushed her away. So I ready myself for disappointment, sitting a little taller and schooling my features into a casual smirk, as I say "we don't tell Jamie."

She glances up at me as she takes a deep breath and her shoulders raise with the inhale.

"Mik?"

I don't like her silence.

Her eyes close as she slumps back onto the cushions and I shift in my seat, unsure of what this all means and feeling a little sick.

"Mik? Say something."

When she laughs it's flooded with relief.

"Thank God," she finally breathes through a giggle. "I was sure you'd want to tell him." Another bubble of amusement. "And then I'd have to plan your freaking funeral before we ever got to have sex." She wipes at her cheeks, her face still to the ceiling and her breath wheezing a little, and I can't look away from her.

The noise that leaves me at her concern is anything but sexy. The choked mixture of a guffaw and a laugh sounds more like a snorted grunt than anything else and she twists her face to look at me. The jade of her eyes is gleaming, like a rainforest at the end of a downpour, and I move to push our little barrier away.

I put the pizza on the table, throw the cushions behind me, and pull on her legs as she yelps. The movement is swift and leaves her laying before me, the shirt now slightly lifted to reveal a sliver of her skin, silver in this light, and I move so I'm hovering over her.

"So, we're agreed on the rules?" I grin as she moves her hands to my face and holds me gently.

"Mhmm." She hums her agreement as she pulls me closer. "But we still do this. We do this a lot or we have no deal." Her lips meet mine with urgency and I groan against her kiss.

Yes. Yes, we do this as often as we can, for as long as we can.

Chapter Seventeen

Ben

Holy shit, this is going to blow up in our faces.

Mikaela sits on the edge of my desk, her skirt riding dangerously high against her bare thigh as she leans forwards, and twists to look through the figures I'm working on. Or trying to work on. In the ten minutes since she walked into my office I've managed to type exactly three things. Instead, I find my fingers dancing over the supple skin of her legs as we whisper about our plans and desperately ignore the danger of behaving so brazenly at work.

The blinds are closed and the door is shut, but Jamie is only next door and the room beyond the glass wall is filled with nosy employees who have to have noticed the increased visits Mikaela's been making to my office over the last week. We've already almost been caught three times in the last five days, first by Jamie, who had a face of thunder for the rest of the day, and then twice by Max. We're playing with fire, but neither of us seem to be able to stop.

"If we get out of here on time, we can meet at my place and maybe catch a late screening at the movies?" She brushes my fingers away from her thigh as I shift closer to her in my seat and take the chance to grab her hand and pull her off of the desk.

Now she's standing between my legs I can hold her like I want to, placing my hands against the back of her thighs and leaning back in my chair to look up at her.

She laughs as she glances to the door and places her hands on my shoulders. "You're going to get us caught, Ben."

"Fuck it," I joke, pulling her closer. "Let them catch us."

She shakes her head and pulls away from me, moving her hands to where mine rest against her and removing my touch. We both know it's too soon to tell anyone anything. We both know we're floating in a heady sort of bliss that comes from sneaking around and neither of us are going to be ready to burst that bubble for a while.

She presses a quick kiss against my lips before pulling back. "Your rules, remember? Besides, I quite like this arrangement and I'd be sad if my brother killed you."

I watch her as she moves to the other side of my desk. She went shopping this week and I had hated the evening I'd spent at home thinking about her, but now? I make a mental note to be a little nicer to Kingston because he'd convinced her to ditch the old outfits and this cream knit and tan skirt combo is driving me insane. The skirt sits just above her knee and hugs tight to her skin and as for the top... Every curve is accentuated and even though the turtle neck definitely screams *workplace,* the fit just screams. Yes. I need to be much, much nicer to her friend.

"So?" Her voice pulls me away from my wandering thoughts.

"So what?" I run my eyes over her again and she laughs as she shakes her head.

"Late screening? Whatever's playing? We can sit in the back and make-out like teenagers?"

I grin at the thought and my dick responds with its own little show, forcing me to shift in my seat and try to picture anything else.

"While I love the sound of that - the last part in particular -" I lean back in my chair and gaze at her as her cheeks flush. "I have other plans tonight."

Her face falls and I roll my eyes.

"With you, Mik. I have other plans with you."

God, I could watch the smile that breaks over her face a thousand times and I wouldn't tire of it. The way her eyes crinkle and her lips curl up to show the smallest dimple in her cheek. It's ethereal.

"Really? What are we doing?" She's practically bouncing with excitement.

"It's top secret," I tease. "Wear something comfortable."

"Comfortable like eating takeout on the couch and watching Fresh Prince re-runs, or comfortable like you're going to make me run? Because, I have news for you, I quit the whole running thing after our little incident. Not sure you noticed, but I really wasn't very good at it." She's rambling like an idiot and I want to kiss her so much it actually hurts my chest.

"Comfortable like whatever makes you feel beautiful, Mik. And be ready by eight."

The door pushes open and our heads snap to the entrance of my office, the smiles wiping from our faces as Jamie pushes into the space and glances between us both. Right now I make myself swear I'll keep my hands off of her at work. If he had walked in just two minutes ago we'd have been caught.

"What have I walked in on?" Jamie looks over his sister in a detailed inspection and I hold my breath. Can he see the slight flush of her skin or the way she crosses her arms over her chest and holds her neck slightly? Did he clock the fact she glanced to me before turning on her most innocent smile and facing him fully?

"Ben has a meeting set for eight am. I told him I'd come in to minute it."

Jamie scowls. "We don't open until nine."

Mikaela shrugs as she saunters to the door and I try to suppress a smile.

"What can I say?" She winks with a wicked grin. "The devil works hard, but Haston works harder. Or maybe he is the devil?"

Jamie rolls his eyes and grimaces towards me. I want to roll my eyes and laugh at her.

"Stop calling him names, Mik. You said you were ready for peace."

She leaves the room with a swing of her hips and Jamie runs his hand over his face.

"I swear it's one step forwards and another two back with you two." He groans when I laugh. "Need me in to mediate?"

"No," I return to the file I have to finish and try to focus. "I'm sure I can handle it."

As Jamie walks out of the office I glance back up at him.

"J?" He pauses in the door and I smile. "Did you need something when you came in or?"

He groans again and rocks back on his feet, practically falling back into the room.

"Yeah. Shit, sorry." He drops himself into the seat opposite me and crosses his leg over as he leans back. "Next month is the big anniversary - five full years of Wilcox Writing - and I want to do something for it. Something big. Wanna see if we have the budget for a party?"

I laugh loudly and his smile gets bigger.

"What sort of party?"

Memories of Jamie and I throwing parties in dorm rooms and off campus housing during our visits to each other somehow don't quite match the occasion.

"Cocktail dresses and suits, champagne on arrival, a DJ. Something sophisticated, you know? Something that says 'we're pretty damn successful actually'. Maybe hire someone to help organise it all. Does that seem doable?"

I can't help myself. When Jamie gets an idea in his head I tend to follow. And who can say no to a party?

"I'm sure it can be done."

"Amazing." He jumps from the chair and claps his hands together. "I'll source everything but run the numbers by you before I spend a dollar?"

"Deal."

"Maybe we can hire a party planner," he muses as he walks out of my office and, immediately, I know the first thing I'll be signing off on is a paycheque for some pretty little firecracker he probably already has his eye on.

Mikaela's face is illuminated by the shifting lights; pinks and soft purples dancing over her and making her seem almost pixie-like in her awe. Dark jeans, torn at the knees cling to her skin and, in her sneakers, she's a good head-and-a-bit smaller than me. The perfect height to pull on that primal part of me that seems to want to claim her and protect her. She moves beside me with graceful steps, even though the ground is uneven and people around us stumble as the lights undulate and pulse. Her t-shirt - an old Metallica shirt I recognise from Jamie's college wardrobe - is torn at the shoulder and hangs off of her, rippling from her curves. It's hard to tear my eyes from her. It might be the most relaxed I've ever seen her.

She reaches out to me, weaving her fingers between mine, as we move past another group gathered in front of one of the performers and make our way to the spot I told her I want to start from. Her eyes dart around us with eager excitement and as we move together she pulls closer to me. I look at her again. I find it hard to look away. I find it hard to breathe. I can't stop smiling.

The exhibit around us is chaotic and wild - a mixture of art and photography, live music and monologues, all inspired by stories I grew up loving - but right in the furthest cornered off tent of the field we are in is the reason we're here; hundreds of images combined to create one. The white rabbit. A figure of curiosity. One of her favourite pieces of Literature.

An intoxicating mix of Mikaela and madness seems to thrum in my veins with every step through the people around us and I sink into the anonymity of the night.

Once we were out of the city, it took us just under an hour to get out here to see it take place, and excitement thrums in my veins as every second of tonight seems to pull us into a new level of this strange fantasy we're sharing; the one where this isn't going to end in tears. The fantasy where this thing between us works.

"Your brother wants to throw a party." I glance over to Mik as we walk through the crowd and she looks around at the throngs of people in clustered spaces of the open air exhibition.

"Is that so?" She smiles to the couple who move alongside us; an elderly pair who glance at our hands interlaced and coo at the promise of *'the early days'*.

"Yep." I pull her closer, draping my arm over her shoulder while still keeping her hand in mine. "Fancy dresses and free champagne kind of thing." The next words snag in my throat. "Everyone at the office gets a plus one."

As we come to a stop in front of the piece I want to show her, she gazes at the images with wide eyes. I release her and she steps forwards. Her eyes dance with wonder. She squints as she looks closer, taking in each scene painted into the tiny cards and whispers to herself with each new image.

"This is incredible." She speaks with reverence when she shakes her head and reaches out, her fingers hovering just out of reach of the art. Immersed in the moment, she is captivating.

"I agree." I can't take my eyes off of her.

She looks up at me, her brows knitting together as she pulls her lip between her teeth, trying to suppress her smile and she moves closer. Her hand slips back into mine as she glances back to the art.

"So this party?" She smiles and I feel my nerves twisting in my gut.

"I mean, it's only been a week and the party won't be until next month so I really don't know why I'm bringing it up, but yeah. Everyone gets a plus one and I - I don't know. I just thought I'd tell you, I guess." I'm beginning to ramble as she stares up at me, the nerves in my stomach amplified by the electric shock of gold that floods over her green eyes from the lights beaming around us.

"Ben?"

"Yeah?"

"I won't be bringing a plus one." She smiles up at me and I can't help but match her as relief floods my senses.

"You won't?"

She twists as she lets go of my hand, reaching up to wrap her arms around my neck and thread her fingers in my hair. She pushes onto her tip-toes as I wrap around her waist and she shakes her head.

"No." She pulls me closer to her lips. "I don't want one. I don't need one."

Her kiss is sweet and reassuring, meant only to soothe my mind, and I melt into it.

"If you want one though..." She smirks against my lips as her words trail off and I squeeze her slightly.

"You aren't even funny, Wilcox." I nip at her lip and she yelps in surprise.

"No?"

"No. Why the fuck would I bring someone else when I've got Mikaela fucking Wilcox in my arms right now?"

I kiss her again, letting myself get lost in the enrapturing feeling of her; her breath mixing with my own, her needs and wants and desires matching the ones I have ignored for so long.

Mikaela

I pull away with reluctance when someone clears their throat behind us, the noise dripping with dissatisfied disinterest, and a groan slips from my lips as Ben's arms loosen around me. I'm not usually a kissing in public kind of person, and discomfort settles in my gut as I turn to apologise.

"I'm so sorry -"

The words are gone. Air is gone. My hands go slack as my entire body becomes clammy and unnaturally warm. My hips sting and my back aches and my stomach, previously alive with butterflies and admissions, is now a dead weight; dragging me down.

I can't move. I need to move.

Why can't I move?

Ben's eyes are trained on me for just a second before he looks up, and then his body is stiff as a board and his grip on me tightens.

He pulls me back so that I'm against his chest and his heartbeat steadies me. I breathe with it. In for four and out for four. Neither of us speak. Neither of us move from this position, but my fingers dig into his arm as I cling to him and try to stave off the darkness creeping over me, and he holds me like he can stop me from crumbling.

"I should have guessed." That voice, like nails dragging underneath my skin, rakes over me and I flinch with his words. Joshua Lucas holds venom in every syllable.

"Don't fucking talk to her." Ben's voice is low and menacing as he stares at Josh and my heart hammers as tears begin to cloud my vision.

"It's a free country, Big Guy." Josh is swimming in sarcasm. "I can do what I want."

"Not with her you can't." Ben moves around me, pushing me behind him as the couple we were walking alongside watches in confusion, and my knees begin to buckle.

I want to hold on to him. My fingers brush against his back just as a hand is placed against my spine and I jolt.

Ben swings back to face me, concern flaring in his eyes and only settling when the elderly man pulling me towards himself and his wife nods at him. He turns back to Josh.

"Tell me, Mr. Haston. How long did it take for her to crawl into your bed?" Josh juts his chin towards me as his glare turns to ice. "A day? An hour?"

Ben steps out of my touch and I reach after him.

"She's shaking like a leaf." The woman holding me whispers to her husband, but I can't focus on her. Ben is closer to Josh than he is to me.

"You're okay, kid." Her husband hushes beside us as he keeps his eyes on Ben's back. All of our eyes are on Ben's back.

"You've got some fucking nerve." Ben's mad. I watch as he glances to the red head standing behind Josh, young and beautiful and innocent, and then his shoulders shake and bitter laughter tears from his chest. This isn't my Ben's laugh - it's full of pity and anger - but when he speaks, his words are soft and filled with unfiltered concern. "If I were you, I'd run far and fast now. He's not the nice guy he pretends to be."

The girls eyes meet mine for just a fraction of a second before she shakes her head and drops her gaze. She's not going to listen.

"Ben." My voice is weak and I hate it. "Let's just go."

He turns back to me instantly, the contempt falling from his face as he moves to my side, and takes my hand in his, he smiles tightly at the couple still holding me up, and they nod before the woman grabs hold of my other hand.

"Whatever he did -" her head juts in Josh's direction "- it was not your fault. You hear me?" Her eyes are filled with understanding as she reaches up and wipes my cheek. "You remember that."

I nod and Ben pulls me away from them, his breath ragged with rage.

We move quickly, despite the crowd seeming to thicken around us, and Josh's gaze sears into my skin, tearing away at the bliss I felt just moments ago.

"Your back seems to have healed nicely, Mikaela."

Ben's hand is no longer in mine and he lurches away from me. I hear the grunt as his fist connects with Josh's face and the girl beside him cries out. The man who had pulled me to his wife voices his approval and, as I spin back, his wife is glaring at him.

My knees shake and I push myself away.

I stumble forwards as I hear him calling out to me, following me back to the car, and I shove through the crowds. I shield my eyes from the light. I shake as I struggle to suck in enough air.

It's all too much.

Chapter Eighteen

Ben

I push the people around me, reds and blues bouncing off of surfaces and blinding me, as I search for her in the sea of people who won't move. The whole night imploded. I brought her here to show her art and performances - to take her down the rabbit hole and into Wonderland - because I know she loves the book and because I wanted to have one moment with her that she would always love, no matter what happens with us. I brought her here and *he* was here. And I acted like a fucking asshole.

My fist aches as I push past the throng and spot her, her golden waves pulled tight into a ponytail that swoops behind her, as she ducks her head and stumbles forwards.

My heart lurches.

I messed up. I really fucking messed up.

"Mik, wait!" I dart past a small group of people gathering in front of a man dressed in a mismatched patchwork coat rambling about madness and people - a performer drinking in his applause - and into a clearing. Three strides. That's all it takes to get to her and I take them quickly, my heart pounding in my throat and my lungs burning with fear. I call out to her again and she finally stops moving.

"Mik." I lower my voice, desperate to make this right - to apologise and keep her safe.

"I'm sorry," she whispers and her words steal reality from me. I've misheard her. I'm sure of it. There's no way that's right.

"What?" My throat cracks as I take that final step until I'm close enough to touch her. Still, my hands remain by my side. Right now, with his voice still fresh in our minds, she doesn't need me to touch her without permission. "Mik, why would you apologise?"

"I ran." She turns to face me and something viscerally painful etches itself into the depths of her eyes. "I just ran and left you there and I'm so sorry, Ben. I just - I couldn't stay there with him and then he said what he said and you..."

Her voice trails off as her eyes drop to my knuckles. They're red from the impact, already swelling slightly, and I curse myself for acting without thinking.

"Mik, I'm the one who needs to apologise. I shouldn't have hit him." I suck in a hard breath as she moves a step closer and takes my hand in her fingers, gently running a thumb over the sting of pain and pausing when I flinch.

"I'm glad you did." Her whisper is confessional. "But I hate that you had to."

Using my good hand, I cup her cheek and duck slightly so I can look at her closely.

"I shouldn't have hit him, Mik." I'm determined with my words and her lip quivers as she looks at me. "I wasn't thinking about what you needed in that moment and I shouldn't have done it."

I watch her eyes as I lean in, pausing before I bridge that gap between us fully, seeking permission. Slowly, Mikaela moves a step closer and tilts her face up to me, brushing her lips against mine with more tenderness than I deserve. This is a kiss for both of us. One to smooth the edges that have been left rough and raw in my moment of hazy rage; a kiss to reassure and remind. I caress her cheek as her lips part and I taste the salt of her tears. She pulls closer to me, her fingers moving to my neck as she anchors us, keeping us together while we give in to the need for connection.

And I feel it.

I feel the world shift slightly, like I've been standing on the wrong mark all this time, as if I have been off centre my entire life and the earth itself has just moved beneath me, correcting me and showing me this is where I have been aiming for all along.

As she pulls back from me, she sighs and I hold her face between my hands, brushing her tears away while she stares up at me.

"I'm so sorry to do this, but can we go home?"

My thumb brushes over her cheek and I smile at her. "Mik, you aren't doing anything that needs an apology. Let's go."

Pulling her into my side, I lead her back to the car, my head swimming with guilt and anger and something so much scarier than either of those two feelings.

Mikaela

In the warm glow of street lamps that intermittently illuminate the pair of us, I sit watching Ben. His eyes roam from the road and over to me every few minutes and each time he smiles softly and moves his hand from the wheel to my leg, caressing my thigh with a softness that leaves my skin singing, before returning back to the wheel. We don't speak. We don't fall into easy conversation or laughter. We don't try to fill the silence with music. We just let the air sit as it is and the world pass by around us.

Ben's hair is mussed from the breeze that pushes in through the open window, dark curls forming in the slightly unkempt lengths and I smile to myself as I wonder what it is that makes him leave his hair a little longer these days. Or if he realises I noticed that he's leaving it longer. When he drives he narrows his eyes as he concentrates on the road ahead and his bottom lip juts forwards slightly when another driver does something to irritate him.

Watching him, breathing in his features like this, brings a semblance of peace to my mind.

My eyes dance over the soft stubble along his jaw before roaming down his neck and over his shoulders. From this angle it's impossible not to notice the strength of his arms; the discipline he has to have to keep the definition of muscle that sits beneath the dark jacket he's wearing. His hands hold the wheel easily, like everything else he does it seems so casual, but the red of his knuckles is slowly turning a soft purple and my eyes linger on the marks as the echo of his fist connecting with Josh's jaw rattles in my mind.

"What are you thinking?" Ben's voice breaks the steady thrum of silence that wraps around us as we sit at a stop sign for longer than necessary and I look up to see his eyes trained on me. Beneath the blue is a babble of something unsure and pained and I want to erase it. I want to soothe him and assure him.

"We need to get some ice on your hand." I try to smile, but it catches on something on the tip of my tongue and doesn't meet my eyes.

"Mik." He twists in his seat and takes hold of my hands where they sit in my lap. "I really am sorry."

I shake my head and watch our fingers entwine.

"I know I acted impulsively and I shouldn't have," he continues in a steady stream of regret and I feel my heart twisting. "I just - I hated hearing him taunt you like that. I don't know what I was thinking. I'm sorry."

"Please stop apologising." It's just a whisper but my voice still cracks. "You really don't need to."

"Then tell me what I need to do, Mik. Please."

I pull one hand back to wipe away the tears I'm getting tired of, and he waits patiently. That's something about Ben I never anticipated: his patience.

"You don't get it. And that's my fault." I laugh sadly.

"What don't I get?" He pulls my knuckles to his lips.

"No one has ever jumped to protect me like that before." I can't look at him when I think of all the times I needed someone to step in. All the times I hadn't let anyone step in. "No one except Jamie, and I just - what if he calls the police, Ben? I'm not worth that." It's not the full story, but it's true all the same.

I hear him suck in a sharp breath and I wait for the knife to drop. I wait for the reality of it all to break me right here, in front of him.

"Mikaela." He pauses and I hold my breath. "Look at me please."

I glance up and my heart stumbles. His eyes are burning with so much care that I feel it in the very centre of me; a soft warmth that starts deep in my chest and spreads through my veins.

"You are worth so much more than you think." He caresses my skin and shifts closer to me. "Why can't you see just how incredible you are?"

My laugh is dismissive and he narrows his eyes.

"I mean it, Mik. You're funny and smart. You're obviously fucking beautiful, you have more balls than most of the men in our office combined and you've never been afraid to put me in my place - even as kids. You're stupidly creative and insanely talented." I open my mouth to protest and he shakes his head. "I've seen your notebooks, Mik, and all the ideas you have. You're incredible. You *are* worth it, Mik. You're worth everything." He sighs and I feel it in my bones. "You used to know all of this, Wilcox. What happened?"

Ben's fingers move to my cheek, holding me as if one caress too heavy might leave me crumbling beneath his touch, and I close my eyes.

The truth is there, lodged in my throat and clawing to get out of me. It tears beneath my skin, drowning itself in the venom left behind, and I try to say it. I really do. My mouth opens, the words hanging between us in a silent string of confessions that have the power to make or break.

Matthew happened.

But that's it. Just a silent sliver of the truth that won't come out. Because saying it could break whatever this is. Saying it still has the power to break *me*. Instead, I settle for something different. Something that only feels like half a lie.

"I grew up." I shrug and Ben shakes his head. When he doesn't say anything else, I pull out of his touch and turn to the world around us. "You know, I think we can safely say we stopped at the stop sign."

He shakes his head again, this time with a soft laugh, and checks for oncoming traffic before driving again.

The rest of the journey is silent.

Ben

Parking by Mikaela's is a nightmare. Parking anywhere that doesn't have its own lot in the city is a nightmare, but Mik's apartment is in the one place that seems to be pre-populated by tow-zones.

When I swear for the sixth time after finding another no-parking zone, she speaks up.

"You do know there's a back alley parking bay for my place, right?" Mik bites her lip as she tries to stop herself from smiling and my forehead meets the steering wheel.

"Mikaela."

"I thought Jamie told you when you crashed move-in day." She laughs and my head feels a little lighter.

"Why would Jamie have told me that?"

"Because he told you to come." She shrugs as I straighten up and turn to her.

"No," I laugh. "He didn't. He was surprised and actually a little pissed I showed up."

Mikaela's jaw drops.

"What?" I'm grinning now, seeing her brighten back to the Mikaela I know. "I wanted to help."

"I was so mad at Jamie." She laughs loudly and points to the alley beside her apartment. "Turn down there and the spaces are at the very end."

"You should probably head home soon," Mikaela sighs as she nuzzles into me on the couch. We've been laying like this for hours now, her curled into my side, my arms wrapped around her with some cooking show playing on the TV, and it almost feels as if the nightmare of this evening never happened. The defrosted bag of peas, tossed into the sink after Mik made me hold it against my hand for half an hour, is the only reminder of it all.

"Not tonight." I feel her heart beat a little harder at my words and laugh a little.

"But rule number two."

"Rule number two," I remind her, "stated that sleepovers were reserved for absolute necessity. Tonight it's necessary."

Pushing up to look at me properly, Mikaela smiles sadly.

"Honestly, Ben. It's not necessary. I'll be okay alone."

"I know you will be." My hand brushes down her spine as I speak. "But it's necessary for me. Is that okay?"

Her mouth twitches at the corner, the tell-tale sign that Mikaela Wilcox is feeling a little shy, and I move my free hand to her face, brushing my thumb over her lips.

"I can go home if you want me to, Mik."

She shakes her head as she leans in slowly.

"No." She kisses me gently. "I want you to stay."

"Good." I pull her so that she's on top of me and she squeals with laughter. "So it's settled. The rules are in tact."

"Mhmm." Mikaela wiggles against me, her legs now straddling my sides. "Yes, they are."

She grins when I roll my eyes and brush my fingers up her sides, pulling her t-shirt up with my movement, and her eyes drop to my lips.

"So," I whisper, "rule number one stays in place. That's a definite. But did we ever settle on what, exactly, rule one covered."

She gulps as my fingers dance over her skin, over the thin lace of her bra, and caress the parts of her I can't see.

"Erm I think -" Her voice is thin and her breathing hitches as my thumb slides beneath the delicate material and brushes against her nipple. "Clothes stay - clothes stay on."

I pull her down to me as she speaks, my lips skimming across her jaw, and she squirms against me.

"Clothes on," she repeats, "or we won't stop."

"Hmm." She tastes of jasmine and honey and salt, and my tongue sweeps over her throat before I kiss and suck at her skin.

"Ben." It's a whisper - just a whisper - and my groin aches in response.

Mikaela pulls my hands from beneath her shirt as she sits up and I push up so that we're face to face, twisting slightly to accommodate for this new angle.

Her eyes are burning in the darkness, liquid emerald, and I am enraptured.

Her lips crash into mine, carnal and untamed, and her fingers weave into my hair, tugging gently as I groan. She knows it drives me crazy when she does that. Feeling her wrapped around me, it's intoxicating. My hands grip her hips, pushing her against the growing erection straining against my jeans, and she gasps against my lips.

I shift again, lifting her slightly as I move, laying her down on the couch and crawling over her. My fingers move from her hips to her hands, moving them so that they're above her head. Breaking the kiss again I move to her neck, nipping and sucking as I push against her and she moans.

Holy shit.

She moans and I am *gone*.

I'm giddy with anticipation, holding her beneath me, my body pressed against hers with the knowledge we can't go further, desperately seeking friction against her.

She twists her wrists in my hold as I pin her with one hand, the other travelling down her body and gripping her waist as her back arches into my touch. Every panting breath that leaves her lips spurs me further. Every touch is frantic, like teenagers in the dark, and my entire body feels like it's surging with electricity. My fingers slip beneath her shirt again, skimming over that scar I've seen once before and her breathing falters.

"Stop," she whispers. The urgency in her voice is like a knife in my gut, and I pull away, releasing her hands and pushing up so that I'm kneeling before her.

"I'm sorry." The words leave my lips in a rush and she shakes her head.

"No." She closes her eyes as she lies there, her hands coming down to rest on her heaving chest. "I'm sorry. It's just - it's just if we carry on I don't know if I'll stop."

I push out a tight chuckle and she smiles slightly.

"Okay." I move away from her and her eyes open as she pushes up on her elbows.

"So." She blinks a few times, as if trying to banish whatever thoughts are darkening those emerald greens. "We have an early day tomorrow. We should sleep."

"Oh yeah. My eight o'clock." I raise a brow at her.

"Oops?" She grins as she moves to her feet, pulling down her shirt and walking away from me.

"You know I'm going to have to make up a client now."

She pauses at the stairs up to her bed. "No, we'll pick someone from this weeks scheduled meetings and tell Jamie they rescheduled. Simple."

I shake my head with a sigh.

"You coming up here or?" She slips out of her jeans, pulling a strained groan from my lips.

"Put on something that covers you up and I'll be there once I've successfully pictured anything other than this image right here." I gesture to her in all of her glory and she grins, moving back to me quickly and grabbing hold of my hand.

"Sorry, Ben." She pulls me gently and I get to my feet. "I'll be sleeping like this tonight. You're just going to have to deal with it."

Whatever noise just left my lips was alarmingly close to a whimper and I breathe deeply, following the tiny tornado of a woman who has so easily pulled me in.

Does she not realise that *dealing with it* is exactly what rule number one prohibits?

I strip down quickly as she climbs beneath the sheets and reaches for the bedside lamp, plunging us into darkness. Crawling in beside her, I can feel every vein in my body thrum with desire, forcing me to take a breath as she wraps her arm around me and nestles her face against my chest.

"I'll have to leave here by six to get home and changed before work," I whisper. "You can either come with me or I can come back and drive you in?"

Mik laughs against my chest and I feel her push her feet against my calf, the chill of her skin jolting against me slightly.

"I'm not getting up before six, Ben. And I can get to the office myself."

Chapter Nineteen

Ben

I press soft kisses against Mikaela's lips as she stretches beneath the sheets and I lean over her. Her eyes flicker open, a small smile ghosting the corner of her mouth, when she reaches out to me and bunches my t-shirt in her fingers.

"Morning." Her voice is thick with sleep as she pulls me in to her again.

"Morning, beautiful." I linger against her lips, my fingers splaying over her side. "I'm just leaving. I didn't want to go without telling you."

Mikaela pouts slightly as she closes her eyes again, her fingers still holding on to me as I try to straighten up.

"Stay." Her demand is undercut by the smirk she's wearing.

"Wish I could, but we both have to be in the office in two hours." I laugh when her fingers drop from my shirt and she tries to push herself up to glance at the clock on the wall.

"Ben. It's five thirty." She grunts as she throws herself back against the pillow. "You said six."

I chuckle as I feel her palm against my chest, half-heartedly pushing me away from her. "I said I need to leave by six."

"Then leave," she grumbles, rolling away from me. "I'll see you at work."

I push myself to my feet where I'm kneeling beside her bed, and grin as she bats me away.

"I'll have coffee ready when you get there."

She's already half asleep when she responds. "I knew there was a reason to keep you around, Haston."

I let myself out with a smile I can't shake.

Mikaela

I rummage through the drawers for what I want: a cherry red, square cut dress with a pencil skirt to my knees that Max insisted I bought. When I'd tried it on I felt ridiculous - far too done up for work - but he'd insisted it looked corporate enough for the office and good enough to ensnare any man's heart. It's the second part I focus on as I pull it from the dresser.

Telling Max I'd finished things with Josh was easy. He'd been relieved, proud even, when I said I didn't want to feel the way he made me feel, but it left Max with a mission and it's one I don't need him to play in: finding me someone good.

As I slip the material over the white lace bra and panties he'd also insisted I needed, his name flashes over the phone on the bed. I grab it quickly as I move to the mirror, putting him on speaker, before reaching for my zipper.

"Mikaela Wilcox." Max's voice is about an octave higher than usual and I find my blood thumping with excitement almost instantly. I love that he does that.

"What?" I grin as I push my hair back and bend down to fish my black heels from under the bed. "What's happened?"

"You're coming to mine tonight, so bring pyjamas to work."

I can hear the clatter of pans and the noise of someone else in the background.

"Why? Who's with you right now?" I can't stop the grin that crosses my lips as I hear a semi-familiar voice whispering about the heat being too high.

"Never you mind right now, Miss Wilcox." Max is definitely ginning too. "I'll fill you in on everything tonight. My sister's in town for once and I want you to meet her."

Ben is sitting at my desk with a lazy grin and a coffee in hand as the elevator doors sweep open and I feel a warm blush creeping up my chest as his eyes rove over my body. His gaze lingers on my chest for a moment too long as I move towards him and place my bag of clothes at the edge of my desk. I push his feet off of the glass surface and he places his free hand on my waist immediately, pulling me over to him and into his lap.

"Ben," I chastise, laughing as he nuzzles his face into my neck and inhales. "Anyone could walk in and see us."

"Nope." He's grinning as he presses a kiss into the skin at the base of my throat. "Friday is staff meeting morning, remember. No one makes it in until nine on the dot on meeting mornings." He pulls back to look at me. "I like your hair like this."

I'm pretty sure my face matches the color of my dress as he catches a lock of my hair between his fingers and tugs it gently. I'd stood in front of my mirror for a full forty minutes pulling the straightening iron through the knots of curls that I usually let hang wild and free, until every kink and inch of frizz was smooth and straight. It had taken longer than I thought it would, but seeing the way his eyes run over me now, it was worth it.

"Thank you." I lean in and kiss him quickly before glancing back to the elevator. "I'll do it more often."

Ben shakes his head, his brow knitting together as he looks at me. "You don't need to do that, Mik. I like it when you leave it natural too. It wasn't me telling you to change."

My stomach lurches a little. He's right. I was offering to do it because he liked it, not because I felt that it would benefit me in any way. Was that who I had allowed myself to become? The girl who would change because *he* wanted me to?

"Oh." I get to my feet and move around the chair, perching against the bookshelf behind him as I try to sort through my thoughts. "Okay."

Ben watches me carefully as he swivels in my chair.

"Talk," he demands simply.

"What?"

"You're being weird, talk to me."

My chest aches. How can he know me so well in such a stupidly short time? I plaster on a smile and shake my head.

"I'm okay, I just had an early wake up call," I tease.

Ben chuckles and reaches for the coffee placed on my desk, handing it to me with a soft smile.

"I'm not sorry about that," he jokes and I grin.

"Me neither."

Ben's eyes drift to my bag and I take a sip from the cup. Smooth and silky, it warms me instantly and I sigh happily.

"What's with the bag?" He looks up at me with a soft smile that tells me it's okay and, for the first time in a long time, I don't feel like I have to hide my plans.

"I'm going to Max's after work. He has gossip and a sister I'm dying to meet." I grin when Ben smiles warmly at me. "We're going to eat our body weight in pasta and talk a whole lot of shit. You know, the usual stuff: hair, fashion, *boys*."

He raises his eyebrows and I sip on my coffee again.

"Boys, huh?" Ben's tone is playfully possessive and my stomach flips. "And what exactly are you telling him about boys?"

"Oh, I don't know." I cross my legs as Ben's eyes trace over the dress again. "I could tell him I'm painfully single." A flash of annoyance darkens his eyes and the flipping turns into a full somersault. "Or I could tell him I'm seeing a mystery man. Someone stupidly good looking and suave."

"Stupidly good looking?" Ben smirks and I stand up, brushing down the skirt of my dress in a deliberate display of preening. "Is that all there is to this guy?"

"Oh no." I lean around him, pressing my hip against his arm as my fingers swipe over the keys of the computer and fire up the screen for the day. "He's also protective and infuriatingly charming. And then there's his soft side. Now that's something really special."

I feel his fingers skim the hem of my dress as I reach past him to the mouse.

"Soft? That doesn't sound right." His voice is husky and as I glance to his crotch it occurs to me that right now very little of Ben is soft.

"You know." I glance up to his eyes and am met with a molten ocean of blue. "You have a very dirty mind, Mr Haston."

Ben grins as he grips my waist and pulls me towards him.

"Is that another trait of this mystery man? A dirty mind?"

He pulls me into his lap again and I wiggle against him, pulling a groan from his lips as he presses a heated kiss into my shoulder.

"Oh definitely. It's intoxicating." I twist my head to the side, searching for his lips, and am rewarded with a tender kiss as his fingers splay over my stomach.

"You know," Ben chuckles, "I think this mystery man is stupidly lucky."

The laugh that breaks through the space around us sends my heart into my throat and I jump to my feet, knocking Ben slightly, making him cry out in a grunt of pain.

"I don't think he's much of a mystery," Max cackles and my face floods with heat.

"Shit." Ben groans again and I glance back to him before looking back to Max.

"This isn't -"

"Mik. I love you, you know that?" Max is wiping tears from his eyes as he laughs and I try not to smile. This is definitely not supposed to be funny. "Thank you for making a great day even better."

"Max, you can't say anything."

"Oh don't worry." He glances to Ben, who's now standing behind me with a look of pure terror plastered across his face. "Your secret is safe with me. I just wish I hadn't heard like half of that."

"Thank you," I breathe out a sigh of relief and Ben's hands find their way to my hips again.

"You're early today, Kingford?" His voice is gruff but kind.

"Yeah, I wanted to get a head start on some admin so that we can leave on time today." Max nods to me and grins. "And now we're definitely leaving on time, because I have so many questions." His attention drifts to the elevator as a green light illuminates the arrow above the doors and his eyes widen. "Oh and that's your brother, so you two might want to find some distance."

Ben's hands drop from my waist immediately and he places a quick kiss on my cheek before turning towards his office. At the last minute he turns and smiles at Max; a warm, friendly kind of smile that melts me on the spot.

"Thanks, Kingford."

"I need details." Max pulls his key from the door as he pushes it open and steps aside. He asked about Ben for the entire cab ride and I kept my lips sealed, unsure of what I could or couldn't say. "Come on, Mik. Please. It's Baby Blue!"

"What's baby blue?" The woman on Max's couch pushes herself up on her elbows and grins at us both as she throws her book to the side. Her smile is wide and spills with energy as she gets to her feet and opens her arms wide. It's Max's smile in a female face, and I feel like I know her in an instant. "You must be Mikaela. I'm Sephy. I can't believe I finally get to meet you!"

She wraps me in a warm embrace and I find myself dropping my bag to hold her. She smells like cinnamon and apple, and a memory of Christmas with my mother stirs in my chest, squeezing my heart.

"Hi," I breathe.

"Mik has a man." Max practically shouts as he scoops up my bag and I glare at him over his sister's shoulder. "And he's gorgeous."

"Oh," Sephy laughs as she pulls out of our hug and holds onto my shoulders. "So Baby Blue's a guy?"

I nod guiltily.

"Well he's one lucky guy to get hold of a beauty like you!" She grins with a wink and I hear the nervousness of my laughter. "Max, make your guest a drink. Mikaela, I'm sure you've got something a little more comfortable than this dress - which I want by the way - so go get changed. The bathroom's the second door on the left. And then, you're telling us everything."

I nod as I grab my bag from the couch and fish out my phone. I dial quickly as I step into the bathroom.

He answers on the second ring.

"What do I tell him?" The words spill from my lips as soon as I hear him breathing and Ben laughs.

"One second, J." He emphasises the name and my heart spikes. "Yeah, it's my girl."

Jamie says something I can't hear - something I don't care about - because all I can hear are those words.

My girl... My girl. Mygirlmygirlmygirl. It's like it's on a loop in my head and my heart patters with the sound of it.

"No," Ben laughs. "You're not meeting her any time soon. I like this one. Don't need you scaring her off."

The chatter behind him disappears and I hear the distinct noise of traffic.

"What do you want to tell him?"

Is he amused? He sounds amused.

"Excuse me," I counter, "my question can wait. Your girl?"

Ben laughs again and I can picture the way he pushes his hair back as he glances back to the group.

"Yeah. My girl. Is that okay?"

I perch on the edge of the sink and press my fingers to my lips as my voice comes out on a whisper. "Yeah, it's okay."

"Good." Ben chuckles and my chest tightens. "Now that's covered, let's circle back to your question. What do you want to tell him?"

"Everything." The word is weighted and I am absolutely terrified of the truth behind it. I want to tell Max every single detail, from the moment I stumbled home to find him on my doorstep to waking up to him this morning. But telling him everything means telling him about Josh, and I realise - with a somewhat painful ache - that I want to tell *someone* all of it.

Ben is silent on the other end of the line.

"Is that okay?"

"Mikaela." He sighs and I close my eyes. "Of course it's okay. I'm glad, actually, that you want to talk about it. It's good."

I sag with relief and listen to Ben breathing.

"Mik?"

"Yeah?"

"Is it too much to say I miss you?" He sounds vulnerable and I smile to myself. "I hardly got to see you at all today."

"The feeling is stupidly mutual, Haston."

"Good." There's a light sound in his laugh and I cling to it.

"I should go." I admit. "Have fun dodging questions about me tonight."

Ben groans loudly as I pull out the sweats and t-shirt I'd brought with me.

"Enjoy talking about me all night," he counters.

"I will."

The silence stretches out between us and I find that I don't want to stop the giggle that is bubbling in my chest.

"Goodbye, Ben."

"Bye, Mik."

Sephy shakes her head as she leans forwards to refill my wine glass for the third time since I started my story and I focus on her as she moves.

She is beautiful. Her skin is a rich brown, lighter than her brother's but beautiful in the depths of warmth in the tone. Her nose has a spattering of freckles, slightly deeper in their darkness than the rest of her face, and when she smiles - even with a hint of sadness - her eyes crinkle around the edges and both cheeks pucker with tiny dimples. Her hair, worn naturally in tight curls, frames her face with a softness that smooths her features into something entirely comforting.

When she turns to face me, she gives me a warm smile and lifts her glass to mine.

"To getting the fuck away from the bad guys." She clinks our glasses together and glances towards Max.

His face is stone. Gone is his easy smile and his warm laugh. Gone is the playful glimmer in his eyes. It's all cold now.

"Max?" I reach out to him and he takes my hand instinctively. "You okay?"

"I hate him, Mikaela." His voice is broken and lifeless. "I hate him so much."

"I know." My chest aches for him. "But I'm glad it happened."

"What?" He recoils from my words as his face contorts in confusion. "How can you be glad about that, Mik? Josh hurt you. He *really* hurt you."

I nod slowly as I glance to Sephy. She smiles in understanding and I swallow.

"I'm glad, because if it hadn't happened, I would never have asked Ben stay that night." I shrug and he closes his eyes.

"Are you okay, Mik?" He huffs and I sniffle.
When did I start crying again?
"Yeah, I'm okay."

Max fell asleep over an hour ago and his soft snores punctuate the air around us. Sephy glances over to me as she gets to her feet, piling up plates on the table and reaching for the empty glasses.

"Let me." I push to my feet and pick up the glasses and the empty bottle, making my way to the kitchen quietly. Sephy follows.

Under the bright light of the kitchen we move as a team, washing and drying plates and glasses after sorting leftovers into plastic containers and putting them in the fridge. For a while theres nothing but the clatter of plates and the soft sounds of water and quiet breathing. We move slowly - taking our time, lost in our thoughts - until Sephy speaks.

"So, Max says you're a writer?" Her voice has a soft lilt that lifts at the end of each sentence.

"He shouldn't say that," I laugh. "I've never written anything to completion. I just keep notebooks with silly ideas."

Sephy chuckles as she reaches into the cupboard under the breakfast bar and slides the plates away. "Don't undersell yourself, Mikaela. There are plenty of people out there to do that for you."

I grin, watching her move around the space, taking items from me as I dry them and slotting them into their various homes.

"Are you working on anything at the moment?"

I nod as I bite my lip. I haven't even told Max about my newest project, it all feels too fresh and too new. I only started it a week ago but even now, as I stand talking to a relative stranger, names and faces and stories scratch at the surface of my mind - itching to be brought to life. It's the most excited I've been to sit and write in a long time.

"It's new and probably won't turn into anything." I shrug.

"But?" She prompts me with a nudge of her hip.

"But I'm excited about it," I admit.

"Tell me about it." Sephy perches on the counter and gestures for me to do the same.

"It's historical romance - World War Two - and it tells the story of a soldier and a nurse." I feel myself coming to life as I think about the characters that had come to life under my fingertips this past week. "They've got the world against them but somehow it works. Somehow they keep finding each other, even through all their pain and suffering, and I just - I haven't been this excited to write something since..." I stop talking, my hands going clammy and my chest squeezing to the point of pain.

Sephy nods solemnly as she eyes me and suddenly her gaze feels sharp, it feels seeing.

"Mikaela." She speaks softly. "You can tell me to shut up if I'm wrong, but I work with a lot of women who have gone through..." She sighs as she looks at me. "Mikaela, I think they're a little like you."

I swallow as she looks at me. There's a knowledge in her dark eyes that doesn't feel pitying, or judgemental. It just feels aware. And awareness is terrifying.

"It's okay." She smiles softly as my hands tremble and I knot them together on my lap. "I'm not going to ask about it, or talk about who he was, but something about the way you spoke about Josh - it just struck me as being almost familiar or expected to you - and I just want you to know that it's okay. And I'm not going to tell Max anything, I love my brother but he doesn't handle these things well. But, you should know how incredible you are for surviving it - if I am right - for finding something outside of it. Okay?"

Staring at this woman who knows far more about me than I have ever shared, I feel my fear shrinking a little. I nod as I take a deep breath.

"I haven't felt this excited to write something since Matthew." Saying it is cathartic.

Sephy nods and smiles and I feel a little less alone in the truth of it all.

Chapter Twenty

Ben

"So you're actually serious about this girl?" Jamie glances from me to Xavier - a friend of Jamie's from college - and then Asher, approaching from the bar. The two men who, out of convenience, took the two free slots in my list of top three people to drink with. One of them is getting bumped for Mikaela. When I nod, Jamie actually looks shocked, like me settling down is the same impossible concept it was when we were idiots in college. "Well, it's settled. We need to meet her then."

"No." I hope Jamie can't hear the hysteria in my laugh. "You're not meeting her any time soon." I take a drink. "I like this one. Don't need any of you scaring her off."

"So, you're really not going to tell us anything about her?" Asher places four beer bottles on the table, nudging me with his elbow as he slips back into his seat. He seems to be taking my silence on the matter as a personal insult, choosing to hound me between each round for details on what she looks like, what she sounds like, where I met her. You name it, Asher wants to know it.

"Nope." I pop the p and finish the end of my last drink. A decision has been made. Asher is being bumped for Mikaela, the nosy shit.

"Come on, Ben." He turns to me with a wicked glint in his eye that tells me he is fishing for more than just a name and I roll my eyes. "She hot? Like on a scale of one to that old camp councillor I showed you."

"First of all," Jamie interrupts, rubbing his temples as if Asher's voice is piercing straight into his brain, "you're a pig. Secondly, that camp councillor you spent the best of three years obsessing over thought of you as an irritating kid and nothing more. It's borderline creepy that you still reference to her, Ash."

I snort in agreement as Xavier laughs. Xavier Russo is the quiet one of our little group - business focused and way too tightly wound ninety percent of the time. I look over to him, painfully aware that his silence has been exasperated these last few months by his own personal issues, and am met with an easy smile. At least he seems okay tonight.

"Aren't you the least bit curious?" Ash continues to press and I groan loudly. "I mean, Ben, with all due respect, you haven't had a girl in what? Five, six years? And when was your last hook up? This development is important."

"Asher, I've dated," I grunt. "I just haven't told you,"

"Yeah, we all know you've *dated*." Jamie grins, looking down at his beer. "But Ash is right. Whoever she is, she's gotta be pretty special to have you wrapped up before any of us even knew she existed."

Xavier nods thoughtfully.

"You must be relieved?" Xavier turns to Jamie and I freeze.

"Why would he be relieved?" Asher voices a question I know the answer to before Jamie even looks at me.

"Up until two days ago Jamie was sure Ben was trying to bang his sister." Xavier's laugh is easy and it makes me feel sick. Almost as sick as Asher's next sentence.

"Wait. Mik's back in town? She single? *Fuck*. What I'd do for a shot at that." He's shuffling forwards in his seat.

Jamie glares at him. I do too.

"Shut the fuck up, Asher."

Was that me? Well, shit.

Jamie is still glaring at Asher, but I watch his jaw clench with my words.

"What?" Asher holds his beer out to Xavier to tap. Xavier just shakes his head.

"Sometimes," Xav mutters, "you're a dickhead, Ash."

"What? Oh come on," Asher laughs. "Mik is hot in that good girl, knows she's hot but doesn't give a shit kind of way."

"To repeat Ben's sentiments," Jamie spits through gritted teeth, "shut the fuck up, Asher."

"Well." Xavier huffs out half a laugh and raises his brows at me. "This is all a little awkward now, isn't it?"

I grunt in response, my mood completely decimated by Asher's stupid fucking mouth. We all know what Ash is like with women. He needs to stay the fuck away from Mik.

"Ben?" Asher turns to face me and I steady my breath. I cannot hit Asher Jones. *I cannot hit Asher Jones.* "A bit defensive of Miss Wilcox there, no?"

I open my mouth to speak but Jamie's voice comes out first. "Ben's known Mik as long as he's known me. They might as well be family. So he can be as defensive as he likes when assholes like you are objectifying her."

There's a brick where my stomach is supposed to be.

When I look over at Jamie he isn't looking at me, or Asher. He's getting to his feet and walking away.

"J?" I shove Asher out of my way, ignoring when he swears at me, and move to follow.

"It's fine, Ben. I'm gonna head home before I smack one of my closest friends for being an ass."

"You sure?" We're at the door and Jamie is shrugging into his jacket.

"Yeah." He forces a smile when he looks at me. "Seriously, it's all good. Thanks for jumping in. And I want to meet this mystery girl soon, okay? Might need to keep Asher away from her though." He chuckles as he runs a hand over his face.

Okay. So this is guilt; a gnawing, nauseating, scratching sensation in the very pit of my stomach that seems to creep its way up into my throat. *Nice*.

"Yeah." I nod. "Soon."

Mikaela

My body aches as I stretch my arms above my head and hit something soft. Jolting upright, I whip my head around to face the person above me and laugh when I find Max sprawled out against the top of the bed. At some point in the night I must have shifted to curl into a ball directly in the middle of the double in his spare room, and at some other point Max clearly decided to climb in with me.

"Max?" I prod him gently in his side and he grunts in return. "Max. Wake up."

"No. We don't have work today. Let me sleep."

I laugh again and push him roughly.

"Max." My voice is whiney and he opens his eyes. "Whatcha doing?"

Something in the grogginess of an unexpected wake up seems to shift in his eyes and Max takes in his surroundings.

"Oh." He smiles a little impishly and I grin. There it is; my best friend is still hiding in there. "I thought you might want company?" He's sheepish as he shuffles along the edge of the pillows he's hogging with his whole body.

"Is that so?"

"Yep." He nods, pushing himself to sit up. "Totally didn't lay there worrying about you until I decided I needed to make sure you weren't alone and upset."

My grin softens and I crawl up the bed beside him, resting my head on his shoulder and settling down next to him. "You're a sweetheart, you know that?"

He weaves his fingers in with mine. "I try."

"So," I clear my throat of the thickness of sleep. "What did you have to tell me yesterday?"

"What?"

"You invited me over to gossip and I derailed it all with my drama."

"Mikaela Wilcox, you did no such thing." His grin is clear in his voice and I nudge him gently.

"Spill your guts, Kingford." I laugh when he groans.

"You've been spending too much time with that boyfriend of yours."

My blush is furious and burns beneath my skin as I scramble for a change in topic.

"What was barman Alex doing in your kitchen yesterday morning?"

"What?" He pulls back to look at me. "How did you -?"

"I recognised his voice from his sage advice that lovely afternoon." I grin when he rolls his eyes. "So Alex, huh?"

"Yep." Max shrugs in feigned nonchalance but his eyes are shining and I stifle a laugh.

"That's all I'm getting? A yep?"

"Yep." He grunts when I elbow him a little harder and the door cracks open.

"Morning guys." Sephy pokes her head into the room and smiles over to us.

"Morning." Max pats the bed and she laughs, swanning into the room in wooly shorts and a crop top. She's wearing a long, thick cardigan that hangs off of her arms where she hasn't pulled it over her shoulders and in the early morning light she looks well rested and beautifully calm. Somehow I think she might always just look beautiful and calm.

"What are we talking about?" She jumps into a free spot at the end of the bed and stretches out.

"Max's new man." I wink at my best friend when he shakes his head.

Between my giggles and Sephy's dramatic sighing, Max groans and tries to roll away from me.

"You mean the hunky, tattooed man I found in the kitchen yesterday morning?" Sephy grabs at his ankle and I giggle.

"That very one." I nod as Max grunts and Sephy squeals.

"He's pretty hot, Max." She props her chin into her hands as she pushes up on her elbows. "Does he have siblings?"

Max grins and Sephy shrugs.

"Weird, Sephy." His laugh is infectious and soon the three of us are curled into fits of laughter and whispers of gossip.

Chapter Twenty-one

Ben

Well, shit.

This is hell.

This is hellfire with a side of sinful torture that burns my veins and has me shifting uncomfortably in my seat as Mikaela moves around the space handing out invites.

Do not stare. Do not stare. Yep. You're staring. And possibly drooling. Smooth.

Mikaela ducks her head as she moves between the desks, ignoring the glances she's getting from every straight male in the room, and placing the small black cards into peoples outstretched hands, and I can't take my eyes off of her.

The electric blue of her shirt is striking against her skin and the material ripples over her in silky waves. She's buttoned the blouse up almost fully and still, the way it clings to her body, it's incredible. Her hair is parted to the side and tucked behind her ear, easy waves falling past her shoulder and down her back and as she walks my eyes trace over her hips and the perfectly peachy curve of her ass. Those trousers... *Shit.*

Clearing his throat, Jamie gets to his feet and claps his hands together, the way he does every week to start the meeting, and I tear my eyes away from her to pretend I'm paying attention.

She continues her circle of the room in silence, smiling over to Max and a few of the other assistants who whisper to her as she passes.

"Okay, so as you all know," Jamie begins, "Wilcox Writings has officially been in business for five years next Saturday. It's been a long road to get here, a lot of set backs, a lot of personal pain and discovery, and a hell of a lot of patience on your part, so, to thank you all, we're throwing a party."

There's a cheer around the room, the assistants whooping and clapping as their bosses roll their eyes, and I glance up as Mikaela takes the open seat beside where Jamie stands. My eyes run over her again as a small grin tugs at the corner of my lips.

She's wearing the heels I bought her last week. The same heels she swore were too much and that I shouldn't have brought. The flash of red beneath her a beautiful reminder that my girl looks good in designer. She looks good in anything.

"Of course every employee has a plus one should they wish to use it and I am so grateful that you all put this into your calendar when Ben and I came up with this hare-brained scheme weeks ago -"

"When you came up with it," I interject with a grin. "I will not be held accountable for anything that goes wrong. I simply signed the cash away."

The blonde from my first week giggles and bats her eyelashes at me, seemingly over my bad manners, and I watch Mikaela straighten a little in her seat; flicking her hair over her shoulder.

"Anyway," Jamie laughs, "there will be no industry talk. Of course our authors have all been invited, as well as the freelance designers and those we call in regularly, but this is a celebration. For all of us."

His eyes drift to his sister and she nods solemnly.

Of course. Five years.

"Do you want to talk about it?"

I'd followed Mikaela into the office kitchen half an hour after the meeting ended and now I'm blocking the door with my body so that no one can come in after us, and she's fidgeting with the coffee machine.

"There's not much to say about it, Ben." She smiles to herself and shakes her head, before reaching up to the shelf where the office staff store a stupid amount of coffee cups.

"Five years isn't a long time, Mik, but it is a big milestone." I move a step closer as she sighs and turns to me.

"I'm fine, Ben, really." She presses her lips into a smile and I nod. "I'm not avoiding talking about it. If I need to, I promise I will. And it's not even the anniversary yet. We've still got two and a half months until I break down over it, okay?"

I roll my eyes and step closer again. "Mikaela."

"Benjamin." She furrows her brow in her best impression of me and I can't help the smile that breaks through my defences.

"I could take you to see her tomorrow?" Hope dances in my chest. Since that morning at the cemetery I've wanted to return. Elizabeth Wilcox was family to me and I miss her. But I also know how difficult it is for Mik to let me close to her like that. "If you would want that?"

Mik's face softens as she steps forwards, placing a hand on my chest and leaning in quickly. I bend down to her height, trapping her lips for the shortest of moments and sighing as I close my eyes.

"I'd like that." She leans against me and I wrap an arm around her. "Thank you."

Mikaela

The week passed in a blur. If I wasn't at work I was with Jamie, hashing out every last detail of this party, so it's no surprise that just four hours before the big event I'm sprawled across my brother's couch, coffee in hand and a guest list the length of my arm.

"I notice a few names that aren't colleagues on here, JimJam," I chastise.

"Yep." He grins over his shoulder as he puts the last of the dishes in the dishwasher and I look back at the list.

"And Stu is happy to work the door?" I check off the box on my to do list that tells me to finalise the guest list, because the party planner Jamie hired insisted Jamie did that part. And he asked me.

"In exchange for advance reader copies of the next hundred books we publish, yeah."

I grin as I picture Stu, the burly doorman who spends most of his working hours hiding in a corner on his phone, with the next big romance novel Jamie is pushing out in a couple of months.

"Fair trade," I muse.

"So," Jamie throws himself over the back of the couch, nearly knocking my laptop off of me in the process and slouches into the cushions. "No one to add to the list, huh?"

"What?" I furrow my brow and my brother stares at me.

"No date? No plus one?"

I groan as I close my eyes and shut the laptop. "No, Jamie."

"Okay." He raises his eyebrows as he shakes his head. "Then I should warn you."

My eyes snap open and my blood pumps through my veins at an alarming speed. "Warn me about what?"

"Asher's coming." Jamie pulls out his phone as he murmurs, no doubt avoiding my glare.

I grimace. Asher Jones is a thorn in my side: an old friend of Jamie's who, despite actually being quite sweet, has a way of looking at me that makes me want to punch him. Regularly.

"I know. He was one of the non-colleagues I was referring to."

"He agreed to sort the catering." Jamie justifies before his face screws up in anticipation of my reaction. "And he knows you're single."

"Why the fuck does he know that?" I kick at my brother playfully and he grins a little.

"A few weeks ago, when we were out for drinks, we were winding Ben up about his new girl and Xav mentioned you and then Asher just wouldn't drop it."

"Oh great." I roll my eyes as I push to my feet and grab my keys from the side.

"Be nice, Mik." Jamie tries to smile at me as I flip him off. "Asher's a dick, but he's genuinely harmless. And you know he's had a thing for you for a while."

"Yeah well he can keep his *thing* far away from me," I grunt as I swing his door open and halt. My heart does a little squeeze before breaking into a happy sprint and I remind myself I cannot touch the man standing right in front of me right now. "Hey."

Ben grins as he looks over my shoulder to what appears to be an empty room. Jamie is still hidden behind cushions and my mouth is dry. He has a garment bag slung over his shoulder and his silly little sideways smile that makes my stomach melt into a puddle of warmth and wanting as his eyes shift over me lazily. How, when I spent an hour on a video call with him this morning, have I missed the blue of his eyes so much today?

"Hey." He winks as he reaches towards me, angling our bodies so the door covers the way his fingers hook into the belt loop of my jeans. "Your brother about?"

"On the couch." Both an answer and a warning. "You're getting ready here?"

"I am." His eyes flick to my lips as his fingers move from my belt loop to the edge of my jeans and skim over my stomach. "You?"

"No." I pray to every deity out there not to let my voice get breathy on me now. "I'm actually heading out now. Max and I have appointments and then we're getting ready at mine."

Ben nods thoughtfully, before glancing over to the couch again and frowning. Jamie still hasn't emerged but that doesn't mean he isn't listening.

"Cool." His attempt to sound indifferent is adorably unbelievable and I fight back a smile. "Well, I guess I'll see you at the party."

"I guess so." I take a step around him and out of the door without a glance at where my brother is, gasping quietly when I feel a firm hand grip my waist and pull me in behind the door.

His lips brush against my neck for just a fraction of a second as he inhales and then he's gone, his laughter booming in my brother's living room as he waltzes in like we weren't just being brazenly obvious in the hallway outside my brother's home.

I lean against the wall as the door closes behind me and take a deep breath. My legs quiver and my heart rate won't settle as my fingers brush over the spot his lips had pressed against and my mind swims in the scent of

Ben. The way heat pools between my legs just with the simplest of touches tells me one thing: we've been slow. Slow has worked. Slow has been good for us. And now? Slow is going to kill me.

"Max?" I shimmy into the emerald dress with a groan as Max digs around in my bathroom cupboard. "Max, come here please."

"Yes?" He pokes his head out of the bathroom and a short cackle bursts from my lips. Beneath his eyes are gold patches, my gold patches I might add, and he has a frown that doesn't fit his face.

"What are you doing in there?"

"What do you think I'm doing?" He bites back, striding out of the bathroom and over to where I stand beside my bed. "I'm seeing how many skincare products you have so I can look my best for Alex. Obviously."

"Didn't you bring your own stuff?" I roll my eyes when he ducks back into the bathroom and more rummaging noises sound out.

"Yes, but you have the good stuff and best friends share their good moisturiser. Right?"

"Of course," I laugh. "Do me a favour and come zip me up please?"

I twist as I turn away from him, my hair still pinned to my head in ridiculously large rollers the woman at the salon insisted needed to stay in until the very last minute, and my make up only half complete. My eyes need shadow and a coating of mascara, and I still haven't decided on nude or red lipstick, but it's hard to choose the perfect one when your body is a mass of bundled nerves.

"Oh my *God*." Max's words leave his lips as a rushed breath.

"What?" My stomach drops. It's been over a month since that night. My back has healed. There are no marks left. Are there?

"Mikaela freaking Wilcox." He lets out a low whistle as my brain kicks back into action and a blush the same shade of red as the lipstick sitting on my vanity spreads over my skin. "Is that -? Are you wearing -? Shit. Haston is going to combust."

I shake my head furiously. "Haston is not going to see it."

Max grunts and I cringe.

"We still haven't - we aren't - listen, I'm wearing it for me, okay. Not him."

It's true. Rule number one has stayed firmly in place for the whole time we've been doing this - whatever this is - and for over a month it has been pure torture. Every other day we're tangled in each other's limbs on my bed - his body pressed against mine, my breath hard to find as I drown in the taste of his skin - but we've kept it strictly clothes on. Much to my dismay. And as far as any recent conversations have gone, there doesn't seem to be any intention to break rule number one just yet. Ben thinks it's too soon. I think his shirts would look much better if they weren't covering up that ridiculously hard chest and those chiseled abs. We're at an impasse... So yes, I put on lingerie tonight that has the power to drive him wild. But no, I do not think he will see it.

"Okay, well, let me state for the record," Max chuckles as he pulls the zipper up and the shimmering green fabric hugs to my skin, " I am all for you wearing it for yourself, but he should definitely get to see it too."

I laugh when he places his hands on my hips and swivels me around to face the mirror.

"So let's get you dolled up and ready for a night we won't forget, yeah?" Max kisses my cheek and I swat him away, grinning like a fool as I run my eyes over my reflection. I don't look half bad.

Chapter Twenty-two

Ben

I have to hand it to the bombshell brunette hanging on to every word Jamie says: she is one hell of a party planner.

When Jamie organised a meeting with her three days after he'd suggested this party of his I'd known it was more than just a celebration. She'd been so nervous, all stammers and clumsy hands, as she'd explained her ideas for tonight and I'd sat watching how Jamie soothed her with little nods, kind smiles and words of encouragement. The man is smitten.

The conference hall of the fanciest hotel in town seemed like a no brainer for a big bash and this *friend* of Jamie's, Emma, managed to get it down to half price because the general manager owed her a favour. Now it looks nothing like a conference hall. The white walls have been covered with sheer billowing material, thin and shimmering with hundreds of lights hidden behind them, and servers walk around the room - moving around tables and crowds of employees, authors and agents - with silver trays of tiny tasters and champagne flutes. At the back of the room a DJ stands behind his set-up, mixing songs I recognise with music I haven't heard before, and watching as people gather in small clusters around the space. To the left are wide French doors, closed for now but sure to be propped open as the space fills out and more air is needed.

Our small celebration turned into a guest list of over one hundred people thanks to plus ones and Jamie's inability to say no to our two idiotic friends, who right at this moment are barrelling through the open doors and whistling as they spin to look around.

Even Xavier looks excited and it's hard to get more than a grunt from him these days.

"Shit." Asher grins as he jabs at Xavier's side. "This is fancy."

I watch as Jamie takes a deep breath and shakes his head at something Emma says. He glances around before pressing a quick kiss against her cheek and moving away from her, towards our two friends. Emma watches him intently and Ash gives her a once over. This is going to be a long night if he decides to be a prick with the party planner.

"Guys!" Jamie's smile is award winning as he pushes between the two men and places a firm hand on each of their shoulders. "I'm glad you could make it. Bar is in the corner there, servers have champagne for now and there's food circulating."

I push away from the group of designers I'm currently surrounded by, excusing myself with a quick nod, and make my way over to the three of them.

"Boys." My acknowledgement may have been a touch condescending and Xav grins. "Glad to see you could find a suit somewhere in that hovel you call an apartment, Ash."

Asher snorts as he reaches for a tray of champagne and passes a glass to each of us.

"Glad you found enough time to pull your head out of your ass to come see us peasants," he retorts and I grin. He's an idiot but I have to admit, I like him. "Your lady coming tonight?"

My face must have flushed because Jamie is looking at me with that inquisitive look that he wears most days now and Asher smirks as he continues. "Or are you worried I'll charm her out from under your nose?"

I snort. "I know you'd try, Ash, but my girl's not easily swayed by one liners and very little follow through."

Xavier grins as he glances around and then he whistles, low and long.

"Holy shit." Xav's voice has a growl to it that sits uncomfortably in my stomach, and I twist to the entry to see what, or who, he's staring at like that.

Holy shit indeed.

I can hear Asher groaning as he grips my arm and I want to turn and push him away, but I can't move.

Mikaela is arm in arm with Max and someone I don't know and don't care to. I can't look away from her and I know I need to.

Her hair is smoothed into simple waves and pinned back on one side of her face, revealing a large amount of her skin down her neck and over her shoulders. Tonight her skin is flawless, other than a tiny silver mark I never noticed that sits just above her collar bone, and a slight gold shimmer is swept across her eyes. Her lips are blood red against the white of her and when she smiles, she is radiant. And then there's the dress. The straps are thin enough I could bite through them and, *oh my God*, I want to bite through them. I want to peel the jewel green from her skin with nothing but my teeth. Every inch of her is hugged perfectly by the silky material, and as she steps forwards my blood races. The dress, which skirts the floor, has a split all the way to the top of her thigh and I am very close to becoming a victim of spontaneous combustion right here, on this very spot.

She looks around the space with wide eyes and that beautiful smile, and when her eyes fall on me I want to step forwards. I want to hold her. A small blush spreads across her cheeks and I swallow the lump forming in my throat. She runs her eyes over me slowly. I can't stop smiling.

This woman is mine.

When she comes to a stop in front of us, Xavier grunts and I shake my head. She looks up at Jamie with that smile that makes her crease her eyes and I am still grinning like an idiot.

"Evening boys." Even her voice is seductive right now. Or is that just me? "Jamie, the place looks better than I imagined."

He pulls her into a hug as he thanks her and I am still staring when her eyes meet mine for a moment too long. Neither of us seem inclined to look away.

"Ben." Xavier elbows me and I glance to him. "If you two don't stop looking at each other like that, Jamie's gonna think his sister is your girl."

I don't speak.

Xavier's eyes bug. "Well, shit."

"Don't." It's a warning.

Xavier glances back to Mik, who's now introducing the stranger as Alex, and then back to me.

"Not my place to comment." He nods tightly and my shoulders sag. "But you are in deep shit when he finds out."

I watch as Mik smiles tightly at something Ash said and note the clipped tone she uses when she answers. I hate the way his eyes run over her and I swallow the burn of jealousy in my throat.

"Yeah. I know."

Mikaela

273

Whoever had the idea to tell Ben to wear all black is officially my favourite person. The striking darkness makes his eyes seem bluer than ever before and as I stop in front of the four men, all gathered by a small section of tables, my heart is in my throat.

You can do this, Mik. Just don't look at him too much.

I can speak to them and not melt into a puddle of desire while he looks at me as if he wants to rip me from the room and devour me here and now. What I can't do though is look at him again because, *Lord give me strength*, he is phenomenal and he is smiling at me like I'm the only person in the room.

"Evening boys." That voice - the huskiness of it - is not mine. Is it? I steal a quick glance in Ben's direction and gulp. Bad idea. Very, *very* bad idea. His gaze penetrates my skin and sets my blood on fire and I can feel my cheeks burning. I turn to my brother quickly, plastering on a smile as he grins at me - completely unaware of my wayward thoughts. "Jamie, the place looks better than I imagined."

When Jamie breaks our hug, I can't stop myself from looking to Ben and I see he's whispering with Xavier. I try to block them out.

"This is Alex. Alex this is my brother Jamie, his friend Asher, and those two are Ben and Xavier." That sounded normal. Kind of. Maybe.

Alex grins.

Asher runs his eyes over me again as he licks his lips and I hold back the urge to roll my eyes.

"Mik. My God am I glad you're back in town. It was getting boring without you." He smirks and I smile tightly at him.

"Now, now Asher. I may have been away but I'm very up to date in your antics. Life seemed anything but boring in my absence. How is Gemma? Still burning her way through your wardrobe or...?"

His grin only widens. "I didn't know you were keeping track of my dalliances, Miss Wilcox."

No, Asher. This is not flirtation.

"But you and I both know, none of my situations hold my attention quite as much as the mysterious Mikaela who disappeared on us all."

Gag.

"How silly that I had your attention when I haven't been in the State for years. Gotta get yourself a life at some point, Ashy." I roll my eyes and Jamie snorts as Ben and Xavier turn back to the conversation.

I chance another glance at Ben and blush when Xavier catches my eye with a raise of his eyebrow.

What just happened between the two of them?

"You look lovely tonight, Mik." Xavier steps forwards to place a quick kiss on my cheek, his hand resting safely on the middle of my spine. "Some of us would say so if we weren't choking on our tongues." His whisper is conspiratorial and when he looks at Ben my cheeks burn.

"Thank you." I try to smile warmly as I glance at the group around me. "You guys don't scrub up too badly yourselves."

Jamie laughs and Max shuffles awkwardly beside me.

"We're going to do a little lap." I offer us an out of the very tense silence that is rolling off of Ben, and Max nods enthusiastically. "But we'll see you in a bit?"

Jamie nods as he pulls his phone out of his breast pocket and turns to face the petite party planner standing in the corner, also staring at her phone screen with a little smile. The very same party planner whose name and number were programmed into his phone long before he'd even considered throwing this party.

I step forwards and place my hand on his arm. "She's pretty." I laugh when he blushes. "I'm assuming you'll introduce her as something other than *work* at some point?"

He rolls his eyes as he places a kiss to my forehead.

"Go enjoy yourself, Mik." He nods to my friends. "Max, Alex. Please, have fun."

The party has been in full swing for a couple of hours and most of the guests have had their fair share of complimentary champagne. Now people crowd the dance floor, laughing and swaying to the heavy beat of some song I don't recognise, and I push away from Alex and Max.

"Where are you going?" Max shouts over the drone as Alex drapes an arm over his shoulder and grins.

"Is she off to find Baby Blue?"

I shoot him a look of exasperation and he holds his hands up in surrender.

"Mikaela," Alex laughs. "It took me nought point two seconds to realise Baby Blue was the one in black staring very intensely at you for the whole introductory chat. Plus, his eyes have hardly left you since." He nods to the corner Ben is lounging in, a glass of clear liquid in his hands as he watches us talking.

A shiver runs the length of my spine as his eyes lock with mine and I try to focus on keeping calm. I turn back to face Alex with a roll of my eyes.

Ben and I have successfully avoided each other all night and it wouldn't take much to figure out why. From the outside our distance is typical: people will assume we pissed each other off in one of the planning meetings again. But something in my bones screams that we are very much in tune when it comes to the real reason.

Something shifted between us when we stood face to face in the entrance tonight. Rule number one is hanging on by the very last threads and this probably isn't the place to test how strong those threads are.

"I'm getting a drink, smart ass." I grin as Max turns back to Alex and pulls him in for a sloppy kiss, before I make my way off of the dance floor and over to the bar.

Out of the crowd I'm grateful for some space. I perch my clutch on the bar and push my hair over one shoulder, scooping it off of my neck to give my skin a second to breathe. It's hot in here.

And then there's a hand on my waist.

My eyes snap to the left and I groan in a very impolite way, right in the face of the guy with his fingers spread over my hip.

Asher Jones is looking for a kick in the groin.

"Asher." I twist to face him, not concealing the scowl on my face as he puts on his most charming smile.

Objectively, Asher is handsome. He's tall - a little less so than Ben, but tall all the same - and his shoulders are broad and strong from years of competitive swimming. His eyes are a delightful silver tone with flecks of dark blue and his skin is permanently sun kissed. His dirty blonde hair has been cropped short for as long as I've known him, a habit picked up from his dad who spent the best part of his youth in the military, and he has the straightest teeth I've ever seen. Objectively, he is handsome, but he does nothing for me. Which only makes him work harder for it.

Asher is sweet too. A bit of a pervert? Probably. Too forward to the point of borderline inappropriateness? Almost always. But he's also the first to put his hand in his pocket for charity, he adores my brother and he always knows to back off when I tell him I've had enough of his attention. Apparently tonight I'll be reminding him that I'm always tired of his attention.

"Can I buy you a drink, Mik?" His eyes dance with flirtation and I roll mine.

"That depends, Asher. Is it just a drink?" I raise my eyebrows and he tries to feign innocence.

"Not sure what you mean, sweetheart."

"No?" I glance at his hand, still holding gently to my hip. "Because your hand on me kind of says otherwise."

He laughs as he shakes his head and pulls his hand back.

"Let me guess," he jokes. "You're flattered, as you always are, but would like to remind me of the last six times you have shot me down?"

I grin as the bartender approaches us. "It's like you read my mind, Asher. I knew there was a brain hidden in there somewhere."

"You know, Mik." He shrugs as he grins. "You teasing me like that only makes me want you more. I love it when you're mean."

I shake my head with a laugh. Pervert, but loveable too. The little shit.

"I'll have whatever cocktail tastes the best for the most money." I smile at the woman waiting for our order. "He's buying."

He gawks at me as I flutter my lashes and smile innocently. Watching him flounder is kind of fun, but also kind of mean.

"I'm kidding. Water please. And put whatever this idiot has on my brothers tab?"

The woman nods with a smile and grabs a bottle from below the bar, untwisting the cap and pouring it out over ice.

I turn to Asher before picking up my glass and give him a quick hug. "It's good to see you too, Ash."

Slipping through the crowd, I crane my neck to find him. He was in the back corner the whole time I was with Asher, I'm sure of it. But now Ben is nowhere to be found. I had hoped we'd be able to stand in a busy little corner, pretend to be blissfully unhappy in each other's presence for a little while, just so I could feel that little bit of comfort that being with him brings, but my hopes are slowly being dashed as I drain my water and place the empty glass on a table.

Maybe I'll go back to Max and Alex.

A small squeak escapes my lips as I feel a warm hand wrap gently around my wrist and tug me through the open doors behind me. The rough pull is partnered with a tender stroke of his thumb over my pulse point, telling me not to panic.

Chapter Twenty-three

Mikaela

"Follow me."

Ben is moving before I have a chance to think. I stumble forwards, my heels making it hard to follow his long strides down the stairs and out into the open air, and glance back to the night unfurling in the room he's just hauled me out of.

No one noticed him drag me through the open glass doors. No one glanced over when I gasped and fell into the darkness. And I find myself grateful no one had seen; grateful no one seems to notice us tearing through the hotel grounds now, as Jamie's celebrations rage on behind us both. Grateful even Max's watchful eyes were preoccupied elsewhere and missed the flush of my cheeks as soon as I had felt Ben's hands on my skin.

"Ben," I grunt, my heels sinking beneath me. "Slow down."

He pauses in the misty glow of string lights wrapped around the trees beside the pond, raking his eyes over me, and I shudder. There's something dark and demanding in the set of his jaw and the gleam in his eyes and my heart throbs as my breathing hitches.

"Ben?"

He smirks as he pulls me closer, his fingers spreading over the small of my back, pinning me against him as his eyes trail over my lips, my neck, my chest.

"You know. I think I might kill Asher Jones." His voice is low and throaty, but the smallest hint of amusement trickles in and it sends shockwaves rippling through me. His other hand releases my wrist and his fingers trail up from my hand to my shoulder, brushing my hair back gently and lingering at the back of my neck as his jealousy fades and something else takes its place; something that steals my breath away.

"He touched you, right here." His voice drops to a whisper as his other hand moves to my hip, squeezing gently and pulling me close. "And I hated it." His fingers dance down the column of my spine, leaving heat where his touch has been, and he leans in slowly, his lips grazing my ear as I hold my breath. "Watching him flirt with you, all I could think-" I whimper as his hand slips between the thin material and my skin right at the top of my thigh and his lips finally caress my neck. "-Was how much I wanted to be him. Touching you. Holding you. In front of everyone."

His kiss dances across my skin between every sentence. Behind us the music throbs and the distant conversations float on the wind, but I don't care. That fire, that desire, is coursing through my veins and he is slowly scraping his fingers up my thigh, pulling the slip of my dress with him. A twig snaps close by - probably a party goer who's wandered outside - and my eyes open as his lips continue to move across my jaw.

"We - we can't." The moan that escapes me only pushes him further. "I - what if - what if someone sees us?"

His fingers still, achingly close to that tantalisingly lustful spot that craves him more than I want to admit to myself, and he whispers against my skin.

"Do you want to stop because someone might see, or because it's me?"

It all comes down to this. Now. All of the secret kisses and stolen seconds together, all of the hiding and testing and waiting. It all boils down to this question. Ben needs to know if I want him.

"I - I -" I can't think. He's still touching me. The heady scent of him invades every word, every argument. Ben is touching me. And rule number one is about to be completely and utterly destroyed. "We..."

"Mikaela." His teeth nip my skin and I yelp as warmth pools deep within. "I need you to tell me if the problem is me, or them. Because, I promise, I will stop if it's me."

His tongue swipes across the sensitive spot he has just bitten and I sigh as his fingers tighten on my thigh.

"Them," I breathe. "The problem is them."

Ben

I smile against her skin, my heart pounding and my head spinning. That damn dress is to thank for this. I want her and I am so tired of slow.

"Okay." I pull away quickly, leaving her bereft and wanting. Part of my brain is caught on the way her breathing is so heavy that she can hardly function, another part of it is planning our escape. "Then let's go."

She seems flustered as I take a step towards the line of cars parked in the driveway and she doesn't move.

"Mik."

"Where?" She watches as I move back to her side, my hand coming up to cup her face gently, a smile ghosting my lips before I lean in and kiss her. I kiss her tenderly, savouring the way her lips meet mine, gently and tentatively. Like one kiss might make this all disappear. Because this is a very fragile line we are choosing to cross now. This makes it real.

Pulling away from her, I catch her hair between my fingers, twisting it as I stare at her. "Somewhere we won't be caught."

She just blinks at me as I smile and roll my eyes. How, in the name of all things holy, is this what leaves her flustered? It's adorable.

"The problem isn't me, correct?"

Mikaela huffs as she glances back to the party we just left, our colleagues and friends continuing on as if the world isn't shifting on its axis.

"No," she admits with a shake of her head. "It's not you."

I brush my fingers against her cheek, pulling her attention back to me. "And do you want to continue this somewhere else? You can say no if you're not ready, Mik."

And I mean it. Despite the fact that every ounce of me aches to continue, to not be pushed away, if she says no that will be okay. I'll wait. For her, I'd wait a million lifetimes.

Mikaela

"Yes," I whisper. "I want to go somewhere else."

It feels like a weight has been lifted from my shoulders. The admission that I want this, want him, has held a heaviness over us for weeks without me realising, all leading to this moment, and, as his lips brush against mine once more, I wrap my fingers around his jacket and pull him close.

Finally, he believes me.

"Then let's go," he mumbles against my lips.

This time I let him lead me away, my hand encased in his own as he stalks towards his car, that Cheshire Cat smile of his never leaving his face. I laugh as I stumble, holding him tightly as we flee Jamie's party under the cover of night.

Under the dim glow of the lights that illuminate the driveway, Ben opens the passenger door but stops me from slipping in.

With no one looking, he pulls me closer to him, grinning when I gasp at the sudden crash into his chest, and places his hand at the base of my spine. Watching my eyes closely, he leans in, searching for something - regret or worry in my gaze? - and presses a tender kiss against my lips. When I melt against his touch he runs his fingers up my spine and smirks at the shiver he pulls from me.

"You have no idea how long I've wanted to do this." His forehead presses against mine as he sighs, and I smile softly.

"If my memory serves me well, Haston, you've been doing this for weeks now." I grin as I kiss him again.

Ben laughs and he pulls away from me, pushing me gently towards the car.

"And a lot of those times were much less PG-13." I continue with a half smile.

"Right." He shakes his head as he rolls his eyes and grins. "Get in the car, Mik."

"Yes, Sir." There's a bubble of laughter hidden in my voice. A bubble that dissipates and catches in my chest as he pauses. His eyes burn, raking over me slowly, deliciously, and he devours the sight of me now waiting in his car, the thigh high slit of my dress exposing a sliver too much of skin. I stare up at him with wide, innocent eyes and he leans in with a smirk on his lips.

"Hmm." He pauses to listen as my breathing becomes heavy, and the cool confident act I've put in place seems to slip and falter with his breath mingling with mine and his lips so close but still not touching me. He straightens suddenly, winking. "I like the sound of that."

With the close of the door, I skip a breath.

The chill of metal bites at my skin as he presses me against the wall. Part of me is screaming that we should stop. Someone could press that button and walk into the elevator and the two of us would be completely unaware as long as we carry this on. But he is on my bare skin, my wrists pinned above my head as he holds me in place and his other hand grips beneath my knee and pulls it to his waist. His lips are everywhere; trailing from my jaw and down my neck, dancing over my shoulder as he licks and bites and kisses, moving swiftly back to my lips, drinking in every soft whimper I release for him.

I moan as he presses against me, the friction of his pants teasing me with every tantalising slip. I can feel him and heat swirls in my core as I arch my back and he pushes harder against me.

"Please..." I pant as his fingers slip beneath my dress, tracing over the lace beneath. I don't care that we could be caught. I don't care that Jamie will kill us both for this. *I. Do. Not. Care.* I want him.

Ben

"Wait." I pull away quickly, my eyes widening and my smile almost painful. I back my hips away slightly, unpinning her as I pull the hem of her dress up a little further and peer at the skimpy black lace that clings to her hips and climbs up her waist in delicate, intricate vines and flowers. It's one of those skimpy, full body things and it's sinful. "Mikaela Wilcox. Who the fuck are you wearing *that* for?"

I let go of her wrists and she covers her face with both hands as a cherry blush spreads across her chest and neck, creeping into her cheeks.

"Oh fuck. Oh *fuck*." Her voice is a choked laugh as she avoids looking at me.

"Mikaela?" My fingers are trailing up her stomach, hitching her dress up with them and my lips twitch at the corners as I fight off the shit eating grin I am desperately trying to hide. "I want an answer to that question because this... Holy *shit*, Mik. This is insane."

I chuckle as she groans, leaning into me and hiding her face further. I let the slip of her dress drop back over her as I bring my fingers to her chin gently and pull her face up so that I can look into her eyes.

She blinks back shadows of nerves and worries, and my voice drops to a whisper.

"Hey, I'm sorry." I shake her chin gently, forcing her to stop chewing on her lower lip as she looks up to me and places her hands on my chest. "I didn't mean to embarrass you. It's just, in all the times I've imagined this, I never imagined you wearing something like that and it's - wow."

"You - erm -" She smiles a little as my fingers brush over her cheeks and the elevator slides to a stop on my floor. "You've imagined this then?"

My laughter rumbles within my chest and I take her hand, guiding her out of the elevator and towards my door.

"You are completely oblivious, aren't you?"

"Oblivious to what?" She does that thing she always does, ducking her head slightly and twisting that ring of hers with her thumb, as she watches me fish my keys out of my jacket and push the door open.

I shake my head and then my hands are on her waist again and I am pulling her to me. I lean in slowly, my eyes burning into hers as I hesitate. She pushes up on her tiptoes, her hand reaching around my neck, holding me gently, and presses her lips against mine.

I whisper against her. "You're completely oblivious to the fact that I've been thinking about this for years, Mikaela."

Mikaela

I don't know what I was expecting, but it wasn't this. It wasn't even close.

Ben watches me silently as I step forwards, my heels now kicked off by the front door and my fingers trailing over the oak unit that stands in the entryway to his home. My eyes dance over the art framed on the walls, mixed between photos of himself and Jamie, of his mother and father on their wedding day, of friends I have never seen him with and smiles that tell a hundred stories. I pause in front of one photograph and something thick lodges itself in my throat. I'm fourteen and it's the very first day of high school. Jamie and Ben are standing on either side of me, their arms folded and fake scowls on their faces. I remember Jamie moaning to Mom that seniors don't do first day pictures. Ben had ruffled my hair as soon as the photo was taken and then told me to stay away from the football team. *"They're gonna love you, Little Mik. And if one of them touches you, J and I will have to beat their asses. So keep your distance,"* he'd warned. And then he'd kicked the quarterback's ass six months later when he and Jamie found me crying in a science lab. I smile at the memory as I move slowly, dedicating each detail of this place to my mind, and step into the wide open living space.

The far wall is almost entirely glass with an uninterrupted view of the East River. It's modern and sleek and completely out of place in this room. The cream couch takes up most of the space and it's drowning in large cushions; none of which match. Nothing has a pattern, they're simply scattered across for comfort. Surrounding his TV are shelves of books, some with spines cracked from repeated use, others so beautifully new it would pain me to hear them break. I don't know why this detail has me so emotional and so shocked.

Not everyone wants to be surrounded by people who compete with flashy cars and homes that feel like museums, I had spat at him once. This doesn't feel like a museum though.

I stand still in the centre of the room, a soft smile lifting my cheeks and a calmness enveloping me where I thought alienation would take hold. This is somewhere I could feel safe and welcome. This is beautiful.

"I was wrong." I whisper more to myself than to him, but he's standing behind me, his hands in his pockets and nerves in his eyes as I turn to him. "I didn't expect this."

Ben

"Well?" I'm unsure why her surveying my home makes me so nervous. I'm unsure why I'm now looking around and noticing that the books are askew and not organised in genre or size or color, or that there is a blanket strewn over the arm of the couch rather than folded neatly and put away. I feel my throat tighten as she gazes up at me.

"It's so..."

"Basic?" I laugh awkwardly.

"I was going to say cozy." Mikaela smiles widely as she turns back to the wall of literature staring at her, and she grins as she runs her eyes over the titles there. Watching her here, my chest squeezes.

It hits me how cold this place seems to me most days. The kind of cold that is only lifting now she's standing barefoot in the middle of my living room. I wrap my arms around her waist and press my lips into her shoulder before she turns back to me.

"Hi." She brushes her fingers against my cheek.

"Hi." I grin.

"So did you bring me here to show off your book collection, or did you -"

She's silenced by my lips crashing into hers and I lift her in my arms. Without breaking contact between us, I sweep an arm under her legs and move swiftly through the hallway. She laughs against my kisses and her hands hold the back of my neck as she pulls herself impossibly close to me and I push the last door open with my foot.

Mikaela

I have no time to think as he places me on my feet before him, spinning me to face away as his fingers make quick work of my zip. I have no time to worry, or panic, or question what we're doing as my dress pools at my feet and his fingers trail down my sides, dancing over the lace of my lingerie. He presses kisses into my shoulder, my neck, my jaw. His hand presses against my stomach, pulling me close to him, and warmth spreads through me with every touch. And then he isn't there. His fingers are gone, his lips are removed, the press of him against me is missing.

Ben

She almost cries out as she turns to me, her eyes betraying how needy she is for more, and I appraise her with what I know are wild eyes.

The lace that hugs against her is delicate and thin. The vines and flowers that crawl over her stomach and across her breasts leave a trail I want to follow with my tongue. I devour the way her breasts heave with each heavy inhale and how she steps towards me confidently. This isn't some timid and shy girl who hid from attention under last season's clothing and quiet observation. It isn't even the Mikaela I've seen for weeks in secret. This is the Mikaela I have thought of only when dreaming; sensual and dripping with confidence. This is the Mikaela I don't deserve.

She is *extraordinary*.

I hold a finger up, stopping her in her tracks as I look at her. I want to appreciate this; the sight of her before me in nothing but lace, wanting me.

Ten years ago I'd been plagued by dreams of this; months went by as I fought off fantasies and daydreams and desires I knew I could not act on.

But reality is so much more than I had ever anticipated.

"You know -" My voice is low and strained, like I'm holding back a guttural, animalistic growl. "You never did tell me who you're wearing that for."

I want her to say it's for me, that she slipped into something so ridiculously tempting thinking of me ripping it off of her. I want to hear that she's been dreaming of this too. I know she's been dreaming of this, really. Mikaela sleep talks. But her true answer steals my breath and shatters me simultaneously. Her true answer dances with sadness.

"For me," she whispers, her eyes wide with honesty and vulnerability. "I - I read it can make you feel..."

As her voice trails away, that familiar look of uncertainty and self-doubt creeps into her eyes. She looks to the floor and I step forwards, closing the distance between us once more. My fingers trace the cup of her breast, skimming the thin line between the lace and her skin.

"Beautiful?" I ask her with a soft smile. When she looks back to me, I see her doubt. "Because you are, Mikaela. You have always been so incredibly beautiful."

I kiss her gently, pulling her closer with a tug of the fabric I hold between my fingertips, and run my hand down the length of her spine. I can show her she is beautiful. I can worship her body so that she never doubts the power she holds again.

Chapter Twenty-four

Mikaela

He works so slowly, lowering himself before me as he kisses my neck and down to my chest. He takes time to kiss my breasts, swirling his tongue over me and tugging gently with his teeth. With every gasp that leaves my lips I feel his curl into a satisfied smile.

I push his shirt from his shoulders and hungrily free him from his trousers, but he traps my wrist in his hands and shakes his head with a wicked grin. He holds my waist tight and tells me to stand still as he peels the lace from my skin, lowering to his knees as he remains before me, his eyes dark and dangerous.

When he's face to face with the puckered pink scar that runs from my sternum to my stomach, Ben doesn't flinch. He doesn't even pause. He simply presses tender kisses down the length of it, whispering about how incredible I am.

That drives me crazy.

His hands slip gently down over my ass and my thighs before he pushes my legs apart and glances up at me. I am staring at him with my mouth open as he presses his lips against the inside of my thigh and then the other. He flicks his tongue over his lower lip and my cheeks flame, and then his mouth is on me and his tongue is moving in deliciously slow strokes and circles and my hands are in his hair.

I gasp as he sucks and licks and kisses and he holds me tight, keeping me still and forcing me to feel every blissful sensation. When my head rolls back and my eyes close, I feel him trail soft fingers over my entrance before pushing inside me; just one finger at first, and then another. Instinctively, I grind my hips against him as his fingers curl and I whimper quietly. Fire consumes me. It burns through my veins and pools in my core. It heats and simmers within me until I am blinded by it. With every lap of his tongue, every push of his fingers, he stokes the flames. He feeds it with every moan that leaves his lips as he tastes me and teases me. I moan again, my hand flying up to stifle the sound.

He stills his movements. My eyes open. I need friction. I need *more*.

"I want to hear you, Mikaela." His words are a command, punctuated by the slow withdrawal of his fingers. "Don't hold back."

He pushes into me roughly and a small cry escapes me as I bite down on my lower lip. Again, he pulls back slowly, swirling his fingers over my heat and up to that spot of beautiful fire before returning to the place I need them most.

"You are allowed to let go, Mikaela." He kisses me there again as his fingers push deeper, slowly this time. "I want you to enjoy this and I want to hear how much you enjoy it."

"I -" My heart is pounding as he curls inside me again, pulling at that thread of pleasure and toying with it. "I can't."

The admission is painful. It's a remnant of my past, as real as the scar he has so easily treated as a piece of art, and I'm not sure which one is more damaging; more permanent.

"Oh but, Mikaela." His fingers continue their blissful torture of me as my knees shake and pleasure beckons to me. "I think you can. I'll help you."

With his tongue back on me and the rhythm of his movements slow and deliberate and so expertly precise, I feel the wave of bliss crash over me and my legs tremble. My cries are strangled and restrained.

I know I'm holding back.

His left hand grips me tightly as he withdraws from me, slowly pulling his dripping fingers into his mouth and grinning as I shake my head with a breathy laugh.

"That's one." He gets to his feet slowly and pushes me towards the bed and down, holding me gently as he presses against me, trapping me beneath him.

"One?" My fingers trail over his broad chest as he pushes my legs apart with his knee and presses a soft kiss against my neck.

"One," he repeats. His fingers rub circles where his tongue has just been and I writhe beneath him. Slowly he positions himself over me and one of my hands moves to his length, stroking, pulling groans of delight from him. He stares down at me as I smirk up at him, fully aware of how desperate he is to finally sink into me and lose himself in the bliss of connection, fully aware of how much power I have over him now. It's thrilling.

He moves swiftly, pulling my hand from him before reaching for the bedside drawer and coming back with a condom. Tearing the packet with his teeth, he wastes no time. One second he's moved away from me, his hand rolling over his length, and the next he's pinning me down, the heat of him pressing against me in perfect anticipation as he holds my wrists over my head in one hand again.

"I wonder how many it will take to have you screaming for me?" He sinks into me slowly, shaking as I suck in a heavy breath. He doesn't move, letting me adjust to the feel of him and I feel myself tighten as he lets out a sigh of pleasure. "Holy shit, Mik. You're incredible."

"Fuck." My moan is whispered as he pulls back slowly and thrusts into me again. I twist my wrists, wanting to feel him, and he frees me instantly. My fingers claw at his back, pulling him closer as my leg wraps over his hips and he moves so gently. With every thrust and grunt, with every bead of sweat that mixes between us, I feel my control slipping away.

"Please," I moan, my nails digging into his shoulders, leaving white half crescents in his skin.

"Mik?" He presses a kiss into the base of my throat. "Tell me what you want."

"Faster." It's a breathy plea as his lips brush against mine and he runs his hand over my hair. "I want you to go faster."

"Fuck." Ben grunts as he thrusts into me, each push harder and faster and I move my hips to match him. His eyes close as he moves, the muscles in his neck strained and throbbing and I can't look away from him. "Mikaela."

Hearing my name on his lips is almost too much and I whimper as I pull him closer, desperate to feel his mouth against mine. This kiss is desperate and broken as the sounds of us fill the air, and I arch my back as his fingers move between us. He presses against me, stroking firmly as he continues to slam into me and when he looks at me I come undone around him, crying out as I cling to him.

Everything tightens. Everything heats. Everything explodes.

Ben's lips trail down my neck as his movement slows and I shake beneath him.

"Two," he whispers, smiling against my skin, and I can't breathe enough to speak.

Instead I bring my hands to his chest as he pulls away from me and I watch him as he smiles softly. His face is so serene in this moment, so joyful and pure, and I want to bathe in the sight of it.

"Your body is so responsive." He grins a little as he trails his fingers up my chest and leaves a trail of goosebumps. "So ready for me."

I nod as he finds a steady rhythm again, hitting me harder but still beautifully slow.

"So fucking perfect, Mik."

As he speaks I bite my lip, only for him to kiss me harshly, pulling my lips apart.

"You're so fucking beautiful when you moan, Mikaela. So beautiful."

My fingers are digging into his skin again as his pace increases and I tighten with his praise.

"Come on, baby." He kisses me again. "One more. Give me one more and then you can sleep. Yeah?"

"No more. I can't." He twists his hips slightly and I moan. "Fuck, Ben." I'm mewling, my nails sinking into him as I feel him clenching and he grins wickedly at the sound of his name.

"One more, Mik. Yes. Just like that. Good girl."

It tears through me violently, ripping my breath from me and plunging the room into darkness as galaxies explode in my mind. I feel his movements stutter as he moans my name with a few more thrusts, and then he's collapsed on top of me, both of us gasping for breath and unable to move.

Ben's laugh is a low rumble in his chest as I shuffle through the room and back to the bed. I've pushed my hair - damp from our shower - back into a messy bun, a chopstick from his kitchen shoved in it to keep it up.

His shirt swamps my frame and, if I'm honest, I've never felt more attractive.

Ben grins as I climb back in beside him, resting my head on his chest as he pulls me closer, and I sigh.

"You know, tonight was -"

"Incredible," Ben interrupts, a smug spark lighting up his face as I chuff out a laugh, pushing up to look at him. My chest fizzes and pops as I watch him laying peacefully. One arm is slung back behind his head, his muscles glistening in the dim light from the street that spills through the window, and the other is wrapped around me. With one finger he traces soft patterns against the thin fabric over my spine. He looks so content with his eyes closed and I shake my head gently.

"What's on your mind, Wilcox?" Ben opens one eye and smiles softly.

"Three." I grin when he smirks and raises an eyebrow.

"I told you I could help you let go." Ben snorts as I swat at his chest and roll my eyes.

"Jamie is going to kill you, you know. It's official." I shrug a little before laying back down, my head on his chest and my fingers brushing against his skin. When he groans I giggle.

"Really? You just had to kill the moment, Mik."

"You were being smug." I kiss his chest before nuzzling closer. "I had to knock your ego down somehow."

"Great." He grumbles as he pulls at the sheets, covering us both as I laugh. "Go to sleep, Mik."

I feel the softness of his lips against my head as he pulls the chopstick from my hair and tosses it aside and I close my eyes, ignoring the chasm that seems to open in my stomach at the thought of how true my words had been.

Jamie is going to kill Ben.

The nutty aroma of fresh coffee and the soft brush of fingertips across my exposed shoulder pulls me from the peaceful haze of dreams. I smile sleepily as I feel the sweet caress of his lips against the freckles that have been warmed by the sun and then the gentle shift of the shirt I stole last night being pulled up to cover me properly.

I open my eyes and push myself up from my place, twisting to look up at the blue eyes that are dancing over my body.

"Good morning." My voice is thick with sleep as I stretch out and Ben smiles, his tongue rolling over his lower lip as he stares at the way the shirt has hoisted up over my hips when I push the sheet from me.

My muscles ache deliciously.

"Good morning." He leans in slowly, trapping my lips beneath his as his hand rests against my waist, pulling me closer. "Sleep well?"

"Hmm." I stretch beneath him, grinning. "Definitely."

Pulling away from me and turning to the bedside unit, Ben laughs a little. I can see his cheeks pull up into a grin as I sit up behind him and run my hands over his shoulders, kissing his neck softly before leaning back and pulling the sheet over myself. He turns to face me with a small tray of fruit and coffee and places it between us both.

"What is all this?" I take the steaming mug he holds out to me in both hands and lift it to my lips.

"Breakfast, obviously." His smile is infectious as he watches me, and I let myself sink into the comfort of this moment. "I was thinking." He watches as I smile over the rim of my cup. "Maybe today we could just stay right here. Skip out on the world, just hide away here and -"

"Repeat certain elements of last night?" I wink at him from above my mug and laugh when he rolls his eyes.

"Maybe." He takes a sip of his own coffee and leans back against the headboard.

Slowly, smirking as I place my coffee down onto the unit beside me and push the tray of fruit away, I shift closer to him. I giggle when Ben half-heartedly protests as I take the mug from his hands, leaning past him to put it down too, before pulling his shirt from my body and straddling him.

His hands move to my sides immediately and I shiver at the touch. Sitting here, wearing nothing, I feel beautiful. I feel beautiful when his eyes trace my lips and my throat, and travel down my body. I feel beautiful when his fingers dance over my skin, leaving trails of heat against me. I feel beautiful when his lips brush against mine and his tongue coaxes my mouth open. I feel beautiful when I am held by him.

Ben sighs as I wraps my arms around his neck, pushing my body against his as his hands grip my backside, and I smile against his lips.

Why the hell had we bothered with rule number one?

Ben

I have dreamed of what it might be like to be with Mikaela so many times in the last decade. I used to wonder if it would be awkward and nerve-wracking, just as it had been in all my failed attempts at relationships before her, just as I thought it always had to be, but it's not. It's simple and easy and normal.

Being with Mik feels normal.

"Just maybe?" She whispers as she twists her fingers in my hair.

"You're killing me, Mik." I groan as she wiggles against me, my body responding to her warmth and proximity with excruciating desire.

I flip her quickly, moving away from her and grabbing the tray balanced against the end of the bed - that can go on the floor for now - before digging in the bedside drawer for a condom and ripping my shorts off. Within no time I am crawling over her again, desperate to feel everything again.

Her eyes trace the shape of me as I lower myself over her, gently pushing her legs apart and I hold my breath. She smiles up at me as her hand moves to cup my face, stroking my cheek, skimming her fingers over my lips. My heart hammers as I gaze down at her.

As my lips brush against hers and I guide us together, the world melts away and I let it.

Chapter Twenty-five

Ben

My kitchen is a mess.

I glance around with a wide smile and take in the domesticity of it all. Flour coats one surface, mixing with chunks of left over pastry, and red smears of some fruity filling coat Mikaela's fingers. She swings her hips from side to side, oblivious to my appreciation, and shimmies towards the sink with pots in her hands. Music blares from the speaker on the counter and her hair is once again twisted and pinned with a chopstick with loose tendrils bouncing around her face. Beneath the white shirt she has stolen from me I know she has nothing on, and as she bends forwards to adjust the volume of her music before starting on the dishes, the shirt hitches up, revealing a puckered river of silver I hadn't noticed before.

It trails down the back of her thigh, thin wire that unwinds below her ass with twisted knots scattering in strange places, and comes to a stop just above the back of her knee. In the light of day it's the faintest trail across her alabaster skin, in the night it had been entirely invisible. But this isn't the only scar on her body and, in the back of my mind, I realise I have slowly catalogued them all as I've given myself to her. I hadn't meant to, but they're all there: listed and noted. The angry pink on her stomach, fresh and healing; the raised ridge that runs beneath her hair; the slash of silver on her collar bone. She has five years of scars and stories I never considered, and watching her dance through my kitchen and bake and wash dishes, as if she has been here one hundred times over, I find myself wondering what the story of Mikaela Wilcox really is. Outside of being Little Mik, outside of Jamie's shadow and in the light of day, outside of *us*, Mikaela has lived a life I know nothing about.

As she turns to the side, reaching for a dish cloth, she spots me. Suds fly into the air when she throws her hands to her chest and huffs out a laugh.

"You're back." She blushes as I walk towards her and wipe soapy bubbles from her shoulder.

"I am." Her shock pulls a smile over my lips as I speak.

"I thought you went for a run."

"I did." I wrap my arms around her waist, squeezing gently as she places her hands on my chest and smiles up at me. "What are you making?"

"Pie." She shrugs as if it's nothing important and not another strangely normal thing for her to do in my home. "Mom's recipe."

I can feel it: my face erupts into an ear to ear grin. The same kind of grin I'd worn countless times in her childhood home. Elizabeth Wilcox made award winning pies when we were kids. She'd even told me once that she considered opening up her own little shop before Mik's dad left and she got sick. I remember staying in Jamie's room when my own father would turn; Elizabeth would make my favorite pie every time. Almost as if she knew I needed it.

"Is it -"

"Cherry," Mik interrupts, turning away from me and grabbing some plastic wrap from a drawer as I follow her through the open space. "For some reason you had the exact ingredients laying around? Was someone hoping

I'd share the recipe?" She teases me as she glances over her shoulder.

"Not at all. Now, remind me why we haven't done this before if it means I get cherry pie?" I lean back against the kitchen island as she rolls the remaining crust into a small ball and wraps it tightly. Her mom taught her to freeze it for later use.

"Because," she muses as she continues to tidy with a smile on her face, "we had rules. And before that, I used to hate you."

I bark out a laugh and Mikaela grins. Last night definitely wiped hate off of the table, as did this morning, and the countless nights we've broken rule number two over the last month.

"Well, let the record reflect that I have never hated you. Not even as kids." As I speak, I push away from my resting place and run my hands across her shoulders and down her arms. My fingers entwine with hers as I wrap myself around her and punctuate the thought with a soft kiss to her neck. When I hold her like this, her muscles relaxing with my embrace, I wonder how I'll ever be able to let go.

I don't think I ever could.

Mikaela

While the shower runs I sit on the couch with my legs crossed. The blanket that had been strewn across the arm of the chair last night is now draped over me and I hold an open book in my hands. Although my eyes skim the words on the page, I take nothing in.

Nothing about the last twenty-four hours has been normal. Nothing about the day I am happily spending baking in his kitchen, and curled up in his arms, and avoiding checking my phone is normal. Nothing. We've stepped over that line into a world we knew would have to change, and panic now settles in my stomach like an old friend returning for a surprise visit. The longer I'm away from him, the more I sink.

When he'd gone to take a shower he'd kissed me again. His lips had been lighter than a feather and his thumb had brushed against my cheek as if I were the most delicate silk that might tear beneath his touch. I'd smiled against his lips and pushed him to the bathroom. He'd made me promise I wouldn't get changed. He said he wanted to see me wearing his clothes for a little while longer. And I agreed. I wanted to keep his shirt on. And besides, the only thing I have here is last night's dress. But now, as I hear him singing off key in the shower and I pretend to read a book I haven't even checked the name of, I want to run. Or hide. Or cry.

And I have a sinking feeling I know why.

I place the book down on the coffee table and get to my feet, leaving the blanket rumpled on the couch behind me.

My bag is still by the door from last night - dropped haphazardly as I had let him pull me into his apartment and bind me with more of those kisses I desperately adore - and I fish my phone from beneath the lipstick and concealer, tissues and business cards. My stomach drops and that desire to cry bubbles to the surface again, face to face with its cause.

Six missed calls from Jamie. Two voicemails. Two texts. Max also called twice and text. I open his first.

Max: You are in trouble. I had to leave that party for you :(call me.

I am panicking. I am definitely panicking. That's why I can't breathe as I dial, and why I slide down the wall and sit between the unit and the front door, curled in on myself as the phone rings. That's why, when Max answers the phone, I find myself whispering.

"Mikaela Wilcox, you are in so much trouble."

"Max?"

"Yes it's Max. Who else would it be, you idiot?" Max is teasing, he's being playful, but it does nothing to settle the nausea threatening to overwhelm me.

"Max, why did you leave the party?" My hand covers my mouth, as if it might somehow hide my conversation should Ben emerge now. As if it can somehow soften the reason I know Max had to leave.

"Because your brother was trying to find you, and then he was trying to find Ben. And considering Alex and I had just seen you two getting a little too hot and heavy in the gardens -"

I feel the sting of my blush as it spreads from my chest to my cheeks.

"Did anyone else see?" I interrupt, only for my voice to disappear. Ben is watching me intently, a forced smile painted over his lips as he stands in grey sweats and nothing else. His dark hair is still wet and tiny droplets of water fall against his broad shoulders.

"Just that Xavier guy. It was his idea for me to do the whole saving your ass thing."

Jamie? Ben mouths the question silently.

I shake my head as I chew my nails. "It's Max."

His smile is no longer forced and uncomfortable. It's breathtaking, and I want to frame it.

"I'll leave you to it then." He strides over quickly and crouches down. "Hey, Kingford." Before I can say a word, he kisses me and I feel something terrifying twist in my stomach.

Oh God, what am I letting myself in for?

"Mik?" Max's voice cuts through my thoughts and snaps my attention back to the line. "Mikaela? Are you still with him? Did he see the lace?" His pitch climbs with every question and his excitement spills from him, washing through the phone and drowning me.

"Yes," I state simply. I'm still whispering despite the fact Ben walked off and into the kitchen, closing the door behind him. "And I think I'm in trouble."

Ben

In the kitchen, I pick at the left over pie from the tin. Something is wrong and I can't put my finger on it. Ten minutes pass as I pace the length of the room, wary of being overbearing if I step out to her again, but desperately wanting to know if the sudden shift in the atmosphere is all in my head.

When she steps in behind me she's twirling her phone in her hands, avoiding my eyes, and my stomach tightens and not in that exciting way I'm growing used to with Mik.

"Whatever you're about to say, can I just say something first?" I step forwards quickly and she sighs.

"Ben."

Shit. Shitshitshit.

"Please, Mik." I stand in front of her, the kitchen island between us, with my hands in my pockets and my heart racing.

She nods.

My words rush from my lips and I can't stop them. "I don't know what's going on in that head of yours now because, well I never really know what you're thinking, and I am terrified you're going to tell me that now you've had a chance to think it over you regret last night and this morning, and you're going to walk out of here and tell me you don't want this. That you don't want me. But I want this, Mik. I want *you* to want this. And I think you do." I should be embarrassed by the way my voice breaks a little there, but I'm not. I just want her to hear this. "But if you don't and you want to leave then that's okay, I'll drive you home and we can go back to whatever we were before. But I want you to know that I want you, Mikaela. I really fucking want you."

Mikaela chews her lower lip when I stop talking. I don't say anything else.

"Max and Alex saw us in the garden. They - erm - they had to leave the party because Jamie -"

"They told Jamie?"

"No."

I sag with relief. "Then what happened?"

"Jamie was looking for me, and then you, and then Xavier told Max to leave so that I could say I left with him. He was offering us a cover story."

I furrow my brow. "Oh."

"Yeah."

We stand there for a moment in silence, awkwardly looking at each other from opposite sides of the room before I sigh.

"It turns out they all kind of want this to happen. Who'd have guessed." She tries to joke, but her smile doesn't reach her eyes.

"What do *you* want, Mik?"

Her voice is a whisper. "I - erm - I don't know."

"I think you do know." I step around the counter and move slowly towards her. I don't want to let her back away now, not when she's already changed me so much. "I think you're just afraid to admit it again. Now that we've crossed that line."

"Why would I be afraid?" Her voice trembles and I want to hold her, to brush away the worries that are swimming behind her eyes. I don't though.

"First there's our history. And then there's the fact that even I'm scared of how easy this feels between us. You're afraid of how relaxed you've been. Not to mention Jamie." I'm towering over her now. "The list goes on and on, Mikaela. You're scared. And I am too."

When my fingertips skim over her cheek and my thumb brushes over her lips she closes her eyes. I feel the warmth of her breath on my skin as I lean in to her and kiss her softly.

Her body responds instantly. Her fingers are pressed against my chest as her lips part and my hand presses against her spine, pulling her closer to me. When we part, I rest my forehead against hers. Neither of us open our eyes as we stand like this, simply existing in the silence around us and the mingling of our breath.

"I'm scared of what happens when Jamie finds out," she admits.

I nod. "We're going to have to tell him at some point, Mik."

Especially now.

She's breaking as she whispers, "he won't understand."

We'll make him understand.

"Maybe not," I admit. "But he doesn't have to."

Mikaela

We're a tangle of limbs on Ben's couch, wrapped in a blanket as we lay quietly. A film plays as the pattering of rain against glass soothes me. My head is on his chest and his arms are wrapped around me and I stare out of the window at the city sprawled out beneath us. My meltdown this morning is now nothing but a blotch in the fabric of our day. A blotch caused by my inability to tell Ben what really scares me.

"Mik?" Ben's hand brushes over my hair and I close my eyes.

"Mhmm?"

"The scar on your stomach. Where did you get that?"

I know he feels it as I tense with the memory, but he waits. I know if I chose not to tell him, he'd respect that.

"I don't have a spleen," I state simply. His brow furrows and he twists his face to see me better.

"Well that would explain part of it."

I laugh a little and he smiles. As painful flashes of red and blue lights flashing in broken glass echo in my mind, I relax back into his hold with a sigh.

"It was a car accident. M- someone rammed into me. It got pretty scary for a while and I lost my spleen. Jamie helped me. Found me somewhere I was able to heal, get some help. He stayed with me for a little while before coming back, and then when I was ready, I just... I moved in with Jamie."

Ben tightens his arms around me as my words sink in. Nothing I've said is untrue, but there's a wave of guilt that threatens to pull me under as I dance around the full story.

"Spleens aren't important anyway," he declares.

I laugh as I push up to look at him and he grins.

"Yeah." I kiss him quickly. "They kinda are."

Ben

"I can do it if you don't want to." I smile and lean back into the cushions as Mikaela paces across my living room. Her phone has been on the coffee table for the last twenty minutes and she still hasn't touched it.

"No." Her curls bounce as she pushes a hand through her hair and comes to a stop. "I mean, how bad can it be?"

Her eyes are wide and she pulls her shoulders up as she tilts her head to the side. I compose myself; creating a facade of cool disinterest when I shrug and glance up at her.

"He could already know. Your brother could be on his way here, right now, to kick my ass and make me stay away from you." I grin when she glares at me. *There she is.* "He could be planning my murder as we speak. He could have hired a hitman. But honestly, the company makes good profit, but I doubt it's enough for a good hitman just yet. Maybe he'll do some saving up for that."

Mikaela groans as she walks over to me and throws herself across the seat. I place my hands on the back of her thighs, kneading and rubbing gently and she laughs when I move to lay on top of her, nuzzling my face into the wild hair that buries her on my couch and kissing whatever skin I can find.

"Ben."

I bury my face further into her neck and nuzzle in close. "Yes, Mik?"

"Can you do it?" She wiggles beneath me as I groan. "Please?"

"Okay." I chuckle. "Give me the phone."

"Mik, where are you?" Jamie's voice is raised over the hammering sound of music and his words are slurred. *"I've been looking for you forever, MikMak, and Ben's gone too."*

As Jamie pauses, I look over to where she sits with a cushion covering the lower half of her face and I smirk. I believe we were in the elevator right around this time.

"Ben's gone. Mik. If you're with Ben I'm going to kill you. Or him. Are you with Ben? Ben has a girl now, Mik. I'm calling Ben and if he doesn't answer I'm gonna -"

"Jamie, that Max guy was looking for you. Said to tell you he's taking your sister to his because she's drunk and lost her keys."

I owe Xavier a drink. Maybe three.

The phone goes dead and Mik grins. "Any chance you can add an accidental extra zero to Max's next payslip?"

My laughter is foreign to me: it has morphed into something easy and light as I tug at the cushion she's holding on to. "Not how that works I'm afraid."

She giggles. "Damn."

"I wonder what the next message is?" I delete the first and wait as the next plays out, placing her phone on the table before resting my head in Mikaela's lap. She combs her fingers through my hair and I stare up at her.

This time Jamie's voice echoes and the sounds of men muttering and taps running makes Mik grimace. *"Mikaela Wilcox. I wouldn't kill you."* He sounds sad and Mikaela's eyes mist almost instantly. I have never heard him sound so broken. *"You know I wouldn't kill you. If I killed you Mom would come back just to kill me."* Even his chuckle is devastating. *"And after everything with Matt I shouldn't ever say I'll kill you. I'm sorry. I love you, MikMak."*

Chapter Twenty-six

Ben

"What does that mean? After everything with Matt?" I watch Mikaela's face drain of any color as I sit upright; my blood thick with ice.

Her eyes are dull and lifeless as she takes a deep breath and plasters a false smile over her lips.

I know her smiles now. I know which pull on the corner of her lips means something amuses her and which subtle downturn means she's going to cry. I know which corner she chews when she's anxious and how easily she draws blood when she does that. I realise now - as her smile spreads over her face with the warmth of a summer sunrise, and her eyes crinkle in the edges, despite the icy void that pulls all heat from the jade - how much I have read and interpreted those smiles over the years. I have *always* known her smiles. And these last weeks I've been drowning in them.

She isn't telling me something.

"Oh, that's nothing." She pushes to her feet and stretches out, turning her back to me as she does so. "Jamie hated Matthew so it's probably just about that. I mean, we didn't speak for a while because of that relationship, you know, so..."

As her voice trails off, I trace that faint scar on her leg with my eyes. I follow each slice and swirl of silver as images flicker in the depth of my mind.

Images that make me sick to my stomach.

Eight Years Ago

Mikaela

"I just don't understand, Mikaela." Mom slips the pie into the oven as she speaks, while I sit at the small table pulled out to the centre of the room. "You love learning."

I tug nervously at the sleeves of my sweatshirt, wrapping the wrists around my fingers and watching as the deep blue shimmers against my skin. "I wasn't enjoying it, Mom."

"Nonsense, Mik. You were absolutely thriving when I came up to see you last month." Her voice drops to a whisper as she takes off her apron and folds it over a chair. "Is it to do with Matthew? He seems like a lovely boy, Mikaela, but sometimes I worry that it's all a little too much, too fast. And I know you and Jamie had words about it all."

I don't look up. My eyes burn with tears I can't cry as I clear my throat and slowly peel back the emotions that are written all over my face.

"It's not about Matty, Mom." My smile is perfectly plain by the time I meet her eyes. "It's about me. I am tired all the time and I hate my lectures. I just want to find a job and start my life."

"In another State?" She folds her arms and raises her eyebrows at me, making me feel about two feet tall in that way that only mother's can.

"Listen, Mom." I stand up, the chair scraping the linoleum beneath me, and move to my mother's side. "I'm twenty and I know it scares you, me being so far

313

away, and it scares me too. But I want to do something. I want to live my life."

A glimmer of hurt flashes behind the blue of Mom's eyes and I feel instant regret. Those words weren't chosen well.

"If it makes you feel better, I'll pick up some classes out there when we're settled or something? Okay?"

She pulls me into her arms and squeezes me tight. "I don't like it, Mikaela, but I appreciate that I can't stop you from living your life. Not after you've done so much for me."

I don't want to do this. I need to do this.

Breaking out of Mom's hold, I move to the counter where a bowl of cooled filling sits with a spoon, and I push myself up. A small smile tugs on my lips as I start to eat. Of course she's making cherry. She makes it for Ben every time she see's him; she dotes on him. I swear, sometimes I think my mother loves that boy more than she loves either of her own kids. Sitting there, my mother ambling around the kitchen, a bowl in my hand, my brother and Ben in the next room over, it hits me that I'm really not sure I'll be able to skip town.

And then the door swings open and Matthew is standing in front of me, his eyes simmering, and my stomach drops.

Has Jamie said something? Ben?

Present

Ben's fingers reach out and trail up my thigh. I know exactly what he's doing. I know where his fingers will twist back on themselves and where they'll catch small knots of scarred skin.

I stop breathing.

"Mik." His voice is low and knowing. "Where did you get *this* scar?"

My head shakes.

"Don't, Ben."

I move away but he follows, his fingers catching my wrist and spinning me gently.

"Talk to me, Mikaela. What am I missing?"

I don't want to do this. I don't want to talk about it. Not when things are going well. And now he's looking at me like that - with sad, painful eyes and too much understanding.

"Please, Ben. Just leave it."

When I pull away from him he lets me. He watches as I step around him, moving to grab my phone from where it sits and deleting every trace of that whispered, garbled, drunk mess that has broken the warmth around me, before grabbing my purse from behind the couch.

"What are you doing?" Ben's voice is pained and he's looking at me like I'm some wounded animal.

My chest aches.

Broken.

It's all broken and he doesn't even know why.

"I should go." I look to the floor and blink back my tears.

He shifts quickly, taking my bag from my hands and placing it on the couch, before putting his hands on my cheeks and ducking to look at me.

"Please don't." His eyes soften and he tries to smile. "I'm sorry, I won't ask again. Just - just don't leave."

I swallow as I shake my head.

"It's different now, Ben." I'm not sure what is different - this strange relationship that we have? Or the way I look at myself? Maybe just the way he looks at me? "This was a mistake."

His fingers drop and he gulps. "Do you - do you really think that?"

I stare at him.

"Mikaela, do you really think this is a mistake? Because if you do, fine. We'll end this and we won't talk about it again. But if you're just saying that because you're afraid of whatever you're not telling me, then that's something we can deal with. I need you to be sure. Because I'm not going to ask you to tell me if you don't want to. I - *shit, Mik* - I think I can put the pieces together myself." He reaches forwards and cups my face again. I close my eyes. "But I don't regret this. I don't regret you and I don't want to lose you. Not when I finally have you."

His fingers brush behind my neck, holding me gently as his thumb traces my jaw.

"Just please don't make me say it." My voice is broken. *Ben knows*.

"Okay." His lips brush against mine as my hand comes up to hold his. "Okay. I'm sorry."

Ben

My blood is boiling and there is nothing I can do about it. Mikaela's face is as white as a sheet and a cold sweat has broken against her neck. I didn't lie when I said I could piece it together - I could and I think I have - but God do I hope I'm wrong.

"I just can't say it." She hasn't opened her eyes but her voice is shaking and I know if she opens them now I'll see pools beneath the green.

"You don't have to." I lean in and kiss her again, thankful that she is letting me. "Ever. Okay? You never have to say it."

Her fingers are wrapped around mine and when I pull back to look at her she leans into me, her head resting against my chest and her breathing unsteady.

"I'm scared, Ben," she confesses against my skin.

"What's scaring you?"

Don't say me. Please don't say me.

"I'm scared that I'll let myself fall for you and then you'll see how broken I really am."

If I ever see her ex, I will kill him.

"You're not broken, Mik."

"Yes." She pulls back to look at me and the pain in her eyes leaves my entire being splintering. "I really am."

Eight Years Ago

"So, J said you're skipping town on us?" I grab a soda can from the refrigerator as Mikaela sorts through pills. Her shoulders are tense and as she reaches up to grab another bottle her sweatshirt lifts slightly. I glance down, my eyes trailing over her and pausing on the yellow stain of an old bruise.

"You know, for it to be skipping town on *you*, you'd have to be in town every once in a while." Her voice drips with sarcasm and I roll my eyes.

I rarely see Mik and it is true, I'm rarely home, but I'm working all the time. And besides, being around her is... difficult.

"Touché." I reach around her to grab the bottle she can't quite catch, my hand falling against her waist to balance myself, and she flinches. "Sorry. Here."

She takes the bottle from me and moves away quickly, glancing over her shoulder at the closed door.

"Matthew seems -" I pause as I search for the right word. "Intense?"

She sighs as she tugs at the hem of her sweatshirt and my stomach twists. Maybe intense isn't the right word. Maybe I should have said nasty, or disgusting, or arrogant. Cruel?

"He's sweet when you get to know him." Her tone is defensive and I regret having said anything.

I watch her for a moment as she moves around me, reaching for a glass from the cupboard and nudging me out of the way of the sink so she can fill it for Elizabeth.

"I'm sure he's super sweet," I tease, smiling as the corner of her lip twitches. "Seems like the guy's a spoonful of sugar away from being Mary freaking Poppins, Mik."

She grins and I nudge her hip with my own.

"I mean would it kill him to crack a smile. He's in there all surly and your poor mom is doing her fussing thing again."

"She's not?" Mikaela rolls her eyes and I smirk.

I like it like this - light and easy.

"Yep. Keeps calling him Sweet Pea and offering to make him cookies. No offer of cherry pie though, so I'm glad that's mine at least." Okay that sounds like I'm thinking about her. And to be fair, I am. Have been for a long time. But I also know I shouldn't be.

Mikaela freezes for just a millisecond before glancing up at me. I don't look away.

We're inches apart, just staring at each other, all traces of humour gone, and a heady sort of thinness in the air, when the door swings open and Mikaela stumbles a step back, her eyes dropping to the floor as my head snaps to the right.

Matthew is glaring at her. Just standing there, silently staring with fire burning in the set of his jaw, as she scurries around me and grabs the pills for her mom. She moves to his side quickly, glancing up at him through long lashes and my stomach sinks.

No matter what I thought I'd just felt between us, she doesn't seem to have felt anything. In fact, she's scared he's misread it. Because, as she looks up at him and he stares silently down at her, she is pleading for him not to react.

It's written all over her face.

Present

I stand in her doorway unsure of what to do. Unsure of what she wants me to do.

"Are you coming in?" She glances over her shoulder with a soft smile and I hesitate. Her smile falls. "Ben?"

"I want to," I admit. "But I have something to say and, depending on how you react to that, I might be safer out here."

She furrows her brow as she comes back to me, reaching for my hand and shaking her head. "I know I freaked out this morning, I'm sorry."

She looks to the floor and I sigh.

"It's not that, Mik. You freaking out was - well it was probably the most normal thing we've done in weeks." I chuckle and she nods slowly. "But I want to say something and it might make you freak out again."

"So far, your prediction is correct." She moves away from me and almost instantly I need her closer again. Hence my own panic. If there is one thing thinking about the past can do to you, it's shove the present down your throat until the truth of it feels like it's going to burst from your skin and spill everywhere. "If you're going to tell me I was right and that we're a mistake, I think I'm going to puke. I was freaking out. You can't use my freak out against me. Not when you worked so hard to get me out of that tailspin."

I am screwing this all up.

"No. Not at all, Mik." The words rush from me as if they have to escape into the air around us just to survive. "The opposite actually."

"The opposite?" She pulls her lip between her teeth and I nod.

"The opposite. I - okay I'm just going to say it - I think - no I'm pretty certain that you're incredible. Right? Like, you're amazing Mik and - God you might not even remember this - but ten years ago - after my dad - you were drunk and I brought you home and you cuddled up to me, Mik. You fell asleep against me, and you were so calm and soft and you. You were just you, Mikaela, and I wanted you then and I don't think I ever stopped. I - holy shit this is a lot messier than I thought it would be." My pulse is drowning out my words and Mikaela takes a slow step towards me.

"Ben?" She reaches up to hold my face in her hands and pulls my lips to hers. "Breathe."

When she kisses me I feel the tension seep out of my shoulders and I wrap my arms around her waist.

"I think I love you, Mikaela."

Chapter Twenty-seven

Mikaela

"What are you doing?" I glance up from the laptop, my fingers stilling as Ben's trace lazy circles up my thigh, his chin resting on my knees while he stares up at me. He's been like this for hours; restless and challenging. Ever since he told me he loves me. Or at least he thinks he loves me. A terrifying concept if there ever was one. Almost as terrifying as the reality of standing there unable to say it back.

"It's okay," he had assured me. *"You don't have to say anything. But I needed to tell you."*

I had tried to say it - I had wanted to - and yet it stuck in my throat like a ball of fire that couldn't escape.

Now his eyes are dark and hooded and, as he smirks, my core clenches and heat pools.

"I'm working here, Haston."

"Mhmm." He moves slowly, positioning himself between my legs on the couch and pulling at my hips so I lay beneath him and I giggle as he presses soft kisses against my stomach. His lips move down as his fingers continue their torturous dance towards his goal. "Carry on, Mik. I'm just doing some work of my own."

His fingers swipe lazily over my panties, pulling a moan from my lips, and Ben grins.

"I can work later," I gasp as he pulls the thin barrier of fabric to the side, moving his fingers over me with tantalisingly slow precision. I feel his laughter brush over the flesh of my thighs before he presses a gentle kiss against one and then the other.

"Nope." He pops the p. "Read it to me."

"What?" I groan again as he slips his index finger down, toying with my arousal and driving me crazy.

"I said -" Another kiss, so close and yet still not where I need him. The swipe of his tongue tells me he is in no rush. "- read your story to me, Mikaela."

The touch of his tongue, flicking that tiny button he knows how to press all too well, partnered with the sinking of his fingers inside me has me panting already, my hips bucking up to meet his lips and my heart racing.

"I - I can't." My voice sounds breathy, whiney, and when he pulls his mouth away from me I whimper.

"Read, or I stop." He shrugs as he stares at me. His eyes are blue flames that warm me to my very core, hypnotising me as I gaze at him. I will do anything this man asks of me in this moment. *In any moment.*

My heart hammers with the intensity of my realisation and I nod quickly.

"There was a chill that clung to the air that night," I begin, struggling to maintain my focus as he pushes another finger inside me and curls them slowly. His tongue laps and my mind spins away from me. I moan. He grins.

"Keep reading, baby."

"The streets were quiet but not empty. Young girls, barely twenty years of age, walked arm in arm in beautiful skirts and sling back heels, eyeing the soldiers who drank together before their deployment. The men paid them little to no mind for the most part."

He releases a throaty groan that vibrates through me, sending trembles up my spine with a searing heat, and I clench around him.

"Good girl. Keep going." He pauses to blow gently on my sensitivity, making my back arch slightly, and I grip my laptop harder.

"Ben, please." I whimper as he resumes his relentless torture. "I want you."

I feel him smile against my skin as he slowly pulls his fingers out of me, curling once more and relishing in the way I push my laptop closed and claw at him.

"And I want to hear your book," he teases. "I love hearing your mind at work."

I shake my head as I grip his t-shirt and pull him up to me. With his lips hovering over mine, and my leg now hooked around him, I press myself up to his body and grin for what greets me.

"Do you really?" I pull him closer, kissing the corner of his lips before whispering in his ear. "Because your little friend seems to want what I want and you can't have both."

Ben groans as I lift my hips slowly, grinding against him, moaning with the delicious feeling of friction against me, before he pushes me down again.

"First of all." He takes my hand, pressing it against the erection bulging through his sweats, and stares at me with a dangerous smile. Ben in sweats is better than Ben in a suit or Ben in jeans. Ben in sweats is entirely mine. "Does that feel little to you, Mikaela?" He shakes his head with a chuckle when I shrug and grin. "And secondly." He kisses me hungrily and pulls my laptop away from it's resting place on my stomach. "I guess I can just get you to read it to me after."

"That's what I thought." I pull his t-shirt up before pushing him back.

"What are you doing?" He groans as I hold him away from me.

"Just admiring you." My fingers trace the defined lines of his abs and I smile when he shivers. "Is that a problem?" There's no give to his flesh and when I trail my nails across the waistband of his trousers, a tortured groan sounds from his lips.

"Well." He grinds against me with a deliciously slow roll of his hips and I gasp at the sensation. "Kinda."

And then his lips are against mine, and I am pushing his sweats away, and his fingers are teasing me again as my pulse races.

"Condoms?" His voice is strained as I move my hand over him slowly, stroking and teasing while his fingers run down my thigh.

"Bathroom cabinet."

He kisses me again before pulling away from me. There is a moment, just one, between us when he stands where he doesn't try to move. He doesn't breathe. He simply looks at me with so much love and wonder that my heart constricts and I wonder how I have gone my entire life not knowing how it feels to be looked at like this. His eyes don't roam over my body or stray from my face. Instead, he stares right into my eyes as a soft smile dawns over his lips and a tender warmth takes root in all of the damaged cracks of my heart. He leans in one last time and I know he hears how my breath hitches as he kisses me with the softest of touches. "When I get back that t-shirt better be long gone, Little Mik."

He walks away and I whisper a response. "Yes, Sir."

He stops in the doorway, his back to me, and I lay watching him move. Every inch of him is well-chiselled perfection - a piece of art he has worked hard to create - and my chest squeezes when he turns to face me.

Mine. All of that is mine.

"If you call me that again, Mikaela, I will not be held accountable for what I do."

There is something deliciously desperate hidden in his eyes, a tugging need or want that surfaces with that word, and under his gaze, I feel heat rise in my cheeks. I nod silently and he chuckles.

This is going to be interesting.

I roll my hips, moving over him at an almost painfully slow pace as my fingers grip his shoulders and he nips the skin of my throat.

"Just like that," he growls.

He squeezes my hips, pushing me over him as I moan, hitting the spot that has pleasure twisting within me, and then strokes my skin again. Like this he has all of the control and every movement, every lift of his hips as he moves beneath me, never letting me have the release that I want, but teasing me with it in every move. Every kiss of his lips against my breasts sends me spiralling further and this time, as he grips my ass tightly, I think he might let me finish. And then he lifts me off of him; the lack of contact jarring me to my senses and silencing the bliss.

"No, I -" A short burst of shocked laughter rips from my chest as he lifts me up and throws me onto the couch. He moves with determination, his eyes lingering on my throat as his fingers scratch up my leg and he hooks my knee against his waist. He presses against me and I gasp as he bites playfully at my neck while his other hand strokes his length slowly.

"I want you to do something for me, Mikaela."

I gulp.

"I'm not going to finish everything I want to do to you -" He rubs the head of himself over me, eliciting a whimper of desire, and grins. "- until you make yourself come."

"What?" I blink what feels like one hundred times as his words sink into my mind and his teeth sink into my flesh again.

"Show me what you like, Mikaela." His voice is velvet against my defences as his breath fans against my chest and his tongue swirls over my nipple. "Please."

This is crazy. He knows what I like. I like everything he does to me.

I can't.

"Come on, Mik," he purrs into my throat as he takes my hand with the one he just had wrapped around himself and moves it slowly down my stomach. "Let me watch you let go."

Ben

I breathe the words against her skin before kissing her gently, my tongue brushing against the seam of her lips, my hand guiding her lower.

My body is fighting electricity as I pull my hand away from her and hold my breath. I want to watch her, to see the spoils of her hard work, before losing myself inside her. I want my Mikaela to be free, and beautiful, and so fucking blissed out that she forgets everything that has ever made her feel any less. I want to pull her out of all of the shit that swims behind those incredible green eyes every time she thinks for a moment too long and, selfishly, I want to see her come apart with my name on her lips and her fingers inside of her just because I asked her to. I want everything she will give me, and as her fingers swipe over her clit, I am terrified I'll break this moment if I so much as fucking breathe.

She's incredible. Absolutely incredible.

She begins slowly, rubbing sensuous circles over herself, and I pull my entire body away from her. She's laying before me, legs spread, with every single inch of her on display and I can't tear my eyes away from the way her fingers move. She touches herself with the gentlest of strokes before slipping her fingers down, inserting one and then another, and her lips part with a breathy moan. Her head presses back into the cushions and her eyes close as she moves her other hand down slowly, her fingernails dragging down her body and leaving tiny pink trails for my eyes to devour.

"Look at me." I'm panting as I watch her; my fists balled against the couch cushions and my cock straining, aching to be touched. When I look up, she's staring at me. "Let go, baby. Think about all the things I'll do for you when you finish, and let go."

"Yes." She's shaking as I shift against her, kissing up her legs as her fingers continue to pump inside her.

"Good girl." I kiss her skin again as her back arches. "Just like that. You are perfect, Mik. Fucking perfect."

"Ben," she moans as her core tightens around her fingers and I wrap my hands around her wrists. I pull her away from herself, kissing her fingertips, tasting her, and groan.

"You taste so good, baby." My voice is caught in my throat as I move over her, pressing kisses into her stomach and over her breasts. I trap her lips with mine as I let go of her wrists and feel her nails claw at my back. When her right hand wraps around me, stroking me gently, I shiver.

"Please," she whispers the softest cry against my lips as her hips lift to meet me, and I groan as she guides me into her. After watching her please herself, feeling her stretch around me, the way her body fits with mine, it's nearly too much. I stop moving.

"Give me a minute, baby. I don't want this to end too quickly." I kiss her again as her hand moves to my chest and she shifts slightly. "Stay still, Mikaela. Or I will have to make you."

Her eyes widen and she bites hard on her lip before mischief flickers and her lips twitch. She rolls her hips again deliberately. Slowly. And I hiss.

"Then make me," she whispers. "Sir."

Well fuck. Challenge fucking accepted.

Mikaela

The way his face shifts seems to release a cage of butterflies in my chest. One second his eyes are wide and pleading and the next? The next Ben is looking at me as if he is going to ruin me. And I have no doubt he will. I have no doubt he already has.

"So it's like that, huh?" His eyes gleam with dark desire and my insides melt. His touch is rough but gentle as he grabs my wrist and pulls it over my head, forcing my back to arch. Instinctively, my other hand flies up to free myself and he catches hold of it, easily trapping me with one firm grip. Once he has me pinned with one hand, the other grabs my hips, pulling me close against him and pinning me there so that I can't move. And I try to move.

"Do you trust me?" He's staring at me as something shifts in his eyes and his worries surface.

My sweet, soft Ben.

Even now, when I test his control and push for more, he holds back for me. His eyes search mine as he breathes hard and my heart races. I nod.

"Use your words, Mikaela." He presses a soft kiss against my lips.

"Yes," I sigh. "Yes. I trust you."

"Tell me to stop and I will," he breathes, his eyes closing briefly. "Okay?"

"I will."

Like this it's almost too much. I can feel him everywhere. But when he opens his eyes again his concern is laced with something desperate and his lips lock onto my flesh; rough kisses searing my skin as he moves down my body. I whimper when his teeth graze against my breast, pulling my nipple before sucking and kissing away the flash of pain, and I want his lips on mine. He moves his attention to my neck, his hips still not moving, and licks and sucks at my skin - marking me lightly. I shift as I try to create some friction.

"Stay still, Mik." He speaks through gritted teeth and I close my eyes.

Pleasure is everywhere as his fingers dig into my skin and his teeth pull at my flesh and I twist my head, cutting off his access to my neck.

"Please." I beg as I open my eyes and am rewarded with what I want. Ben's lips crash down over mine with almost painful force as he squeezes my hands tighter over my head. His hips pull back quickly before he slams back into me and I moan into his mouth.

The hand that has hold of my hips moves to my leg and, with a speed and level of flexibility I wasn't aware I had, Ben pushes my knee onto his shoulder before burying himself in me to the hilt.

I cry out at the instant hit of pleasure and feel myself tightening around him, pulling everything I can from him, and his lips leave mine.

"Fuck. Ben. Yes." My voice trembles as he rams into me again and again and I shake violently. *Fuck*.

My whole body is aching, twisting and knotting with anticipation of the high that he is tearing from me.

"Fucking perfect." He grunts as he presses his forehead against mine and my mouth opens in another loud moan. Every word is punctuated with another thrust. "You're. Fucking. Perfect."

And he is my undoing. As his thrusts become more erratic and his words slip into grunts of effort and pleasure, the dam bursts and fireworks illuminate every inch of my skin. My veins thrum as my heart stutters, and my breathing hitches with every tremor. I ride the high he has given me until I can only see stars in a blue ocean. He leans in to kiss me fiercely.

"Oh my God." I mumble against his lips as he frees my hands and they find their way to his face. His stubble scratches against my skin when he pulls back to look at me, and I hold onto him. Both of us are breathing heavy, eyes locked, as every hidden facet of emotion we have pushed aside and buried for years spins out between us. And I can't stop myself when the tears come.

His eyes are gentle with understanding as he brushes my tears away as quickly as they fall and pulls out of me. Within seconds he's disposed of the condom and is wrapping me up in his arms. He holds me against his chest, his lips brushing against my hair, and while the silence of the moment wraps around us, something that had been dark and cracked inside of me fuses together in blinding, golden waves. Somehow he knows I don't need words right now. Somehow he knows these are not the tears of a broken girl too afraid to admit what she wants. Ben sees me and he knows me and he loves me. And I have *never* felt so full in my life.

Ben's fingers move along my spine when I move to kiss him and his lips taste like summer - sunlight and happiness and warmth - and I am finding myself in him.

Chapter Twenty-eight

Ben

"We're going to get caught." Mikaela is giggling as I wrap my arm around her shoulders and pull her closer to me. The wind is still, but there's a bitterness in the air and the lavender dress she's wearing is thin silk against her skin.

"Jamie's out of town, Mik. For the rest of the week." I stop walking, shrugging out of my jacket and earning grunts and complaints from people who have to move around us on the busy sidewalk, before wrapping it around her. "I refuse to hide in your apartment for another three days." I lean in, my lips a breath away from hers, and smile. "I want to show you off a little, Mik. Let me?"

As she kisses me I feel her step closer. She takes a steadying breath when she pulls away and glances to the people going about their evenings around us. My hands move to her cheeks, brushing her hair aside and holding her close.

"No one is looking, Mik." I kiss her gently. "Stop worrying."

The trill of my phone pulls us apart and Mikaela runs her fingers through the long waves of sun-kissed gold as she sighs. She's nervous and it pinches at my heart.

"Hey." I grin as she wraps her arm around my waist and pulls me to start walking again. "Yeah, we're five minutes away. Have they seated you?" Mikaela glances up at me, a soft smile on her lips, and I wink. "No, go tell them the table is under my name. They should have asked you when you arrived."

She steps a little closer as she makes space for a small family to sweep past us on the sidewalk.

"Yeah, she's with me now." I chuckle at his excitement. "Yes, she remembers you."

She laughs when I roll my eyes dramatically.

"I can hear you grinning, Norman."

His laughter is full of energy and enthusiasm and Mikaela smiles to herself at the sound of it, distant but clear.

Norman is glancing around the restaurant as we enter, his eyes skimming over tables where families sit laughing and joking, and corner booths where teenagers share bowls of pasta and a bill their parents will probably wince at later.

As we approach the table, waving off the twenty-something year old waiter who seems far too keen to shed Mikaela of my jacket, he gets to his feet.

Time has been good to Norman. His eyes still glisten with troublesome youth and his smile is wide in the warmth of his features. His skin is worn by age, wrinkled and softened after years pulled a thin veil of wariness over him, but he stands tall and he speaks loudly. He is a man of pride and experience, and the light lift of his Dublin accent - never dulled by his decades here - drifts over the cacophony of patrons, welcoming me into the comfort of his presence as if I'm a troubled teenager all over again; desperately seeking some kindness.

"There's my boy." His hand claps against my shoulder as he pulls me into his embrace, holding me for a moment as he breathes in. Overwhelming comfort spills over me. It's been too long since we last did this. "Let me look at you."

Norman holds me at arms length, his eyes slowly running over my face, my arms, my shoulders. He drinks in the sight of me as a smile dances over his lips, before turning to where Mikaela is standing beside me.

Her eyes glance between us as she fidgets with the sleeves of my jacket and takes a deep breath.

Norman nods at her, but doesn't move forwards. It's like he reads her nerves perfectly and gives her the space to process the moment as she needs to. His voice is softer with her than it's ever been with me. "I trust that you're taking good care of my boy, Miss Wilcox?"

Her answering smile is shy and demure. It's coy and I want to kiss the edges of it. I want to draw out her brilliance again.

Mikaela

Norman's eyes are alight with suggestion and I feel my cheeks burn with my blush as I smile.

"I'm trying," I admit sheepishly. Truthfully, in the week since Jamie's party, Ben has had to take more care of me than I deserve. Especially when I cried after sex. In the days since, he has been attentive and gentle and so loving that my heart just keeps filling with more and more of him, even when the darkness creeps in again.

The fact Ben now knows about Matthew unwittingly unearthed memories that keep crawling into my dreams, twisting them into something dark and damaged, until I wake screaming. But Ben never asks what tears me from sleep. He never makes me explain. He just holds me. He cares for me. He loves me. And each night I keep the details hidden and locked away.

I keep keeping them from him.

"It's so good to see you again, Missy." Norman releases Ben from his grip and steps towards me, his arms outstretched.

Folding into him is easy and strangely familiar. In the years of him ferrying the boys around, I had very little to do with this man. He was always sweet and kind, but we spoke rarely. A brief memory of him smiling knowingly in the rear-view mirror from that night ten years ago pulls a small laugh from my lips as the scent of leather and pine mix around me. Norman is somehow a wash of soothing warmth and I hug him back with enthusiasm as one warm hand rubs firmly against my shoulder.

"Now, let me look at you." Just as he had held Ben, he now holds me, pulling back as his hands splay gently over my shoulders and his eyes give me a once over. "Well, aren't you a beauty!"

I drop my eyes as I laugh out an awkward thank you and Ben's arms wrap around my waist as he pulls me back gently.

"Stop staring at my girl, Norman. You're going to make her run for the hills." He presses a soft kiss into my cheek as Norman laughs heartily and moves back to his seat.

"Your girl." He muses aloud as he shakes his head and a devilish smile tugs at his features. "I remember one night, about eight years ago - so just before I retired - having to drive around town for three whole hours with this one." He gestures to Ben with his thumb as Ben pulls my chair out for me. "He was going out of his mind. Kept telling me the girl he was desperately in love with was leaving town with the wrong guy. You know where I picked him up from before that drive, Miss Wilcox?"

My chest aches.

"Please, call me Mik." I shake my head in a lie. Of course I know where Ben had been that day. I remember everything about that day and the nightmare that followed.

"Well, Mik." Norman smiles softly as Ben groans. "I picked him up from your apartment."

"Norman." Ben's tone is light and playful, but there's a warning there; a way of telling him not to say anything else. And I suspect it isn't to save him from further embarrassment.

I glance towards him, and although my eyes meet Ben's for just a second, I can see it there. He knows that this particular memory ties too closely to memories of Matthew.

"I'm saying nothing, and I'm saying it well." Norman sips from his glass as the waiter approaches and I try to smile softly as I pick up my menu.

Ben places his hand on my thigh below the table, a small token of comfort, and squeezes gently.

I breathe.

Eight Years Ago

"Yeah right." Matthew practically spits his anger over me. "I didn't fucking walk in on nothing, Mikaela. Tell me, if I hadn't walked in would you have fucked him right there, or do you think you would have at least pretended to give a shit that I was in the same fucking house and fucked off somewhere to screw him?"

My eyes are stinging with his venom and I try to hold back the pain his words bring. "Matty, I promise you, nothing happened. Nothing was going to happen. Ben was just helping me with Mom's pills."

Matthew scoffs as he storms out of the living room, past the boxes piled high and belongings all sorted for tomorrow's drive.

"Please don't do that," I plead with him as I crash through our stuff, chasing after him. "Please don't walk away when I'm talking to you. I need you to listen to me."

I know I should stop talking. I know I should let him walk away. *Why am I always doing the wrong thing?*

"You need me to listen?" His eyes are dark and dangerous and I feel my throat tighten. "I need you to keep your fucking legs shut and stop acting like a ten dollar whore."

His words snatch the breath from me.

"What?" My voice is barely a whisper, barely a sound.

"You heard me." He steps forwards and I flinch.

He freezes.

"Matty," I plead. "I promise you, Ben and I have never - we would never -"

His breath is hot on my face as his fingers wrap around my arms and he pulls me closer. "I don't believe you."

He pushes me away, into the boxes behind me, and I stumble as I try to correct my footing. Piles of pots and plates come crashing down over me as I throw my hands out to stop my fall and I feel it; the pop and grind of something deep in my wrist.

As I cry out, my eyes blurring with instant pain, I hear the door slam behind him and I lay breaking under the crashing chaos of our lives.

I hold my wrist against my chest, my whole being protesting each time I move, as I place the last pot back in a box and bend down to pick up the crumpled cardboard from this evening. My eyes sting and my fingers tingle with a fuzzy numbness as the door creaks open.

It's hours after midnight. The van is getting here at six and then we're leaving. Leaving all of *this* behind us. We'll leave the anger and the jealousy, we'll leave the misunderstandings and the history we can't seem to escape. All of it will be behind us once we were out of this place. I'm sure of it.

Matthew slinks through the space with dull eyes and a tight frown. In his hands is a bunch of tulips, the same flowers he bought me on our first date, and my heart splinters a little. *How did he get them this late?*

"I'm sorry, Mik."

He can't look at me.

"I know."

"I just - I hate him."

"I know," I repeat.

I sigh as I try to lift the box I have just re-packed and my wrist protests, a shooting pain burrowing up my arm. Matthew moves to my side the second the box drops from my grip. His touch is gentle and soothing as he moves it, placing it on the coffee table, before taking my hand and running his fingers up my skin.

"Mik, your wrist is swollen."

"I know." *Where are my words? Where is my voice when I want to tell him it's broken? I am broken.*

"Let's go." He pulls me to his side and wraps an arm around me.

I close my eyes. "Where?"

We haven't finished packing the bedroom.

"The ER. You need someone to look at it."

I stop moving. "What do we tell them?"

Matthew looks into my eyes and I find sincerity in his. "The truth."

"The truth?"

"Yeah, Mik. You fell into the packing boxes and tried to stop your fall. The truth."

My throat constricts as I nod and try not to cry.

When we're gone it will all be different. I'm sure.

Present

Ben

Mikaela's head is thrown back in laughter as she leans into my side and Norman sits back in his chair, watching us both.

"You didn't?" She wipes at the tears that escape her in her laughter and Norman nods.

"He did. Thought he was super smooth about it too. Didn't dream that I'd catch him. And let me tell you now, Julia Haston is not a woman to mess with." He laughs with complete ease as he watches Mikaela for every reaction she has. He drinks in her laughter and her smiles, and he comes to life in front of her; her excitement feeding into his own. "When she found out he'd stolen my car - not even the one I was paid to drive around in, mind you, but my Mustang - she went nuts. The boy was cleaning floors with a toothbrush for a month."

Mikaela rests her head against my shoulder as Norman speaks and I run my hand over her neck and across her shoulder, goose-pimples trailing where my touch has been, before I reach back for my jacket draped over her chair, and wrap it around her shoulders.

"How did I not know about this?" She nuzzles closer beside me as I wrap an arm around her, a beautifully easy smile ghosting her lips.

"Because it happened when I was fifteen and you were your very bookish, very scary self who spent all of her time telling her brother I was a privileged little douchebag who would inevitably end up in jail." She blushes as I recall her words and I grin. "I was terrified I'd be proving you right, so I swore Jamie to secrecy."

She laughs as she shakes her head and Norman mirrors her. "Did you two do that a lot? Swear not to tell me things."

Only twice.

Only if it would hurt you.

"Wouldn't you love to know?" I tease her lightly before leaning in to press a small kiss against her lips.

"I was going to order dessert," Norman guffaws and Mik blushes as she looks over to the old man teasing us, "but I think that filled my sweet allowance for the night."

Norman turns, fishing in his jacket to retrieve his wallet, and I place my hand on the bill in the middle of the table. I pull it towards myself as he shakes his head.

"You said last time that I could pay," he protests.

"No chance, Norman." I slip my card into the leather holder and hold it up for our waiter. "Maybe next time."

"Let me guess." Mikaela leans forwards and whispers as if conspiring against me. "He says that every time?"

"Without fail." Norman nods with a roll of his eyes. "And every time I remind him."

Mikaela's laugh is like light itself as it washes over me, but darkness falls in an instant as she looks over Norman's shoulder and her back straightens.

"Mik?" My hand is on her spine instantly. "What's wrong?"

My eyes follow hers to the door. Outside the silhouettes of strangers bundling into their coats are muted by the shadowed windows, and my heart starts to sprint.

Mikaela shakes her head and releases a breathy laugh. And I want to believe it.

"Nothing," she sighs. "I - I just thought - never mind. I'm fine."

When she turns back to me, her smile is dazzling. It's one of her rarest smiles. The one that has no secrets, no burdens, no worries. It simply exists because we exist.

Mikaela

I glance over my shoulder as we leave the restaurant and confirm what I already know: it was a trick of lighting. My stomach settles, as it had inside when the presence I thought he'd left behind drifted out of the restaurant and away from my chest, and I turn to face Ben as he helps his old driver into the back of a private car.

"You know, Benjamin, you don't have to hire me a car every time I see you." Norman grins and I relax even more. "It's a fecking waste."

Watching Ben with this man soothes me. He's kind with him, patient and doting. It's like watching a grandfather and his favourite grandchild at play; calm and easy and beautiful.

"Yeah, but I can, so I do." Ben shrugs as he holds onto the door and Norman smiles up at him.

"I say it every time I see you, but I'm so proud of you, boy." Norman releases a deep sigh and my eyes mist as Ben clears his throat. I smile when he nods over at me before continuing. "Even more so now you finally got the girl. Don't screw it up. She's precious."

"I know." Ben's voice is gruff and emotional and I step to his side.

"Thank you, Norman, for a lovely evening." I smile at him and he winks.

Ben closes the door and we watch as the driver moves steadily down the busy road before turning to make our way home.

"I had fun tonight." I wrap my arms around his forearm, hugging close to him as we walk, and he pushes his hands into his pockets.

"Yeah?" His apprehension is scrawled over his face as he stares ahead and, for a moment, Ben seems vulnerable.

I tug his sleeve as I stare up at him and wait for the blue of his eyes to find me.

"Yes." My voice is calm and steady as we walk together, hardly watching where we're going, and I ease his mind. "Norman's like this bomb of chaotic stories and kindness, and I really like him. Thank you for wanting me here tonight."

Ben pulls his arm out of my hold, only to wrap it around my shoulders and pull me closer.

"You know, he was the best example of a good man that I had growing up." It sounds confessional, as if he's afraid to admit it. "Still is. And he's always liked you. Even when Jamie and I were shoving you away and demanding he drove off without you. He would lay into us for that shit every time."

I grin as he rolls his eyes and holds me close.

"Your place or mine?" I glance up at him as I ask and he smirks.

I know that look.

"Your place." His voice drips with promises. "It's so much closer."

Chapter Twenty-nine

Ben

Sex with Mikaela will never grow old. Hearing her little high-pitch moan as I hold her close to me, feeling her wrapped around me - tightening around me - it's everything.

I lay kisses down her neck, sucking and nipping as we move together. Her arms wrap around my shoulders as she rolls her hips, sinking over me again, and I pull my face back to look at her. Like this, face to face, her chest pressed against mine and our eyes locked, is the happiest I have been in a long time. Holding her, watching as her eyes cloud with bliss and she bites down on her lip, I move my hand to where we were connected and brush the pad of my thumb against that little spot that I know will detonate her. Enthralled, I watch as a warm blush spreads over her cheeks.

"Fuck," she moans loudly, her head rolling back, her eyes closed.

"Look at me." I sound desperate, strained, but I want to see it happen. I need to see her come undone for me.

Her smile is completely peaceful and her eyes are dancing forests of pleasure. I cup her face with my free hand as she moves slowly, lost in our connection, and my heart splinters.

I love her.

In this moment, in every moment I have ever shared with Mikaela Wilcox, there is one thing I can be sure of: my heart was, is, and always will be, irrevocably hers.

And I don't care that she hasn't said it back. I don't care that when I said it she stammered through an awkward thank you until I put my hand over her mouth and rolled my eyes.

I love her. *So fucking much.*

I pull her towards me, my chest burning with the weight of it all, and I kiss her softly. I kiss her with adoration and worship and the undying need to hold her close, and as she kisses me she tightens around me and whimpers into my mouth. She comes undone with the words dancing at the tip of my tongue, and then it happens.

By the time we hear the keys it's too late.

Mikaela rips away from me, pulling the throw from the couch up over herself just as he drops his bag to the floor. I grab my sweats from where they've been thrown, yanking them up and on without even thinking about what's already been seen and step in front of her.

His eyes are glued to her - not me, not us, *her* - and his jaw is tight.

I've seen Jamie like this before - pain and anger rolling off of him - and a year later I know why. I know why heat poured from him at the same terrifying pace as icy pain. Why he ran from the bar and drove three hours out of state. Why she came home six months ago and ended up working for her brother a few months later. Why our paths crossed again.

Mik had called him.

For the first time in three years her number had lit up his phone screen and he bolted right to her side. I'd pieced together enough information to know it was when she had the accident, but the rage he'd held in that moment went unexplained for so long.

Except now I have an idea. And now that pain and anger isn't *for* her, it's directed at her, and I don't know what to do.

"Jamie, it isn't -"

"It isn't what it looks like?" He spits his words at me, cutting me off as he glares past me to where Mikaela's sitting, frozen like ice. "Really? Because it looks like you're *fucking* my little sister."

I take a step forwards just as Mik reaches for me, her hand skimming along the base of my spine as I move out of her reach.

"Ben," she whispers, almost as if warning me not to say anything.

"Jamie. I know what you're thinking, I know what you think I'm like with girls, but it's not like that. Okay? I'm not like that." I keep my voice calm and measured and when his eyes snap to me, all that burning fire now aimed at me, I feel the pressure in my chest ease. "Mik and I, we're-"

"*Mik and I?*" Jamie grunts taking another step back. The laugh that follows is acidic. "How long?"

"Jamie." Her voice is small and afraid, and I feel sick.

"How fucking long, Ben?" Jamie shouts, his whole body lurching forwards. "How long has my best friend been screwing my little sister behind my back? Fucking hell. *She's* the girl? Fuck you, Ben."

He shoves at my chest and I stumble slightly.

"Jamie, stop." Mikaela's standing now, the blanket wrapped tightly around her as she comes up behind me. "It's not like that." Her fingers wrap around mine as she pulls closer to me and Jamie watches us with incredulous eyes. "He - we - Jamie, I love him."

My whole body is on fire. Those three little words slipped so quietly from her I'm not sure I heard her correctly.

I look down to her and she's staring up at me with the smallest smile, despite everything going on with her brother, and my heart is soaring.

"You do?" My face is aching from the width of my smile as I meet the burning intensity of her eyes.

She simply nods and for a moment I don't care that Jamie is here. I don't care that we've been caught. I don't care that he hates me right now. I only care about one thing: *Mikaela Wilcox loves me and I have never felt so much at once.*

"Love!" Jamie barks an acidic laugh and Mikaela flinches. "Fucking hell, Mikaela. You sure know how to pick them."

My skin bristles with his words.

This will go one of two ways: either Jamie is about to insult her again, which will, no doubt about it, end our friendship completely, or, Jamie is going to say something that he can't take back that may well shatter the very strange, fragile surface their relationship has been skating on for the last year.

Either way, I need him to stop talking. *He* needs me to get him to stop talking.

"Jamie, don't." My tone is firm but my eyes are open books, pleading with him to stop.

"You love him, Mik?" He scoffs as he steps up to us, his chest practically against my own as he pushes me back again and glares down at her.

"Jamie." I push back. Just slightly. Moving him away from her.

"Would you still love him if you knew he was lying to you, Mik? That he's been lying to you all this time?"

Her fingers are gone and I can't look at her. Not as Jamie floods the space with the one confession that could destroy it all; us, them, everything.

Chapter Thirty

Eight Years Ago

Jamie

"Mik's dropping out of college." I pass another beer to Ben as he drags his eyes from the football game on the screen and furrows his brow.

"What?" His confusion would be amusing if it wasn't the same fucking face Mom and I have been wearing for the last six days.

"Don't ask." I sigh as Ben glances to the door closed between us and the women of my family. "I'm guessing it's something to do with the boyfriend."

Ben's eyes dart back to me and I roll my eyes. Of course that's news to him. And of course he looks like I've just slapped him with a cold fish.

"Boyfriend?"

I bring my bottle to my lips. "Mhmm. They've been pretty serious for about a year. Seriously, this is why you need to come home more often. You need to catch up."

Ben shifts in his seat and drags his eyes back to the screen.

Two years.

Two long fucking years of this sulky shit whenever Mik comes up in conversation. I'm honestly not sure if he hates her or wants her, but either way; it's getting old.

"Anyway," I continue, "he's moving out of state now he's graduating. Got some fancy role in a tech start-up and she wants to follow. She swears she'll pick up classes there but I don't know, dude. He's very-"

A loud rapping on the door cuts me off and I push to my feet. A long, low groan threatens to erupt as I'm faced with the very same man hell-bent on killing my sister's future.

"Hey, Matthew." I grumble, making my way back to the couch and not bothering to look to see if he follows.

"Mik about?" Not even a hi. *Nice.*

"In the kitchen with Mom." I glance to Ben and see his eyes roll over Matthew, no doubt sussing him out. "This is Ben."

Matthew's eyes are ice when they meet Ben's and he makes no attempt to hide the distain that mars his features. He nods tightly and grunts at us both.

"Yeah." He turns back to the kitchen, his muscles suddenly tense and a distinct aura of intolerance waving off of him. "I know who he is."

He pushes his way into the kitchen and I watch as Mikaela instantly jumps off of the counter and glances back to us. Whatever she's told Matthew about Ben, she definitely doesn't want them in the same room.

Five Years Ago

"Jamie, where are you? It's Mom. Jamie you need to get here. Please. I - I can't do this without you and..."

The air is not breathable.

I haven't heard from Mik in months. Not since Matthew and I got into it again. Not since he broke my nose. Now we take turns with Mom. We have a schedule. A schedule that Mik's voicemail throws out of the window.

I can't breathe.

"I don't know how long she's got left in her Jamie and I'm all alone here. Matthew - Matthew wasn't able to come with me and I need you. I know we haven't spoken in a while but I need you, JimJam. I need my brother. Please."

I can hear the words she doesn't want to say hanging in the dead air before the message cuts out: it's time.

Suddenly I can't move fast enough. My shoulder isn't aching in the same way it was seconds ago, my head isn't pounding.

It's clear.

Everything is painfully clear and I need to get out of here.

That message was left three hours ago. Just as we'd been sitting in the back of an ambulance. Three hours. So much can change in three hours.

"What's wrong?" Ben follows quickly behind me as I throw my discharge papers on the nearest nurses station and race down the corridor. I don't know this place well enough - Mik takes Mom for her appointments and recent renovations left her turning in circles in the last month too - and I feel like I'm walking through quicksand.

"I've got to go. I've got to find Mik and - and -" My voice cracks as my chest does. Pain floors me and drags me down, and I know. I know within the very bones of my being that it's too late.

I'm too late.

"Jamie." Ben's pulling me up, his eyes darting around the space for somewhere to take me. "What do I do?"

"I need air." I choke on the words as he pulls me with him, guiding me out to the nearest exit.

She's standing in the rain. Just standing there. And my body seems to shatter as I step towards her.

One step pushes me closer, then another, and then I'm running to her and she's staring at me with empty eyes.

"Mik! Mikaela! I'm so sorry. I - Mik." I reach out for her, crashing into her as she flinches away and pushes. She pushes hard.

"Don't touch me." Her voice is lifeless, dull.

"Mik -"

"I called you." Her eyes are hollow as she tilts her head to the side. Her anger is seeping out with the rain, clinging to her skin but never reaching in. It doesn't warm her with any fire. "I called you so many times, Jamie. Where were you?"

"We were in the emergency room." I admit, far too aware of the smell of whiskey breathing from me. I reach towards her and she pulls away again. "My phone was on silent and I was getting my shoulder fixed and I - Mik, I'm so sorry. I should have been there."

"We?" She laughs bitterly as a spark of something fans behind her eyes. Emotion, however small, takes hold and she stares at Ben. "Of course. I should have known Ben was involved."

When I step closer this time she hits me.

Her fist smashes into my chest again and again as agony rises within her and her whispers become wails.

"Don't fucking touch me." She sobs. "Don't touch me." Its a knife in my chest. "You were supposed to be there." Twisting. "You promised her." Eviscerating. "You promised her you'd be there, Jamie. But you weren't. You fucking weren't." She whimpers. "I hate you." Whispers. "I hate you so much."

I stand and I take every blow. I wrap around her as she pummels into my chest. I hold her as pain screams in my shoulder.

I let her break me because she is broken.

"I'm sorry. I'm so sorry. I'm sorry." My whispers are nothing, but they are truth. I sweep my hand over her hair and I hold her.

I hold my sister as she falls apart.

"You said you'd be there." She crumbles. "Why weren't you there, Jamie?"

I try to tell her. But when Ben speaks and tells her it was him - when Ben takes the fall for me again, like the time I stole his driver's car - I can't say the words. I can't tell her the truth. Because even now, with this lie hanging over us, a lie I know is to save what little there is left of us, Mikaela freezes against me and pushes me away.

When she looks at me it's as if she died too.

She backs away and moves towards Matthew's car.

"I'll let you know the funeral arrangements when they're finalised." My heart implodes as her lifeless voice fills the space between us. "And then we're done, Jamie."

A strangled sob catches in my throat as I step towards her, my whole world going up in flames as she shakes her head.

"And Ben?"

"Yes, Mikaela?"

Is the world still turning?

"Stay the fuck away. You are not welcome anywhere near her. Do you understand me?" Ben nods and I'm shaking.

Matthew is smug and self-satisfied as he laughs. He really laughs. Like he gets some kick out of this pain. Because he wins. With Mom gone she has nothing keeping her here. I stumble forwards and she looks back to me.

"Get in babe." He's cold and detached, and I want to kill him.

"Mik, please." I plead as I race to her door, desperately hoping I can make her stay. "Please don't leave."

"I want to go home." She's empty.

Three Years Ago

"Mik, please open the door." My forehead is pressed against the chipped and broken wood of their apartment door. My chest aches with the same emptiness I felt two years ago. My chest aches for my sister. "Please."

Behind the thin wood I hear her whimpering. I hear as she desperately tries to silence her tears and my heart burns. I know that she will be sitting against the door with her knees pulled to her chest, rocking gently.

I need to hold her, to help her.

My mind races over the words she spilled to me hours ago and I try to think of a way in, a way to get my sister back, as her voice echoes in my mind.

Jamie, I'm scared. I'm scared and I don't know what to do. I don't know what to do.

"I can hear you, Mik." My whisper is fraught as I place my hand against the wood and slip to my knees. "Please just let me in. I can help."

Silence.

"I love you Mik. I love you so much, okay? And I'm here." I whisper as a new kind of pain burns through me. "I love you. I am here and I will be here when you are ready to come home."

I'm scared and I don't know what to do.

"I'm sorry." I apologise for not being here sooner. For not fighting to get my sister back. For hiding away out of shame and guilt. I apologise for the lies that dance between us, taunting us both, and for the words I haven't been able to say. I apologise for two years of silence and tears. I apologise for not protecting her; for not keeping his hands off of her. "I'm so sorry."

One Year Ago

"Is this Jamie Wilcox?"

The voice on the end of the line is not my sister's and my blood stops pumping through my veins.

"Speaking?"

"Mr Wilcox, my name is Samantha, I'm calling from Massachusetts General Hospital. You're currently listed as next of kin for a Miss Mikaela Wilcox." Ice. My veins are stopped with ice. "I'm sorry to say she's been in an accident."

"I'll be there." My voice is thin. "Four hours. I'll be there in four hours."

I shut off my phone and dive from our booth, pushing past Ben as he makes his way back with drinks.

"Jamie?" He calls after me.

I don't stop.

Xavier and Asher stare at me.

"Jamie!"

She's pale. And small.

I never realised how small my sister is.

Her chest rises and falls with a mechanical whirl and I close my eyes.

A ventilator. That's what it's called. The machine helping her breathe is a ventilator. In the morning they'll try to take her off of it. But for now, while she's lying in the post-op suite, wires running out of her and tubes pushing into her, her face bruised and torn and her skin a deathly white, a machine is helping her to breathe.

I want to soothe her. I want to run my fingers through her hair like Mom used to but I can't. I can't because there's white gauze wrapped around her scalp and the doctors said she'd needed stitches.

I'm not sure how long I sit with her before I fall asleep, but at some point I do. And when I do, I dream of it. I dream of him.

His face, his eyes, his car.

I dream of the moment he decided to smash his car into the drivers side of the tiny heap of junk my sister scraped coins together to buy.

I dream of her scream as the door crumples, and her tears as the fire department try to cut her out. I dream of the stranger who watched it all unfold and waited with her until the police came.

I dream of Matthew stumbling out of his car, unscathed. Sitting on the sidewalk, crying.

I dream of it all until a sharp beeping noise pulls me out of one nightmare and into another.

"Get him out of here!" A doctor shouts over her shoulder as she pushes hard on Mikaela's chest and someone pulls me from the room.

Blinds are drawn and time is frozen and I am left to wait.

I am left to wait to find out if my world will cease to exist.

Present

"He wasn't driving, Mik." I spit the words with all my anger as Ben glares at me.

I know what he thinks: I'm destroying me and her all over again, I'm letting go of my sister out of spite and anger and disappointment. And maybe he's right. Maybe I am doing all of that, but I know something Ben doesn't. I know Mikaela will stay this time.

I know that we're stronger than before.

"What - what do you mean?" Her eyes dart between us both and I watch as she takes a step back.

"When Mom died. He lied, Mik. We both did." I stare directly at him as his shoulders tense and his eyes darken. "He lied to save my ass. I was driving that night. I crashed his car. Ben was in the passenger seat, and he lied. You brought him to see Mom and he was lying to you. You're *fucking* him and he is lying to you."

"I don't understand." Mikaela is shaking, the chill from the evening air only amplified by my confession.

"Mik." Ben turns to her and moves quickly, his fingers splaying over her hips as she shakes her head over and over. I want to punch him. "Mik, I'm sorry. I wanted to tell you, but you were in so much pain and I thought - I thought it was the right thing to do. I wanted to tell you. I did."

"But you didn't." Her voice is low and whispered and drowning in anguish. "Or you would have told me."

"Mik." He ducks to her level.

"Get out." She steps back and he lets go.

"Wait please, Mik."

I've never seen Ben beg before. It sinks in my stomach.

"I said get out!" The volume knocks the breath from me. Mikaela isn't a shouter. She never has been, not once growing up, never with Matthew. Not even when Mom died. But now? This? I've made a mistake.

"Mikaela." I choke on my own voice.

"Both of you! Get out. Now!" She shoves at Ben's chest with one hand, tears streaming as he moves towards her and his own tears begin to fall. "Get the fuck out!"

With the door slammed in our faces, we both stand in silence. Ben stares numbly at the door as I stare at my feet, shame flooding through me.

"Shoes."

He looks at me in a blind stupor. "What?"

"Your shoes. And your top. They're in there."

He nods as his eyes drift back to her door.

I sigh. "I'll drive you home."

Chapter Thirty-one

Ben

"You really think so little of me?" My head is in my hands as Jamie paces back and forth across my living room. In the hour since we left Mik, his temper has settled and given way to pure, unadulterated panic. But mine? Mine has simmered and bubbled to boiling point.

"No." He huffs as he pushes his hair back and glances back to the door. He's tried to leave three times already, but I keep stopping him - if Mik wants to be alone, she needs it, and we will respect that. It's the least we can do. "But I also don't want you screwing my sister."

When he looks at me there's a shimmer of fear behind the honesty and it enrages me. When he says it like that it's seedy and disgusting, and that isn't what's been happening.

"Jamie, what the fuck is your problem?" I shake my head as I suck in a deep breath. "Why do you insist on thinking so little of me? I'm not who I was in college - fucking different girls every other night and partying too hard and making shit choices. I haven't been him in a long time, J, and you know that. So, what the hell are you so afraid of?"

He sinks to the seat beside me. "I can't lose her again, Ben."

"And what? You think I'll drive her away?"

Jamie sighs, long and drawn out, and I stare at him.

"Honestly? Yeah. I do." He swallows and I wait. "I think she's been through more shit than you're ready to deal with, Ben. I think you won't mean to, but you'll hurt her. And then she'll run."

"Tell me." I say it simply, like my chest hasn't been housing a lump of cement where my heart is for the last twenty seconds.

"What?"

"You're so scared I'll hurt her, that whatever she's been through will be too much for me. Tell me what it is. Because I know it's bad, J. I know whatever it is is why she's got scars on her stomach and the back of her legs. And her shoulder, her neck, her scalp. I know it's why she ended up living with you again. I know it's Matthew. I know he was like my dad. *Fuck, J.* I know he was one hundred times worse than my dad. So tell me. Tell me everything, because I am telling you I can handle it. For her, I will handle it."

"Ben." Jamie's hands run over his face as he groans and throws himself back on my couch. "I don't even know where I'd start."

"Try the beginning."

Mikaela

"I'm glad you called." Sephy drops a bag full of tissues and magazines and chocolate onto my coffee table as I sit and stare at the shoes by the door. "What can I do?"

"I don't know," I whisper.

"Okay." She shrugs and sits next to me. She makes no effort to push me to talk. She doesn't try to coax any more of an explanation than the weeping, heaving disaster of a phone call she received as soon as I was sure they were gone. She just lets me be. I'm glad I called her.

"Sephy?" *Where is the life in my voice?* "He lied. They both lied."

"I'm assuming 'he' is this Baby Blue guy?"

My arms wrap tighter around myself, clinging to the t-shirt I pulled on almost as soon as he'd left, and inhale the smell of him. Why, when I am reeling, when my world is crumbling because of him, do I need him closer?

I nod.

"And who else?"

"Jamie, my brother."

Sephy breathes in deeply. "And what was the lie?"

"The lie isn't what's important." I choke on another sob as the image of Jamie's face, rain soaked and broken, swirls behind my vision. "I can't do lies again, Sephy. I won't."

She nods thoughtfully before turning to face me. When I look at her, her face is a mask of compassion and kindness, but she's detached too. This is the mark of her profession; the shoulder to cry on who knows what questions to ask and what questions to avoid.

"The lie matters, Mik. Even if you don't think it does. What was the lie?"

I take a steadying breath and close my eyes.

"When my mom died, Jamie wasn't there. I called and I called and he didn't answer. And she begged for him, Sephy. Her last words were just his name over and over. She wanted her son and he wasn't there. And then I found out he was in the hospital all along. They'd been in an accident. Drink driving. Ben said he was driving."

"I take it he wasn't?"

I shake my head as my tears spill, my mothers croaked whisper is stuck in my throat.

"And he just told you."

"No," I whimper. "Jamie did."

For a moment Sephy doesn't say anything. She just processes it all and lets me sit in my pain.

"What happened after Ben told you he was driving?"

I look at her and shake my head. Why are we rehashing the past when the present is the problem?

"Just trust me, Mik. It's important."

"I cut them both off. I didn't see Ben for five years and I didn't speak to Jamie for three."

"Okay. And you were with Matthew?"

I nod as more tears come and Sephy moves closer, her hand rubbing gentle circles against my spine.

"Things were bad then. I had no one and Matthew used that to keep me stuck. And one night I just - I couldn't handle it and I called J. He drove for hours to get to me and I -" My throat closes with the weight of the memory. "I panicked and I wouldn't let him in. I pushed him away again." My whole body is shaking. "We've only just got each other back."

Sephy takes one of my hands in both of hers and waits for me to look at her. "If Jamie had told you he was driving, what would you have done differently?"

I stare.

"What would it have changed, Mik?" Her tone is persistent and my chest is tight. I know what it would have changed. I also know what would have stayed the same.

"I don't know if I would have called Jamie two years ago."

"Okay." She nods as she smiles. "So Ben's lie meant you were able to bring your brother back into your life?"

I rock forwards and place my forehead against my hands.

"I guess." I sniffle.

"Do you think maybe that's why he did it?"

I shrug and Sephy laughs.

"I don't know, Sephy."

"Do you think maybe you can get past the lie if you knew it was to protect you? To protect you both?"

I groan as I feel her shifting and Sephy sighs.

"It's not an excuse, Mik. I'm not saying it was right. But I am saying that maybe he had his reasons." Her voice is light as she pulls one hand to my hair, brushing through it to comfort me as I lean into her touch.

"He should have told me." It's a weak defence, but it's all I have.

"And you would have left him before he had a chance to explain."

"You know, I should have called Max," I grumble.

"He would have been just as dramatic as you are, Mik."

My phone rings between us for the seventh time and I close my eyes.

"You know he's just going to keep calling." Sephy pauses the film and looks over to me.

She's right. Every few minutes my phone rings and it's always Ben. He's left messages. He's text. I've not looked at any of it.

"At least read the texts," Sephy suggests.

I untuck my feet from beneath the cushions, reaching for the phone I don't want to look at, and take a deep breath.

Five messages.

Ben: Mik, please just let me explain. I'm so sorry. Just call me back.

My eyes burn.

Ben: I know I should have told you, baby. I know. I screwed up.

My heart pinches.

Ben: I can't bear this. Please just call me. Please. I fucked up and I'm so sorry. Please.

I can't get enough air.

Ben: I know you're mad. I know Jamie is too. Please don't push me away, Mik. Please.

Everything is broken.

Ben: I love you. I love you so much.

Sephy holds me as I cry. She holds me until there's nothing left to leave me and my heart is just an empty shell. She holds me until I slip into a painful, broken sleep and dream of crystal blues and rain soaked sidewalks.

Ben

Jamie isn't talking to me. He made it clear when he left mine last night that our friendship is done.
And I don't blame him.
I've lied to him for too long.
And I lied to her.
And Jamie needs her.

My relationship with Jamie Wilcox is now, well and truly, business only.

I sit in the chair behind my desk, my eyes burning from exhaustion and my clothes scruffy, as I wait.

Eight fifty seven.

She's never this late.

I just need to talk to her. I need to have one moment alone with her so that she can see why I did it.

Fuck that.

I need one minute alone with her so that I can apologise and beg and grovel. Nothing I did was right. I should have told her. I should have come clean the second she asked me to go to Elizabeth's grave. I should have just told her. But then I would have lost her. Jamie would have lost her. The mist of confusion is a never ending chasm of desperate bidding and pleading for answers I don't have and don't know how to find.

All I know is that I need her.

And I feel like my lungs are collapsing without her.

Mikaela

"I can't do this." I choke on my fear. "I shouldn't have come in."

Max's hand tightens around my fingers as the elevator doors split open and I stare up at him.

"Max, I want to go."

"No." He doesn't elaborate. He simply pulls me through the doors and to my desk as Ben pushes himself out of his office and straight towards me.

"Mik. Can we talk?"

"No." Max is firm with him as he stands between us and I sink into my seat. "Back away, Blue. She needs space and this isn't the time or place."

"Kingford, please. Get out of the way."

"Ben." I can't look at him. "Not here."

"Then where, Mikaela?" Ben doesn't move closer. He lets Max shield me with his body and my heart is hammering in my chest. "Where and when? Because we need to talk. I need to talk, Mik. Please."

I look over my shoulder and my stomach drops. People are staring, eyes wide and lips pressed behind hands as they lean over desks to whisper to their friends.

People are talking.

"I don't know." My throat is closing.

"Talk to me, Mik." He pushes around Max this time, shaking him off as a hand wraps around his arm to pull him back, and crouches beside my chair. He spins me quickly, forcing me to look at him, away from the eyes that are watching us and my heart stutters. "Tell me how to fix this."

"Please don't make me do this here." I whisper and his fingers brush over my cheek, wiping away the strength I am clinging to for dear life.

"Don't do it at all."

"I have to, Ben."

His eyes - so blue and inviting, so calm and warming - are glued to mine, and I watch as his own strength shatters into a million pieces. His tears fall quickly as he shakes his head, holding me gently when I wrap my hands around his fingers and remove his hold on me.

"We're over, Ben."

Pain. I just see pain.

"No. No, Mik. We can fix this."

His hands are clinging to my chair now and I close my eyes. Every single fibre of my being wants to wrap around him and hold him. Every single aching pit of my soul craves and calls for him. My chest caves as I speak and his whispered pleas seep into my skin.

"We don't work, Ben. When there's no one around us - when there's nothing else - we work. But that's not reality."

"Mik, please don't do this."

"We don't exist in this reality. We never did."

"We can." He places his head in my lap, his hands clinging to my thighs and I am hurting. This is hurting. "I want you, Mik. I love you. We can fix this."

"There's nothing to fix, Ben. I don't want you."

I feel him leave. I feel the pressure of his hands leave my chair and the air shift around me. I feel as Max moves to my side and wraps around me. And I feel the stares. I feel every single knife of their whispers and every single pointed look.

Once I could feel nothing, now I feel it all.

Jamie wrings his hands as he sits at my kitchen table, the chamomile tea between us cold, both mugs full. I left work just five minutes after I'd arrived. I walked out. Jamie followed. And now we're here and, for the first time in a long time, we're being honest.

As clouds outside blanket the sky, and the brisk air turns dark and heavy, we are talking.

"I don't get it, Mik. You hate each other. You always have." His voice is pained and exhausted, and I feel it too.

"I think that, maybe, I never really hated him." My admission comes with agony. "It was just easier to pretend I did than it was to face what was really going on in my mind."

"And what is really going on?" He looks up to me with those open, honest eyes and I sigh. I should never have lied to him.

He should never have lied to me.

"Ben was unexpected and terrifying. He's always scared me because I think I've always known that he is soft and kind and safe. He saw all my broken edges for what they were, Jamie; he saw them as pieces of me. Just as you are a piece of me, and Mom, even Dad. He saw them and he accepted them." My tears start to swim as my lungs heave and I feel like I'm drowning. "He never wanted to fix me, Jamie. He just wanted me. And I could never hate him."

"And you what? You want to be with him?"

I take a deep breath and raise my shoulders as I wrap my blanket tighter around myself.

"I do." I admit. "I want him so much that it scares me. I want his smiles and his *really* stupid jokes and the way he can stop me from spiralling before I even know I'm doing it. I want him. But I want my brother more."

"Mik, I -"

"I chose wrong once." My voice cracks and I reach for Jamie's hand. "I won't choose someone over you again."

When Jamie's phone rings he closes his eyes and rests his head on our hands. "I don't know what to say to fix this, Mik. I don't like it, but I don't want you to be unhappy."

I take a deep breath before pulling away and clearing up our mugs.

Is that what I'm choosing? Unhappiness?

"Just answer your phone and we'll put this all behind us."

Chapter Thirty-two

Ben

This is like sitting under water. Like being submerged while the world keeps turning around me, conversations keep flowing, but I can't hear them. They are nothing more than a distant hum echoing around me. Punctuated by a high pitched keening. It's like breathing under water... I can't.

My head is heavy. Too heavy. And my chest. *Why is my chest so tight?*

I try to move but the groan and crunch of something underneath me - no above me? both? - seems to intensify when I do.

Maybe if I can just get my phone?

Another shift.

Another scream in the world around me. Heat. There's so much heat.

My head is spinning.

What was I doing?

Right.

My phone.

I need my...

Someone is talking.

I don't know the voice.

And the heat is back.

It's so hot. Am I sweating? No. That's blood. I'm bleeding. But it's running backwards. How? Or am I - I'm upside down. That makes sense.

I'm upside down and bleeding and it is warm.

And now someone is talking.

I can't make out what they're saying.

They seem far away. And I'm tired. So tired.

I still haven't opened my eyes.

If I rest for a minute, I can get enough strength to shout or speak.

Or whisper.

I let myself slip and as I slip, I think only one thing.

Mikaela.

"Sir. Can you tell me your name?"

My hand moves to my face. There's something covering my mouth. There's a pressure in my chest.

I blink but all I can see is light. Too much light.

It had been getting darker. Right?

A hand wraps around mine.

"Sir, that's helping you to breathe. You need to keep that on. Can you tell me your name?"

"Ben." My throat rasps. "My name is Ben."

"Okay, Ben." Her voice is soothing. Calming. "My name's Alyssa. We're on our way to the hospital. You've been in an accident."

That feels familiar. An accident. I was driving. I'd stopped at the stop sign, hadn't I?

"Ben, I need you to stay with us now, okay? Talk to me. Tell me who we need to call for you, okay?"

My eyes are heavy and my chest is still burning.

"Ben. Stay with me. Is this your phone?"

Alyssa holds up a shattered screen as my head rolls to the side. I can't speak again. I can't.

"Just blink for me, once is no, twice is yes. Ben, is this your phone?"

One blink. Then another.

"Okay," she breathes. "You're doing great, Ben. We're almost there. Just stay with me."

"No."

I know the voice above the water.

"I don't know. Half an hour ago maybe?"

Hysteria. That's the sound of hysteria. The pitch that sits just above acceptable, the pace that's too rushed. Everything suggests pain and panic.

"Haston. Yes. Benjamin Haston."

Someone else responds; telling her what she needs to know.

Her voice is so distant. "Thank you."

Mikaela

"Hey." I brush his knuckles with my thumbs as I look up at him. His skin is dry and pale and cracked. Dark circles hang like shadows beneath his eyes. Those eyes are still closed; so closed. "I'm so sorry, Ben."

Every single part of me is dying with each and every beep and whir of machinery that he's hooked up to. Wires and tubes and bruises spatter his skin. He's had stitches under his left eye and over his lip and the black marks of the collision are spreading over his face.

My eyes run over his chest, moving in even breaths, and I feel the rise of nausea.

Three.

That's how many ribs are broken.

Three.

And then there's his leg.

His leg is lifted in some contraption that keeps it elevated; the cast that has been wrapped around it is still drying.

The pain of it all hits me like a brick to the chest and the air is stripped from my lungs as I bury my head in the sheets beside him.

I cling to his hand as I cry, my chest heaving and my words tumbling out of me between each broken sob.

"I'm so sorry. Please, *please* just be okay. I need you." I choke on my breath and squeeze his hand tight. "I need you, so you can't go and do stupid shit like getting into accidents, Ben. You can't do that to me."

A shift of the sheets and a groan of pain pulls me up from where I've buried my face and my heart sputters as I stand.

He blinks as he looks at me, his gaze showing something life-like beneath waves of pain, and I choke on another sob.

"You're here." It's all he says.

"I'm here," I repeat, my fingers brushing gently over his face, soaking in the fact he's awake. He's awake and speaking and his eyes are so blue.

"Mik. I - I'm so sorry" His voice shakes and my heart aches.

"It's okay. It's all okay" Soft groans pull from his chest as he tries to sit and I place my hand on him. A gentle way of telling him not to move. He coughs and groans, and I try not to hurt him as I pull away.

"No." His hand lifts and he reaches for me. I take it in both hands. "Don't. Don't go, Mik."

"I'm not. I'm not going anywhere." My voice is thick with tears as he nods and closes his eyes. "I'm right here."

He sighs as I sit and, eventually, he slips into a morphine induced sleep.

I watch him and I hold onto his hand as tight as I can.

"Now, while I wish it were under better circumstances, I am glad to see this."

My head snaps up. I must have fallen asleep. Ben's chest moves steadily and my hand is still tucked into his. And Julia Haston is standing in the doorway, her hair dishevelled and a wild gleam in her eyes.

"Mrs Haston." I stand quickly and glance back to Ben. How much does she know?

"Well, tickle me pink. Mikaela Wilcox is the girl who has my son's heart in a twist."

"I - erm - Ben's stable. He was awake a little while ago. He's - he -" And then her arms are around me as I cry.

"Oh, shh. Don't cry darling. The nurses told me everything." Her hand brushes over my hair as I wrap around her and bury my face in the warmth of her. "It's okay. He's going to be okay."

I nod as she holds me, soothing me, before she pulls us over to the chairs behind me.

Even in a disaster, with her hair tied back and yet still full of chaos, with her heart on the sleeve of the pyjama top she's still wearing, her feet shoved into trainers clearly used for gardening, her body shaking with shock, Julia Haston holds herself together. She digs through her purse, her eyes glancing up at her son as he lay sleeping, before pulling out a pack of tissues and handing me one.

"Are you okay, Mikaela?"

I blink a few times, trying to find an answer to her question.

"I don't know," I admit as more tears come. "I - erm - I don't know how much he told you."

"Oh, absolutely nothing." She smiles as she glances to Ben and pushes to her feet before running her fingers through the dishevelled mop of his hair and closing her eyes. "You know how he is. Won't be vulnerable until he needs to be."

I nod quietly.

He had been vulnerable with me and I pushed him away.

"Mrs Haston, I - erm - we..." I gulp as I watch her fuss over him.

"It's okay, Mikaela. You can let Ben explain when he's awake." She smiles softly over her shoulder at me and I nod.

"Thank you."

Ben's Mom is kind and calm as she speaks and I listen. "Mikaela. My son, the stubborn creature that he is, has had you in his sights for a long time. And for a while, I won't lie to you, I didn't really approve." She sighs when I glance to my hands. "Not because of you. Understand, dear, you are exactly what my son needs. But, for a long while, I was worried he wasn't what you needed."

I feel my face screw into a contortion of confusion and shake my head, still watching my fingers twist.

"Your momma spoke to me when you left, Mikaela. And Ben spoke to Norman."

I blink back my tears.

"That boyfriend of yours was a piece of work." Her fingers comb through Ben's hair as she tuts. "And Ben had his own demons to fight. He - his father had a streak and Ben was so angry for a very long time." My hands are shaking. "So I told him to back off. I told him to listen to Jamie and to give you space and time. And then your momma... I'm so sorry you lost her, darling. She was a good woman."

"I - I think I'm in love with him." I breathe my admission with my eyes closed and Julia Haston laughs.

"Oh, I know, dear. I saw the way you looked at him years ago." She sits back beside me and takes my hand as we slip into silence.

Hours pass as we sit in cracked and broken vinyl chairs. At some point Ben's mom fell into a restless sleep and I moved her slowly, tucking a cushion behind her head and laying a blanket over her. Then I crept to Ben's side as he slept, just to watch him breathe. Sitting here, I count every rise of his chest.

"Ma'am. We operate a one overnight visitor policy here." The older of his nurses whispers to me from the doorway as I place my hand on his forehead, checking he isn't too warm.

"Okay. I can go." My heart is in my throat. The last thing I want to do is walk away right now, when he isn't awake to know I'm not running out on him. "I just need to gather my stuff."

The woman nods, her white cloud of hair bobbing slightly with the movement, and smiles.

Moving carefully, desperate not to wake Ben when he needs rest, I crouch beside his mother and hesitate with my hand hovering over hers.

"Mrs Haston?" Nothing. Not even a groan. "Mrs Haston?"

I place my hand over hers and her eyes open instantly as she bolts upright in her chair.

"What's wrong? Is he okay?" Her voice is a croak and her eyes are wild again. When her sight settles on her son, still sleeping soundly, she exhales in one long breath and holds her free hand over her heart.

"I'm so sorry, Mrs Haston. I didn't want to startle you. I - erm - I have to leave." I glance back to the nurses station, the corner visible just outside through the window between us and the hallway, before shaking my head. "I'll be back first thing. Okay?"

"Why are you leaving?" For a moment, as she furrows her brow and cocks her head to the side, I see where Ben got his most striking features. Her eyes are darker than his, but they are still a striking blue - stormy and weathered but beautifully inviting - and the way she smiles even when she's breaking is so painfully *him.*

"It's hospital rules." I try to smile too, but it doesn't feel right on my lips - too stretched and taut - too forced. "If he wakes up can you tell him I'll be back? Please?"

I can't bear to look over my shoulder to him without more tears coming.

"Of course, dear." Julia cups my cheek with her hand and nods slightly. "I'll give you regular updates too. What's your number?" She leans over the side of her chair to retrieve her purse and digs for her phone, handing it to me quickly. "I'll give you a moment with him before you go, if you'd like?"

Her eyes trace the way he rests behind me and I take a deep breath.

"Thank you."

Ben

Something soft brushes my forehead once, twice, three times. There's a calming rhythm to the touches, little brushes of affection that I know aren't meant to wake me. And yet with every touch, I feel myself being pulled out of my groggy haze of sleep and back to the room I know she's waiting in.

"I've got to go." She's talking in hushed tones and I hold on to her voice. "But I'm coming right back in the morning and I'm going to keep coming back, okay?"

Is she crying?

I don't want her to cry.

"I said some really stupid things, Haston. Really stupid." I feel her lips press into my forehead and I want to open my eyes. I want to see her. "But I didn't mean them. I was stupid and scared, and it was all so messy. But I love you. I love you so much that it makes me say stupid, stupid things and I just - I really hope I can fix this."

Her hand is wrapped gently around mine and I feel her slipping away. I need her to stay. So I focus. I focus on her fingers and holding onto them.

It takes a second for the cloud to lift from my mind and my muscles to move, but she freezes.

"Ben?"

Holy shit my throat is dry. "Hey."

Gravel. My throat feels like I'm dragging up grit and gravel. It sounds like it too.

I blink against the darkness, my eyes unfocussed and struggling to adjust as I search for her, and then it's right there. My favorite shade of green, misty and clouded in worry, but staring down at me.

"You should be sleeping." Her voice is fractured and I shake my head gently.

"You're leaving?"

She nods silently as her free hand comes up to my face again, gently pushing my hair back and holding onto me. I close my eyes and lean in against her touch.

"Please don't."

She pulls her touch away and my eyes flick open.

"No," I clarify. "I mean don't go. Please."

"I have to," she sighs, her fingers weaving back into my hair in a soft caress. "You're only allowed one overnighter."

"Wait." I glance at the empty room and try to shuffle into a seated position. My chest protests and a low moan slips from my lips. "Who else is here?"

"That would be me." Mom's voice is tight, like a coil ready to unravel at any second, and I look to the doorway.

She's a mess.

In all my years, I've never seen my mother leave the house in anything other than a well-pressed suit, or at least co-ordinating colours. Today though she's anything but put together.

Her blue silk pyjama shirt hangs over a pair of jeans I didn't even know she owned and her shoes are caked in days of mud. Her hair, usually coiffed perfection, is pulled into a ratty bun on top of her head. She's not wearing a scrap of make up and her eyes are dim from exhaustion.

"Mom." I breathe a harsh sigh and she shakes her head as she comes to stand beside me.

"You stupid, *stupid* boy." Her voice wavers and her eyes mist. "If you ever do something like this again, I swear on your grandmother's grave, I will kill you with my bare hands. Do you understand me?"

I grin: a real, dopey, drug induced kind of smile that has my cheeks hurting almost as much as my chest. "Yes, Ma'am."

She presses her lips to my forehead as she squeezes my hand and glances to Mikaela.

"I found someone wandering the halls. He said he wanted to make sure you were okay." Mom speaks softly to Mik, as if she's fragile. "I told him that you're going to stay tonight and he's going to bring me home instead."

Mik opens her mouth to speak but Mom holds her hand up.

"He filled me in on some of this." She gestures between Mikaela and I with a raised eyebrow and I grimace. "And I think you two need to speak. So does he."

"Ma, you keep saying he. Who?" I grunt as I shift again and both Mikaela and Mom place a hand on my arm, rolling their eyes at me as I grin.

"Jamie, of course." Mom doesn't seem impressed.

Mik tucks her hair behind her ears and I look to her for clarification. "You know, he was pretty surprised to find out he's one of your emergency contacts." She shrugs as if it's nothing. "He brought me straight here."

Mik is in the seat beside my bed, her fingers entwined with mine, and silence has wrapped around us.

I want to hold her and never let her go, but each shift in the bed reminds me I can't.

"So." I clear my throat and she looks up to me, green meeting me with warm intensity. "How bad is it?"

"Three broken ribs." She clears her throat and I nod as I wait. "You broke your leg, but doctors don't think it requires surgery. They said they'll need to monitor it though. And then there are the cuts and bruises, and the smoke inhalation. I - I thought I'd lost you, Ben."

A broken sob rips from her chest and I break with her.

I need her closer, I want to take care of her and comfort her, but I also need to feel her warmth - to know she's really here with me and not running from us.

"Hey," I squeeze her hand gently and pull her closer.

She stands by the bed, her hand flapping over my chest as she traces the wires connecting me to various machines, and I pull again. "In. Now."

"What?" Her eyes widen in alarm. "Ben, no. I can't. Did you miss the part where I said you have broken ribs and a broken leg? I can't just climb in with you."

"Yes." I push myself over slightly and suck in a breath. I will not let her see the pain if it means I can't hold her. "You can. Now get over here or I'm not going to sleep and then you'll tell me off because I need to rest and we'll just go in circles all night."

I tug her arm again and she sighs before kicking off her shoes and crawling in beside me. She moves gently, careful not to jostle me or tug on the blankets. She doesn't wrap around me or nuzzle in like I want her to. Instead she lies on her side, inches away from me, and she watches me closely.

"Hey, Mik?" I turn my face to her and try not to grin as she sighs.

"Yes, Ben?"

"I love you too."

Her blush is beautifully refreshing as I pull our hands to my lips and press soft kisses against her knuckles.

"You heard that then?"

"Yep." I close my eyes and let the haziness come for me again. "And there's no need to fix anything. Now I think we should sleep."

"Okay," she whispers and I feel her shift closer before pressing her lips against mine for a second. "Goodnight, Ben."

I hum as she settles beside me and darkness washes over me with a comforting warmth.

Chapter Thirty-three

Mikaela

I blink back against the rising sun pouring in through the wide window on the other side of the room. For a moment confusion flits across my mind, dragging me through a weird limbo without clarity, and my heart hurts a little.

And then I feel it.

Ben's hand is wrapped around mine, holding it gently against his chest as it rises and falls in deep movements, and I peek through heavy lashes to watch him sleep.

My body aches from laying on the smallest sliver of bed, as far from his bruised and beaten body as I can be, but that one point of contact... That brings me a comfort that warms my bones.

I smile to myself, closing my eyes again as I focus on the way he's clinging to me in his sleep, before jolting upright.

"You look good, Mik."

The sound of blood rushing seems to scream behind my ears and the thickness of my throat dries into nothing but parched heat.

"Cat got your tongue, babe?"

My heart stops for a second before picking up in a painful sprint. I glance around, aware that in the quiet lull of the early hours of the morning less doctors and nurses roam the hallways. Less families wait for results and news.

We are completely alone in this corner of the hospital.

We have been undisturbed for hours.

And I have no idea when someone will come to check on Ben.

We are alone and he is here, his head low and his hands shoved deep into his pockets, and I can't breathe or move or scream. I can only stare and shake. I can only panic. I can only freeze.

My mind scrambles for escape. My tongue ties over words I can't say. My fingers brush against Ben's hand.

Ben. Ben who is bruised and broken. Ben who is vulnerable. Ben who sees me and loves me and protects me. My Ben.

Ben pulls me back to myself.

"Get away from me." My voice is strangled; stuck in my throat. My chest seems to cave under the pressure of his presence and my hand shakes as I grab hold of myself, too afraid to move or shout or scream. Too afraid to pull Ben into this when he can't defend himself.

"You know, I really missed you." He doesn't make a move to step away, he just stares at me through thick lashes as I struggle to breathe.

"You need to leave." I can hardly hear myself.

His eyes drop to Ben, breathing deeply with his eyes closed and bruises splattering his cheekbones, and he smiles.

Matthew *smiles*.

I force myself to move, to push between Ben and the man who stole who I was, and I look at him. I really look at him.

Matthew is hunching forwards as he holds his side as if he's in pain and his lip is split. Across his neck is a cluster of scratches, surface deep but painful looking. Under his jaw is a bruise that is turning a thick black. And his arm is bruised and torn in a way I remember my chest and cheek had been after the accident. His hair, a shock of autumn red, is caked in his own blood in places.

My stomach twists as bile rises in my throat.

"How long did it take you, Mik?" His voice is splintering and my gut is churning.

I don't answer.

"I asked you a question." His eyes flash with liquid ice and his smirk has me sick to my stomach. "It's Ben right? I recognise him from that dinner at your Mom's. What was it? Eight? No, nine years ago? God. He was like a fucking dog with a bone. Should have known you'd open your legs for him eventually."

"Matthew -"

"What happened to Matty, Mik? You used to call me Matty."

"What did you do, Matthew?" My legs are shaking as I get to my feet and, for a second, I think I might pass out or collapse or puke.

I think I might do all three.

He watches Ben so closely that my skin prickles.

"I saw you two. In that restaurant." His voice is eerily quiet as he steps forwards.

I stumble back, my hip crashing against the bedside table as I grasp for the lamp that almost falls.

Matthew tilts his head to the side. "For months I told myself you didn't want me to find you. But then I realised you went back to Jamie. Why would you go somewhere I knew if you didn't want me to find you? You wouldn't. So I came to find you, Mik. And I watched you."

"Matthew."

"I watched you with some other guy and I watched that guy too. And I waited. You weren't *with* him so I thought I'd give you time, Mikaela. You wanted time, right?"

"Matthew."

"And then one day *he* was with you." His jaw twitches as he stares at Ben. "And I watched you fuck about with him, Mik. I watched you in the garden at that party. How you let him touch you..." He looks back to me and his cheeks are wet. "And I saw you in that restaurant. And you wore purple. The exact same shade we painted our bedroom. Remember that?"

"Matty." The name burns my throat as I say it. "What did you do?"

"I didn't mean to do it." His voice is cool and controlled, and I take a shaking step towards him. "I didn't mean to hit his car. I just kept thinking about the way he handled you, Mik. He keeps putting his hands on you and you're not his to touch like that. You're mine."

Hot tears roll down my cheeks as I shake my head.

"You need to leave." It's just a whisper but I see the way it ignites that spark of fury that's never too far beneath the surface.

He lurches forwards and a small cry escapes my lips as his hands wrap tightly around my arms.

Jamie

"What do you mean you don't know where he is?" An officer is walking down the hall towards me, peering in to every room as his partner stands over the nurses computer, glaring at the screen. "He should never have been left alone."

"With all due respect, sir, we're short staffed and we're nurses. If you wanted him monitored, you should have left an officer posted," the nurse bites.

I smirk. She's feisty.

"Yes, we should have," the officer snaps back.

And then a familiar voice cuts me in half. "You're not his to touch like that. You're mine."

I drop the coffees where I stand.

I need to move. Why can't I move?

"Who are you looking for?" My voice is shaking.

The officer glances my way.

"What?"

"Who are you looking for?" I turn to Ben's room. Just three doors down from where I'm standing. And I run.

Mikaela

"Get your fucking hands off of my sister before you lose them. *Now*."

Jamie's hands are balled into fists and his cheeks are flushed as I lock eyes with him.

Matthew doesn't move.

"Now, now, JimJam." He smirks as he runs his eyes over me. "You don't want to start something you can't finish. You never did manage to win against me."

"Maybe not." Jamie spits through his teeth and I can see he's shaking. "But this time I'm not alone."

I'm glued to the spot, my heart hammering and tears streaming as two police officers step around my brother, and Matthew glares at me as he holds me tighter.

My chest heaves and my head spins.

The thick fingers of the taller officer wrap around Matthew's uninjured wrist and within an instant that spark of anger turns into a blaze. Shock tears through Matthew's face as he swings an arm out in a blind attempt to hit the officer who has hold of him now and I flinch away as the back of his hand connects with my jaw. I stumble backwards, heaving for breath, as the officer drags him from the room and Jamie rushes to my side.

"Breathe." His command is partnered with his palm against my chest as the other rests on my back, holding me tight as I try to regain my focus, the same way he'd been coached to before, and I hold tight to his arm. "You're okay. We're right here. You're okay."

I stare at the white crescents my nails are leaving in his skin and try to loosen my grip.

When Jamie speaks I can't focus. I can think of nothing but the fact he was here and Ben is laying here broken and bruised because of him.

Ben is here because of me.

Jamie's words are hurried and muffled and his hand never leaves the spot against my heart as he looks over my shoulder.

I follow his breathing blindly and struggle against the hold of panic that chokes me. And then a hand brushes against my waist and I am somehow sitting on the edge of Ben's bed and his hand is on my skin.

He is back beside me, pulling me against him despite his pain as Jamie guides me to him.

His arms wrap around me as he pulls me to his chest, his eyes swimming with concern, and I can see his pain etched into the depths of the blue.

His lips move but I have no idea what he said.

"Mik?"

I blink as his fingers brush gently over my cheek and Jamie sinks into the chair beside us.

"Why didn't you wake me, Mik?" Ben whispers.

When I open my lips to speak, pain rips through me and my remaining composure buckles. Ben holds me, wrapping me in him, shushing into my hair as I fall apart.

"It's okay. You're okay. He won't touch you again, Mik. He's not going to touch you." He brushes his fingers over my skin as I cling to him and presses kisses into my hair.

Eventually my sobs subside, my heart stops its violent thudding in my chest, I calm my shaking, and Ben is still holding me. Still whispering to me. "You're okay."

Silence has its grips on Ben as he shakes his head in defiance. He knows I'm right. My bones ache with the weight of what isn't being said. And he knows I'm right. Why won't he just admit it?

"You asked about my scars, Ben." My voice trembles as I lay with him and he sighs a deep, pained sigh. "They're all from him. And now he's hurt you."

"You're still not getting the point, Mikaela." Jamie groans from the chair and Ben nods silently. "He did it. Not you. This isn't on you."

"I should have told you everything sooner." My entire body is exhausted and every muscle seems to scream at me to release the tension I know I've been holding on to.

"Mik," Ben sighs. "I already knew. I told you I'd figured it out. I knew."

"I never told you," I whisper.

The silence that falls over the three of us is weighted and worn. It's a thick fog that engulfs the room and leaves the hair on my arms standing. It's secretive and saddening.

Eventually Jamie grunts.

"What?" I twist to look at my brother, still reeling from Matthew's presence, and note the distant look in his eyes.

"I did."

I turn back to Ben. His eyes are closed.

"What?" My voice is quiet.

"I told him, Mik." Jamie sighs. "After I - erm - after you two - when I found out. I told him."

I move slowly, removing myself from Ben's embrace as I sit up and twist to face Jamie. I wipe my face, brushing away tears as they fall, and take a deep breath.

"How much?" My voice wavers and my breathing is shaky.

"Mik." He glances up to me through tear stained lashes.

"How much, Jamie?"

Jamie closes his eyes as his own cry sticks in his throat. "Bits and pieces."

I nod slowly and feel Ben behind me, his body leaning towards me as he tries to comfort me, his hand pressing gently against my spine, and I wrap my arms around myself.

When I close my eyes I try to put myself in his shoes. I try to revisit every painful memory, every bruise and fight and scar, through Jamie's eyes. I try to recall those memories of whispered phone calls as if I had received them; as if I had listened while the person I love most in the world, the person I lost once before, begged for help. Begged for someone to just get him out of the hell he was living in. How I would have felt if, when I'd shown up to help, he'd refused to let me in. I try to imagine it was Jamie's burden that I carry.

The weight of it is crushing.

When I lay back beside Ben he makes no move to touch me and guilt gnaws at my skin. He is in so much pain - too much to hold me through this - so I take his hand in mine and squeeze gently.

"Okay, then I guess you have questions I should answer," I sigh as Ben brings my knuckles to his lips.

"You don't have to, Mikaela." He smiles sweetly at me and I run my fingers up his arm and shake my head.

"I kind of do though. Just, maybe not right now?"

"Not now," Ben agrees.

Behind me, Jamie sighs and I hold out my hand. He takes it instantly and we wait like this together.

Ben

"Mom." I groan as Mikaela laughs and runs her fingers through my hair.

The nurses helped me get into a seated position a little while ago, and now Mikaela is curled up beside me, carefully distant in her touch but still connected, and I never want to let her go.

"Mikaela Wilcox." She pats Mik's hand gently. "Honestly, I'm just glad he got it together in time. It was a constant worry he'd still be a mess and you'd find your Prince Charming."

I grunt a weak denial and Mikaela smiles sweetly before pressing a kiss into my cheek.

A light rap on the door pulls our attention away from the playful teasing - teasing that has been lifting Mikaela out of her panic - to the officer standing behind a nurse. My stomach drops.

"I thought you guys said Benjamin could give you a statement when he's better?" Mom squares her shoulders and sits taller as her eyes roam over the man who won't smile.

I shake my head gently as Mikaela disengages her fingers from my own and apologises quietly.

"I'm so sorry, Mrs Haston." She slips from the bed and takes a step towards the man in the doorway. "I just need to deal with this. I'll be right back."

As Mik moves towards the door and away from me, I reach out, wrapping my fingers around her wrist and stopping her in her tracks.

She closes her eyes.

I'm already itching to get out of this bed, trying to swing my broken leg off the side, so she steps back towards me quickly.

"Stay," she whispers. "You can't get out of this bed and your Mom needs to have some time with you, okay?"

"But you need me, Mik." I counter with a pleading glance to the door. The idea of her having to relive it all without support makes me sick to my stomach.

"I'll be fine. I promise. And if they need you, I promise I'll bring them straight to you, okay?"

My hand cups her face as I pull her lips to mine, kissing her softly as Mom smiles to herself and Jamie groans.

"Okay. But if you need me..." My forehead is pressed against hers as she wraps her fingers around my hand and holds me for a moment.

"Then you're right here. I know."

Mikaela

"And then what happened, Miss Wilcox?"

The officer hardly looks up from his notepad as we sit in the small on call room the nurse had lead us to.

I wring my hands together repeatedly as I relive the events of a few hours ago, my breath hitching at strange places with each retelling.

"And then Jamie was there. He told him to let go of me - he had police with him already. I don't know how. And they got Matthew off of me and Ben was awake. I'm sorry. This is all just a lot right now."

The officer nods as his pen skims over the notes he already has. "And Mr Kaden told you he crashed into Mr Haston's car?"

"Yes," I breathe. We have gone over this countless times now and I'm growing restless. I want to go back to Ben. "And that he's been following me for a while now."

"And your relationship with Mr Haston is what, precisely?"

"He's my boyfriend."

"Okay." The officer clicks his pen and closes his notebook with a sigh, before turning off the device on the table that's been recording this whole ordeal and smiling gently towards me. "You did great, Miss Wilcox. I'm sorry you had to go through all that. We just have to be thorough in these reports."

I note that his eyes are warm brown, like melted chocolate, and his skin has a deep tan that etches kindness into the wrinkles forming around his mouth and eyes. His hair, dark and short, is speckled with grey and white, and the slight bend in the bridge of his nose gives his crooked smile a soft edge. He's kind.

"I understand." My breath leaves me in a gush as I slump forwards, finally done having to speak it all back into existence. "What happens now?"

"Well." The man leans back slightly as he speaks and his tone is swift and matter-of-fact. "Violation of a protection order is a Class 1 Misdemeanour. I'll head back to the precinct and file a criminal complaint against Mr Kaden which will put him in contempt of court. He will be arrested and a date will be set for him to face a judge. You may be called as a witness. The judge will decide if he will go to prison or pay a fine or both.

In addition to this, charges of Reckless Driving will be brought against Mr Kaden. As this will be his first offence in this state he could face an additional thirty days on top of any prison sentence handed to him. However, a judge may rule to include his previous conviction, for which he has already served a four week sentence, which would allow for a further ninety days incarceration to be applied."

I rock back in my chair. It's information overload and my mind is reeling. Court. Fines. Misdemeanours and criminal complaints. I feel sick.

"Prison?" I glance at the man smiling softly at me and he nods.

"Six to eighteen months, Ma'am."

"There she is." Ben's mom has a small smile aimed at me as I slip back into his room quietly. Instant warmth spreads through me at the sight. There's a sadness in her eyes though; a sadness that I recognise all too well. "Ben was just filling me in, dear. How are you holding up?"

I sigh as I run my hands through my hair and close my eyes.

"I don't know," I admit, leaning against the wall. I can feel them looking at me as I try to breathe through that building bubble of anxiety.

When I open my eyes I see two things. First I see the shame in Ben's eyes. The shadow of painful regret dances in the waves of blue, no doubt a remnant of telling his mother this story, although it is partially his to tell. I smile sadly at him as I move closer and lean in to him. His expression softens as I do so and I press a soft kiss against his cheek.

Everything is okay.

Then I notice the way Mrs Haston moves. She shuffles in her chair, moving to the side to make enough space for me to sink in beside her, and pulls back the knitted blanket that's thrown over her lap. While I stand beside Ben, his mother motions to space beside her and opens her arms.

"Any girl who has been through what you have been through today needs a mother's hug, dear."

My heart clenches and a small whimper sounds as I find myself curling in beside her, crying as the blanket is pulled over me and a warm embrace envelopes me.

"It's okay, darling girl," she soothes. "Get it out of your system."

Chapter Thirty-four

One Year Later

Ben

"We're going to be late, Mik." I shout over my shoulder as the sound of the hairdryer turning on tells me I was right to say we need to be there half an hour before we really do. "You know they said we can't be late."

I fasten my tie, a soft baby blue that I know is her favorite, as I roll my eyes and focus on getting our stuff together.

Mikaela's bag is on the couch, her scarf and jacket thrown over the arm, and her phone on the coffee table. I gather it all up, laughing as I hear her swear in the bedroom.

In the four months since she moved in she hasn't made it a single week without walking into the corner of the bed. Today breaks her longest streak yet.

"You okay in there?"

"Just peachy," she grumbles as she stomps down the hallway, one hand behind her back and reaching for her zipper while the other tugs at the hem of her dress. "Can you?"

I know I should move to her aid quickly, especially as I am the one bugging her to get out of the damn door on time, but looking at her - all grumpy and pouty as she leaves *our* bedroom - I just need to breathe her in before we face tonight.

"What?" The quirk of her lips as she tries not to smile is really adorable.

"Nothing." I shrug as I take a step towards her and place my hands on her hips. "Just thinking that I might be the luckiest man in the world."

"Oh yeah?" She rolls her eyes and I grin. "Well if you don't zip me up the luckiest man in the world won't be getting lucky for a week."

My chuckle is low as I twist her around to gain access to this tricky zipper she's complaining about before I groan loudly. I pinch the bridge of my nose as I look to the ceiling and grunt.

"Mikaela fucking Wilcox, we are going to be late for your fucking dinner and you are wearing *that* under your dress? Is this a ploy? You can do this dress up yourself, can't you? You just want sex."

My eyes trail over the red lace that peeks out from beneath the matching crimson dress that is currently being held up only by her hands. Fuck what she wants. I want sex now. Little tease.

A sweet little laugh slips from her pouty lips and I push her hair aside before kissing her shoulder. "You drive me absolutely crazy, you know that?"

"Yep." She takes a deep breath and leans back into my touch. "But you love me."

"I do." I wrap around her and close my eyes, revelling in the moment before it passes.

Mikaela

I clear my throat as I stand up and raise my glass. Everyone falls silent and turns to face me, and suddenly I feel a little nauseous. This is why I didn't want to do this tonight. Ben insisted we had reason to celebrate. *"You've done two incredible things,"* he had enthused, *"you need to take a minute to breathe it in, Mik."* But right now, I just want to be at home on the couch with my boyfriend, with one of our Friday Night cooking shows on... Even if Jamie has pulled this whole thing together for me - well, Jamie and Emma.

The latter, who very quickly fell into the role of doting sister with ease and love a little after Ben got out of the hospital, rests her head on my brother's shoulder as he pulls her close to him. Her hand rests over the tiny bump she's carrying around these days - my perfect little niece all tucked up safe and cozy in there - and she smiles encouragingly at me. Slowly, she lifts her shoulders for three beats and then releases; a reminder to breathe.

Ben's hand slips over the back of my thigh, a gentle reminder that he's right beside me, and I square my shoulders before taking a deep breath.

"I just want to thank all of you for coming tonight." My eyes drift over the friends and family who came to celebrate with us - Max, Alex, Sephy, Xavier and Asher, Julia, Norman, even a couple of the other assistants from Wilcox Writings. Even Dr. Walsh came, her dark hair loose around her shoulders and her smile no longer that detached, polite smile from our sessions. Now she is positively beaming with pride. Beside her, Harry, my agent, sits in the corner, a conspiratorial smile on her lips as she glances up from her phone and nods at me. My stomach flips. "If you'd have told me a year ago that I would be sitting here with you all, having finally finished college, I think I would have laughed and told you all to fuck off."

Ben groans and Jamie cackles, earning him a swift smack from Emma.

"Sorry." I grin. "I'd have told you all to politely leave."

Ben rolls his eyes and squeezes my thigh gently. My heart stumbles as I glance at him. He has done so much for me - so, so much - and my heart aches with how full it is. He'd done this. He'd found Dr Walsh. He'd attended every hour of therapy with me until I didn't need him there anymore. Then he came up with this idea. He did the math. He realised I just needed thirty credits to graduate. He completed the applications to every Creative Writing course in the State of New York for me. He organised my schedule. He stayed up late for months, reading my assignments and building stories with me. He helped me to find myself again and because of him I am here. I have my degree. I have my future.

"I am so eternally grateful for each and every one of you here tonight." My voice wavers and I clear my throat. "You have all been so supportive of me, from reading my earliest drafts of every assignment, to listening to countless breakdowns where I really thought I couldn't do it. But it's more than that, because today something major happened."

Harry leans forwards in her seat and Ben grins from ear to ear as everyone else stares in confusion.

"Today, a publishing house - one that isn't owned by my brother - made me an offer, and Harry just accepted it for me. Thanks to each of you, I'm finally doing what I set out to do. Thanks to each of you, I get the chance to do this. You all got me through a really dark time when I had to face my demons and I wouldn't be here without each of you. Especially my Ben." I turn to face him where he's sitting, his eyes glued to me and a sad smile on his lips, and my heart squeezes tight in my chest. "A little over a year ago I faced the scariest day of my life. In the space of a few hours I walked away from the most incredible man, realised I was hopelessly in love with him, and then thought I'd lost him. Falling in love with you was a collision, Ben. It was sudden and unexpected and, at times, absolutely terrifying, but I don't know what I would do if I didn't have you. I definitely wouldn't be standing here having finally done something I stopped believing I could do. I love you so much and I am so grateful for every day I get to keep you in my life." I brush my fingers through his hair before cupping his cheek and winking at him. "You are my constant inspiration."

He turns his face quickly, pressing a soft kiss against my palm and smiles up at me.

"To inspiration," Jamie calls out, lifting his glass while others follow suit, and I gaze into my favourite sea of blue.

I kick off my heels as soon as we're in the elevator, grinning as Ben's fingers roam over my hips when he pulls me against him, my back against his chest, and his face nuzzles into my neck.

"So, how does it feel to be an author?" His breath fans over my skin as he speaks and I hold onto his arms as I close my eyes.

"Honestly?"

I feel his laugh.

"Yes, Mik. Honestly."

"I'm exhausted and nauseous."

"Of course you are." He sighs as the doors slip open and he reaches down to scoop up my shoes. "Because you overthink everything, Mik."

I laugh as he pulls me through the hallway and down to our apartment, and shuffle impatiently while he unlocks the door. "Ben?"

"Yes, Mik?"

"I'm hungry."

Ben groans as he hangs up his jacket and turns to face me. "Mik, we literally just spent the night at a beautiful restaurant with fancy food and wine."

As he speaks I slip my hands up his chest, staring up at him with doe eyes, and Ben's words slow.

"And you are nervous, so you hardly touched your food, and now I'm going to have to make you grilled cheese at one in the morning, aren't I?"

I push up on my tip-toes as his arms wrap around my waist and he leans into my kiss with a gentle eye roll.

He kisses me slowly, with his hands pressed against my ass and a resigned smile against his lips. This is my favourite kind of kiss - the lazy kind that takes its time to spread a warm, buzzing electricity through my veins - and I sigh as he pulls away.

"You know, I don't think you realise that you're pretty perfect, Benjamin Haston."

"Oh, I know I'm perfect, Mikaela." He smirks before kissing me again and pushing me towards the couch. "Now sit that pretty butt down and let me make you a sandwich, Little Miss Author."

I flop onto the couch as instructed and tug the blanket from where it's thrown over the side. In this moment, with Ben in the kitchen and my face buried in our couch cushions, I finally let myself breathe.

Epilogue

Ben

Two more weeks. That's all. I only have to wait two more weeks and then I have the go ahead.

Waking up beside her this morning feels different somehow - like the day knows I am antsy with anticipation - and I roll onto my side to look at her.

The freckles that climb her spine are a constellation I have memorised, and yet, each time I trail my eyes over her skin I focus on each one as if I've never seen her before. I trace my fingers over the curve of her spine as she lays beside me, brushing past the old scar on her shoulder and pushing her hair aside, and a soft smile breaks through her semi-sleepy state.

"Morning, baby." I press a kiss against the button of her nose before she rolls onto her side and the sheets bunch at her waist. I pull my hands over her side, the pad of my thumb skimming the underside of her breast as I move closer. "Big day today."

"Mhmm." She shuffles closer, hooking her leg over my waist without even opening her eyes, and pulls my lips to hers. "Big day. Yep."

"You've got a deadline now. Gotta get up and go be a little superstar." I mumble against her lips as I grin and Mik groans.

"Less talking. More kissing." Her fingers wind into my hair, tugging gently as she rocks her hips against me and I chuckle.

"Yes, Ma'am." I roll so that she's beneath me, my teeth grazing her jaw as I begin to suck and nip my way down her body, making her squirm beneath me.

Yes.

I could wake up like this every morning for the rest of forever. I want to wake up like this every morning. And for my plan to work, and for Jamie not to kick my ass for taking the focus away from the big birthday he's got planned for her, I just have to wait two more weeks before I can ask her to be mine forever. And I will ask, because no matter what obstacles the universe throws at me I know one thing for sure. I will walk every single path placed in front of me, I will break every rule placed down and face every storm, to make sure that Mikaela Wilcox spends the rest of her days smiling.

Two roads diverged in a wood and I -

I took the one less traveled by,

And that has made all the difference.

Robert Lee Frost

Author Note

Thank you so much for reading my debut novel and supporting me on my journey as an independent author. It means the world to me to have shared this story with you all and I hope that you have found as much joy in reading it as I did in writing it.

Collision has been a labour of love. I began this story on a whim. I had an idea of a woman whose story I wanted to tell at a point in my life when I needed an escape, and I found that once I started I simply couldn't stop.

Mikaela and Ben were characters I fell in love with. They each have shades of darkness in their lives and yet they find light in each other. Writing their journey has been an outpour of love and fear and worries and adoration, and at times I had to let the characters decide their own fates. To do that I needed to be sure of just one thing: who is Mikaela Wilcox?

Mikaela is a woman of strength and substance, but she has been hurt. I have known Mikaela's. You have known Mikaela's. Globally, it is estimated that 736 million women - that's one in three - have been subjected to violence at the hands of their partners and/or strangers at least once in their life, and many victims never report.

Instead these women seek help from friends and family, if they ever do seek help at all. It was important to me that Mikaela's story told the truth of this narrative and I can only hope that you feel it did.

Acknowledgements

Mum: You let me disappear for months and months into this world of pretend when I really needed to. You let me tell these character's lives as if they were my closest friends and hold myself together with this story when we both felt ourselves falling apart. You helped me to become a writer when I wasn't sure I knew how. Without you I wouldn't have gotten through this and I cannot express how much I love you. I am who I am today because I get to call you mine.

Dad: You get to hear me speak like a crazy person about people and places that don't exist and you always do it with a smile. Thank you for always thinking I can achieve my dreams, even when I'm not so sure, and for driving me everywhere which ultimately means you heard 90% of this story before it was written. Thank you for your love and guidance and rubbish sense of humour. I get a lot of that from you.

My brothers and sisters: When I told you all I was writing a book, did you think I'd really do it? I'm not sure I did. Thank you for encouraging me to step away from this when I needed to, and for realising that when I was disappearing from our world it was because I was so engrossed in this one. It was because I *needed* this one. Thank you for being the best siblings I could ask for. And if you read this book, thank you for never, *ever* discussing certain scenes with me.

Granny Olive: Did you really think I'd leave you out? Thank you for always making me laugh, for encouraging every single thing I have ever attempted to do, and for essentially being behind the entire Irish sales of this book. You, my wonderful Granny, are incredible. You are strong, and loving, and absolutely beautiful – inside and out – and I am so proud to be your granddaughter.

Grandad Norman: I began *Collision* after we lost you. You were my biggest fan and my loudest supporter and I cannot tell you how much I wish you got to see me achieve my dreams. There is not one thing I could write that you wouldn't have shouted from the rooftops about and I know we would have enjoyed the fact you would have told everyone to read this, only to read it yourself after suggesting it to the world. I miss you, but I am so grateful for the wonderful 27 years I had with you and everything you taught me. I think of you constantly.

Lizzie: We may live miles and miles apart and we might have to contend with time-zones, but I know I have a friend for life in you. You have been with me from the very first chapter all the way up until now and I am eternally grateful for the love and support you have shown me. Thank you for coming into my life and staying.

Emily Wittig: Thank you for a beautiful cover design and helping me to bring this book to life. You are a creative genius and I am in awe of you.

My colleagues: Oh my god you read my book. I might just run and hide... Thank you for understanding all of my quirks and catastrophes and for knowing when to tell me I am working myself into the ground. Thank you for also making countless jokes about the nature of some of my writing - I have never laughed so much at my own expense and I love you all for it.

My beta readers, ARC readers and incredible Street Team: You know who you are. You are so important to me and I will never know love like the love I have for a group of strangers who agreed to help me with this. Thank you so much.

And to you, my readers: Thank you for reading this. Thank you for supporting me. Thank you for giving me a chance. I have always loved to write and somewhere along the line I kind of lost sight of that. Your responses on social media and in feedback helped me to find that voice again. This story exists because of you, so thank you for bringing me Mik and Ben and all of their beautiful friends.

Possession

Xavier Russo and Katerina Zamfir were a one time thing. They were strangers. They would never see each other again. Right?

When their lives intwine in ways neither expected, paths change and choices are made. But can they find the calm in all of the chaos and will they finally possess enough courage to take what is theirs?

Follow their story in *Possession*, book 2 in The Confession Series.

Coming Soon.

About The Author

T. S. Reed yearns for lives she hasn't lived and love stories that only really happen in books. Growing up she often hid in the worlds of other people's words and found solace in the magic of a well told story. She's a bit of a coffee addict and dreams of running away to New York City, but naturally she's a homing pigeon and is happiest with her family around her.

Her debut novel, *Collision*, is a story of love, loss and finding yourself in the darkest of times.

Find Me

If you fancy tagging along with my journey, or just fancy having a good giggle as I fall head over heels for a new book each day, find me here:

Instagram – @t.s.reedauthor

TikTok – @t.s.reedauthor

Website – www.tsreed.co.uk

Printed in Great Britain
by Amazon